TROUBLED WATERS

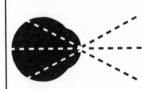

This Large Print Book carries the
Seal of Approval of N.A.V.H.

TROUBLED WATERS

DEWEY LAMBDIN

**CUYAHOGA COUNTY
PUBLIC LIBRARY**
2111 Snow Road
Parma, Ohio 44134

THORNDIKE PRESS

A part of Gale, Cengage Learning

GALE
CENGAGE Learning

Detroit • New York • San Francisco • New Haven, Conn • Waterville, Maine • London

GALE
CENGAGE Learning

Copyright © 2007 by Dewey Lambdin.
Map copyright © 2007 by Jeffrey L. Ward.
Thorndike Press, a part of Gale, Cengage Learning.

ALL RIGHTS RESERVED
This is a work of fiction. All of the characters, organizations, and events portrayed in this book are either products of the author's imagination or are used fictitiously.
Thorndike Press® Large Print Core.
The text of this Large Print edition is unabridged.
Other aspects of the book may vary from the original edition.
Set in 16 pt. Plantin.
Printed on permanent paper.

LIBRARY OF CONGRESS CATALOGING-IN-PUBLICATION DATA
Lambdin, Dewey.
Troubled waters : an Alan Lewrie naval adventure / by Dewey Lambdin.
p. cm. — (Thorndike Press large print core)
ISBN-13: 978-1-4104-0534-0 (hardcover : alk. paper)
ISBN-10: 1-4104-0534-6 (hardcover : alk. paper)
1. Lewrie, Alan (Fictitious character) — Fiction. 2. Ship captains — Fiction. 3. Great Britain — History, Naval — 18th century — Fiction. 4. Large type books. I. Title.
PS3562.A435T76 2008b
813'.54—dc22   2007046962

Published in 2008 by arrangement with St. Martin's Press, LLC.

Printed in the United States of America
1 2 3 4 5 6 7 12 11 10 09 08

To the memory of
CAPTAIN FREDERICK MARRYAT,
Royal Navy
(1792–1848)

a veteran of the Napoleonic Wars,
a wry wit, and the man who started
the genre of nautical fiction . . .
with both high adventure and *humour!*

Law is a bottomless pit.

John Arbuthnot (1667–1735),
The History of John Bull, 1712

Full-Rigged Ship: Starboard (right) side view

1. Mizen Topgallant
2. Mizen Topsail
3. Spanker
4. Main Royal
5. Main Topgallant
6. Mizen T'gallant Staysail
7. Main Topsail
8. Main Course
9. Main T'gallant Staysail
10. Middle Staysail

11. Main Topmast Staysail
12. Fore Royal
13. Fore Topgallant
14. Fore Topsail
15. Fore Course
16. Fore Topmast Staysail
17. Inner Jib
18. Outer Flying Jib
19. Spritsail

A. Taffrail & Lanterns
B. Stern & Quarter-galleries
C. Poop Deck/Great Cabins Under
D. Rudder & Transom Post
E. Quarterdeck
F. Mizen Chains & Stays
G. Main Chains & Stays
H. Boarding Battens/Entry Port
I. Cargo Loading Skids
J. Shrouds & Ratlines
K. Fore Chains & Stays

L. Waist
M. Gripe & Cutwater
N. Figurehead & Beakhead Rails
O. Bow Sprit
P. Jib Boom
Q. Foc's'le & Anchor Cat-heads
R. Cro'jack Yard (no sail fitted)
S. Top Platforms
T. Cross-Trees
U. Spanker Gaff

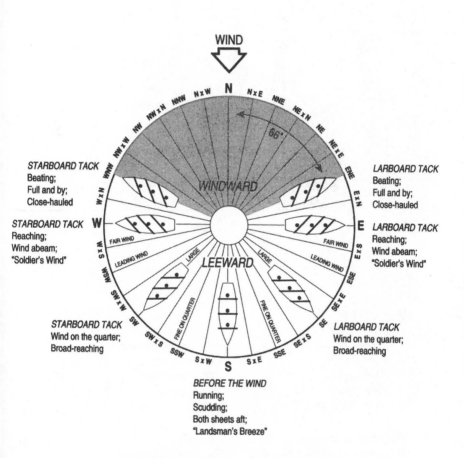

WIND

STARBOARD TACK
Beating;
Full and by;
Close-hauled

STARBOARD TACK
Reaching;
Wind abeam;
"Soldier's Wind"

STARBOARD TACK
Wind on the quarter;
Broad-reaching

LARBOARD TACK
Beating;
Full and by;
Close-hauled

LARBOARD TACK
Reaching;
Wind abeam;
"Soldier's Wind"

LARBOARD TACK
Wind on the quarter;
Broad-reaching

BEFORE THE WIND
Running;
Scudding;
Both sheets aft;
"Landsman's Breeze"

WINDWARD

LEEWARD

FAIR WIND

LEADING WIND

LARGE

FINE ON QUARTER

FAIR WIND

LEADING WIND

LARGE

FINE ON QUARTER

66°

N   NxE   NNE   NExN   NE   NExE   ENE   ExN   E   ExS   ESE   SExE   SE   SExS   SSE   SxE   S   SxW   SSW   SWxS   SW   SWxW   WSW   WxS   W   WxN   WNW   NWxW   NW   NWxN   NNW   NxW

POINTS OF SAIL AND 32-POINT WIND-ROSE

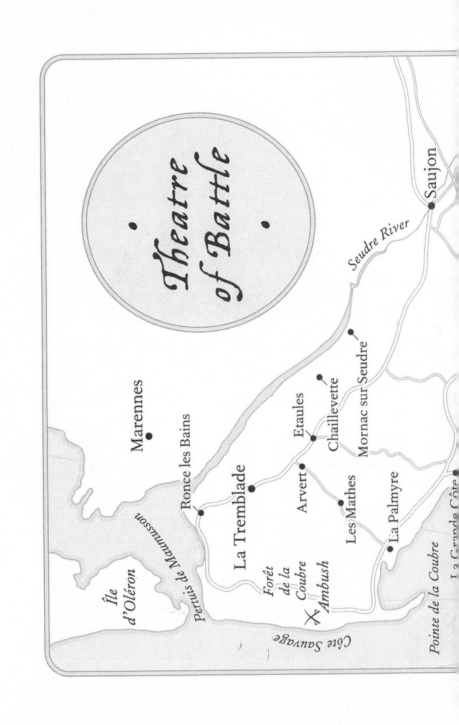

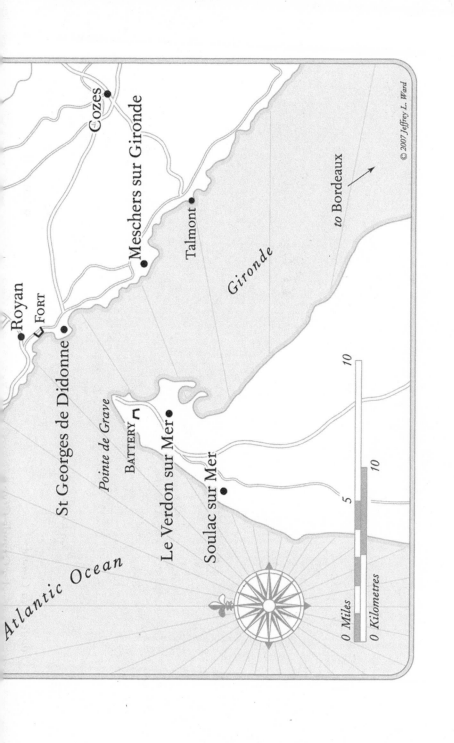

Cozes

Meschers sur Gironde

Talmont

Gironde

to Bordeaux

© 2007 Jeffrey L. Ward

Royan

FORT

St Georges de Didonne

Pointe de Grave

BATTERY

Le Verdon sur Mer

Soulac sur Mer

Atlantic Ocean

5

10

10

0 Miles

0 Kilometres

PROLOGUE

Alexander Iden (to Jack Cade):

How much thou wrong'st me, heaven be my
    judge.
Die, damned wretch, the curse of her that
    bare thee!
And as I thrust thy body in with my sword,
So wish I, I might thrust thy soul to hell!
Hence will I drag thee head long by the
    heels
Unto a dung hill, which shall be thy grave.
And there cut off thy most ungracious head,
Which I will bear in triumph to the King,
Leaving thy trunk for crows to feed upon.

William Shakespeare,
The Second Part of King Henry VI
Act IV, Scene X

CHAPTER ONE

Captain Alan Lewrie, RN, stepped out of the doors of the George Inn, just as the watch bells of a myriad of warships and merchant vessels in Portsmouth Harbour began to chime the end of the Morning Watch — Eight Bells, and the start of the Forenoon — in a distant, jangly ting-tinging much like what a rider near London might hear from church bells of a Sunday morning.

Not exactly a sound to set one's pocket-watch by, that chiming, for each ship depended on the turning of sand-glasses to measure hours and half hours, quarter hours for the Dog Watches, the initial turning of the glasses dependent on the vagaries of masters' and captains' time pieces, all of varying quality, accuracy, and cost.

Lewrie unconsciously drew his watch from a waist-coat pocket and found the time to be two and a half minutes *past* 8 a.m. Then he, as half a dozen other officers nearby did, put it to his ear to see if it was still ticking strongly. One much older Post-Captain growled under his breath, gave his a hard shake, and damned its maker with a muttered "Christ . . . bloody cogs!" before stalking off.

Lewrie merely shrugged, put his back in his waist-coat pocket, and lifted his gaze to savour the morning. And a fine morning it was, by Jove! There was ample early summer sunshine, and the sky was barely dappled with thinly scattered and quick-scudding light clouds. Flags and vanes showed the wind had come about from the Nor'east, and in some strength, too, for the flies of those flags were snapping chearly, the halliards chattering against the flagpoles. Weather vanes on rooves squeaked and jiggled to a relatively brisk breeze.

Lewrie resettled his cocked hat on his head, and, now alone on the walkway as the other officers headed away on their own occasions, allowed himself a most satisfying belch — not a well-stifled, gentlemanly thing, but a rather long, and loud, eructation; for in all of Portsmouth there was no breakfast finer than that served at the George Inn, and his morning repast of two eggs fried not quite to hard, with fried and grated potatoes, a chop-sized hank of flank beef, and bread sliced two finger-joints thick, toasted to perfection, then slathered with fresh butter and Kentish apple preserves, had been perfection . . . *and,* sluiced down with three cups of coffee fetched to his table half-scalding, to boot . . . well!

That belch, in point of fact, was so savoury that Lewrie allowed himself a second before taking hold of the scabbard of his hundred-guinea presentation small-sword to restrict its swinging, and set off towards the quays, and the King's Stairs, where he would take a hired boat back to his new frigate.

The morning was so clear and bright that even before he got to the King's Stairs, Lewrie could espy dozens of sail making the most of the shift of wind to head down-Channel for the Atlantic. Nearer to, at least a dozen warships were falling down to St. Helen's Patch, down to the Isle of Wight and the open sea, after being cooped up in port for a fortnight or more, awaiting a favourable slant of wind and a moderation in the weather.

To be back at sea! Were *Savage* in *any* respects ready to sail, what a grand morning's departure it would be, but, alas, his frigate still lay to anchor with both bowers and both stern kedges down, with her upper masts and rigging stripped "to a gant-line" for re-rigging and re-masting to his satisfaction. Her jib-boom and bowsprit had been steeved to a lower angle, whole new sets of inner and outer jibs cut and sewn, and the Sailmaker and his crew ready to make new fore-and-aft stays'ls to Lewrie's requirements, once the upper masts were set in place . . . all to aid

HMS *Savage* to "point" just a half, or a quarter, point closer to the eyes of the winds.

The sooner, the better, pray Jesus! Lewrie fretfully thought, his good mood and joy of a good breakfast curdled by the dread that he might not stay free long enough to skitter over the horizon, out of reach of his pending legal troubles . . . and the adamantine wrath of the Beauman family.

No wonder the others were peerin' at me so odd, Lewrie thought as he reached the stone quays; *wond'rin' whether I'm saint or felon.*

The George Inn was one of the better establishments in Portsmouth, the favourite of senior naval officers, so he had been among an host of Rear-Admirals, a Commodore or three, and Post-Captains of more than Three Years' Seniority, like himself, "salted enough" to wear a pair of gilt-lace epaulets on their shoulders. They'd *seemed* polite and civil enough, some smiling as they pointed him out to their table companions and gave him a nod. Others, well . . .

"That's Lewrie, don't ye know . . . pile o' 'tin' in the West Indies . . . the 'Ram-Cat,' he's called, and God pity his poor wife . . . at Cape Saint Vincent and Camperdown, both, with the medals for 'em . . . a fight near Cape Town in early spring, took a bigger French frigate . . . two-hour fight in a blowin' gale, I heard . . . got *his* frigate out from the Nore during the Mutiny . . . oh, in all the papers, and such 'cause he *stole* Jamaican slaves t'crew his ship . . . darlin' of the Abolition crowd, and Wilberforce, so please ye! 'Black Alan' Lewrie now, haw-haw . . . soon t'hang, I heard, God rot 'im! Aye, and Wilberforce, too . . . demned 'reformers' and 'kill-joys'!"

Lewrie had heard rumours from his new allies in the Society for the Abolition of Slavery in the British Empire, the Reverend William Wilberforce and his coterie, that the Beauman family, already about as fond of him as cold, boiled mutton, had departed Jamaica for England.

Now they'd finally discovered just who it was who stole their dozen prime field hands from one of their many plantations, the one on the shore of Portland Bight (well, sort of, kind of, *recruited* or *received,* not stolen *exactly!*), they were come with vengeance running hot in their spleens to see him tried, convicted, stripped of all of his wealth and property, cashiered from the Royal Navy, then most publicly and satisfyingly carted to Tyburn and hung from a gibbet, to the taunts from the Mob, and the Huzzahs of the Beaumans.

Never should've shot their damned cousin in that duel, Lewrie silently rued, grimly recalling when he'd seconded his old friend Kit Cashman, who'd drilled the youngest Beauman brother, Ledyard, right in the belly, too, who'd taken five agonising days to die after they had scandalously violated the rules of honour with a back-shot, and extra, hidden pistols. *Though it was satisfyin'* . . .

Most of the bumboats and boats for hire were scurrying about from vessel to vessel, and for the moment, only two remained tied to the landing, their shabby bundled or furled sails rustling and snapping to the breeze, and frayed rope halliards chattering against their short masts, the blocks clattering and squealing. Lewrie paused from choosing, taking a long look seaward. It was such a clear and sunny day that he could even see far up-channel into the main anchorage of Spithead, past Gilkicker Point into the little-used and shallow channel of Needles Passage round the west end of the Isle of Wight. Redcoats standing sentry-go on the ramparts of the Monckton Fort could be spotted individually. To the east, he could even make out the heights of Selsey Bill, for a rare wonder.

And there was his brand-new frigate, HMS *Savage,* anchored not five cables offshore, and as shiny as a new-minted penny, just fresh from the graving docks. Her new hull paint, tar, and pitch shone in the morning light, every glitter of sunshine on the cat's-pawed harbour waters reflected down her sleek flanks like a continual shower of diamond chips. She floated light and high, less her guns and stores, which still sat ashore in warehouses and armouries at Gun Wharf, or among the goods from the Victualling Board's vast depot, and fresh copper cladding, normally below the waterline, flickered with dapples of sun like a horizontal sheet of gold or brass.

She was a Fifth Rate 18-pounder of over 950 tons burthen, the largest, longest, best-armed ship Lewrie had ever been appointed to command, and the thought of losing captaincy over her was as painful as the dread of dying. She was long, lean, and powerful-looking with such a sweet, aggressive curve to her sheerline and gunwale, with an entry and forefoot finer and leaner than the usual bluff bowed ships built in British yards. She was a leashed greyhound! A *French greyhound,* Lewrie had to remind himself; *even so, though . . .*

The French had built her at Brest, of stout Hamburg oak before the outbreak of the war in 1792, and commissioned in the vicious and bloody turmoil of the Terror in '93, named in honour of the crackpot ideas of the philosopher Rousseau as *Le Sauvage Noble.* Sent out to an ignoble sacrifice, Lewrie had learned, for with all the former aristocratic or Royalist-leaning officers of the French Navy dismissed from the service, hunted down for trial and humiliation by the revolutionaries, imprisoned for a time were they lucky . . . their heads chopped off by the heavy, wicked

21

blade of the guillotine were they not . . . she had been captained, and her semi-hapless crew led, by former Bosun's Mates and *matelots* with the "proper" revolutionary attitudes and viewpoints. When she ran afoul of a lighter-gunned British frigate off Rochefort a year later, in '94, all her grace and power had gone for nought and she had abjectly surrendered after a mere quarter-hour's pounding!

Re-named HMS *Savage,* taking the name of a much older Sixth Rate of 16 guns that had gone to the breakers after serving since 1761, she'd been "bought in" and commissioned into the Royal Navy for a full three years of active service before requiring a "truck to keel" refit, a new crew, and a new captain, and Lewrie *had* thought himself as fortunate to get her, but . . .

"Hoy there, fellow!" someone cried nearby. "A boat, at once, I say!" Lewrie turned away from admiring his frigate to espy an officer, a Lieutenant in best-dress uniform, trotting along the quay, chivvying a much older, gap-toothed and one-eyed civilian in charge of a broken-down hand-cart piled with the officer's dunnage, the Lieutenant lending a hand on one of the shafts to speed the hand-cart along. Lewrie noted the typical sea-chest, much battered and scraped, with its original gay and martial paint nearly faded away; a large canvas sea-bag, and a pair of stuffed-tobursting *portmanteaus* made of scrap carpet, to boot, atop the precarious and wobbly cart.

"I'm late, I'm late!" the younger officer could be heard to say. "Christ, a quarter past Eight Bells! I'm fucked, so bloody fucked . . . *oh!*" he exclaimed as he took note of Lewrie and his pair of epaulets. He visibly blanched, almost slammed to a stop in chagrin to use blasphemy *and* Billingsate in the presence of a Post-Captain.

"Joining a ship, are you?" Lewrie enquired, putting a "stern" expression on his phyz. "Cuttin' it rather *fine,* ain't you?"

"Aye, sir," the Lieutenant replied, doffing his cocked hat in salute, to which Lewrie replied with two fingers touching the brim of his own. "Got the last coach, skin o' me teeth, that, and arrived at a late hour last night, sir. Some old friends at the Blue Posts . . ."

"Indeed," Lewrie primly drawled, quite enjoying himself, for a rare once lately. *Damme, this is fun!* he thought. "And they simply *had* to 'wet you down' to your new posting, hmm?"

"Aye, sir," the Lieutenant shamefacedly replied.

"A damned bad beginning, sir," Lewrie admonished. To punctuate his shammed disdain for such, he drew out his pocket-watch and peered at its face, then turned and waved at the last remaining hired boat at the foot of the landing, for, during their brief

23

conversation, another Lieutenant and two Midshipmen had engaged the other, better boat.

"I, ah . . . ," the Lieutenant began to say, realising that he was going to be even later reporting aboard his new ship, for he was out-ranked and would have to wait for the return of anything that floated.

"I s'pose I *could* offer you a ride, Mister, ah . . . ?" Lewrie idly offered.

"Urquhart, sir. Ed'ard Urquhart," the other told him, looking desperately into the middle distance to see if anything *resembling* a hired boat was coming back to the foot of the King's Stairs empty. "Edward, mean t'say . . . ," he babbled on. "Might I enquire as to where your ship is anchored, sir? Mine own is quite near at hand . . . that frigate just yonder, sir . . . *Savage*."

Aha! Lewrie exultantly thought; *they've finally got round to sendin' me a First Officer, at last!* One *had* turned up, weeks before, but that'un had pleaded off sick after the first week, and had departed looking like Death's Head On A Mop-Stick, hacking, wheezing, coughing, and hoicking up phlegm by the bucket. *He's mine, damn his eyes!*

"What? Captain Alan Lewrie's ship?" Lewrie pretended to scoff.

"Aye, sir."

"Under *that* scoundrel, that rogue?" Lewrie mock-sneered. "That rakehell Corinthian?

24

Hah! God have mercy on your soul, then, sir!"

Lt. Edward (or Ed'ard) Urquhart blushed and gulped, timorously replying, "I was given to understand, though, sir, that Captain Lewrie is a most distinguished and capable captain. A *renowned . . .*"

"Any fool can be brave and dashin', don't ye know, sir," Lewrie pooh-poohed. "Well, then, Mister Urquhart. I will, this once, mind, take mercy 'pon ye, and allow you to board that shiny wee barge, before attending to mine own urgent return to *my* ship. Bargee! Two passengers . . . and all this . . . jetsam."

The boatman and his assistant helped place the heavy sea-chest amidships of their scruffy little launch, while Lt. Urquhart saw to his own sea-bag and carpet bags, an act that secretly pleased Lewrie, for most young men of the squirearchy, who made up the bulk of the Navy's officers, would have stood aloof on their dignity and depended on the lesser sorts to hew and haul.

Lt. Urquhart stepped down into the rustling boat, following the time-honoured tradition that senior officers would be "Last In, First Out" when transferring from a ship or shore.

"W'ichship, Cap'm?" the bargee at the tiller asked, once they were settled upon their respective thwarts.

"We'll go to *Savage* first," Lewrie stated.

"A short sail for you. The 'gant-lined' frigate, yonder."

"Four pence apiece, sirs," the bargee said, horny and grubby hand out to receive their coin, no matter how short a trip it would be. Once paid, he nodded to his assistant, who cast them off and shoved on the landing stage, then whirled to hoist the single lug-sail.

"A *pretty* thing," Lewrie said in seeming disparagement. "French, ye know."

"She's absolutely beautiful, sir," Lt. Urquhart replied, gazing at her with delight, despite the reception he would most-like receive for reporting aboard so late in the morning.

"Note her bows, though, Mister Urquhart," Lewrie went on as if to point out her flaws. "Much too fine. Fast, aye, but perhaps with less buoyancy than ye'd need t'ride a heavy sea, when it ships over the bow. She'll bury her 'nose,' like as not. And the Frogs don't space their hull timbers close, or thick, enough t'take heavy poundin'. She'll flex, in a full gale, and fill herself with scantling timber in a fight, without close-spaced, stout bracing. Kill a lot of men?"

"If Captain Lewrie has no qualms about her, sir, well . . . ," Lt. Urquhart declared, before catching himself at being too argumentative with a strange Post-Captain. "After all, sir, do not our own naval architects take off

26

the lines of the newest French National Ships that we are able to capture, and emulate them? Better to serve aboard such a frigate than one of those much weaker and lighter-timbered new brig-sloops, sir," he added, with an attempt at a disarming smile.

"Like Lucifer said in Dante's poem, Mister Urquhart," Lewrie quickly riposted. " 'Better to rule in Hell than serve in Heaven'? I assume by your age, and the condition of your sea-chest, that you are to be her First?"

"Aye, sir . . . my first such commission," Lt. Urquhart proudly stated.

"Oo's fer 'is *Savitch* barkee, then, sirs?" the boatman at the tiller asked as his sole assistant handed the launch's lug-sail as the boat swung up to approach the frigate's starboard entry-port.

"Both of us," Lewrie told him with a taut grin of mischief.

"Boat ahoy!" came a shout from the quarterdeck.

"Savitch!" the assistant in the bow shouted back, showing four fingers as well to indicate that a Post-Captain was coming aboard.

"Oh, my soul!" Lt. Urquhart whispered. His eyes blared in alarm as he swivelled about on his thwart to look at Lewrie.

"*Told* you Lewrie was a scoundrel, Mister Urquhart," he grinned.

CHAPTER TWO

After that shocking chance meeting, Lt. Edward (or Ed'ard) Urquhart had had a rather trying day. His proper reporting aboard was not so bad, nor was his reception in Capt. Lewrie's great-cabins, where he had been offered a glass of *cool* tea with lemon and sugar, been told he would be one of the rare "Johnny New-Comes" aboard *Savage*, after most of the officers and crew of Lewrie's old ship, HMS *Proteus*, had volunteered to turn over into this new frigate . . . a great honour to Lewrie, to elicit such loyalty. But for those of warrant or petty officer rank who pretty much stayed with one ship, commission after commission, such as the Bosun and his Mate, Cooper, Sailmaker, Master Gunner, and lived aboard even when a warship was laid up in-ordinary, HMS *Savage* was now manned by officers and hands who had "rubbed together" for three years, and would squint with chary eyes at an interloper. 'Til they had had a chance to take his measure.

Capt. Lewrie had informed him that he destested tyrannical, "flogging" officers, and had found that *his* "people" had never been of the insubordinate sort; that the necessity for corporal punishment was rare aboard, and that he'd found "firm but fair" treatment from solidly experienced officers, not Tartars, worked better than anything else.

Lt. Urquhart had heard scads about Capt. Alan Lewrie from his fellow officers, not just from the newspapers and such. He was not as famed as the gallant Pellew, or Collingwood, not quite the nationally cheered Nelson, but he had a reputation as a fighter, so Urquhart had come aboard feeling rather fortunate to have a chance to serve under a man who had a fairly well-known name in the clannish family of fellow Royal Navy officers. Capt. Lewrie was also possessed of a repute that was, well . . . *colourful,* to put it charitably.

Lt. Urquhart beheld a man in his mid- to late thirties who owned a charming and easy smile; a captain who "wore his own hair" 'stead of a wig, whose hair was mid-brown, where the sun had not lightened the shade to light brown, and the merriest blue eyes surrounded by laugh lines and the crow's-feet of perpetual sea-squinting — though they did, when Lewrie turned more serious about professional matters, seem to go frostier and greyer. Lewrie was three inches shorter than

Lt. Urquhart's own six feet even, a fellow who might weigh eleven or twelve stone, with a fit build, without the beginnings of a senior Post-Captain's pot belly, bred of higher pay, prize-money, or private means natural to the typical squirearchy background of most captains his age; born of the ability to purchase more wine, brandy, and rich viands, consumed alone in a ship-captain's traditional aloofness from others aboard; from the richness of suppers shared with fellow captains and foreign dignitaries when "showing the flag," with junior officers and Midshipmen on a weekly rotation when at sea, where one was forced to show off open-handed hospitality, even a touch of splendour, from one's own purse.

Or, as Edward Urquhart had always suspected, from sheer boredom to fill the lonely, aloof hours spent so often alone at-table in one's great-cabins. Or the gluttony that followed *years* of plain commons!

Capt. Lewrie had done most of the talking, asking the usual questions about Urquhart's previous service, and Urquhart had responded as firmly as he could without veering off into too *many* inessential digressions. After that disastrous first meeting ashore, he had a false impression to correct, an urgent need to *please* and to reassure his new captain that he would be a worthy addition; *and,* the hope that he fit in.

It did not help Lt. Urquhart's efforts that Lewrie's two cats, a stout black-and-white one named Toulon (*and where had that odd name come from?* he wondered) and a mostly white younger one named Chalky (*much more obvious, that'un*), had come trotting to the desk in the day-cabin from the transom settee where they had been sunning themselves, and had discovered that they simply *adored* the new First Officer, the scent of his fresh-blacked Hessian boots, the leather scabbard of his sword, the tails of his uniform coat, then the suitability of his lap! From whence they had explored his coat lapels, shirt collar, and neck-stock, and had even gone so far as to nuzzle and paw at his hair!

Lt. Urquhart, it was sad to say, was a huntin' dog man, and had no use for cats, except for killing stable rats.

"We're fresh from the graving docks, and expect the barges and water hoys alongside this morning, Mister Urquhart," Capt. Lewrie had concluded, rising to his feet to most charitably walk Urquhart to the exit door, which had required Urquhart to rise as well, giving him a chance to peel the two wee beasts off — gently, rather than following his instinct to seize them by their scruffs and hurl them from one end of the great-cabins to the other. "I expect you'll be hard-pressed to see all loaded by sunset. We've a well-

31

drilled and experienced crew, so the work should go orderly, and your fellow officers, whom I expect you'll soon meet, know what they're about, so it shouldn't be all that demanding, really. Welcome aboard, and I'm looking forward to having you as First Officer, sir."

Well, it hadn't gone *that* smoothly. Urquhart suspected that he was on trial by every leery Man-Jack, Midshipman, and officer. *Everybody* had seemed to suffer from sudden ignorance of ropes, blocks, and such, requiring him to see to everything. The "test," if testing it was, had felt more tongue-in-cheek than mutely insubordinate, and Lt. Urquhart had swallowed his spleen and patiently endured it . . . mostly.

By the end of the day, at Eight Bells of the Day Watch and the start of the usually idle First Dog, the holds had been filled. Water butts stowed and firmly wedged in, then filled with fresh water pumped from the ungainly hoys; great casks of salt-meats treated much in the same manner. Chests and bags of fresh-baked biscuit, a vast array of Bosun's stores and spare timbers, miles of spare cordage and replacement blocks all had gone below, settling HMS *Savage* a few inches lower in the harbour waters. The day after, and kegs of gunpowder, flannel cartridge bagging, gun-carriages, and the frigate's artillery would come aboard.

Last into the ship, late in the day, had come a load of fresh loaves, a bellowing bullock whose hooves had barely touched the deck before he was slaughtered for supper, and a cage of live chickens for the officers' mess. Lt. Urquhart had mopped his brow, nodded to his new fellows, and had gone below to his deal-and-canvas partitioned cabin (rather grand in size after the ones he had bunked in whilst a junior officer!) and had finally had a chance to unpack and sponge himself down before dressing for a proper meal in the wardroom. One where he must begin to enforce his own stamp upon the others. "Firm but fair," sober and nearly humourless, relentless in the pursuit of duty no matter his private nature. He had it all planned out.

Unfortunately, his curiosity got the better of him, for there was too much to learn about his new captain from the ones who'd been with him so long.

CHAPTER THREE

Mr. Maurice Durant, the ship's Surgeon, a rather laconic French *émigré* finally promoted from Surgeon's Mate (it helped to be a Protestant Huguenot), had made a guarded comment about Capt. Lewrie's pending legal troubles anent some dozen "stolen" slaves, seven of whom still survived among *Savage*'s crew, which resulted in an equally cautious discussion of the how and the when of the matter. And, whether their captain might *remain* captain for very much longer, or might be relieved to face trial in London, and where would they be, then?

Lt. Urquhart was struck by how *fond* the others seemed to feel about Capt. Lewrie, despite the notoriety attached to him, the tracts and pamphlets put out by the Abolitionists, and the lurid accounts in the newspapers. The seeming depth of their feelings went beyond the usual dread of serving under a new captain of unknown abilities, temperament, or aggressiveness that might not be equal to Lewrie's when it came to seeking action, glory, or prize-money. Quite expectedly, they would fear dull, humdrum service or anything that took the gloss off the reputation they had made in HMS *Proteus.*

Some of it, Urquhart suspected, was the comfort of "old shoes," and "better the devil you know . . . ," along with their rightful pride.

Together so long, *Savage's* wardroom did not *exactly* follow the traditional narrow strictures on table conversation, either. Captains and senior officers usually were *never* discussed, except in the most careful, praiseful way. Their foibles and idiosyncracies, "warts and all," were definitely off-limits, but . . . *Savage's* officers knew their captain extremely well by then, and seemed to take a perverse pride in his . . . weaker moments.

A glass more than he'd planned to imbibe had fuzzled Urquhart's wits just enough to mangle his attempt to quash such improper nattering. It came out as "Well, I dare say that Captain Lewrie has made himself a fair name in the Fleet." Said with a sober face, at least, and with the merest hint that they treaded on taboo territory as his brow furrowed. "Such is *not,* usually, a thing junior officers *should* bandy about. I will allow, however, that I am not cognisant of every deed which has created such a sterling reputation. I was right proud to receive orders into *Savage* as First Officer, and . . . when I learned that Captain Lewrie commands her, I did, indeed, say to myself, 'Aha, I've heard of him,' and thought myself quite fortunate . . . as I gather that you gentlemen feel, about serving under him. Though I cannot say that I knew much beyond the fact that I *had* heard the Captain's name mentioned at one time or t'other. What-all have you and the Captain done in your old ship, then? What are the high-water marks you might recall?"

It was off to the races after that.

Alan Lewrie had always been reckoned an extremely lucky fellow, Urquhart was rather eagerly informed by Lt. Adair, the Second Officer, a dark and curly-haired Scot; by the Third Officer, Mr. D'arcy Gamble, who had been an "upwards of twenty" and capable Midshipman aboard HMS *Proteus* 'til their last battle in the South Atlantic off the coast of Africa; by the elegant Marine officer, Lt. Blase Devereux; by Mr. Durant the Surgeon; and by the Purser, the prim little Mr. Coote. Even Sailing Master Mr. Winwood, a most taciturn and sober-sided fellow of the new "Strenuous Christian" bent, lauded cautious praise for Capt. Lewrie . . . though with some reservations anent his "extra-curricular" activities.

Lucky, aye, reckoned so by fellow officers,

and especially so by the people who shipped "before the mast," from the lower deck, for hadn't Lewrie been blessed with a *geas* in the Bay of Biscay when he'd captained HMS *Jester* way back in '94? Why, 'twas rumoured that *seals* — hundreds of miles from any beach! — had come alongside and spoken to Commander Alan Lewrie at the end of a sea burial of a Midshipman of Cornwall who might've, *might've* mind, been born a *selkie,* one of those ancient cursed souls who had angered the mythic, half-forgotten Celtic sea-god, Lir, and were doomed to live lives in the sea as seals, crying for a life on land, then shedding their skins and becoming human just long enough to suffer longings for a life in the sea, 'til the end of time. Silly, pagan, and heretical, but Cornish and Irish tars walked in awe of Lewrie as one of Lir's blessed, to this very day. And how hellish-odd it was that they'd heard other officers eerily recall the barking of seals whenever HMS *Jester* needed an omen of danger ahead!

Lucky in battle, and in prize-money, too, Lewrie was. How had he gotten *Jester* in the first place? He'd been First Lieutenant into HMS *Cockerel,* but had ended up seconded ashore — or in charge of a captured French mortar boat, some had heard tell — during the siege of Toulon in '93, and had been captured by the bastard Frog Napoleon

Bonaparte himself when the mortar vessel blew up, but saved by Spanish cavalry. Blown sky-high, but lived! *There's* luck for you.

Days before the evacuation of the First Coalition forces, he'd been put in charge of a leaky, half-armed French frigate, barely manned and crammed with French Royalist refugees. Chased down by a squadron of two *corvettes* and a frigate, Lewrie'd not only held his own, but hammered one *corvette* to ruin, then swung cross the bows of the next, boarded her with a scratch assault force of British soldiers and refugee Frenchmen, and *took* her for his own!

His patron at the time, Vice-Admiral Sir Samuel Hood, had made Lewrie a Commander once back at Gibraltar, and re-named her HMS *Jester* 'stead of *Sans Culottes* or something revolutionary.

"No, wasn't *Sans Culottes*," Lt. Gamble chortled. "The way that I heard it was, there were some japes 'bout how ridiculous some of the French warships' names were, and Captain Lewrie said that it would not do to have an HMS '*Bare-Arsed*' in the Fleet, and Admiral Hood thought him too *much* a wag, and called her *Jester* as his own little joke."

Despite the impropriety of such talk, Lt. Urquhart found that he was quite intrigued — perhaps half a bottle of claret over, but intrigued — and even essayed an appreciative little chuckle, which only encouraged them, for this was miles beyond the usual carefully written official after-action accounts sent to Admiralty and printed in the *Marine Chronicle* and the *Gazette.*

Lewrie and *Jester* had been a terror to the French during the First Italian Campaign, when Napoleon had routed and annihilated the Genoese, Piedmontese, and Savoian armies, and had defeated the might of Austria, too. Raids along the coasts, shelling the few roads that could support supply waggons, capturing coastal shipping, which bore the bulk of French supplies; routing and reaping French vessels sent to support their army on Corsica against British invasion.

"Though I did hear that he did *something* that angered Nelson, who was in overall command," Lt. Adair said with a puzzled shrug of incomplete knowledge. "Made him kick furniture and *swear,* one time, or more."

"Went ashore and shot some Frenchman he was pursuing, someone told *me,*" Lt. Gamble offered. "Got caught up in the battle that ran the whole Austrian army twenty miles in a perfect panic, 'fore noon, but got back to the coast and was picked up by one of our boats that wasn't even looking for him. Speak of Captain Lewrie's good fortune!"

"Why, that fellow he shot was the very same Guillaume Choundas we dealt with in the Caribbean," Adair added. "Shot his arm clean off with that Ferguson breech-loading rifle, from two hundred yards away, or better. Choundas was in charge of all the privateers working out of the isle of Guadeloupe, and 'twas *his* frigate we battered to kindling right in the harbour of Bas-Terre before she could get a way on. And that Captain Choundas, the ugly bastard, well . . . 'tween the American Revolution and the French'un, Choundas and the Captain crossed hawses somewhere in the Far East, too. We put paid to that ogre . . . even if the Americans *did* end up capturing him."

"But 'twas the Captain's doing, Mister Adair," Mr. Winwood stuck in, "that we cooperated so closely . . . yet so carefully . . . with the new American Navy during their brief little not-quite-a-war with the French back in '98. Bless me, but we *led* the Yankee Doodles out of English Harbour, right to that French arms convoy bound for Saint Domingue, and Choundas's clutch of warships and privateers, too."

"Don't forget Saint Vincent," Lt. Devereux said, after he'd topped up his port and passed it leftwards down the table. "*Jester,* I'd heard, was on her way home with despatches, in need of a refit at the time, when she stumbled into Admiral Jervis's fleet. Think of it, Mister Urquhart . . . Nelson in HMS *Captain,* with the *Culloden,* daunting a whole wing of the Spanish fleet, up against two-decker, three-decker ships of the line, and the *Santissima*

40

Trinidad, the world's only *four*-decker, before they could assail the rear of *our* fleet. And, right by their side was Captain Lewrie, and HMS *Jester!* A Sixth Rate, by Heaven, which *had* no business engaging anything bigger than her, especially not a ship of the line, blazing away with her nine-pounders and drawing the fire of the world's biggest warship!"

"Captain'd tell ye different," Mr. Winwood countered, coming as close as he might to an outright laugh. "I mentioned it once whilst we dined, and he swore that *Jester* was just sailing along alee of Nelson, minding her own business, and acting as a signals-repeating ship, but Nelson suddenly wheeled out of line and nigh would have rammed *Jester* amidships, had she not hauled her own wind and come about as well. As the Captain told it, it was 'ram you, or damn you' . . . that *Jester* and he were *pushed,* and courage had nothing to do with it. He *did* fire on the *Santissima Trinidad,* since it seemed the thing to do, but that she was far out of range of *Jester's* guns, and *far* out of range of her own, and why the Dons would waste an entire four-deck broadside on his wee ship, he still has no idea. Took 'em a *month* to re-load and run out."

"But Admiral Jervis *thought* it brave," Lt. Adair said. "That's why the Captain wears the gold medal for the Battle of Cape Saint

Vincent. Told he was daft as bats, in point of fact, and not to do *that* sort of thing again, but he *did* put his name forward for the medal."

"After that . . . before it, I can't quite recall," Lt. Gamble said with a frown of concentration, "*Jester* was in the Adriatic with a small squadron. A few months before 'Old Jarvy' had to fall back on Gibraltar and abandon the Mediterranean. Oh! That was *definitely* during Napoleon's Italian Campaign, and the French badly needed Adriatic oak to build new warships, or repair the ones they still had, and the Captain went through their merchantmen like a hot knife through butter. Fought a vicious pack of local pirates . . . Serbian or something . . . to save a bunch of English men and women. Got lured ashore by them, and almost lost his life before his First Lieutenant got leery, and sent a Marine party ashore. The pirates had taken a Venetian ship, just full of Catholics and 'White Muslims,' whom they hated worse than anything, and were simply *butchering,* for *fun,* 'fore the Captain got there. *That* is where Captain Lewrie met Mistress Theoni Connor, widow of a man in the Ionian Islands' currant trade, and, ahem . . . well, saved her, and her little boy's, life. The pirates put her up for auction, and the Captain bought time by bidding her price up, *I* heard."

Lt. Urquhart raised a brow over that'un,

for, while he was not a rakehell, and had been raised in a strict but loving, religiously observant home, still and all, he was a young man of all his parts, and not averse to a "run ashore," so long as precautions were taken, and pleasures could be taken discreetly. *That* was one incident that he'd heard about Capt. Lewrie. A *Greek* woman, a *hellish-fetching* widow, rich as King Croesus off the currant trade, and Britons' insatiable desire for them, who lived so flambouyantly in London, had had a child out of wedlock with a Navy officer, was his mistress during the time he was ashore . . . ? Capt. Alan Lewrie's name had been linked to her, and the boy-child was, so he'd heard, named Michael *Alan* Connor! Aha!

"Theoni *Kavares* Connor, the one you mean, sir?" he asked the only-slightly-discomfited Lt. Gamble. "She and the Captain . . . ?"

"Aye, that's the one," Lt. Adair supplied. "She came down to Sheerness and took shore lodgings, once *Proteus* was repaired after the Battle of Camperdown, and got orders for the West Indies. The Captain *did,* ah . . . spend a night or two ashore, but . . ."

"Long before that, just as *Proteus* was fitting out, just before the Nore Mutiny, well . . . ," Mr. Winwood intoned, and heaved a deep sigh. "Now, foolish as it sounds, there was something *fey* about her, too, a . . . Celtic,

43

pagan thing that was extremely odd and . . . disturbing."

"Tell it me," Lt. Urquhart asked of him, even more intrigued.

The Mutiny at the great naval anchorage of the Nore, which was much more dangerous and rebellious against King and Country than ever the more respectful Spithead Mutiny had been, had begun just as demands had been fulfilled among the Channel Fleet. Lewrie had just been "Made Post" into HMS *Proteus,* fresh from the private yards at Chatham, where she had first tasted water under another captain, and the manner of her launching had, as Mr. Winwood had said, been extremely odd.

The Admiralty's chosen name was to be *Proteus,* a Greek sea-god, but, came the day when the bands, the crowds, the dignitaries, and the Church representatives had turned out for the celebration, a retired Rear-Admiral who, at the moment, had been filled with more brandy than sense, and at the nagging of his myth-laden wife, who had been simply *besotted* with the newly popular tales published by the blind Irish poet O'Carolan and an host of others, cried out, "Success to his Majesty's Ship . . . *Merlin!*" as he hoisted his glass to her and drained it off, just as the last restraining props had been sawn through, and a gasp had arisen, and the band nigh-stumbled to a cacophonous halt.

One simply *didn't* name a Protestant Christian King's ship, one specifically built to kill Catholic Spaniards and atheistic Frenchmen in the most efficient manner, after a pagan wizard and heathen *Druid* . . . even if Merlin *had* been such a boon to fabled old King Arthur!

HMS "*Merlin*" had begun to slide down the greasy ways into the Medway, 'til another senior officer in better mental takings, and relative sobriety (perhaps one without a termagant wife in tow!), quickly got to his feet, seized a full glass, and corrected things with a loud cry of "Success to His Majesty's ship *Proteus*!"

At the instant, the frigate had stuck quite solidly on the ways!

Talk of *greater* consternation! It was not until an Irish sawyer who'd helped build her, with his little boy at his side, had gone down the slipway and had stood under the ship's bows, right beside her cutwater; had *whispered* something to her to this day unknowable, then the wee lad had given her the tiniest shove, more like a love pat, in point of fact, before *Proteus/Merlin* had given out a soft groan, then had *allowed* herself to be launched, sliding into the river, as sweet as anything!

Newly "posted" Alan Lewrie was, in fact, her second captain. A bit after her launch, whilst still completing rigging, her first commanding officer and his cousin, her Chaplain, both Anglo-Irishmen landowners in the *big* way over hundreds of poor Irish cottagers, rowed back from shore one dead-calm night. Not a breath of wind stirred, with not a ripple to disturb the Medway's surface, yet *Proteus* had heaved a slow roll starboard, steepening the boarding battens to dead-vertical, and the first captain and her Chaplain and been heard to utter shouts, as both suddenly lost their grips — both were abstemious, and sober as judges, so it was reported later. The Chaplain well . . .

He fell backwards, striking his head on the gunnel of the ship's boat. He sank out of sight at once, and his body was *never* found, and, while her first captain had managed to cling to the boarding batten steps, he had claimed that it felt as if the man-ropes had *stung* him or *bit* him as hurtful as wasps!

And, not a week after, said captain was found raving and crying in his nightshirt, dashing about the quarterdeck, or cowering in sheer terror in his cabins, swearing that *Proteus* had murdered his cousin, and was out to kill him, too! Were his family not rich, he could have ended up in Bedlam in London, supplementing his half-pay (it took rather a bit of doing for a senior officer to be struck off the Navy List for any cause other than dropping stone-cold dead in those days!) off the poking-stick and water-squirt conces-

46

sions offered those who toured the place and wished to stir the inmates up from catatonia.

At that point, enter Capt. Alan Lewrie, lucky, again, to get himself such a fine, spanking-new frigate. Or, so he had thought, for not a fortnight later, *Proteus* had fallen down the snaking Medway to the Nore anchorage, right into the heart of the Mutiny! One mutineer in particular, whom Lewrie himself had recruited off the receiving ship (he'd turned out to be a former Midshipman Rolston back in 1780, when Lewrie first donned King's Coat as a "Mid," a little fiend who had been responsible for a sailor's death and broken to Ordinary Seaman), stoked *Proteus*'s own rebellious cabal of mutineers, and had tried to arrange the murder of *all* her officers, warrants, and gentlemanly Midshipmen.

In the end, Capt. Lewrie, kept from being sent ashore as the other officers and captains were by the rebellious committee, had won enough loyal sailors and Marines to launch a rebellion of his own . . . with the rather embarrassing help from the roughly two dozen prostitutes fetched out to the ship by the bumboatmen-pimps, who'd usually serve as temporary "wives" by sailors with money for their "socket fees," supporting them on shares of their rations, rum issues, and smuggled spirits. The mutineer committee had declared that all women must stay aboard the rebelling warships, long after the sailors' last coins had been, spent, so the doxies had been feeling a touch rebellious themselves!

Indeed, HMS *Proteus* was one of the few warships that had managed to escape, under fire from mutinous ships of the line, to join up with Adm. Duncan's much-reduced squadron, which kept watch on the Batavian Dutch Republic's coasts to daunt the Dutch Navy from leaving port to join with a French fleet . . . after dropping off the whores, and those mutineers they'd made prisoners. It *had* been reckoned notorious that Capt. Lewrie had sent letters to both Admiralty and Parliament asking that the women receive monetary rewards and letters of thanks for the patriotic and courageous aid they'd offered!

The Captain had also sent a note-of-hand to his London solicitor, ordering that each of the prostitutes be paid a more-than-decent sum "for services rendered!" and what the Crown, Society, and Capt. Lewrie's *wife* thought of *that,* well. . . .

And when that Rolston had died, now that was eerie, too . . .

A transfer from *Proteus* to a coaster they'd met, hired to take prisoners to the authorities at Sheerness; Rolston coming on deck in chains and shackles, cursing Lewrie for his luck — there it was, again — for how else could one explain how Rolston could swing his cutlass for a killing, beheading blow, but

48

damme if the Captain hadn't deflected it with his *tin penny-whistle!* and if the Good Lord, or the pagan sea-god Lir, hadn't been looking out for him, then please explain it!

Then, when Rolston had started down the boarding battens, with man-ropes in hand, damme if *Proteus* hadn't heaved a slow roll to *windward,* and Rolston had cried out, hands springing open as if something had stung his palms, and had fallen into a round pool of lanthorn light 'tween both vessels, surfacing one last time, and looking as if he was floating in a circle of odd yellow-green light, as if sinking into the very eye of a great sea-monster, then had seemed to be *sucked* down, and howling a final shriek of utter horror!

After a collective shudder of recalled awe, the bottle of port made another quick circuit of the table, all of them feeling as dry as dust, of a sudden.

"After that, we played the Dutch a merry jape, sir," Lt. Devereux of the Marines told Urquhart. "We spent weeks close inshore of the Texel, hoisting false flag signals to the fleet they feared was just over the horizon, and pretending to reply to questions . . . even if Admiral Duncan had barely a handful of old sixty-four gunners present, 'til the Nore Mutiny was settled, and he was re-enforced."

Urquhart certainly knew what had happened, once the winds had come fair; the

Dutch fleet had sailed, but had been caught upon a lee shore and nearly annihilated, and *Proteus,* it seemed, had played her own significant part in the battle, engaging a larger Dutch frigate and forcing her to strike after a boarding action. Capt. Lewrie had been seriously wounded in the arm, but had lived. His uncanny luck had held once more, for his arm had *not* required amputation, as most broken-bone wounds would have done. And that was why the gold medal for the Battle of Camperdown hung on his chest alongside the one for Cape St. Vincent!

Lewrie . . . Mistress Theoni Connor . . . Hyde Park . . . the Captain and his wife, yes! Urquhart suddenly recalled. A hero with his arm in a sling, a wife with a furled umbrella employing it like a sword after seeing her man's mistress and bastard by-blow at close quarters, making Lewrie hop, duck, and back up briskly! There'd been many salacious snickers in his favourite coffee-house when *that* tale had been told! He hid his smile as the others touched upon Lewrie's doings in the West Indies, and Lt. Urquhart once more went wide-eyed.

An outbreak of Yellow Jack, that was why Lewrie had needed the dozen Blacks so badly. Was it before, or after, the Captain's friend had duelled Ledyard Beauman and slain him, when the Captain had had to shoot Beauman's second, too? No matter; that was one reason there was so much bad blood. Against the French, though . . . *Proteus* had swept the north coast of St. Domingue (what the rebel ex-slaves were now calling Haiti) of any shipping larger than a canoe; had captured American arms smugglers; captured, sank, or burned French merchantmen and privateers; had crippled that Choundas fellow's big, proud frigate as they had already related, and had put paid to that cruel fiend, too!

"And weren't there *seals* barking," Lt. Adair said, with a face full of wonder (and rather red with claret and port), "the night that our boats went ashore to fetch out our Black fellows? Seals in the West Indies have been hunted nigh to extinction, but I swear I heard them, and their splashings, to boot."

"Some of the lads . . . ," Mr. Coote, the Purser, who had spent the last hour entire in contented and companionable, nodding silence, said. "They swore they *saw* seals in the water, and even I thought I saw one head, and disturbance in the water. I certainly am sure that I heard them. Mister Langlie's boat crews . . . our former First, sir . . . vowed that seals swam to either side of their boats on the way back aboard."

"Saint Nicholas Mole," Lt. Devereux reminded them.

One of ex-slave General Toussaint L'Ouverture's armies tried to oust the British

Army garrison at the port on the northwest coast, and *Proteus* had caught a signal asking for help, and had sailed into the roadstead. Close ashore, with the fighting lines hidden in dense forests, Lewrie had sent a signalling party ashore to aid the Army and wig-wag. With their frigate's guns at extreme elevation, *Proteus* had fired both solid round-shot and bags of grape-shot, adjusting according to the shore party's signal flags, and allowing their own troops to fall back behind a screen of plunging shot and re-form their lines, and, in the process, decimating the slave army. With springs on her cables, *Proteus* had swung in a wide arc, firing off nearly all of her grape-shot, cartridge flannels, and a whole tier of powder casks from morning 'til sunset, saving the port, and the British garrison in the process!

"And those French Creole pirates," Lt. Adair suggested with a wry shake of his head. "Had we been quicker about it, there'd have been nigh a *million* pounds sterling in silver captured, not a mere two hundred thousand!"

"Barataria Bay, d'ye mean?" Lt. Urquhart cried. "Aye, I read of *that'un!*" Courageous sea-fights, prize-money, and slews of captured enemy *specie* brought in had ever caught his eye in the *Marine Chronicle* . . . especially since Lt. Urquhart had never even come within hailing distance of anything so adventurous, or profitable . . . yet. Though, under Capt.

Alan Lewrie, it sounded better odds that he *could* be part of such glorious doings. And reaping the monetary benefits.

"Mad as hatters, the lot of them," Lt. Gamble said with a sniff. "Rich, bored young grandees, none older than me or Adair, there, but determined to seize Louisiana back from the Spanish and turn it over to France again. And the way they tried to finance their rebellion was to turn pirate!"

"Play-actors," Lt. Adair sneered. "Murderous, cold-blooded, and capricious little bastards. And one bitch."

"Stole a prize of ours, as far abroad as Dominica!" Lt. Gamble continued. "Marooned the hands of her Harbour Watch on the Dry Tortugas . . . 'cause they'd yet to *do* a marooning, so please you! Laughed and hooted, our sailors said once they'd been rescued, like it was a grand game. One shot our Midshipman Mister Burns . . . poor tyke . . . just to try his hand at long range, and it took him three days to die. Well, we made them pay, when we finally ran them to earth. Slew the lot of them. 'Twas only the girl that got away, and she nearly slew the Captain for revenge . . . for scotching their plans."

"Why are foiled plots always 'scotched'?" Scot Lt. Adair carped.

" 'Cause you Scots plot so bloody much!" Lt. Devereux hooted.

"Per'aps it was more ze wrath of a woman scorned, and betrayed, than mere revenge, sirs," Surgeon Mr. Durant slyly suggested, wreathed in a cloud of smoke from his clay pipe. "*N'est-ce pas?* After all, ze Captain 'ad made her acquaintance in New Orleans before rejoining ze ship."

"In New Orleans?" a puzzled Urquhart gawped. "But that's more than an hundred miles up the Mississippi, in *Spanish* Louisiana!"

"Foreign Office doings, that," Mr. Winwood heavily said, with a sage tap aside his nose. "The Captain, I gather, has been involved with their agents *several* times during his career. Something in the Far East 'tween the wars, something that involved that Choundas chap . . . again in the Mediterranean, I heard, when in *Jester.* It might've involved Choundas, again. In the West Indies, a pair of Foreign Office agents spent rather a long time aboard *Proteus,* that James Peel especially. The Captain was temporarily supplanted in command by a more senior Captain Nicely, and sent to New Orleans in civilian disguise as a cashiered British officer looking for employment on the Mississippi, with just a small party of our sailors . . . three of whom proved false in the end, and ran . . . guarded by a merchant agent from the Panton, Leslie Company, who was half a spy himself."

"Charité de Guilleri, she was," Devereux

stuck in. "And a most *hellish-fetching* wench of nineteen years or so. The Captain managed to *meet* her, her brothers and cousins, who were all in on it, and . . . I *gather* that he and she even might have conducted an, ah . . . *liaison* for a time, before they set off on their last foray, and he rejoined the ship."

"I'm certain that the Captain would not have, ah . . . ," Winwood grumbled with a blush. The others smirked at the Sailing Master and his squeamishness; which led Lt. Urquhart to reckon that his Captain was a man of *many* parts!

"Saw her only the once, myself," Marine Lieuterent Devereux said with a rather wistful expression. "When we assaulted their camp, on Grand Isle. Standing atop an ancient Indian burial mound or something . . . chestnut hair flowing in the breeze, dressed mannish, in breeches and boots . . . and shooting at us with a Girandoni air-rifle."

"And all honours to Lieuterent Devereux and his Marines, and late Lieutenant Catterall and his party of sailors, for conquering them," the Purser cried, which made them pound fists on the wardroom table.

"A toast, gentlemen . . . to Mister Catterall," Devereux called for. "To 'Bully,' God rest him," he added when all the glasses were charged. And they drank in remembrance of their old companion.

"The Captain boarded one of their schooners and slew one of the older pirate leaders, sword to sword," Lt. Adair narrated, after the port bottle had made another round. "Then, took off in a native boat after the wench, and he almost closed with her, too, before she shot him. Right in the centre of his chest!"

"*Shot* him?" Lt. Urquhart marvelled, a tad wall-eyed, by then. "In the centre of his chest, and he *lived?* Surely, sir, you're not saying that his . . . what'd ye call it? . . . his *geas* for good fortune made him bullet-proof?"

"All she did was knock him flat, and make a bruise as big as a mush-melon," the Surgeon, Mr. Durant, said with a wry chuckle.

"Fortunately for the Captain, the butt-flask of compressed air which provides the motive force was nearly spent," Lt. Devereux related, with a chuckle of his own. "I put it down to *extreme* good fortune, no more, Mister Urquhart, for, had Mademoiselle de Guilleri had a spare flask, we'd have lost him, certain."

"You should have been there to see the pirates' captured Spanish treasure ship explode, sir!" Lt. Adair told Urquhart. "She took light somehow, as she drifted off, and when her powder magazine went up, she was blown to kindling. And God knows *how* many new-minted silver coins went flying sky-high . . . bright as a royal fireworks, and plopping in the bay in a circle a mile across, and lost forever!"

"After that, 'twas a rather, dull year,

though." Gamble frowned. "Off to Halifax last summer with despatches . . ."

He was interrupted by the lone chime of One Bell in the Evening Watch — half past eight, leaving them another half hour before a call for Lights Out at nine, observed in harbour or at sea.

". . . a partial refit, and a full re-coppering, there," Gamble went on. "To Portsmouth, then orders to join the escort of an East India Company trade."

"We might have gone as far as Bombay, Calcutta, or Canton, but for getting our rudder shot clean off by a French frigate one night off Cape Town," Adair supplied with a pouty look. "Though we did touch at Recife and Saint Helena on the way, and that was enjoyable."

"*And* there was the circus," Lt. Gamble said with a twinkle.

"Circus?" Urquhart, by then rather bleary, enquired, at a loss once more.

"Why, Mister Daniel Wigmore's Travelling Extravaganza, sir!" Lt. Adair replied. "Surely, you've heard of it, the most famous circus in all the British Isles!"

"Circus, menagerie of exotic beasts, and theatrical troupe, in one," Lt. Gamble happily mused. "Comedies, dramas, aerial acts, knife throwers, dancing bears, and lion taming . . . clowns, mimes, and bareback riders. Some barer than others, hmm?" He leered.

"Oh, 'Princess' *Eudoxia!*" Adair gaily joined in. "Bow and arrows, and *never* missed, standing bareback, from under the belly of her huge white stallion, facing aft like a Parthian, what a wonder she was!"

"Billed as Scythian, Circassian royalty, but really a Roosian Cossack," Gamble stated with equal enthusiasm. "An absolutely *stunning,* dark-haired beauty, slim and tall, with the most cunning long legs, in skin-tight breeches, knee-high moccasin boots, a corsety thing, and see-through gauze . . . what-ye-may-call-it long shirt. And wasn't she hot after the Captain! *Threw* herself at him . . . 'til she learned he was married, o' course."

"He *did* pick up a smattering of Roosian, though." Adair leered suggestively. "Curse-words, mostly, from that vicious old lion tamer father of hers."

"Their slow old tub, the *Festival,* was bound for Cape Town to capture new beasts, and attached itself to our convoy on our way for Recife," Lt. Devereux explained. "She sailed with our home-bound trade, too, once we'd replaced our rudder and set the ship to rights, and was there the night we fought and made prize of the *L'Uranie* frigate. The second Frenchman went after the slowest ship in the convoy . . . the *Festival* . . . but, when they tried to board her, they ran into a hornet's nest of trained, bears, baboons, and a loosed *lion.* Knife throwers, sharpshooters, and

Mistress Eudoxia's bow and arrows, too. The Frogs were so terrified, they tumbled back aboard their ship and sheered off, just as the other escort, the old *Jamaica* sixty-four, got about and closed with them, and I doubt they fired more than a single broadside for honour's sake before they struck, as well.

"Why, Wigmore's Circus received Thanks of the Crown, Thanks of Parliament and 'John Company,' and even did a command performance for King George," Devereux said with a laugh, "and now Wigmore's future is made forever. I must own surprise, Mister Urquhart, that you haven't heard of them."

"I was at sea aboard *Albion,* and out of reach of the papers," Urquhart had to admit. "Though I did read the official account about *Proteus's* defence of the convoy. Well, gentlemen . . . ," he said, with a glance upwards to the stubs of the candles in the overhead lamps, instead of drawing out his pocketwatch. "This had been a most enlightening evening, one which assures me that as *Savage's* First Lieutenant I run no risk of lacking excitement, hey? And I look forward eagerly to whatever new adventures our gallant Captain Lewrie may lead us in future."

"We will follow him anywhere," Lt. Gamble said with a taut grin, and his tongue firmly in cheek, "if only to see what he'll get into, next, ha ha!" Which jest raised a general round of laughter from all the men at-table, but for

59

the dour Mr. Winwood.

"I, ah . . . ," Urquhart flummoxed, his now-fuzzy thoughts put off pace by Lt. Gamble's smirky comment. "A toast, may I be so bold . . . a *last* one, for the Captain assured me that tomorrow will be a strenuous day . . . to the gallant Captain Alan Lewrie, and to further Glory and Fame for HMS *Savage!*"

He raised his glass on high, as did the others, but . . .

"And to 'Mother' Green's best, sirs!" Lt. Devereux amended. "*And* our Captain's favourites!"

Urquhart gawped once more, mouth agape for a moment, for Mother Green (God rest her patriotic soul!) had made and sold the finest and safest sheep-gut cundums from the Green Lantern in Half Moon Street in London for years, had come out of retirement at the urging of her old clients when the American Revolution had erupted in 1776 to make "protections" for their officer sons, so they could "rantipole" Yankee Doodle wenches in perfect assurance of safety, too.

Urquhart also blushed, for did he not have a round dozen from that selfsame source, now manufactured by Mother Green's heirs, down in the bottom of his sea-chest, 'cause one never knew when the chance might arise . . . not with women of the better sort, certainly, but . . . ?

"The Captain . . . *Savage* . . . and Mother

Green!" he proposed.

"Boat ahoy!" came a muffled cry from the unfortunate Midshipman who stood Harbour Watch in the officers' stead. The reply could not be made out as they tossed back their last glass-fuls to "heel-taps," but moments later came the faint thud of a boat coming alongside the entry-port, and at such a late hour, too.

CHAPTER FOUR

Alan Lewrie was ready for bed, after a rather succulent supper taken alone in his great-cabins. A whole jointed chicken, dredged in flour and crumbled biscuit, then pan-fried the way his wife from North Carolina had cooked it, a method happily re-discovered when he'd been dined aboard ships of the fledgling United States Navy in the Indies, among officers from South Carolina or Georgia. Fresh garden peas and young spring carrots, intermixed, had accompanied it, supported by a baked potato smeared with mustard, and a basket of dainty shore rolls.

His Cox'n, Liam Desmond, had talked their "Free Black" volunteer cook, so aptly re-named Cooke, into baking a few apple tarts, as well; all sluiced down with one of the bottles of Cape Town white wines that Lewrie had purchased just before sailing back to England, and a couple of brandies, after, when catching up on the last of the day's unending flow of official paperwork from the warehouses ashore, a chapter or two of a new novel, and a game of chase with a champagne cork on a string with Toulon and Chalky 'til they'd tired of it, had rolled their eyes at him, and had flopped down on the canvas deck chequer, exhausted.

He was in his nightshirt, the coverlet and top sheet of his hanging bed-cot turned down, and was just about to roll into that bed that was wide enough for two (and a sure eye-opener for any senior officer who espied it) when there came the sharp rap of a musket-butt on the deck without his cabins, and the loud cry from the Marine sentry of "Vis'tor fer th' Cap'm . . . SAH!"

"Enter," Lewrie cautiously replied, not without an eye towards his weapons rack, for if the Beaumans had landed in England, and had laid charges against him, it could be someone from a Lord Justice, or one of those new-fangled Police Magistrates, come to arrest him!

Thankfully (perhaps) it was only a lone, rather weedy-looking civilian who entered the great-cabins, hat in hand and blinking his eyes as he took in his surroundings; surely a civilian fellow who'd never been aboard a ship of war, by the way he bore himself so mouse-shy and curious. Lewrie noted, though, that he bore under his arm a leather portfolio of a very pale dye, what attorneys jokingly called "law calf." Lewrie looked even *sharper* towards his weapons rack.

"And you are, sir?" Lewrie had to demand at last, putting on a stern "phyz" with one quizzical brow raised.

"Beg pardons," the pale-skinned civilian all but stammered as he came forward. "But, am I speaking with Captain Alan Lewrie of the *Savage* frigate?"

"Of *course* you are, sir!" Lewrie snapped, appalled at such an inane question. "Your boatman brought you to *Savage,* not the *Victory.*"

"Beg pardons," the weedy fellow reiterated; though he didn't look daunted in the least. "Allow to name myself to you . . ."

"Aye, that'd help," Lewrie drawled, summoning up as much dignity as one could when clad in a loose-flapping nightshirt and his bare feet.

"George Sadler, sir . . . clerk to Mister Andrew MacDougall, Esquire, in London. Your barrister, sir?"

"Aye, Mister Sadler? And what is so urgent that he sent you down?" Lewrie enquired, with one hand hidden behind his back with his fingers crossed, and a sudden cold and empty fear-void in his innards.

"News has come from Jamaica, Captain Lewrie," Sadler announced as he opened his "law calf" brief and withdrew a sheaf of documents.

"The Beaumans haven't landed in England,

then? Not yet?"

"No, sir. Not yet. Word of proceedings instituted on Jamaica have, however, come. Along with most-helpful information anent them provided by, ah . . . a certain friend of yours from the Foreign Office on Jamaica . . . a Mister James Peel?"

"What sort of proceedings, sir?" Lewrie asked.

"Why, your trial, Captain Lewrie," Mr. Sadler said, wide-eyed.

"I haven't even been charged with anything yet!" Lewrie barked.

"Oh my, but you *have,* Captain Lewrie," Sadler sadly told him as he referred to his sheaf of documents and allowed himself a pleased little "Aha!" as he found the pertinent one, which he held out in offering for Lewrie to take. "Charged, I fear, with the theft of a dozen slaves, and tried in the High Court at Kingston, Jamaica, nearly six months past, found guilty, and are sentenced to be hung."

"What?" Lewrie spluttered. "How can I be *tried* if I wasn't . . . ?"

"*In absentia,* Captain Lewrie," Sadler replied, much too calmly, and with a wee shake of his head over Lewrie's lack of knowledge of the intricacies of the law. "It happens all the time, when a felon flees the jurisdiction of the —"

"Flee, mine arse!" Lewrie roared. "I sailed away under naval *orders!* Got 'em in my desk,

65

t'prove it, by . . . ! Mine arse on a *band-box!* Of all the . . . shit, shit . . . *shit!*"

He sank onto his leather-padded chair behind his desk, feeling badly in need of another brandy, some civilian clothing, and a ticket for overseas. *Wonder if the Yankee Navy's in need of experienced men?* he shudderingly thought; *see one o' their consuls, get a certificate o' citizenship, and huzzah, George Washington!*

"Under the circumstances, Captain Lewrie, Mister MacDougall is in need of your presence in London, as soon as possible, he told me to relate to you," Sadler went on; legal cases and trials were his work-a-day experience, mostly piles of paperwork to him, and the personality of the accused was of no matter; nor were the accused's *feelings!* "He also told me to assure you that the informations supplied by Mister Peel, including a complete copy of the trial transcript, reveal a most 'colourable' proceeding. He is certain that perjury was committed . . . though, to determine the full nature of that, it is vital that he speak with you in person, sir."

"I was . . . what is it called?" Lewrie managed to say from a dry throat; one that he massaged to see if a hempen noose was already about his neck. "What's the legal term for . . . ?"

"Falsely convicted, Captain Lewrie," Sadler

said with a simper of esoteric amusement for a second. "Though the informal term would be 'framed.' I fear you must come up to London at once, sir."

"Oh, bugger!" Lewrie bemoaned. "I just can't leave my ship at the drop of a hat, the Navy'd have my 'nutmegs' off, relieve me of my command, whether I request leave, or not, just . . . ! Couldn't MacDougall simply sue for more time?"

"Believe me when I tell you that time is *precious,* sir," Sadler said with a negative shake of his head. "Your poor relationship with the Beaumans, and their brutal and vengeful nature which you described to my employer in letters, must be fleshed out by direct questions put to you, *before* the Beaumans and their representatives arrive and lay the charges, the verdict, and the sentence before a court. This can't be done by post, any longer."

"Christ shit on a biscuit," Lewrie muttered under his breath as he rose and headed for his wine-cabinet for a restorative glass of *something* . . . any spirit that fell first to hand. "The *bastards!*"

"They seem to be, sir," Sadler primly agreed, with a longing eye on the squat bottle of brandy that Lewrie dug out. He brightened as Lewrie waved the bottle in his direction and fetched out a second glass. "It would appear that *we,* meaning your legal representatives, have received the transcript, and the verdict, *beforehand* of its being laid before a Lord Justice in King's Bench, where all criminal trials are held. Which happy fact will allow us perhaps enough time to find flaws in your trial, which *may* result in the sentence being ruled null and void, and a second trial held *here,* or your being acquitted."

"Really?" Lewrie piped, with a faint glimmer of hope.

"And, until your foes actually arrive, and are allowed to lay the sentence of death before a Lord Justice, you will remain a free man, Captain Lewrie," Sadler assured him (sort of) as he accepted the glass of brandy and did, for a weedy sort, a manly job of drinking off half of it at once. "And there is the matter of which law term will have space on its docket before an evidentiary hearing . . . before you are brought to dock, that is to say . . ."

"Damme, I could be at *sea* long afore that!" Lewrie gleefully cried. "Out of reach of . . . !"

"Though, sir . . . perhaps under a death-sentence," Sadler had to point out. "Until we may challenge the result of your trial, and stay its execution."

"*Ba-ad* choice o' words, Mister Sadler," Lewrie said, blanching. "Bloody-bad choice o' words!"

Christ, am I fucked! Lewrie thought to

68

himself; *think o' going to Sophie's and Lang-lie's wedding with* this *hangin' over me! Shit! Did I say "hanging"? Now th' bastard's got* me *doin' it!*

■ ■ ■ ■

Book I

■ ■ ■ ■

Dick Butcher: The first thing we do, let's kill all the lawyers.

> William Shakespeare,
> *The Second Part of King Henry VI*
> Act IV, Scene II

CHAPTER FIVE

It had been extremely crowded in the diligence coach up from Portsmouth to London; "arseholes to elbows" as Lewrie grumbled at the coaching inn at Petersfield, where the horse teams had been changed. A few passengers got off there, but a horde of new'uns had gotten on, and Lewrie had been crammed into a *tiny* corner by a window, with the bench seat normally fit for three abreast jam-packed with four, and nary a one of them seemed to have bathed, the last week entire!

He had taken lodgings at an inn suggested by Mr. Sadler, who had made a *bad* travelling companion. The man simply *could* not silence his cheery babbling; towards Lewrie, who grunted back, lost in his own brown study and ready to throttle the wee bastard; with each and every passenger — male, female, child or toddler, wizened, droop-eyed, and wheezing dodderers, simpering matron-hags, adult men, new mothers with "drool fountains" on their laps — anyone was fare for him, from rich to poor, and generally goggling out the windows at every passing sight like a simpleton who'd found himself on an aristocrat's Grand Tour of the Continent by mistake!

Well, perhaps Mr. Sadler had never *been* outside London before, Lewrie could speculate, and he *was* on a Grand Tour. And, slaving away over special pleadings, all ink and rustling paper, from dawn to dusk as a law *clerk* just might be a stiflingly drab life, in a sober-sided profession. Sadler was like a boy just up from school!

He ate like one, too, for Lewrie had been given to understand that the "honorarium" already paid to his employer, Andrew Mac-Dougall, Esq., did not cover travel expenses, meals and lodging, etc., and etc., so it was Lewrie's *not*-bottomless purse that had gotten Sadler back to shore and into decent lodgings after they had completed their business aboard *Savage,* had repaid his downward fare to Portsmouth, and their coach fares to London, Sadler's hearty breakfast, their mid-day meal at Petersfield, and a basket of treats to take the edge off any wants the rest of the way up to London, as well as a pint of ale here, then a bottle of porter aboard the coach (to keep Sadler's touchy throat condition wet), Lewrie's rooms in London, *and* another hearty evening meal taken together at a rather fashionable new chop-house near Somerset House in the Strand . . . a chop-house that seemed dedicated to settling the National Debt off the price of its victuals, and one Lewrie was mortal-certain had *never* been one of Sadler's haunts, without one of his employer's clients to pay for all . . . the damned fool!

He'd even shown up at Lewrie's lodgings for a "pre-consultation" breakfast, by God!

"Mister MacDougall will be out shortly, Captain Lewrie," Sadler said with a simper as he hung up his hat and greatcoat on a hall-tree in the outer "office," and saw to Lewrie's as well. They had coached the short distance from Lewrie's inn. Well, *Sadler* had coached in rare style from whatever miserable garret he occupied to the inn, then had the cabman *wait* (for an extra fee) 'til they had eat, and for a small fellow, Sadler *could* put it away like a modern-day Sir John Falstaff, then taken the coach up the Strand to Fleet Street, then into narrower Whitefriars Street, where MacDougall had his "digs."

It was not quite the "offices" where Lewrie had expected to find himself; the first room he entered was more a parlour or sitting room than anything else, all prim and clean, with an Axminster carpet on the floor, a marble fireplace, and fresh-looking and brightly upholstered settees and wing-back chairs set about, with two large windows facing the

75

street, and God only knew how much Mac-Dougall paid in Window Tax for such a lot of light, and a good view.

Sadler parted a set of double doors in the back wall, stepped through, then closed them, leaving Lewrie to pace about the parlour, peer into the bookcases, and fret with his shirt collar and neck-stock. A moment later, Sadler was back, leaving the doors open this time and saying most formally, "If you will step this way, sir?"

Hmmph . . . got his work-a-day face back on, I s'pose, Lewrie had to think; *thank God there'll be no more blathering.*

He followed Sadler into a room of equal size to the parlour, one featuring a dining area, a wee butler's pantry, and a large sideboard. Past that'un into a third, a bedroom with an old-style curtained four-poster, then through a final set of double doors to yet another large room furnished as a proper office, a book-lined study with a fireplace and yet *another* pair of windows looking west onto Bouverie Street. *Damme, how much is his fee?* Lewrie wondered, and felt thankful that Reverend William Wilberforce and his charitable, and fervent, anti-slavery followers had so far footed the bill!

"Aha, Captain Lewrie, do you come in, sir!" his barrister gayly exclaimed, broadly gesturing him to a wing-back chair before his desk, which was piled high with stacks of legal *octavos* and folders of that pudding-crust "law calf" leather. "Your servant, sir, and I am Andrew MacDougall. Will you take coffee or tea, Captain Lewrie? Take a pew, sir, and be comfortable whilst we begin about it, ha ha!"

And he's *the one t'save mine arse?* Lewrie gawped to himself as he took in Mr. Andrew MacDougall, Esquire, for MacDougall looked more like a puckish public school *boy* than what Lewrie expected an attorney to be. MacDougall looked no older than his middle-twenties, his face round, with dimpled cheeks and chin, under a head of curly dark blond hair that spilled over his forehead in an unkempt mop — one that he swiped back at least twice before Lewrie could seat himself — and was so curly that Lewrie could conjure that he really wore a peruke-styled court wig of unconventional colour, were it not for the fact that his lawyer's formal black court robe and peruke already rested on a stand in one corner, a stand formed much like a mast with one crossed yardarm. Lewrie found it oddly disconcerting, that mute display; more of a legal scare-crow with "arms" spread wide to net the unfortunate, and the peruke with its three tight side-curls, short queue bound with a black ribbon resting on a pad atop the stand, a faceless intimation of future horror. It was so ghoulish that Lewrie felt a tiny shiver.

Scare-crow, or the Grim Reaper? Lewrie thought with a gulp.

"Well now, isn't this delightful?" MacDougall most happily said as Sadler hovered over Lewrie's right shoulder. "Coffee or tea, sir?"

"Umm . . . coffee'd suit," Lewrie decided. "Delightful, sir?"

"Why, to meet one of Britain's heroic sea-dogs, Captain Lewrie!" MacDougall exclaimed again, making Lewrie even uneasier with the dread that his new attorney did rather a *lot* of exclaiming, and had less of the requisite *gravitas* than God had promised a March Hare!

"A sea-dog now under a sentence of death, sir," Lewrie replied with a squirm of impatience to get past the politenesses to the meat of the matter.

"Oh, that!" MacDougall said with a wave of his hand as he took hold of a matching wing-back chair and dragged it round the desk quite near Lewrie's, plumped himself down in it, and crossed his legs "club-man" fashion, with one ankle resting on a knee. "Stuff and nonsense!"

"Stuff, and non— ?" Lewrie gawped . . . aloud, this time.

"Slavery was outlawed in the British Isles nigh fifty years ago, Captain Lewrie, and the condition of slavery is no longer recognised under Common Law," MacDougall was quick to assure him, leaning over to tap Lewrie on the knee, and bestowing on him a very wide grin. "Also, there is the fact that the Committee of Privy Council for the Colonies . . . , dis-banded long ago, by the by . . . , allowed Jamaica, and certain other colonies and plantations, use of their own local Grant Law, *but,* such law has no standing in English jurisprudence, d'ye see, Captain Lewrie! Oh, for cases concerning commerce, those presented in Courts of Common Pleas, or Chancery Court should such Grant Law cases concern inheritances and disputed wills, jury decisions or local justices' rulings *might* stand if appealed in England, but certainly *not* anent your case, which *would* go to King's Bench for confirmation, most usually. Ah, the coffee! Capital! Thankee, Sadler."

"So . . . no one's to snatch me up and march me off to Tyburn?" Lewrie asked, suddenly feeling a *lot* better.

"Newgate, sir," MacDougall corrected him, with another swipe at his unruly locks, and yet another of his disarming smiles. "Tyburn's out, and Newgate Prison, near the Old Bailey, is London's new site of executions. Closer and more convenient to everyone needful of instruction in the sureness, and majesty, of the law, ha ha! There's nothing finer than a series of hangings to keep our criminal class daunted, ha ha! Well, sometimes in Horsemonger Lane . . ."

"Beats the theatre all hollow, too, does it?" Lewrie shied away, wondering just what *sort* of a tom-fool his supporters had engaged.

"Entertainment for some, surely, Captain Lewrie . . . grim warning to others," Mac-Dougall chummily agreed as he shovelled four spoonfuls of sugar into his coffee and stirred it up. "Ah, just right. Brazilian, and thank God the Portuguese are still neutral in this war."

Lewrie took a sip of his and found it not *quite* as scalding-hot as he preferred, but it was close, so he dashed two spoonfuls of sugar into his own, stirred it up, and sipped again.

"So . . . ," Lewrie reiterated, "*could* someone take me up?"

"Oh, there is a remote possibility," Mac-Dougall allowed with a shrug, "*very* remote, mind. Any fool may lay an 'information' with one of our new-fangled Police Magistrates, but that sort of arrest usually involves *petty* crimes . . . or revenge 'twixt thieves who've fallen out. Even were you to be denounced, and the Bow Street Runners come snatch you, you'd be back on the streets, in a trice . . . or, as my good old granther always said . . . 'in twa shakes o' th' wee sheep's tail, an' th' feerst ain a'ready been shook,' ha ha!"

"Uhm . . . why?" Lewrie had to ask, not reassured a whit.

"Fear, sir! Fear!" MacDougall told him

with a great chortling laugh. "Now, 'tis a crime the Runners are already pursuing, yes, they would hold you 'til trial . . . one of those King's Bench 'justice mills' that prosecutes twenty or thirty cases a day. But, you, sir! Ha! We do not treat our well-born, or our *heroes,* in such a fashion. Most of the criminal class, the lower classes, well . . . their crimes are evident, as usually is their guilt, God help them. But for a *gentleman,* a member of the landed gentry and the well-to-do, most of the magistrates start to tremble in their boots! Deference to the 'better sorts,' and members of the nobility, would result in a quick *remand* to higher authorities, and, with the presence of legal counsel at your side upon such remand, would have you free in an eye-blink.

"Unless you had committed a heinous crime here in England, sir," MacDougall cautioned in a (rare) sober moment, then not a second later guffawed and slapped his knee. "And, of course we both know that you didn't, and any Police Magistrate would drop you like red-hot shot and not care a *fig* what transpired on Jamaica, unless *told* to do so."

"I may safely walk the streets of London, then?" Lewrie asked.

"*No* one walks London streets in *perfect* safety, given how many criminals we have abouts, Captain Lewrie," MacDougall said, finding a new cause for amusement, "but, in

81

your case, such a taking-up, as I've already said, would be a very remote possibility."

"Well, that's something, then," Lewrie said with a relieved sigh.

"There is also the commonly held fear of the old 'Star Chamber' tyranny and official oppression, Captain Lewrie," MacDougall told him as he rose to liven the fire in the grate with a poker, then sat back down. "You are aware that there are no *government* prosecutors under Common Law? Every person put on trial, whether in King's Bench for criminal cases, in Common Pleas or Chancery Court, is prosecuted by an objective attorney engaged by the aggrieved party. *And* every person brought to court is *supposed* to be represented by yet another objective attorney engaged by the accused, his family and supporters, or, in some cases by a barrister, sarjeant, or advocate appointed by the Lord Justices should the accused be indigent."

"As I supposedly was back in Kingston?" Lewrie charily asked.

"The conduct of your trial *in absentia* on Jamaica, I tell you, sir, was the very *epitome* of the worst abuses of Star Chamber proceedings!" MacDougall intoned in a sudden pique. "From what I was able to gather from friends and allies of yours in the West Indies, your legal counsel, a locally schooled 'Johnny New-Come' to the Jamaican bar, was whistled up from a tavern cross the street from the courthouses, given but half an hour to familiarise himself with little more than your name and background, and presented no witnesses on your behalf, not even any witnesses who might attest to your character or qualities, before your trial began. Oh, there's a whole *host* of irregularities which I have gleaned from the transcript of your trial, sir . . . rather a short one, given the fact that the entire proceedings did not last much more than three hours, from 'Oyez' to verdict, to sentencing, and the justice's 'God have mercy on his soul, wheresoever he may be at this moment'!"

"Three . . . hours?" Lewrie blanched, that wonderful coffee curdling in his stomach. "Three bloody *hours?*"

"Not as odd as you'd think, sir," MacDougall replied, laughing again. "Why, the first complex criminal case in King's Bench, with a slew of witnesses on both sides, that actually lasted more than a lone *day,* did not occur 'til 1794! Sat in on it, whilst I was 'eating my terms' at Grey's Inn, and what a show it was, ha ha! Fascinating!"

"Oh, Christ," Lewrie weakly croaked.

"Nought to fear, Captain Lewrie," MacDougall soothingly said. " 'Eating my terms' was not *all* I did before being called to the bar."

MacDougall then proceeded to lay out the

usual *cursus lex* that most aspiring attorneys were required to pursue . . . which did nothing much to reassure Lewrie that *any* lawyer was worth a pinch of pig shit.

A first or second son, usually from a well-to-do family, *might* attend university for a decent grounding in a gentlemanly education in rhetoric, Latin, and Greek. Whether graduate or not, anyone wishing to become a proper lawyer would approach one of the great Inns of Court — Lincoln's Inn, Grey's Inn, Middle Temple, or Inner Temple — whichever suited his tastes, and where the members seemed more of a like mind to his than any of the others, then ingratiate himself by merely *hanging about,* reading precedent from past proceedings on his own time with *no real schedule of instruction,* and *dine-in* often enough for the elder members — those called "Benchers" who had already earned their honourifics of "King's Counsel" — to "vet" them and decide, usually after a period of three years of social dining "in hall" with other members, whether they should be "called to the bar" or not! Oh, *some* more aspiring *might* spend their time as "special pleaders," the ones who wrote up presentations to be submitted to court for their elders, but it wasn't really all *that* necessary, after all. There were many well-born aspirants who avoided the drudgery of such menial work, but became lawyers on the strength of their supper conversation, and their ability to *look* sober after those communal dinners!

Andrew MacDougall, though, was the son of a Scottish magistrate who had actually bothered to read the law, and for a time apprenticed himself to a real, successful attorney before inheriting the estate and becoming a respected local magistrate. The father's respect for the law, and his incessant talk of what had occurred in his local court, his explaining the intricacies of the differences between English Common Law and Scottish — and long evenings in his study spent wrangling what current law was, and what a fair-minded man felt it *should* be — had enflamed young Andrew MacDougall to be a barrister. He had spent time at a good public school (or what passed for one in Scotland), then had done two terms at university in Edinburgh before coaching down to Oxford to complete his studies, *then* had approached Grey's Inn. And while "eating his terms," he had deeply immersed himself in studying, in attending Court sessions, in long and earnest discussions with the "Benchers" and writers of his lodge, *eagerly* offering to take on the drab finger-pinching work of a special pleader for more than a year before being called to the bar, and, MacDougall was quick to inform Lewrie, had been successful in most of his cases, since!

"My gown's yonder, sir," MacDougall concluded with a hint of pride as he pointed to that spooky black robe with outstretched arms on the stand in the corner, "though I am still required to wear one of 'stuff,' not silk, and have yet to earn the title of King's Counsel, yet I do assure you that I will do my absolute best to represent your cause, Captain Lewrie, and *my* absolute best is, dare I say it, rather a cut *above* what you may encounter from some other of my colleagues, whether I held strong personal views on the justice of your actions in recruiting those slaves and making free men of them, or not . . . which act I not only approve, but applaud, by the by, ha ha!"

"Though . . . whether you approve or not, Mister MacDougall, you sound to me more than capable," Lewrie told him. "Thank *God* for it!"

"Thankee kindly for your words, Captain Lewrie, and I trust you will be of the same mind once your time before the bench is over," Mr. MacDougall said. "Now. We may need send Sadler for a second pot, or a third, as we get to the meat of the matter. For I must glean all I may from you concerning the theft . . . well, shall we say, rather, the 'obtaining' of those dozen former slaves, ha ha! How, and when, was the idea concocted, and with whom . . . every last particular that happened on the night you, ah . . . closed the

86

coast, what evidence still in your possession I might present as testimony, that sort of thing? I know you are fitting out a new ship of war, and your time is short, so today, perhaps tomorrow as well but no longer, it is vital that we make the most of your presence here in London."

"Let's be at it, then," Lewrie was quick to agree.

CHAPTER SIX

Surviving witnesses; there were plenty of them, for Lewrie's old crew and wardroom had mostly turned-over entire from *Proteus* to *Savage.* MacDougall was delighted to hear that all Lieutenants and Midshipmen were required to keep daily journals noting wind, weather, sea states, and what happened during their times on watch, or out-of-the-ordinary events that their ship met. While Lt. Catterall was dead and gone and his journals were unavailable, Adair and Grace could testify, and Lt. Langlie, no longer on the ship but still fitting out his own new warship, could send his old journals to MacDougall, if he was quick to ask for them. "Hell's Bells," Lewrie spat, "I'll be seeing Langlie before that . . . he's to wed my ward, Sophie de Maubeuge, this weekend in Portsmouth!"

"And did you keep journals of your own, sir? Did you write down what your purposes were that evening?" MacDougall pointedly enquired.

"Not *really!*" Lewrie explained, squirming. "Once a commission is done, logs and journals are sent to Admiralty for perusal and storage, so . . ."

"No, it wouldn't do, would it, to write down 'May first at Eight p.m., turned slave-monger,' hey?" MacDougall said with a *moue,* followed by a schoolboy's giggle.

"I noted the course steered from Kingston, closing the coast at night, dousing all lanthorns . . . how far offshore it was when we came-to, sending boats ashore under Mister Langlie, and, ah . . . being received of a round dozen . . . volunteers," he concluded, blushing a bit.

"What? Doused all lanthorns?" MacDougall suddenly enthused as he scribbled that down on a sheet of foolscap, so madly that he slung ink droplets. "Now that's *extremely* interesting!"

"It is?" Lewrie asked, at a loss.

"And," MacDougall eagerly pressed, "did you, or any of your surviving witnesses, see any lights *ashore,* sir?"

"Well, there were some porch lamps and such, a half-mile or so back from the beach," Lewrie recalled. "Where, I assumed, the overseer had his lodgings, perhaps one or two round the main house's porch gallery, where the Beaumans would reside, if they'd been there. It wasn't their *only* plantation, d'ye see, but the one nearest to my friend Christopher

Cashman's plantation. I'd not have tried it on, else, for he'd sent word to them that, if they wished to run and join the Navy, they'd get the Joining Bounty as volunteers, and get the same treatment as any White volunteer. Could've taken twenty or more, the whole *lot* of 'em, if Admiralty wouldn't notice sooner or later that I was paying twice the number of hands that *Proteus* was rated."

"But . . . other than *those* few lamps, did you see any other light ashore?" MacDougall squirmed like a puppy as he insisted on an answer.

"Nary a one, sir," Lewrie could firmly aver, for he had spent the hours from sunset to dawn in a funk-sweat to be discovered, and it had been a *huge* relief at the time for *Proteus* to have stolen in, then stolen out, without waking a cricket.

"Saw no hand-carried lanthorns or torches, no hue and cry?" Mr. MacDougall repeated, as if a life hung on the answer. "Hounds barking, gunshots, anything like that?"

"God, no! 'Twas quiet as the grave," Lewrie told him.

"Ah *ha!*" MacDougall sharply cried, slapping his palm on his desk and guffawing as he swiped his hair out of his eyes once more.

"Well, there were *seals* on the beach, *they* barked a bit, but no dogs," Lewrie further informed him.

"Never saw a living soul coming to that

beach, other than your volunteers, Captain Lewrie?" MacDougall demanded, suddenly not sounding so young and schoolboy-ish. "What other lights were there? A moon?"

"Starlight," Lewrie related, pouring himself another coffee as he did so, even if the pot had gone tepid. " 'Twas a new moon at that time. It was, ah . . . taken into account for the success of the enterprise," Lewrie admitted, a trifle shame-faced, and talking chin-down to his shirt collar.

"And your own ship's lights were all extinguished, ah *ha!* Yes?"

"Yes, of course," Lewrie assured him, one brow up.

"Would it surprise you very much, Captain Lewrie, to learn that the Beauman family's overseer on that plantation, and his son, claimed in their testimony at your sham trial that they were awakened by sounds of the slave population, ah . . . celebrating? That they testified that they quickly roused themselves, took up arms, a hand-lanthorn, and lit a rag torch? That they rushed down to the beach, but arrived too late to re-capture their runaways?"

"What? That's utter shite!" Lewrie spat. "We didn't . . . !"

"Fired off a pair of shots at the boats, they swore," MacDougall rushed on to relate. "And, though they hit nothing, your ship was so close ashore, they knew her for a frigate, a

British frigate, at once. More damaging to you, they swore they could mark *your* appearance . . . by the light of your ship's taffrail lanthorns, because you were standing right by one of them, *fully illumined!*"

"Mine arse on a band-box if they could!" Lewrie erupted.

"Now, sir . . . another matter," MacDougall demanded, picking up a not-so-thick *octavo* and flipping through the pages to the section he wanted quickly. He rose and paced, tossing hair out of his eyes, and looking like a cherubic, rotund Puck, for he was a young man of substantial girth and heft. "In what position, relative to the coast, did your frigate lie? Sideways to the beach? How close?"

"Well, as to how close," Lewrie growled, still fuming over those bald-faced lies. *I'm a better skulker than* that, *by God!* he assured himself as he got to his own feet, too exercised to sit any longer. Lewrie and MacDougall began a slow, stomping "minuet" about the parlour office, mostly circling the un-used chairs before the desk as if participating in a game of "Odd Man Out," when the music suddenly stops. "There was a broken shoal of reef and rocks a cable distant from the beach, and we fetched-to into the wind three cables shy of that, as I recall."

"And a cable would be . . . ?"

"Why, one hundred and twenty fathoms," Lewrie supplied, shocked that such was not common knowledge. "Six feet to the fathom, that'd be seven hundred and twenty feet. Well, the nautical mile is divided into *ten* cables of *six hundred feet* each, so, say the reefs and shoals lay six hundred feet offshore, and *Proteus* was fetched-to eighteen hundred feet further out. There was a break in the reef, right between *Proteus* and the beach, and we could see the phosphoresence of the waves breaking on the reef and rocks . . . high tide, round midnight, and we planned for that, too, d'ye see, a much dimmer rim of phosphoresence where the waves rolled in on the sand . . ."

"Twenty-four hundred feet from shore, on a *dark* night, ah *ha!*" MacDougall crowed, stopping to wet his quill in an ink-pot before he began tramping a circle of his offices again. "Sideways, were you?"

"Uh, no," Lewrie told him, feeling as if he was forced to chase his barrister round the office. "Usually, the Nor'east Trades blow to the Sou'west, but for the Blue Mountains, and the shape of the coast, so we had winds out of the East that night, and to fetch-to, we had to place our bows into the Nor-Nor'east, with the fore-and-aft sails forcin' her forrud, but the fore-tops'l laid aback t'keep her idlin' in place, and makin' a slow stern-way, away from those shoals. A person on the beach would've seen us close to bows-on, not abeam."

"And you could not have gone any closer, I

93

take it," MacDougall asked, juggling loose transcript pages. "The danger of the reef, I'd suppose?"

"Less than ten feet of water, inshore of the reef, as I recall from the chart," Lewrie answered, "and only twelve to fifteen feet of water to seaward of it, even at high tide. We fetched-to as soon as the lead-line showed six fathoms. *Proteus* drew eighteen feet, right aft, so we had a safe margin, with deeper water clear of hazards astern, so an hour or so of drifting wouldn't set us on anything that could rip our hull open. Right *along* the reef, 'twas three feet or less, even at high tide, so . . . *will* you sit down, sir, or must I trot *after* you?"

MacDougall came to a full stop suddenly, looking round his offices as if wondering why he was there, and where was the nearest chair.

"So, your ship did *not* lie in profile to the shore," MacDougall pondered, after he'd settled himself once more. "In profile with her bows pointing West towards the cape, or the point, or whatever you . . . ?"

"God, no!" Lewrie hooted. "The shoreline swings in a great arc in Portland Bight," he continued, taking a welcome chair himself. "To the West of Kingston, is roughly East-to-West, then begins to jut South down to Portland Point. The Beauman plantation, and Cashman's, are on the coast, quite near the

Point. Uhm, have you a pen and paper I may borrow? I'll draw you a rough sketch, though a proper chart of the —"

"A *chart?*" MacDougall cried of a sudden. "But, of course! You still have the chart you used that night?"

"Aye," Lewrie told him, puzzled by his attorney's enthusiasm; wouldn't that chart, still with his pencilled markings, prove that he had premeditated the crime, after all? And, he had to wonder why Mr. Andrew MacDougall, Esq., burbled with laughter, rocked on his chair, and kicked his thick legs in seeming joy. To Lewrie, MacDougall looked about to pop like a *haggis,* all swollen with steam, and a poke with a sharp-tined fork would do him in!

"One *never* throws away an accurate chart," Lewrie said, hoping that MacDougall's glee was a good sign. "They're rather *rare,* d'ye see. Certainly, my Sailing Master, Mister Winwood, has his, as well. Never throws *anything* away, even pencil stubs, he doesn't. He was my Sailing Master in *Proteus,* and turned-over into *Savage.* While he may not need charts of the West Indies for now, I'm sure his charts are still aboard."

"You *must* send it me, yours and his, at once, sir!" MacDougall urged, swiping hair from his eyes again, and about ready to leap from his chair and start that infernal pacing once more. "We must have *him,* this Winwood fellow, too! He was there that night? Oh, capital!"

"Well, in fact 'twas Mister Winwood who took the most interest in the former slaves' welfare, and their spiritual improvement. None had more than a smattering of knowledge of Christianity, before comin' aboard," Lewrie related, made more at ease by Mac-Dougall's elation.

"Denied the Good News of Christ?" Mac-Dougall scowled. "Why? By omission, or calculated *commission,* one wonders. If told they're equal in the Lord's sight, might slaves begin to *think,* and wonder why they are slaves, and whether their own humanity is the equal of a master's, perhaps? Is that common, d'ye think, Captain Lewrie? As a means for their continued oppression?"

"It may vary from master to master, sir," Lewrie said, digging round the top of Mac-Dougall's desk to find a spare lead pencil, paper, and enough space in which to begin to draw. "Some, I'm told, don't go much beyond one of Saint Paul's letters, the one about 'slaves, obey your masters,' hey? Mister Winwood 'twas the one who helped them take new, freemen's names for ship's books, even used the usual hosing-off under the wash-deck pump that new-come hands get as a sort of baptism.

"He's Low Church," Lewrie had to caution. "Halfway to 'Leaping Methodist,' mind."

"Such a character witness, though," Mr. MacDougall mused, with his arms about his chest, rocking once again as if in transports of a heavenly rapture at a Welsh revival meeting. "Oh, capital! Capital! I shall swoon with joy, swear I will, to have him in the box! What a scandal 'gainst the Beaumans I could make!"

MacDougall stopped rocking, turned grave, and peered anxiously at Lewrie. "Charts. Maps. Where does one get them, from Admiralty?"

"They don't print their own," Lewrie told him, happily drawing. "But there are plenty of printers who do. Sayer and Bennett in Fleet Street are very good, very up-to-date, if they're still in business."

"How large are they, Captain Lewrie?" MacDougall pressed.

"Oh, 'bout three foot square, most of 'em, though it depends," Lewrie said, intent on his depiction of the reef and beach. "Harbour charts and their approaches might not be more than eighteen inches by eighteen, some even smaller."

"We must have one *much* larger," MacDougall petulantly declared. "A *gigantic* reproduction for all in the courtroom to be able to take in . . . judge, jury, and, most especially, the audience, ha ha! They, ah . . . ever make charts that large?"

"Doubt it," Lewrie replied, looking up from

his sketch. "It'd be dear." *And,* he wondered; *will you be billing* me *for that?*

"*Hang* the cost!" MacDougall exclaimed, leaping to his feet at last, unable to contain his urgency; which outburst made Lewrie wince. "The Reverend Wilberforce will surely see the necessity. Cost is no object, compared to true justice . . . for you, the former slaves, and the cause of ultimate Empire-wide Abolition.

"Yes, Captain Lewrie, I, too, support the cause of Abolition," MacDougall quite proudly stated, looking as if he was posing for an heroic portrait. "In this one instance, I may not be *quite* the dry and objective lawyer who presents the most compelling argument in his client's best interests. I *am* enthusiastic in court, others tell me. Though, *not* to my detriment, nor to the interests of those who engage me. And I have found that visual evidence is more compelling than dull, yawn-inducing blather, d'ye see?"

"The 'picture's worth a thousand words,' d'ye mean, sir?" Lewrie supposed aloud.

"Exactly, my dear Captain Lewrie," Mac-Dougall replied, guffawing with great pleasure, abandoning his stiff "noble" pose as quickly as a poster could be ripped from a tavern wall. "If the printers cannot reproduce your charts large enough, perhaps a canvas, as big as a bedsheet, may serve, and a journeyman artist or sign painter could draw it all in broad strokes. Something on which the jury may gaze as any false evidence is reiterated. Do the Beaumans not bring their witnesses with them, and depend upon a dry reading of their testimony from the Jamaican transcript, well . . . there's confrontation standing mutely in the centre of the courtroom. Do they fetch 'em along, and testify anew, I'll present your officers, and that Mister Winwood, in stark rebuttal."

"Or, tear them to pieces when you put your question to 'em?"

"Beg pardon, Captain Lewrie?"

"When you question them yourself," Lewrie re-stated.

"Oh, heavens no, sir!" MacDougall pooh-poohed. "The prosecuting attorney puts questions to *his* witnesses to form a case, then I, as a defence attorney, put *our* witnesses in the box to refute. Prosecutors under English Common Law cannot examine my witnesses or attestors, nor may I examine his!"

"What?"

"I fear you've had little exposure to the law, and courts, Captain Lewrie," MacDougall said, with one of those simpering little "how ignorant of you" laughs.

"Not 'til now, no," Lewrie sarcastically replied. *And, why that is, God only* knows, *the things* I've *got up to!* he thought a tick later. "Well, at least I'll have no fear of scathing questions from whoever it is the Beaumans hire as prosecutor," he concluded with a resigned sigh.

"Uhm . . . beg pardon again, Captain Lewrie, but . . . ," MacDougall said, looking a bit *sorry* for his new client. "The accused only speaks upon his own behalf *after* the verdict is announced . . . most usually in King's Bench cases to plead for mercy . . . transportation to Australia, 'stead of the New Market gallows."

"What?" Lewrie gawped in alarm. "I just sit in the dock, while everybody else gets t'lie their arses off? Stay mum as a tailor's dummy, while . . . ?"

"That, ah . . . is the custom, Captain Lewrie," MacDougall sadly informed him. "Ah, look at the time!" he cried as a mantel clock atop the fireplace chimed the hours. "I *thought* I was beginning to feel a tad peckish. Oh, there's an hundred, a thousand, more matters which I must ask of you in the short time allotted us, but I do believe we may repair to the most excellent chop-house . . . quite nearby . . . and take our mid-day meal. I took the liberty of reserving private rooms where we, and Mister Sadler, who shall prove to be instrumental to the preparation of our presentation, good fellow, may dine. I swear, all you have related to me, and what stir such has caused in my wits, has made me *famished.* Shall we adjourn for the nonce, Captain Lewrie?"

Sadler and his tape-worm, Lewrie morosely thought as he gathered up hat and sword in the outer parlour; *and you, MacDougall, a dab-hand trencherman yourself. Still a growin' lad, in need o' stuffin', hey? Good thing I brought a* full *purse t'ondon, 'cause I doubt* any *attorney treats, or even go shares! Can't* speak *for myself . . . my* God, *but I'm bloody doomed!*

CHAPTER SEVEN

"I really can't . . . ?" Lewrie whinged once they were seated in the small but well-appointed private dining room.

"Not a word, sorry," MacDougall tossed off, intent on the hand-written day's menu and wine list. "Aha! They've fresh oysters up from Sheerness, and a dozen apiece sounds lovely, don't you think, Sadler?"

"Capital, as you always say, sir," his clerk happily seconded.

"Their veal's always toothsome, hmm . . . ," MacDougall mused aloud, "perhaps only the *brace* of roast squab, before the main course. Rhenish with that, it goes without saying, *and,* I see they've still a few dozen of the Château Lafites to go with the veal. Any favourites, sir?" he asked Lewrie. "Anything else catch your fancy? The lobster, perhaps? It is done to perfection, here."

"Not all *that* hungry, really," Lewrie replied, ready to finger his purse, to weigh what he had remaining, for the way MacDougall and his perpetually starved clerk were thinking, this mid-day meal might cost as much as the wedding breakfast for Langlie and Sophie down in Portsmouth. "Soup, salad, perhaps the veal with some shore vegetables. Can't get fresh, at sea."

"Nonsense!" MacDougall said with a snort. "Can't think, can't plot, on an empty stomach, and we've a long afternoon ahead."

A waiter arrived, took their orders, and set out glasses and chargers, silverware, and napkins, then re-closed the doors to scurry off. Not a tick later, another waiter arrived with a bottle of that grand St. Emilion Bordeaux for them to sample, then disappeared just as softly as the first.

"Now, sir," MacDougall said, "along with the transcript of your fraudulent trial, and the utter uselessness of your putative counsel dredged up from a Kingston tavern, your friend, Mister James Peel, of the Foreign Office, provided me with some even more intriguing information, most particularly the makeup of the jury that convicted you."

MacDougall seemed to preen, and, like most people with a secret that you did not yet know, withheld his news with a most smug smile.

"And, pray, what is that, Mister MacDougall?" Lewrie enquired, fighting down his urge to grab the lout by the lapels and give him a brisk shaking. *Why do I always run into the "beg me to tell you" type?* Lewrie cynically asked himself. It was hard enough to tolerate it when it came from Peel, or Peel's former superior, the archly inscrutable Zachariah Twigg, but by God he didn't have to take it from a civilian!

"Peel provided me with the entire list, sir," MacDougall preened a bit more, tapping his noggin sagaciously, "*and,* their backgrounds and connexions to the Beaumans. While I did not bring it with me, and cannot cite you chapter and verse from memory, I can relate a few of the most suspicious.

"Your jury consisted of a dozen local gentlemen . . . though what constitutes a gentleman on Jamaica is rather a *broader* definition than that which obtains in the British Isles," MacDougall half-whispered as he leaned a bit closer. "One, for instance, was a captain of a slaving ship . . . a ship 'husbanded' by several rich planters, the Beaumans and their close kin, principally. One gentleman was editor and part owner of a Kingston newspaper . . . the other owner being —"

"Hugh Beauman, aye," Lewrie grimly interrupted, for he and his friend Christopher Cashman had both suffered that paper's attentions, both before and after the duel. "A damned lyin' rag!"

"The jury even included tradesmen . . . an importer and chandler who sells 'shoddy' and cast-offs with which to feed and clothe slaves," MacDougall grimly intoned, "and, an *overseer,* a slave *driver* from one of the Sellers family's plantations, hey?"

"The Sellers!" Lewrie spat. "More Beauman kin, and a Captain Sellers was the one I and the judges at that duel had to shoot down!"

"More reason for the overseer, and another from that family to be disqualified," Mac-Dougall said in an outraged huff. "The rest of the panel consisted of slave-owning planters, all of whom Mister Peel pointed out to me in his affidavit most suspiciously selected from the immediate neighbourhood of the Beaumans' main plantings, and supplied us with their bonds of long affinity, direct or indirect kinship, and ties to business interests or indebtedness, most carefully delineated."

"A sham from start to finish, sir," Sadler stuck in.

"I would not have thought such a travesty of justice *possible* in our more enlightened times," Mr. MacDougall gravelled with a derisive snort, "without the active collusion of the court itself! But, quite happily for your cause, Captain Lewrie, your friend Peel's attestations were all done on paper bearing the letterhead of Lord Balcarres, the island's Governor-General, lending the *imprimatur,* the 'Guinea Stamp,' of official interest, *and* dis-approval, by the local representative of

H.M. Government . . . and his own affidavit was witnessed by the secretary to Lord Balcarres, to boot, ha ha!"

"Nothing from Lord Balcarres, though," Mr. Sadler was quick to add, taking the edge off Lewrie's joy, "but, the Reverend Wilberforce and his patrons in the House of Lords have written him, requesting he delve into the matter, and, hopefully, return a denouncement of . . ."

The doors to their private dining room opened, and in came the rolls, three bowls of "cock-a-leekie" soup (the chop-house must have had MacDougall's Scottish tastes graven in stone, by then), and a round ball of butter the size of a man's fist. And it was a close-run thing as to who scored the first roll, Sadler or MacDougall, with another contest to see who could usurp the fresh-sweating butter!

The soup deserved a glass of Rhenish, each, no need for a full bottle, really; a *second* glass to accompany the salad of fresh greens drizzled with oil and vinegar, and, hang it . . . fetch a *whole* bottle of Rhenish to accompany the pair of squabs that each of them ended up ordering. And, when the plates of oysters arrived — a dozen for each — why, they were so succulent that to forego a bottle of Portuguese sparkling wine to sluice them down, and cut the edge of the horseradish sauce, would be a mortal sin!

And, of course, the roast veal, the seasoned fried potato quarters and asparagus, *demanded* that rare Château Lafite, laid down long before the war supposedly (and *not* smuggled from the south of revolutionary France last month!), so delightful on the palate that two more bottles were necessary!

Dessert was apple dowdy and ginger snaps, and MacDougall swore that the very best thing with hot, sweet apple dowdy would be a light, sweet Canary — a single glass, no more, thankee Jesus.

"Coffee for three?" MacDougall asked, once all that repast had finally disappeared. "Clear heads for the afternoon's doings, what?" he jovially suggested, swiping hair from his shiny forehead, dabbing a fine sheen from his cheeks, and a last flick of apple dowdy from his lips. "It is my custom to save the nuts, fruit, and port for supper."

"Worse things happen at sea," Lewrie commented, feeling a bit glassy-eyed by that point, and his belly constricted like a vise by the waistband of his breeches.

The doors closed as a waiter went for cups, new spoons, and a coffee service. Once gone, MacDougall leaned over, all chummy-like and more than a bit pie-eyed himself, to simper at Lewrie for a moment, and snicker whilst he stared holes in Lewrie's direction.

"Aye, sir?" Lewrie at last had to ask, believing that if the man kept eying him so intently, he'd fall out of his chair.

"Saved the very best for last, Captain Lewrie," MacDougall said, touching a finger to his lips as if to shush everyone. "Your former Leftenant-Colonel Christopher Cashman . . . the fellow who, as you say, instigated the plan for your dozen slaves to flee their masters, and volunteer 'board your frigate . . . your Mister Peel has *found* him!"

" 'Kit'?" Lewrie whooped (rather loud for conspiratoral whispers but, given the circumstances, and the load he'd "taken aboard," could be forgiven this once) in utter astonishment. "*Found* him, d'ye say! I've been tryin' the most of two years. Where'd he light, sir?"

"The reason none of your letters ever caught up with him was due to his peripatetic rambles, Captain Lewrie." MacDougall chuckled. "From what Mister Peel wrote, Colonel Cashman first tried Charleston, South Carolina, wandered down to Savannah, Georgia, looked over commercial prospects as far north as the Chesapeake Bay, before settling in Wilmington, North Carolina. Requests to various British consuls finally found a mention of a business firm in Wilmington by the name of Seabright & Cashman. A further request determined that the fellow partnered in that firm was, indeed, one *Christopher* Cashman, English as roast beef, and formerly of Jamaica, ha ha!"

"The old rascal!" Lewrie chortled with glee,

wondering if his old friend had gotten at least *one* of his letters, begging "Kit" to hunt down Guillaume Choundas, then in American custody after capture by a monstrous Yankee frigate in the West Indies, and murder him, by fair means or foul, to save Britain future troubles should the man get free of his parole and return to French service . . . that, and to save his bastard half-Lewrie, half-Cherokee son, Desmond McGilliveray, from murder, should Choundas ever discover that the promising lad was his!

Must write the boy, Lewrie blearily reminded himself; *see what he's up to. First thing tomorrow.* A promise he'd made and re-made, monthly, since departing the Caribbean.

"Saw-mills, pitch, tar, and turpentine . . . ," MacDougall related, pausing to belch, then quickly excuse himself, "import and export, and rice-mills, iron forging . . . land speculation, that sort of thing."

"I must write him at once," Lewrie vowed, cringing to admit that young Desmond would be taking "long straws" for a bit longer, but at the moment, saving his own neck by getting corroboration from "Kit" was more important. "Do you have the address? But, of *course,* just send it care of Seabright & Cashman. Wilmington can't have grown so big as when I was there during the Revolution!"

"*Peel's* written him," MacDougall countered, leaning back into his chair with an ominous creaking noise of tortured joinings. "Just two months ago, as he said in his last letter to me, and 'twill take two months more, or better, to get a first reply, then another period of time for either Peel or Cashman to contact *me*. Do I have a certified declaration from your old friend to present in court, I may prove beyond all question that you are most definitely not guilty of theft.

"Though . . . ," he added after a deep breath, and taking a second to run his tongue round the inside of his mouth, most-like looking for a last crumb or morsel, "you could still face the risk of new charges of unlawful Conversion, but not theft or robbery."

"Conversion . . . ?" Lewrie frowned, never having heard the term.

"Of being the person who *received* the stolen goods, then used them for his own purposes," Mr. Sadler softly supplied from the other side of the table.

"Might as well say that *King George* 'converted' 'em, then," Lewrie sneered, "for *he's* the one who's gotten service from 'em!"

"Hmm . . . scribble that down, will you, Mister Sadler, lest we forget it?" MacDougall said with a giggle and an inspired expression. "A ludicrous argument, but . . . not *completely* implausible. They *are* his Majesty's sailors, are they not, ha ha? No matter . . ." The attorney suddenly sobered (though with a bit of visible difficulty, that). "Your friend Cashman is now a citizen of the United States of America, and the state of North Carolina, not a subject of the Crown, and beyond the reach of British law, unless and until he voluntarily returns to Great Britain, or any British colony or possession, so, he would run absolutely no risk were he to supply us with an affidavit stating his role in the matter. We must keep our fingers crossed."

"Well, of course he would!" Lewrie countered. "Once you write him and suggest it, he'd be . . ."

"Ah, but I may not, Captain Lewrie," MacDougall interrupted as he put on his stern and formal "pose for a noble picture" phyz. "For me to elicit testimony which I know to be fraudulent would go against the grain with me. I will do all I can for you, but to suggest to a witness that he 'cut his cloth' to suit my purposes would be to suborn perjury, and that would be dishonourable to the profession of the law, and would redound to my complete discredit.

"Besides," MacDougall said with a lopsided cherub's grin, "we have so much perjury, obfuscation, and collusion done by the Beaumans, already, that any jury in the land may smell the rot. Whilst we, on the other hand, *must* be above all that, and appear as pure as Caesar's wife."

"Along with our usual antics, sir?" Sadler

mystifyingly added, stifling a chuckle of his own with his napkin.

"Goes without saying, Mister Sadler, indeed, ha ha!" MacDougall chearly replied, guffawing right out loud.

"So, does Cashman send us an . . . affidavit what-ye-call-'em," Lewrie asked, too fuddled to pay much attention to that cryptic statement, "sayin' that 'twas he who roused the slaves to run, and arranged for me t'be there to collect 'em, I *don't* get 'scragged'?"

"My dear Captain Lewrie," MacDougall smugly assured him, "by the time I'm done, you'll be chaired and cheered through the streets, and 'twill be the *Beaumans* who'll be lucky to get aboard a ship back to Jamaica with clothes on their backs, a step ahead of 'Captain Tom' of the Mob!"

"Well, if you're sure . . ." Lewrie pondered.

"Certain as tomorrow's sunrise, sir!" MacDougall vowed. Then, both he and Sadler turned their gazes on him, just as a waiter fetched them their coffee, milk, sugar, cups, and spoons. The waiter carried the reckoning, scribbled on a quarter-page of foolscap, as well, which he withdrew from a chest pocket of his traditional blue apron. Sadler and MacDougall both put their heads down as the waiter poured coffee for them, and got grossly intent upon the sugaring and the milking of their beverages, paying the waiter no mind.

Christ! Lewrie sarcastically thought; *my bloody treat, sure!*

The waiter, obviously a fellow very familiar with the ways of the barrister and his clerk, made but a small, sly nod, and turned his attention to Lewrie, coughed into his fist as if to prompt Lewrie, and plastered a benign, but expectant, smile on his face.

"Oh, give it me," Lewrie resignedly said, pulling his leather purse from his snug breeches' pocket.

Mine arse on a band-box, I could buy a blooded hunter, at these prices! he groaned inwardly, regretting that he and Caroline had made up their minds to settle a "dot" of an hundred pounds a year on young Sophie, to match the hundred that Langlie's parents had settled on him. A trip to Coutts' Bank would be in order, soonest, to replenish before returning to his expensive lodgings that evening, else he'd not be able to pay that reckoning, either!

"Well, after coffee, we'll retire to my lodgings," MacDougall suggested, once the waiter was gone. "A hard afternoon's work, then supper? I know a wonderful new establishment near the 'Change, sir."

I don't feed him proper, I end up swingin' in the breeze? Alan Lewrie cynically wondered.

"But, of course," he had to say, and grin as he did it. "That sounds simply delightful. I am completely in your hands."

CHAPTER EIGHT

It was a passing-fair day for a wedding. Rain had poured down in buckets the early evening prior, just about the time that Lewrie had returned to Portsmouth in the diligence coach, slithering down the road from Portdown Hill. Thankfully though, the rain had eased off to misty, light showers round midnight, and had quit in the early hours of the dawn, just afore "first sparrow fart."

By proper sunrise, the skies had mostly cleared, displaying patches of lighter-coloured clouds, through which the sun broke, now and again. The town, and the seaport, smelled fresh-laundered without the usual accumulated reeks. Horse dung and ordure had been flushed away (for a little while, anyway) and the street cobbles and narrow brick sidewalks bore a damp sheen, with here and there puddles, some rather large but shallow, that acted like mirrors to the now-benign sky.

Lt. Urquhart, who had never met Langlie, volunteered to remain aboard, along with the new-come Midshipmen, to keep an eye on the ship, whilst *Savage*'s Commission Sea Officers, Marine Lieutenant Devereux and Mr. Winwood the Sailing Master, along with Mr. Midshipman Grace, accompanied Lewrie ashore in the ship's boats, buffed up, polished, brushed down, and clad in their best uniforms. For a rather rare once, except for Sunday Divisions, they had even bathed, closely shaved, and gotten their hair trimmed and combed into presentable order.

Caroline had insisted upon the services being held at the church of St. Thomas A'Becket's, that grand and prominent Portsmouth landmark. If hoary old St. George's in their home village of Anglesgreen was not convenient to Langlie's family, who lived in Kent, and if Langlie could not get free of his new ship long enough during her own fitting-out . . . and if a London parish church was equally inconvenient, then St. Thomas A'Becket's it would be, and *hang* the cost! she had determinedly insisted . . . rather *strongly*, in point of fact; turned as chilly as a Greenland blizzard, high-nosed and imperious, and playing upon her husband's guilt like a master violinist. Hadn't Lewrie made a "pile of tin" off Creole pirate silver, his prize-money from the Mediterranean as well been freed by the Prize-Courts, at long last, so . . . ? "What is money for, if not to spend on such an occasion . . . dear?" she had pouted.

115

■ ■ ■ ■

Lewrie and his well-groomed party shambled into the appointed inn, the Blue Posts, to meet up with the groom and his party, and there Langlie was, dressed in a spanking-new uniform, with the single bright gold epaulet upon his left shoulder, his shirt, waist-coat, and breeches as white as snow, his Hessian boots new-blacked, and his long and curly dark hair brushed back, with a dab or two of pomade to keep it in good order, and a mere sprig of a queue at the back of his neck and uniform coat collar in the new style.

And looking as fretful and nervous as a treed cat, even if his two Lieutenants and four Midshipmen off the brig-sloop HMS *Orpheus* were gently joshing him at the moment.

"Captain Lewrie, sir!" Langlie exclaimed, flea-quick to cross the room and offer his hand, 'stead of waiting to receive that honour.

"Commander Langlie!" Lewrie replied in like manner, taking that offered hand and giving it a warm shake. "Ye look well in your new rank, and both well-deserved and about time, too, sir!" Lewrie said in normal tones, then leaned closer to whisper, "but about as nervous as a feagued horse. Marriage'll do that, or so I'm told, though."

"More gladsome anticipation than fret, sir,"

116

Langlie admitted in equally guarded voice, beaming fit to bust. "May I make you known to my parents, sir, my sister, and my officers and 'Mids'?"

"Be delighted," Lewrie happily agreed.

It had come as rather a surprise, when Lt. Langlie had spoken to his captain, just days after his commission and orders had come down from Admiralty, hemming and hawing, coughing into his fist and turning as red as rare beef, to formally ask Lewrie for his ward's, Sophie de Maubeuge's, hand in marriage. Oh, Lewrie had long ago given both of them permission to *write* each other, but then Sophie and Caroline had gone all wroth with each other, and Sophie had fled to London, to live with his father, Sir Hugo St. George Willoughby, and had been (for Sir Hugo and his unsavoury repute) introduced into London society, Lewrie had figured that the girl surely had struck upon another, by then; one with richer estate and prospects, perhaps, who would not turn his nose up at a penniless "foreign" girl with but a mediocre paraphernalia to bring to the marriage, and but a miserly "dot" of annual support, no matter how radiantly fetching and lovely, how well-schooled in social graces, but . . . it seemed that "absence makes the heart grow fonder."

Lewrie could *almost* understand it; when he'd first met her at Toulon in '93, Sophie and her firebrand brother and woeful mother had been living with an equally impoverished cousin, Baron Charles Auguste de Crillart, one of those "Royalist" French naval officers hounded from the service during the Terror, and ejected from his seat in the People's Assembly for being too damned reasonable and moderate . . . stances both highly suspect and *rare* in those bloody days.

Sophie had evinced all the signs of being in teenaged "cream-pot love" with her older cousin. In defending the hundreds of refugees of the fall of Toulon, de Crillart had sacrificed his life, and poor wee Sophie had lost her brother in the final boarding of the lone French *corvette* that had caught up with their weary old, half-armed frigate, as well. To make things even more grievous, a last broadside from the *corvette* had smashed in the stern, down low, slaughtering her mother, to boot, and Sophie would have had no one to look after her, if not for Lewrie honouring his pledge to the dying Charles de Crillart to see to his kinfolk. Lewrie and Caroline had been her saviours; Caroline in the beginning with her whole-hearted charity, and Lewrie streaked with their common foes' blood, smudged with spent gunpowder, hatless, and a sword in his hand at the end of that battle . . . the battle that resulted in the *corvette* becoming HMS *Jester,* Lewrie's first wartime command.

Did I seem a replacement for poor Charles? Lewrie took time to maunder; *was an officer from* someone's *navy Sophie's destiny?*

He gave himself a mental shake, plastering a smile upon his phyz for the introductions. Mr. Anthony Langlie, Senior, was a squire-archy gentleman-farmer of good appearance, an equal to his son's handsomeness, well dressed and obviously a man of some means, whose lands — 640 acres in freehold — lay close by to Horsham. Mrs. Langlie made just as impressive an appearance, not the typical "country dumpling" he expected; still a quite fetching and tastefully dressed lady in her fourties. The Langlies were the sort of educated and polished couple one might meet in a fashionable drawing room in London, yet not so grand and high-nosed. If they were to be in-law kin, Lewrie could contemplate future time with them *might* present him with conversation that did not consist solely of sheep husbandry and how the apple crop was doing!

Admittedly, the Langlies *did* eye him in a fashion that Lewrie could only deem . . . chary. No matter the good reports they had of him through their son during his service as First Lieutenant aboard *Proteus,* there *were* those many articles in the newspapers, some hints of infamy, the taints of the "tar brush," and all.

"Well, then . . . Mister Langlie, sir . . .

Mistress Langlie, ma'am, quite delighted to meet you, at last," Lewrie said after the requisite bows and hand clasps and pledges of "yer servant" and such. "After a three-year commission with your son, I feel deeply honoured for him to become my son-in-law, for there's no finer officer in the Navy, to my lights, nor a finer gentleman. Didn't *exactly* realise the depths of their feelings for each other . . . the drudgery of duty, and all that . . . that they'd sent each other miniature portraits, and such, 'til he asked for Sophie's hand. They'll make a grand couple, let me assure you, and you'll be getting a sweet and honest daughter-in-law, good in the pantry, still-room, at housewifery? My wife, Caroline, has seen to that."

Like shakin' fins with a shark, they're thinkin', Lewrie could conjure as they simpered polite agreement with him; *or marryin' into a tribe o' head-huntin' cannibals from the Great South Seas!*

Lewrie was introduced to Langlie's officers and Midshipmen, and got a much better, almost hero-worshipping, reception from them, young "Mids" especially, who all but goggled and gulped, as if being presented to Nelson, for all they'd heard of his derring-do. Lewrie made the introductions of his own officers, and the "Mids" off *Orpheus* looked upon those worthies, heroes in their own right during the fight that had taken the

French frigate *L'Uranie* after nigh a two-hour battle in the middle of a raging gale, much the same, Langlie's Midshipmen in awe of the saltiness of Mr. Grace, even though he had come up from the Nore fisheries, and was several grades of "gentility" below their own typical squirearchy or low-order nobility backgrounds.

"Ah, hmm," Langlie quibbled, looking at his pocket-watch.

"Ah, indeed, sir," Lewrie agreed, looking at his own. "I fear that I'm due away to the George to collect the bridal party. You will excuse me, Mister Langlie . . . Ma'am? And, I will see you all at the church quite soon. Mister Adair?"

"Aye, sir," his Second Officer piped up.

"Coffee or tea only, do you please, or my wife will kill me," Lewrie cautioned.

"Keep 'em somewhat sober, Mister Whitney," Langlie also said in like vein to his First Officer.

"Aye aye, sir."

And, for a brief, shared moment of inner amusement, Lewrie and Langlie looked each other in the eye, taut grins breaking out on both their faces and nodding (winking, on Lewrie's part) in recognition of the fact that both of them, Post-Captain or new-minted Commander, were in command of King's ships, and were mature leaders of men.

Moulded ye, Langlie . . . damned if I didn't,

121

Lewrie could think as he took his leave; *though I had better than good material to work with. You're on yer own bottom, now . . . in more ways than one. And, God help the French . . . Sophie excepted, o' course.*

CHAPTER NINE

At the grander George Inn, where the wedding breakfast would be held, Lewrie spoke with the owner, took a peek into the private dining rooms, already laid for the celebration, then trotted abovestairs to his family's lodgings.

"Ah, there ye are, at long last," his father, Major-General Sir Hugo St. George Willoughby, grumbled as he entered their rooms.

"Father," Lewrie answered, heading for the bedrooms.

"I'd not *dare* go in there, at the moment, me lad," his father cautioned. "A massive bout of the vapours, all's not quite 'tiddly,' and I heard voices raised in high dudgeon not a minute past. Brandy?" Sir Hugo laconically offered, lifting a squat bottle to him.

"Ah, no, thankee," Lewrie demurred. "Not before the ceremony's done'd be best. They're in a pet? At logger-heads, or . . . ?"

At one time, Caroline had been all Christian sympathy and welcoming, doting "step-mother" to Sophie, when she'd first arrived from Gibraltar. But, once those anonymous "you must know of your husband's doings" letters had come, and *kept* coming, and had suggested that he and Sophie had been lovers, Caroline had turned spiteful on the girl, which was why Sophie had fled Anglesgreen in tears of betrayed trust, and ended up with Lewrie's father, the most unimaginable "port in the storm," for Sir Hugo was known far and wide as an infamous lecher and "beard-splitting" rakehell. It was Caroline's duty to stand in lieu of her real mother at such a time as Sophie's wedding, and to every outward sign, she was fulfilling that role, but . . . what she actually thought was anyone's guess.

Lewrie took a dithering step closer to the bedrooms.

"Suit yourself," Sir Hugo said with a sigh as he leaned back in his chair and crossed one knee-booted leg over the other. " 'Tis not a *shrieking* pet, thankee Jesus. Last-minute 'where's me pearl drops?' — I gather — a *general* bout of the 'fantods.' Women's nerves," he scoffed. "So . . . now you've met the Langlies, what was your impression?"

"Not the 'Chaw-Bacon Country-Puts' I expected," Lewrie said as he made the wise decision to seat himself at the table with his father. "So gracious and straight-forward, the French'd call 'em *suave*. I do imagine, do we dine 'em in back home, they'll even eat with knives and forks, as mannerly as kiss my hand."

"And, did they goggle when they clapped eyes on you?" Sir Hugo asked with a snicker.

"Like greetin' a crocodile, aye," Lewrie told him, chuckling in spite of his own twangy nerves. He'd not had that much experience at getting people married off, could barely recall his own, and getting Anthony Langlie and Sophie de Maubeuge "long-spliced" was as demanding a proposition as arming, rigging, and commissioning a warship. And, as pleasing an occasion as it was, it took time *away* from seeing to that proper commissioning of HMS *Savage;* kept him pent ashore whilst awaiting the Beaumans' arrival, was a day stolen from possible escape on the King's Business once *Savage* was able to sail . . . !

"Well, won't be a patch on what the Langlies think, when they clap eyes on *me,* haw haw," Sir Hugo said with an evil little smile.

"You'll do nothing to spoil the . . . ?" Lewrie fretted. He'd seen his father in action before; his eyes glittered something Satanic!

"I will simply be my usual self," Sir Hugo archly replied.

"God help us, then," Lewrie muttered under his breath, for his Corinthian sire, despite his sterling success in the field in Indian Army service, the *nabob's* pile of plunder he'd fetched home, and his long-ago knighthood for bravery during the Seven

Years' War to scrub the smuts off his repute among the "better sorts," *had* been a member of Lord Sandwich's Hell-Fire Club in his early days, and had whored and rantipoled with the strumpets and "bare-back riders" in the undercroft cells of Medmenham Abbey, before the club had been exposed and broken up. Indeed, so eager a member was he that, after a night or two of swilling, gorging, and "putting the leg over," Sir Hugo had been one of the few orgyasts who rose Sunday morning to attend the "Divine Services" that Lord Sandwich, in "dominee ditto" attire, preached against fornication and other deadly sins . . . mostly to the hundreds of farm cats that his labourers would herd into the church to improve their own amoral natures!

And, despite the good service Sir Hugo had rendered the Crown in the field during the Nore Mutiny at Sheerness, people *would* gossip and goggle him, women gasp behind their fans (whether in disgust or carnal curiosity, it was sometimes hard to tell), men cut him "direct" or displayed taut grins of envy, to this very day, for once a rogue, always a rogue; an unsavable sinner bound to Hell on the *fast* coach, or the man one might like to spend an evening with, just to pick up some pointers!

Least he's turned out proper, Lewrie told himself as he turned a leery eye on his father; *damme if he ain't sober, too! Mostly.*

To match the uniformed naval members of the wedding, Sir Hugo had donned his very best Army uniform; a smartly tailored red coat all adrip with gilt lace and gilded chain gimp, lace and gilt buttons up the sleeves above the blue cuffs; blue facings and collar with gilt-outlined button holes, atop a scarlet waist-sash, and breeches, shirt and waist-coat as white as snow. There was also the star of the Order of the Garter, and the cross-chest sash that went with it. Sitting on the table between them was a cocked hat the size of a watermelon, just as laced with gold trim and gilt cords as his coat, and a gold-bound black silk cockade on its left-hand forward face.

At his hip, the sly old rogue sported not the usual hundred-guinea straight small-sword like everyone else, but a Moghul *tulwar,* reputedly one he had taken off the corpse of a Rajput *rajah* whom he'd chopped to *chautney* sauce. It was a short sabre with a shiny Damascene blade, but so studded with pearls, emeralds, and rubies that it was worth a *rajah's* ransom in its own right, and Lewrie hadn't seen a gaudier one in Zachariah Twigg's vast collection at Spyglass Bungalow when he'd been forced to ride up to consult the old cut-throat a year before. Gilt hilt and hand-guard, an engraved and gold-inlaid blade, sheathed in a bright-steel scabbard with gold (not gilt) throat and drag, with even *more* inlays, engravings, and inset gems.

Pretty as it was, it was no toy, and was as keen-edged and dangerous as a barber's razor.

And, of course, Sir Hugo also sported a tight-curled white peruke with short queue, for his own hair was mostly a thing of the past, and his nigh-bare pate was now age-spotted. All in all, did one meet him on a daytime street, and be unaware of his scurrilous nature, one might be mightily impressed . . . almost to the point of gambling with him, or loaning him money!

There came the thuds of travelling chests being shut, a light patter of soft-soled shoes, then the bedroom door was flung open, and Caroline emerged, followed not a tick later by the bride, and a brace of maid-servants, one a stout and red-faced country girl from Anglesgreen who did for his wife, and a slimmer, darker, but just as shiny-faced and beaming maid-servant whom Sophie had engaged in London, all cooing and twittering at the joy of the occasion, and how splendidly the bride had been arrayed, how radiant she was at that instant.

"Sophie, Sophie, Sophie," Lewrie commented as he and Sir Hugo got to their feet, "give ye joy of the day, my dear! And, allow me to say how absolutely lovely ye are!"

"*Merci* . . . thank you, Captain Lewrie," Sophie replied, shiny-eyed, as if about to burst out in tears of sheer delight, or tears of last-minute qualms.

"Breathtakin', ye are, dear girl," Sir Hugo added. "Pretty as a picture. This Langlie fellow's a fortunate dog, damned if he ain't."

"Merci, grand-père . . . merci beaucoup," she said to him, for she had always been closest to the old *roué,* depending on him to learn how to adjust to being British. She gave him a twinkling smile and bowed a graceful curtsy to punctuate her gratitude for the compliment, along with his years of amusing aid.

"And, Caroline . . . ," Lewrie dared venture, for despite the giddy air coming from the bride-to-be and the maids, his wife sported that worrisome furrow 'twixt her brows. "How utterly splendid and lovely you look this day, as well. Smashin'!"

"Why, thankee, husband," Caroline replied, dipping him a curtsy as fine as Sophie's, and *sounding* pleased, with a *sketch* of a smile on her face. *Does she* still *suspect Sophie . . . and glad t'be shot of her?*

Indeed, both of them were a "picture."

Sophie, with her reddish auburn hair and bright green eyes, had chosen a bridal gown of aquamarine satin with the puffy upper sleeves and skin-tight lower sleeves that were now in fashion; high-waisted and square-cut at the bodice, all ruched and awash in white lace. Her hair was done up under a fetching, matching bonnet with fake flowers, fruit, and ribbons, bound under her chin by more ribbon. In Sophie's travelling chest lay more gowns; for the coach trip to where they'd honeymoon, for their first supper together as a couple, dainties for morning-after lounging, more gowns for enlightening tours of whatever was famous where they were going, and, surely some even daintier bed gowns to entice her new husband into starting a naval dynasty.

No wonder Caroline's "fashed," Lewrie understood; *she's spent a month slave-drivin' seamstresses an' milliners, and payin' out a year's farm rent on the girl!*

Caroline had chosen a soberer gown of dark blue satin with matching bonnet, trimmed in gilt lace. Hers was in much the same high-waisted and low-cut style, but with wide, shawl-like pleats over both of her shoulders, more's the pity.

Damn trepidation! Lewrie told himself, going to take hands with both of them, bestowing a chaste kiss on Sophie's cheek, then another upon his wife's. "Both of you are as lovely as the occasion merits," he reiterated, and Sophie squeezed his hand in shy thanks. There *was,* though, a slight shying away from his kiss on Caroline's part, a faint stiffening of her spine, and limpness to her hand. She all but uttered a resigned sigh! Sure sign of a whole gale to come when she and Lewrie were alone, *but over what?* he tried to puzzle; *some reconciliation!*

"And, there's my children!" Lewrie exclaimed, taking the arrival of his sons and his daughter as a convenient excuse to break free, and shove what dread he had of his wife's iciness down to his "orlop" for later . . . *much* later, could he manage it.

Sewallis, his first-born, was now thirteen, a lean and primmish lad just entering that awkward time 'twixt childhood and maturity . . . though he had always been too sober-sided for Lewrie to fathom exactly why. His suitings were dark grey "ditto," as stark as a parson.

Hugh, his middle child and ever-rambunctious imp, was now ten, and more flambouyant, dressed in a blue coat and buff waist-coat and new-fangled trousers, booted not shod, and though Caroline had spent a fair amount of time getting them spruced up, and warning them both to behave, Hugh already looked mussed, with his blonder hair in his eyes and his neck-stock come halfway undone.

Little Charlotte, well . . . at seven, she was definitely made in her mother's spitting image, her long light brown hair controlled by a pale blue bonnet and ribbons, dressed adult-like in a pale blue gown very much like Caroline's. Her amber eyes glowed as her gaze devoured every detail of Sophie's *ensemble,* mesmerised by a real-life bride.

Lewrie shook hands with the boys, knelt to

give Charlotte a hug, and gave them all a congratulating jape or compliment. Naval service had spaced their births so far apart . . . that, and the use of cundums.

After Sewallis's birth in the Bahamas in '87, he'd been off on patrol duties for the most part, as far south as the Turks & Caicos, for months on end, so Hugh had not been quickened 'til the early months of '89 (in *Alacrity's* great-cabins and hanging-cot, to be truthful) and born just after he'd paid off, taken half-pay, and rented their house and lands from Caroline's uncle, Phineas Chiswick, in Anglesgreen. Where he had spent the most miserable years of his life as a know-nothing gentleman-farmer, of whom it was said that he knew how to "raise his hat, but little else," a useless drone and hanger-on to his much cleverer wife, who had grown up with a bountiful knowledge of agriculture from her childhood in the Cape Fear region of North Carolina.

It was a wonder to Lewrie, so bored had he been in those days, that, for want of anything better to do, there weren't *more* children, but . . . after Charlotte's birth, and Caroline had survived the perils of childbed fever, *she* had suggested that three was enough, and wished him to obtain cundums; so much to do on the farm, in the still-room and truck gardens, the flower beds and decorative plantings, care for the children already born, their mutual joy of horseback riding . . .

The annual Bills of Mortality listed most deaths for young women as childbed fever, which usually took the infant, too. They had already birthed Sewallis as heir, Hugh to go Army, Navy, or take Holy Orders, and a lovely daughter, and they *seemed* to thrive, thank God, and might live to adulthood and have children of their own someday, so, why take the risk? And, Lewrie had been so much in love with Caroline in those days and so loath to risk her life, so selfish to keep him with her for all the years the Lord gave them (and, selfish to keep her the slim, tempting lass who'd come to their marriage bed, too) that he had been more than willing to go along with her wishes . . . his only worry had been how he could portray ignorance of what cundums did, and where they might be obtained!

Charlotte, Lewrie supposed, was a happy accident, the result of an unguarded night as the stormclouds of the French Revolution and the Terror loomed. The Nootka Sound Incident 'twixt Spain and England in far-off northwestern North America in 1790, his temporary recall to the colours, then the sureness of war coming with France, too, after the revolutionaries had beheaded King Louis and Queen Marie Antoinette. After the war did erupt in February of '93, Lewrie doubted if he had been home with Caroline more than five months, altogether, in the past seven years!

He could step back and admire his well-groomed (well, there *was* Hugh!) and well-behaved, properly educated children (well, there also was Hugh's boisterousness, and Charlotte's penchant for blurting out whatever thought crossed her wee mind, usually at the worst possible moment!) and call himself fortunate.

He could take pride and visual pleasure in Caroline, too, for she had not battened or thickened into the typical country housewife and matron. Were the lines on her face more noticeable, they were not as prominent as those of women her age, and they were, mostly, laugh lines and crow's-feet 'round her usually merry eyes. Her hair was yet glossy, her amber brown eyes bright, her form straight and slim . . .

I'm judgin' her like a fox hound! Lewrie chid himself; *ready to see how even she trots! Thirty-seven's not* that *old, after all; me* or *her. Why can't we . . . ?*

"I pray one of you gentlemen has confirmed that the coaches we contracted are arrived?" she rather vexedly enquired, more than ready to believe that her husband or father-in-law had forgotten that detail.

"Waiting at the kerb as I came up, dear," Lewrie was glad to be able to tell her.

"Saw to it," Sir Hugo drawled as he tossed back the last dregs of his fortifying brandy and tucked his ornate cocked hat under his arm. That worthy looked as if he *needed* fortifying, for with Lewrie slaving away like a Trojan to fit out his new frigate, it had fallen to him to be the go-between, the hewer of wood and the drawer of water to supply what the women needed from London, the fetcher and carrier, and guide to the better shops when Caroline and Sophie came up to the city.

And, there'd been little love lost 'twixt Caroline and Sir Hugo since he'd come back from India, and just popped up as a land *owner* and immediate neighbour to their *rented* lands. To Caroline, Sir Hugo was, if not Satan himself, then one of his unsavoury minions, and ever the slightly shameful burden to be borne!

"Grand-père?" Sophie prompted, with a twinkle.

"Of course, *ma chérie,*" Sir Hugo replied with a wide smile, and offered his free arm to her to escort her downstairs to the coaches.

"Children, next," Lewrie ordered. "Sewallis, see to your sister. Caroline and me, last. We'll debark at the church in the reverse order. First in, last out, like an Admiral, hey? You're to give her away, father?" He got a firm nod from both Sophie and Sir Hugo.

He could understand that; his father had

ever been charming and delightfully droll, erudite and surprisingly patient with Sophie as she made her adjustments to English country living. Besides, his father's French was infinitely better than Caroline's. He'd played the "Dutch Uncle" to the girl ever since his arrival, and had kept her chastely amused. Of all Lewrie's household, Sophie, surprisingly, had adored the old rogue the very fondest.

Lewrie offered his own arm to Caroline, and she laid hers atop it . . . lightly, so *very* lightly, as if averse. *Buggery, buggery, and buggery!* Lewrie thought, irked; *what's the bloody trouble now?*

"You did not ask of Mother, nor Uncle Phineas," Caroline said in a whisper as they trooped in rough order towards the door. "Nor did you ask why Governour and Millicent are not here."

"Well, in the excitement of the occasion, I s'pose I didn't," he whispered back. "Governour, I may assume, thinks me a traitor for spiriting away my Black sailors, undermining slavery worldwide . . ."

"Mother Charlotte will not see Midsummer's Day," Caroline told him, her whisper turning harsher, "and cannot travel. Yes, Governour will not attend any event where you are also present, and forbade Millicent to come, as well. I know you have no love for Uncle Phineas, nor he for you. Burgess . . ."

"In London, last I heard," Lewrie responded. Carefully.

"Beguiled by *you* to purchase Colours in a British regiment, and risk his life all over again, no matter the perils he faced in India," she accused. "He's done *enough,* God save us, he's *done* his duty . . ."

"Entirely his desire, Caroline, I did not . . . beguile him. He also wishes to wed. I'd think you'd be happy for him," Lewrie said.

"Wed some trull of *your* acquaintance, pah!" Caroline spat as vehemently as she could get away with as they descended the stairs to the entry hall, to the smiles and bows of the servitors and innkeeper. For them, at least, his wife plastered on a serene and happy smile.

Family! Lewrie scoffed to himself; *ain't they* so *much fun?*

CHAPTER TEN

Very few people stopped to ogle as the parade of coaches drew up to the entry of Saint Thomas A'Becket's, for in these wartime days, one more naval wedding was two-a-penny. Perhaps a few wives whose husbands were away overseas paused, and smiled in reverie or bitterness. Maybe a bachelor officer or sailor, perhaps an idle civilian lecher or two, stopped just long enough to leer at the bride as she emerged and was handed down, grinning to themselves, and wishing to be in the groom's boots that night.

Langlie's Second Officer (his name escaped Lewrie entirely) put out his Spanish *cigaro* beneath his shoe, then came to hold the doors to the church for them, and doff his hat in salute.

Inside, one of Langlie's Midshipmen ushered them down the aisle to the left-hand pew boxes in the front, whilst Sir Hugo spoke with a curate, then led Sophie to a private room outside the nave where she'd wait 'til the music began.

Once seated, Lewrie checked breast pockets of his uniform coat for the sheaf of folded-over letters he carried; notice from their own church, St. George's, in Anglesgreen, attesting that the Banns had been read three times; the rector's fee for the ceremony, the fees for the organist and bellowsman, the bell-ringers, and small gratuities for the crucifer and acolytes. He looked across the aisle to the groom's side and found Mr. Anthony Langlie, Senior, fidgetting with a thinner stack of letters, as well, and they shared a smile together.

For all his time passing through Portsmouth, it was the first time Lewrie had actually been *in* St. Thomas A'Becket's, so he simply had to crane his neck and take in all its splendours, the décor of the ceilings, nave, apse, ambo and high pulpit, the carvings of its columns and the intricacies of the stained-glass windows, most so nautical in nature, to match the famous golden galleon atop the spire outside.

Such a *wee* wedding party, in such a large edifice, nigh *echoing* empty, with so few relatives or neighbours able to attend. Counting acolytes, musicians, even dustmen, there weren't above two dozen folk present. Behind the immediate family on the Langlie side, there was no one except officers, Midshipmen, and a few sailors off HMS *Orpheus.*

"Pardons, pardons . . . by your leave," someone whispered behind them, and Lewrie turned his head to discover that Burgess Chiswick had managed to make it down from London, after all! He slid into the pew box just behind their full one, making Caroline all but squeal with open delight. "Coach was late, sorry, can you feature a 'dilly' that runs behind? Hallo, Alan! Oh, sister, you're looking *splendid!* Just *did* find lodgings at the Black Spread Eagle, and freshen up, first!"

Burgess no longer wore East India Company uniform, but was most nattily attired in a snug double-breasted tail-coat of bottle green, a sedate but shimmery fabric that Lewrie didn't recognise; equally snug grey trousers and top-boots, with a new-fangled cravat that completely hid whatever sort of shirt he wore.

Maybe that'll mollify her, Lewrie hopefully thought.

"How do things go, in London?" Lewrie asked, whispering softer than before.

"Won't be a *grand* regiment, but it looks as if I may purchase a majority for a *reasonable* sum," Burgess whispered back, sounding as if he was chortling all the same. "Army's not doing much, at present, so Horse Guards is a buyer's market. And, I met the Trencher family."

"Aha!" Lewrie congratulated, much too loud for the occasion.

"Joined the Abolitionist Society . . . sent my *carte de visite* up and finally wangled an invitation, and you're right, Alan, Theodora's damned . . . 'scuse me, nearly *perfect!* Thankee for the suggestion."

"Well . . . ," Lewrie said, come over all modest, swivelling so he could face Burgess and see his eager smile, but . . .

Christ Almighty! he gawped; *what the bloody Hell are* they *doin' here?*

For there, a couple of pew boxes "astern" of those where men off *Savage* impatiently sat, were Mr. Sadler from his barrister's office, a bird of ill omen to be certain, and . . . in the same box with him . . . Mr. Zachariah Twigg, the devious, cold-blooded, murderous, arrogant, and duplicitous, haughty old master spy who had bedeviled Lewrie's very existence since their first encounter in 1784 in the Far East!

Lewrie's jaw dropped open, and he could *feel* the blood drain from his face; to which struck-dumb expression the cadaverous-looking Twigg responded with a grim nod, a flex of his spidery fingers on top of his silver walking-stick handle which rested between his knees, and then did the *very* worst thing for Lewrie's equanimity . . . that cruel visage, so usually set in thin-lipped asperity and high-nosed disdain for the world in general, and sometimes for Lewrie in the particular, twisted up into a *rictus* of a sly smile . . . the sort of smile Lewrie might conjure that would appear upon a starving tiger or a nettled cobra just before the leap, strike, or spit. In Lewrie's harshly won experience with the man over the years, nothing good had *ever* come of a smiling Zachariah Twigg!

There came a wheezing sound from the organ bellows, the ringing of the bells in the steeple and loft, giving Lewrie a welcome excuse to snap back front, and pass a hand over his ashen face.

"Whatever *is* the matter, Lewrie?" Caroline rasp-whispered, inclining her head towards him as if *meaning* to share both prayer book and hymnal with him, but with a fierce look normally reserved for any misbehaving children: Act-Up-Now-And-I-Promise-That-You-Will-Pay! Too much was invested in time and money, in prestige and decorum, in frets and labour on her part, to let *anyone* spoil this wedding. It was hers as much as it was Sophie's, by God, and the person who ruins it will get drawn and quartered by the horses of the bridal coach!

"Er, uhm . . . nothing, my dear," Lewrie muttered as the organ music drew them to their feet, awaiting the bride's entrance on the arm of the splendidly turned-out Sir Hugo. "Surprise, I must own, to see an old . . . companion attending. I will introduce you later, love."

"Hmmf!" was her comment on that; sure

that whoever it was, was he a companion of his, he *must* be a fellow sinner and adulterer, hence, not *worth* an introduction.

Lewrie? he silently groaned to himself; *she called me Lewrie? Have we come to that, like all t'other fed-up-with-the-bastard wives do? Whatever happened to Alan, or "dear," or . . . oh, right, all* that *happened.*

Why *was* Sadler here, 'less the news from the courts was dire? Why would Twigg attend, and how bad could his news turn out to be, as well? Sadly, Lewrie was certain he'd discover the whys, not a second after the happy couple coached off into wedded bliss.

CHAPTER ELEVEN

The ceremony went well, as did the new couple's departure, with both ship's officers and Midshipmen forming an arch of bared swords or dirks . . . though forcing Commander and Mrs. Langlie to duck when they got to the shorter Midshipmen, whose arms and shorter dirks threatened hats, shoulders, and noses.

Once at the George Inn, the wine began to flow almost from the instant that hats, swords (dirks), and walking-sticks were deposited with the doorkeeper, people still sober enough to read the place cards got themselves sorted out, and took their seats, with some of the men, principally Zachariah Twigg, Sir Hugo, and Mr. Sadler, heading straight for the sideboard and its restorative brandy bottle. Lewrie wished he could do the same, but he still had host duties, the requisite speech to make in praise of Langlie and Sophie, toasts to propose . . . and his wife to puzzle out, for though she appeared gay and chirpy, he could recognise the secret signs that Caroline was missish over *something.* Too, there were the children to keep an eye on, and there were Sadler and Twigg to avoid 'til the last minute, like rosied plague carriers or peeling lepers!

"A lovely setting for the ceremony, what, Captain Lewrie?" Mr. Langlie the elder remarked with a glass of wine in his hand. "My Missus quite relished it. A most pleasing compromise location, in all."

"Oh, absolutely, sir," Lewrie agreed. "Why, in all my years of passing through Portsmouth, I cannot actually recall my being inside of Saint Thomas A'Becket's before. A most impressive place, indeed."

Langlie slightly cocked an eyebrow over that statement, keeping a mostly serene expression, though implying, *I dare say* your *sort would have not!* anyway. Or so Lewrie deduced; he *refused* to cringe.

"Your father, Sir Hugo?" Langlie continued. Lewrie managed not to wince as that name was mentioned, as was his usual wont. "A most, ah . . . colourful character, or so I have heard?"

"Colourful ain't the half of it, Mister Langlie." There came a faint guffaw from over Mr. Langlie's left shoulder as Sir Hugo came to join them. Colourful, indeed, for Sir Hugo's long-time Sikh orderly/valet, Trilochan Singh, he of the swarthy complexion, bristling mustachios, and evil eye patch, stood just off Sir

145

Hugo's larboard quarter in full regimental fig of his old 19th Native Infantry.

"And, never lend him, or let him hold, any monies, either," Mr. Zachariah Twigg chuckled as he joined them, too, and damned if his own personal man, *Sri* Ajit Roy, wasn't there, as well, right down to those elephant hide sandals of his, red cotton "celebration" stockings, suit of dark buff broadcloth with baggy *pyjammy* breeches. His mustachios, though greyer than Singh's, were as stiff as anchor cat-heads, too, and it looked as if Roy and Singh had been having an "old boy" reunion much like *almuni* of Harrow or Eton. Langlie's jaw dropped; so much for serenity!

"*Namaste,* El-Looey *sahib,* best wishes," Singh said in a gravelly voice, palms together, and bowing.

"*Namaste,* Cap-tain El-Looey," Ajit Roy added. "Oh, springing joy to the happy pair!"

"*Namaste, Sri* Ajit Roy, *Sri* Trilochan Singh," Lewrie replied as he put his palms together before his face and bowed in return. "*Dhanyavaad* . . . thank you for coming so far, and your wishes."

"Colourful runs in the family, Mister Langlie," Sir Hugo said.

"I dare say!" Langlie replied, unsure whether to smile or flee.

"You've met my father at the church, sir," Lewrie said, attending to the social niceties,

146

"but, allow me to name to you Mister Zachariah Twigg, late of the Foreign Office. Mister Twigg, the father of the groom, and, I am proud to say, my new in-law, Mister Anthony Langlie of Horsham, in Kent."

"Your servant, sir," from Langlie, then from Twigg. "Delighted to make your acquaintance, Mister Langlie," as Twigg prosed on, smooth and benign as a sated tiger. "Allow me to express my congratulations to you and your wife upon this happy occasion, and remark that you and Mistress Langlie have raised a praiseworthy son, one with great promise to the Crown, and the Navy, whose name has figured prominently in official reports from Captain Lewrie, the last three years, to my superiors, and Admiralty, as well."

"Ah, well?" Langlie puffed up with pride. "Thankee kindly, sir, for your best wishes, and for that information, too."

"Ahem" came a faint throat clearing, a timid cough into a fist from Mr. Sadler, who hovered nearby.

"My old orderly from my time in East India Company service, and a long-time friend, Mister Langlie," Sir Hugo stuck in, "former Sergeant . . . *Havildar* Trilochan Singh?"

Twigg was quick to introduce Ajit Roy as well, *outré* though an introduction of a servant to a gentleman was, requiring Mr. Langlie to try on the pressed-together palms, head bow, and stab at pronouncing a Hindu greeting, with Langlie looking dazedly bemused, as if wondering whether his son's wedding day could get *any* stranger.

"Ahem?" Sadler coughed a tad louder. He wasn't exotic, merely impertinent, but evidently thought his case urgent enough to violate the niceties, this once.

"Oh, yes," Twigg said. "May I also name to you another friend of Captain Lewrie's, Mister Langlie, who coached down from London with us?"

He did? Lewrie fearfully gawped to himself; *Twigg, father, and Sadler in the same coach? With Ajit Roy and Singh, to boot? Christ, I must* really *be in the legal "quag"!* The two former orderlies/valets surely would have ridden *in* the coach, not been stuck in the cheap seats atop in the rain; vile as they were, both Sir Hugo and Twigg held high regard and respect for their manservants. *Sadler's such a chatterbox away from work, 'tis a bloody wonder he ain't fluent in Hindi or Urdu by now!*

"Bless me, Mister Twigg, but 'tis a rare thing, indeed, to see a solicitor be so, ah . . . solicitous, as to coach all the way down to Portsmouth for a client's ward's wedding," Mr. Langlie marvelled, and making Sadler turn *several* livid colours, after Twigg had made but the sketchiest explanation of Sadler's relationship to Lewrie; "financial aspects" was the way he'd phrased it.

"C . . . Captain Lewrie is a client of long standing, sir," Mr. Sadler managed to say with a straight face. "And, so successful with prizes taken over the years, that, ah . . . ," he trailed off with a sheepish grin.

"I see," Langlie said, chin lifting and eyes glazing over after meeting one too many below his station. Sadler *handled* money, so he was a "tradesman," perhaps only a cut above an apothecary or tailor, and not *quite* a gentleman. "Your servant, Mister Sadler," he said as he turned to Lewrie once more. "A small matter, sir, speaking of financial doings . . . you are agreed, Captain Lewrie, that we each settle one hundred pounds *per annum* on our newlyweds . . . an hundred from me upon my son, an hundred from you upon Sophie?"

"Absolutely, Mister Langlie," Lewrie agreed.

In much better humour, Langlie cocked a brow again, and posed a better offer. "Care to go guineas, instead, Captain Lewrie?"

Twenty-one shillings to the guinea, as opposed to twenty to the pound, would be £105 *per annum*, £210 total, in addition to the pay of a Commander in active commission, 8 shillings a day, or a little over £134 *per annum,* less all the damned deductions, of course, so Sophie and her new husband would start out life on a firm financial footing, even if Sophie chose to reside apart from either set of in-laws.

I get acquitted, it's not that much more, Lewrie told himself; *I get convicted and hung, and it don't matter a toss.*

"Guineas it is, then," Lewrie agreed with a smile, offering his hand to seal the bargain. He could not resist turning to the hovering Sadler and adding, "You'll see to that arrangement, will you, Sadler? There's a good fellow."

"But of course, Captain Lewrie," Sadler had to respond to keep with the spirit of things, bowing himself away, his neck turned red.

"Well, shall we seat ourselves, join the ladies, and allow the festivities to begin, sir?" Langlie suggested, main-well pleased.

"Must speak," Twigg rasped in a harsh, business-like whisper in Lewrie's ear as Langlie preceded him to the table. "Later, hmm?"

"If we must," Lewrie said with a resigned sigh. "You, father, and Sadler all came down togeth— ?"

"Later," Twigg shushed him. "All will be discovered."

CHAPTER TWELVE

Praiseful speeches from Lewrie, from Langlie's father, one shy shamble of thanks from
the bridegroom, and even Sophie broke tradition to tap her wineglass with a spoon and
rise to express eternal gratitude to the Lew-
ries for her adoption as their ward, which
touched upon how courageous Captain Lewrie had fought to conquer the French, who
would have butchered the Royalist refugees,
but for him; the pledge to her dying cousin
to see her safe and protected in life, and,
finally . . .

". . . to have been so welcomed that I have
quite forgotten those times when I was
French, and may now make the proud boast
that I have been raised as English as — as
plum pudding! — and am now as equally
proud to be the wife of an heroic British sea-
dog. *Merci* to you, Captain Lewrie . . . to you,
Mistress Caroline," she said, tearing up just a
bit as she lifted a champagne glass. "To Sir
Hugo, my jolly mentor, and to you and your

company, Sewallis . . . Hugh . . . Charlotte. Darling and playful companions, all, and, to my many happy years in your family in Anglesgreen, that dear and lovely place, which will remain with me forever, no matter where Anthony and I go. *Merci, merci beaucoup,* to you all, and *bonne chance* to all of us!"

They toasted the King, with the youngest of Langlie's Midshipmen at the foot of the long table proposing it; followed by carefully chosen wardroom toasts — Monday's "To Our Ships at Sea"; Tuesday's "To Our Men"; and Sunday's "Absent Friends." Studiously avoiding, of course, "A Bloody War or a Sickly Season" (which was too much of a reminder of the bridegroom's trade), "Hunting and Old Port" (which wasn't *apropos*), and most certainly *not* "Sweethearts and Wives, May They Never Meet!"

After that, things degenerated to the usual "a glass with you, sir (or ma'am)," and offers of "may I interest you in another slice (serving) of this delectable . . ." ham, goose, roast beef, force meat pie, sausages, bacon, or removes of hashed potatoes, dainty made dishes, or platters of eggs, either fried, scrambled, poached, or Frenchified into *omelettes.*

At long last, not long before most people in Portsmouth would be thinking of their mid-day meals, when every attendee and guest had been sufficiently stuffed, and was "nigh-squiffy" with spirits, Langlie and his bride retired abovestairs to refresh themselves and change into travelling clothes, and the wedding party began to break up, in search of ease of their own, or another glass of something wet. Snickering Mids and young officers, with Burgess Chiswick leading Lewrie's children, went out to "decorate" the coach.

About a quarter-hour later, Sophie and her new husband had come back down, into a shower of rice and good wishes, some wishes verging on the ribald, said their good-byes, shook the last hands, shared their last hugs and kisses, and departed.

Thank bloody Christ that's *over!* Lewrie thought, nearly "half-foxed" himself, and in need of a restorative nap with his boots off, and the waistband of his breeches undone.

"Done, and done," his father said, beaming with pride over how well things had turned out.

"You did warn Langlie 'bout Sophie?" Lewrie asked him, thinking that Sir Hugo looked a tad off-centre, too.

"Whene'er she lapses into French, or gets a thicker accent, he should be on guard, yes," Sir Hugo rumbled, swaying a little. "Guard his purse, too, haw haw! Where will they lodge?"

"A posting-house in Brighton," Lewrie told

him. " 'Tis summer, so it should be pleasant. Salt-water bathes, flash crowds, even if the King or the Prince ain't there. Then, back to his ship on Monday, and Sophie's to move in with the Langlies near Horsham."

"Pity," Sir Hugo said, sighing. "Still, I don't s'pose Langlie will begrudge an hour or two of his time. Sadler'll have to go speak with him."

"Sadler? Why?" Lewrie scoffed.

"Didn't get his Lieutenant's journals, or get a shot at deposing him for your trial," Sir Hugo explained, as if he'd *surely* already told his son all about it. "Recall that wee matter, do ye?"

Here, Anthony, have my lovely ward, Lewrie thought sarcastically; *oh, by the by, could you testify t'save my neck? Good trade, hey what?*

"Ahem." Sadler announced his continual, pestiferous presence by coughing into his fist again.

"Ha, hmm?" Zachariah Twigg cleared *his* throat from slightly aft of Mr. Sadler, with an impatient and imperious look on his phyz.

And, to top things off, there also stood Caroline, arms crossed above her waist, tapping a neatly shod foot with one demanding brow up, and that furrow of "Right-Bloody-Now!" between her eyes!

Oh, Christ, Lewrie groaned to himself; *which of 'em can I afford t'shrug off? Eeny-meeny-*

miney-mo?

"Captain Lewrie," Twigg said, right-snappishly, when it appeared that he'd have to wait 'til Epiphany for *Lewrie* to make up his mind. "I believe there are matters of the greatest import which I, Mister Sadler, and Sir Hugo need to discuss with you. Mistress Lewrie, might I implore your kind indulgence? Half an hour, perhaps but a single hour, at the utmost, I assure you, dear lady." For Caroline, Twigg came over all cooing and gracious, delivering an over-formal bow with a hand on his chest.

"Oh, do what you wish with him!" Caroline snapped, bestowing on Lewrie a very frosty glare, heaving a dramatic sigh of resignation, and narrowing her eyes. She spun on her heels to leave, stiffly bound up the stairs.

Ouch! Lewrie thought, for officers and Midshipmen off both warships had trooped back into the dining room for a last pocketful from the leftovers, for later, or to take a last celebratory glass of spirits down to "heel-taps," and had witnessed that little *contre-temps.*

"Mister Adair, I will see you and the rest back aboard ship, sir . . . gentlemen," he said to dismiss his people, then made awkward good-byes to those off HMS *Orpheus,* who followed his own out the doors, some much worse for wear, "short-tacking" for the piers "three sheets to the wind." Thankfully, Langlie's parents had already departed for their lodgings, for a lie-down, and an easing of corsets or shoes. "Go with your mother, children," Lewrie bade his offspring. "Navy work."

"I've my own rooms at the Black Spread Eagle," Twigg said, once they were relatively alone. "My coach is waiting. Let us all repair there. With any luck at all, our own business shall be done well before dark, so Mister Sadler may coach to Brighton and speak with Commander Langlie tomorrow, after their first night of connubial bliss and a very late breakfast, hmm?" he suggested with a leer.

"Just how bad is it?" Lewrie had to ask, sounding as if musing more on his wife's chilly departure statement, instead.

"The Beaumans, and their entourage, are landed in London, and are hot after your immediate arrest, sir," Twigg bluntly told him, but with a rarely heard tinge of sympathy in his voice. "We must put our heads together to determine the best course of action. Let us go."

Once they were in Twigg's lodgings, a bottle of brandy made an immediate appearance, and a vital contribution towards calmness for every set of frazzled nerves, Lewrie's most especially. They seated themselves on the hard settees and half-sprung chairs near the tiny fireplace, with the bottle and extra glasses

156

on a side-table dragged up between them.

"Now, Mister Sadler," Twigg began, "what does your employer say of this development?"

"It was expected, Mister Twigg," Sadler said with a grim nod of his head. "Mister Mac-Dougall was certain that they would not be satisfied with a ruling from Jamaican courts, and must pursue the sentence of death *in absentia* in King's Bench, here, to obtain what *passes* for justice. Mister MacDougall, of course, has already made strenuous effort to deter the Beaumans' case from appearing on this Law Term's docket, hence delaying any need for Captain Lewrie to be taken up and put in prison. You know of the Law Terms, sirs?"

"No," from Lewrie; an abrupt nod from Twigg; a certain shifty look from Sir Hugo; and, from Burgess Chiswick, who had joined them at the last second, a cocked head and a negative shake.

"There are four official Law Terms each calendar year, sirs," Mr. Sadler solemnly explained, "when Court Sessions are held. There is Hilary Term, which begins in January . . . Easter Term, which is sat just after Easter, and is self-explanatory. We are now in the Trinity Term, which began on Whitsunday, and which will continue to try cases 'til late autumn, and, thankfully for the good Captain here, is full."

"Well, right then!" Burgess exclaimed, as if

it was all over.

"Lastly, there is Michaelmas Term, which begins in October, and does not conclude 'til Christmas, sirs," Sadler continued in the same tones, ignoring the enthusiastic interruption. "Trinity Term is also the time when the Lord Justices remove themselves to the major cities of each shire to conduct trials of those imprisoned for major crimes beyond the scope of local magistrates."

"So, the Lord Justices are now away?" Lewrie puzzled. "In that case, who sits in London while they're gone? And, who could doom me to hanging on the strength of the Beaumans' lying packet?"

"Magistrates, mostly, sir," Sadler told him, shifting about to face him. "Though, at least one or two Lord Justices who do not care for protracted stays in the countryside remain."

"And, do the Beaumans lay their case before one of them, Alan here gets taken up and slung into gaol 'til . . . ?" Burgess asked.

"One of the remaining Lord Justices would be perfectly capable of accepting the transcript and verdict of the Jamaica court," Sadler informed him, turning in his chair again, "and pronouncing sentence, Mister Chiswick."

"Upholding a *travesty* of justice?" Sir Hugo all but yelped.

"That is why my employer, Mister MacDougall, was so eager to lay hands on a copy of the transcript, Sir Hugo," Sadler said with a prim pride, though having to swivel to face yet another interlocutor, "as well as receiving an affidavit from the Jamaican barrister who represented Captain Lewrie during that sham of a trial. An affidavit which was obtained by Mister James Peel of the Foreign Office at Kingston, and the deposition performed by Lord Balcarres's . . . the island's Governor-General's . . . personal attorney, one Mister Johnathon Porter, Esquire, a most respected member of the bar, and formerly King's Counsel from Temple Bar, before accepting Lord Balcarres's offer of employment overseas. Trust me, gentlemen," Sadler said, spreading his hands, and letting a wee smile cross his solemn, at-work features. "Every Lord Justice in the land has dealt with Mister Porter, and hold him in the highest esteem.

"It does not harm our cause, either," Sadler continued, turning just a big smug, "that both Mister Peel and Mister Porter had the deposition transcribed to papers bearing the Governor-General's seal and letterhead, copies of which Mister MacDougall already has in hand, and stands ready to lay them before any Lord Justice who may adjudge the matter. Such imprint, sirs, while not bearing Lord Balcarres's *signature,* will go a long way towards lending a taint of official, though tacit, displeasure with the conduct of the

Jamaica trial."

"And what did this local barrister have t'say for himself 'bout the matter?" Burgess pressed.

"Why, that he was hired on by the Court, dredged up from taking a pint or two of mild in a tavern close by, Mister Chiswick," Sadler said with what almost approached a sly snicker, "given less than ten minutes to familiarise himself with the charges and the identity of his absent client, and was unable to present much beyond a *pro forma* defence. Poor Mister Pruett, a new-come to the Jamaica bar, about as unschooled as they come, sirs! Poor in abilities, I should suspect, as well as pelf, and only paid his honorarium months later, after persistent dunning of the local court system for his meagre thirty pounds.

"And, *that* miserly honorarium, gentlemen," Sadler said with an air of gleeful triumph, "was finally paid by Mister Hugh *Beauman's* local attorney, in part, at least, since the local Justices didn't deem Pruett's services worth even such a low amount!"

"Why, that's . . . that's . . . !" Lewrie spluttered, jerking erect from his dismal slump in a hard chair so quick that he spilled a bit of brandy on his waist-coat.

"Evidence of a criminal collusion 'twixt prosecuting barrister and defence barrister so vile that poor Mister Pruett could be brought

160

up on charges, and slung into prison himself," Sadler crowed. "Loss of membership in the bar, at the very least. Both of them, really . . . Pruett, *and* Beauman's barrister, Mister George Cotton."

"And he said *that* in his deposition, Mister Sadler?" Sir Hugo chortled, rocking back and forth with excitement on his chair.

"Indeed he did, Sir Hugo, sir," Sadler exulted. "My employer believes that Pruett's presence at any trial, or delaying evidentiary hearing, is so important to Captain Lewrie's defence that he wrote to Mister Peel, along with a sum of money, to see to it that Pruett must take passage to England, and be lodged in London until such time that he testify in *person,* exposing how one-sidedly was the trial conducted, how scanty were his chances to present a credible defence, and what a travesty was the whole affair, sirs!"

"Right, then!" Burgess erupted. "Huzzah! A glass with you, Mister Sadler . . . and a glass with you, next, Alan old son!"

"Toast . . . toast!" Sir Hugo insisted. "Top up your glasses, so we may make a double toast! To the poor Mister Pruett of Jamacia, and the sagacious Mister Andrew MacDougall, Esquire!"

He's t'have room, board and spirits on my *purse?* Lewrie thought, utterly appalled at how eager other people were to spend his money, even on his own behalf. Recalling how lavishly MacDougall and Sadler had already regaled themselves at his expense, he didn't know whether to laugh with relief, or weep in fear of future poverty.

After that gala toast, though, Mr. Sadler shyly called for their attention for a bit longer, for he had more to relate.

"Mister MacDougall, sirs, has already ascertained who it will be who prosecutes the Beaumans' case, as well," Sadler said in sober takings. "Evidently, their Mister Cotton on Jamaica had written their London solicitor and agent before taking ship, whom they authorised to engage a barrister upon his own judgement and recommendation, to speed things along whilst they made their sailing arrangements."

"Who is the bastard?" Sir Hugo snarled.

"Sir George Norman, K.C., sirs," Sadler informed them. "He is also a member of Grey's Inn, as is Mister MacDougall. Very well known at the bar. And, to Mister Mac-Dougall, too, so . . ."

"Ain't that . . . illegal, or something?" Sir Hugo asked, snorting in disbelief. "Mean t'say . . . !"

"Not at all, Sir Hugo . . . gentlemen!" Sadler quickly responded with a prim dislike for the honourable conduct of members of the bar to be questioned. "One might as well question the validity of two former students of Cambridge opposing each other, of two

162

congregants of the same church parish, or
—"

"It happens all the time, Sir Hugo," Twigg,
sitting and listening silently for the most part,
assured the nettled old fellow, giving him a
calming pat on the arm. "One must remember that both MacDougall and this Norman
fellow gain their livelihood from their *suc-
cesses* for their clients, and their best interests. Ain't that so, Sadler?"

"Indeed, Mister Twigg."

"Their livelihoods, and their reputes,
rather," Twigg went on, leaning back in the
padded armchair *he* had appropriated as if
musing. "Lose a prominent case, and one's
repute is diminished. As is their ability to at-
tract clients, or stick in the mind of solicitors,
who engage them."

"Oh," Burgess Chiswick commented, seeing the light. "I should think their *pride* suf-
fers, too. How important and brilliant others
in their line o' work think 'em . . . how
shameful a loss would be to their souls?"

"Exactly so, Mister Chiswick," Sadler said,
taking charge of the conversation once more.
"A man recognised as King's Counsel, or
barrister, might be engaged to prosecute one
time, defend another . . . so, for all those
reasons which you and Mister Twigg have laid
out, it would be impossible, and a grave offence 'gainst the dignity of law, and their
personal sacred honour, to collude. Sir

George Norman 'ate his terms' the requisite three years at Grey's Inn, and was called to the bar three years before my employer applied, and Mister MacDougall was still a special pleader and writer when Sir George was made King's Counsel. They are not colleagues, in the familiar sense, gentlemen."

"Don't sup t'gether?" a dubious Sir Hugo asked. "Shoot, fish, go on country retreats with each other?"

"Sir George and Mister MacDougall do not socialise at *all*, Sir Hugo," Sadler could say with confidence, and a certain sly humour. "I do not think that such would be possible, in point of fact, for, ah . . . well, Sir George holds rather low opinion of Scots, or anyone who has risen from beneath his own class, in general. Sir George's father is Viscount Selby, his elder brother a Baron, and Sir George, I should have said, is Sir George Norman, *Baronet* . . . long before he attained the honourific of King's Counsel, and became a Bencher in Grey's Inn."

"Aha!" Twigg said, with a derisive bark. "What our man here, Captain Lewrie, might nautically term a 'top-lofty,' is he?"

"The 'top-loftiest,' Mister Twigg," Sadler said, snickering a trifle.

"Reckoned a capable man?" Lewrie had to ask, so he could know his odds, and his opponent.

"At *some* things, Captain Lewrie," Sadler

replied, tapping his nose. "Sir George did a few terms at Oxford, to no special honours earned . . . no Blues won, d'ye see. Mister MacDougall heard a lot of him during his early years at Grey's Inn . . . for Sir George dined in diligently, and was reputed to *toady* diligently with the Benchers of the time, but . . . without much in the way of proper legal study. Sir George's family is close friends and cater-cousins to a great many at the law, though, and . . . one might charitably say that he was called to the bar more on the strength of his connexions than his abilities.

"Do not mistake my meaning, gentlemen . . . Captain Lewrie," Mr. Sadler gravely cautioned. "Sir George Norman is not a fool, nor easy to outwit in court. He is not an opponent to dismiss, or underestimate . . . though . . . ," he said, looking as if he wished he could chew on a thumbnail in such company.

"Though *what?*" Burgess prompted, impatient and intrigued.

"Well, Sir George has done rather a lot of cases in the Court of Common Pleas, for rather well-connected clients from his own social set, and the peerage. One case in Chancery Court, a most convoluted and intricate affair of inheritances, multiple wills, the upkeep for distraught and penniless heirs during its slow procession through the courts, has been *so* lucrative, *and* protracted, that no

165

one doubts it will outlast Sir George's life-
time, and keep him independently wealthy
apart from what his own family might settle
upon him!"

"He hasn't tried cases in King's Bench,
then?" Twigg posed with a frown on his face,
his spidery long fingers flexing on his glass.

"Oh, many, sir!" Sadler countered. "For
those accused who may meet his honorarium,
or who have family and friends who may have
the wherewithal to support their kinsman's,
or friend's, cause. Not that often on the
defence, mind you, gentlemen. Mister Mac-
Dougall says he suspects that placing one's
reputation at risk, should he lose, might not
suit Sir George's cautious nature. No, he has
been engaged most often to prosecute, and
has an estimable record of success at it. As
Mister MacDougall says, though, most of
those were open-and-shut cases with but little
doubt of the accused's guilt, nor the outcome
of the proceedings."

"I see," Twigg said slowly, drawing out the
phrase, and with a sly grin spreading on his
skeletal face, thin lips drawn upward. "And,
after seeing Captain Lewrie's name featured
so prominently in the newspapers, perhaps
even in some of those Abolitionist Society
tracts, and such, he scented a chance to shine
in a *most* prestigious case, certain that the
fame resulting from the successful prosecution of a well-known figure would polish his

repute to a *high* gloss, aha!"

"And, if he read the transcript, and took the Beaumans' lies as Gospel *Truth* . . . !" Lewrie exclaimed, snatching at sudden hope, after a dismal few hours.

". . . not realising how despicably and shamefully the Beaumans cheated, and colluded . . . !" Burgess, ever a staunch ally, cried in like glee. "Why, it must've looked as easy as a stroll in Hyde Park! And, thousands of pounds in his bank account for two hours' work, to boot!"

"Yayss," Mr. Twigg drawled, "for I am sure that the solicitor who engaged him for the Beaumans made known to him how King Croesus–wealthy the Beaumans are, and how large an honorarium he could demand."

"Mister MacDougall, sirs, is confident that Sir George is not *yet* cognisant of how weak his case really is," Sadler stated, "nor how colourable is the testimony, and the veracity of the witnesses quoted in that transcript. Mister MacDougall said for me to tell you, Captain Lewrie, and I quote, 'that, forearmed as we now are, I fully expect to eat Sir George Norman, and the Beaumans, alive, in court.' "

"Thank bloody Christ!" Lewrie breathed, ready to leap to his feet, raise his arms in victory, and perform a spastic dance around the room!

"That is why your presence in London is

urgently necessary, sir," Sadler went on, pouring cold water on *that* wee horn-pipe of joy.

"D'ye mean, now the Beaumans are in England, we're goin' t'court right *now?*" Lewrie spluttered, visibly paling a trifle, and with a sinking feeling under his heart. "To-morrow, or . . . ?"

"Oh no, sir!" Sadler countered, his attempt at a sympathetic and reassuring smile more of a leer at clients' ignorance of the law, than anything else. "As I said earlier, the Michael-mas Term, in October, is the earliest we may expect. No, this would be more in the way of an evidentiary hearing, a *preliminary,* to stave off the prosecution. My employer wishes you to be in London no later than day after tomorrow . . . in your best fig, he told me to tell you, Captain Lewrie. Best of your uni-forms . . . I'd suppose today's, for the wed-ding, will suffice. Though, ah . . . ," Sadler cautioned with an "ahem," and a cough into his fist, "perhaps it might be best did you coach up in civilian clothes."

"In *mufti,*" Lewrie's father said with a knowing nod, and a bit of Hindee slang. "So any *bazaari badmashes* the Beaumans might have hired don't recognise him, aha."

"Surely, you do not imagine that *any* En-glish gentleman, even if reared in the Colo-nies, would stoop to violence, or murder, sir!" Mr. Sadler gasped. "The Law grinds slow, but fine, and to go *outside* of the Rule of Law would be. . . ."

"Revenge is the reason for half the murders, Mister Sadler, and yes, dignified, home-grown English gentlemen do it all the time," Mr. Twigg harshly told the naïve Sadler (and he should know what he was talking about, after all his deeds and experiences!). "Or, they hire on bully-bucks, so their own hands stay clean."

"Ye don't know the Beaumans, if ye think *they're* civilised. I was ordered out of port after Kit Cashman shot Hugh Beauman's brother, and I shot his cousin," Lewrie sourly commented. "Else, I'd have ended up dead in a dark Kingston alley, with my throat slit, a second duel for revenge bedamned. They're vicious brutes, for all the money, land, and slaves they own . . . English-born or not."

"The high-handedness of Lewrie's trial, Mister Sadler," Mister Twigg archly said, "as if they *own* the courts on Jamaica? If they may present such calumnies in a court of law, so prideful as to think they may get away with anything so fraudulent, should be proof enough for you as to what innate English respect they hold for the Rule of Law, and how unscrupulous, and dangerous, the Beaumans may be when rowed beyond all temperance."

"*What* temperance?" Lewrie scoffed. "Never *had* any."

"I see," Sadler murmured, both enlightened

and appalled.

"Alan and I shall coach together," Sir Hugo offered, "with my man, Trilochan Singh. B'tween the three of us, the Beaumans'd need a *squad* o' cut-throats t'do him in."

"Why not hire a band t'lead the way, while we're at it?" Lewrie gravelled, heading for the brandy, too fretful to sit any longer. "We could stand out like a royal *fireworks!* 'Ooh, Da . . . lookit th' foreign feller! Oo's 'at wif 'im, 'at Lewrie git?' Mine arse on a. . . ."

"To the contrary," Mr. Twigg interjected with a sly expression. "A grand show's the very thing. Sir Hugo and I came down together in a hired coach, not the diligence, with Singh, and my man, Ajit Roy . . . who, I may dare say, is as dangerous an opponent as Singh, though not a Sikh sworn by his faith to wear the 'seven steels.' Mild appearance on Ajit's part has led many a foe to under-estimate him. *Dead* foes, I am happy to relate, hmm? No, we shall coach to London as grand as any lord and his retinue. Sir Hugo in his uniform, Singh in his, and Ajit Roy in his best native, holiday suiting. You, Lewrie, in the clothing you now stand in. T'would take an *extremely* well-paid gang of bully-bucks who'd dare attack such a party.

"Lewrie!" Twigg snapped, turning his gaze as quickly as a famished falcon in his direction. "Have you, among your crew, any tars who'd relish a fight, does it come to it?

170

Sailors who'd kill, if it is required? Any who might enjoy a melee . . . to the knife?"

"Bloody dozens, I suspect," Lewrie said with a sly smile of his own, recalling past battles, and those possessed of the hottest blood-lust during a boarding action. "My Cox'n, Liam Desmond, he's a battler . . . his mate Patrick Furfy. Not the sharpest thinker, but he is big, strong, and like most Irish, dearly loves a good scrap. And, there's Jones Nelson, one o' my Black, uh . . . volunteers. Monstrous-big, and very strong. Not so good with cutlass or pistol, but Nelson is daunting, just t'look at, and does wonders with mauls, logger-heads, and wooden rammer staffs."

"The more exotic, the better," Mr. Twigg agreed, nigh purring. "Good, we are agreed, then. Dawn, day after tomorrow, we shall, with those additions, coach to London."

"Make room for me," Burgess Chiswick offered. "I did not pack my own uniform, but I did fetch along a brace of double-barreled pistols, and, may one of you gentlemen lend me a sword . . . ?"

"I've some spare French officers' swords aboard my ship. Pick whichever you like, Burge," Lewrie offered.

"We'll be arseholes to elbows, but . . . ," Sir Hugo said, flexing his fingers on the hilt of his costly *tulwar,* as if looking forward to a violent encounter somewhere 'twixt Portsmouth and the Elephant and Castle posting-house in London. "Perhaps anyone sent to intercept us might think that Lewrie and his armed sailors are the Impress, looking for fresh muscles for the Navy, and shy off, haw haw!"

"Should I also fetch cutlasses for Singh and Ajit Roy?" Lewrie asked.

"No need," Sir Hugo told him with a grin. "A hanger sword's a part of his seven blades. In his luggage already."

"Ajit Roy and I, ah . . . are always . . . prepared," Twigg added.

Just bet ye are, Lewrie thought; *daggers, swords, pistols, and a pair o' swivel-guns, t'boot! Mounted t'either beam o'yer coach?*

"Well then, gentlemen," Sadler said, draining the last of his brandy and setting his glass aside with a determined thump, as if the meeting was gavelled to adjournment. "I must be off in pursuit of the happy groom, to obtain his deposition and Lieutenant's journals, then join' you in London as soon as possible. It is obvious that I depart, leaving Captain Lewrie in the safest of hands."

"And I could use a lie-down, 'fore supper," Sir Hugo said with a yawn as he finished his own brandy and rose to see the others out of his rooms.

"Well, then," Lewrie said, as well, ready to head back to the George Inn. Oddly, he didn't feel *that* much in danger; not in Portsmouth, not in a Navy seaport, surely!

He had his frigate and her crew, and a most secure place to sleep soundly, where any lurking assassin couldn't reach him. There'd be so many senior officers and their own attendants at the George that even a lone knife-man would feel daunted to enter. No, it would only be on the road that danger lay, right?

Oh, shit, Lewrie suddenly recalled; *Caroline's still waitin' to tear a strip o' hide off mine arse, for* some *reason.*

He had no decent excuse for haring back to *Savage* for shelter from her simmering displeasure, either. Not for *long,* at any rate!

This ain't goin' t'be pretty, he told himself.

CHAPTER THIRTEEN

"Tea, please, Abigail," Lewrie requested, once he had shed his hat, coat, presentation sword, and snake-clasp belt. At least, he *thought* Caroline's new maid-servant's name was Abigail; it was hard to recall, since he'd only clapped "top-lights" on her two days before . . . though for convenience sake, most housemaids got called "Abigail" no matter what their bloody names really were.

"Jane, sir," the stout girl with a bulldog's face meekly said.

"Jane, then, and yer pardons," Lewrie corrected himself.

They're gettin' uglier, he thought as he steeled himself to see his wife. Evidently, Caroline would not trust him to keep his fingers off any live-in household help but trolls, or the women who'd win the side of bacon at the annual village ugly-face contest without trying.

"Jane" returned with the tea, but Lewrie only had a sip or two to restore himself, and appear soberer after all that palaver with Mr. Twigg & Co., before Caroline emerged from her bedroom in an "at-home" dress and more comfortable slippers.

"You may go, Jane," Caroline said in a level tone. "The children are now changed, and ready for a stroll. Take them, please."

"Yes'm."

Lewrie studiously applied himself to sugaring and creaming his tea, slurping down one cup as the children thundered from their rooms, and tromped noisily belowstairs for the outside world . . . and God help Jane, and Portsmouth . . . and got a second cup ready for consumption before Caroline swept to a settee and sat . . . arms crossed, her brow furrowed, and her gaze piercing.

"And what was of such import that required the better part of two hours, husband?" Caroline coolly enquired.

"Savin' my bloody neck from the noose," Lewrie told her. "That the Beaumans are in London, and what my attorney plans t'do about 'em. How we're t'go, and when . . ."

"You're just dashing off again?" his wife scoffed. "When?"

"T'morrow, very early," Lewrie told her. She wasn't yet so hot she was throwing things, so he dared to amble over to a wing-back chair by the fireplace with his cup and saucer, and sit himself down. Not in *easy* reach, it went without saying!

"I see," Caroline muttered with a nod of her head, then heaved one of her exasperated sighs. "I suppose I should expect no better of you, after all these years. Absence, and indifference."

"I *could* stay with you here, dearest, but the next time ye saw me'd be swingin' in the wind at Newgate," Lewrie posed. "Rather see me hang?" he tried to jape, with a lop-sided grin.

"Hmm" was her answer to that.

"Oh, for God's sake, Caroline!" Lewrie griped, crossing his legs and shifting uneasily on his chair. "We were makin' *some* progress on a reconciliation. Now, you . . . you've been in a pet ever since you came down from home. What's the matter? The weddin's over, and it came off damn' near perfect. I'd've thought ye'd feel relieved, 'stead o' . . ."

"It did," Caroline said, with no joy of arranging a successful ceremony, breakfast, and beginning on good terms with the new in-laws. "Now I'm shot of her, and God help the Langlies. The coy . . . jade is now *their* worry," she spat, and Lewrie could read "bitch" or "whore" in place of the term she chose.

"Caroline . . . there never was a single *thing* 'twixt Sophie and me," Lewrie assured her, as he had dozens of times before. "I made a solemn oath to a dyin' man . . . a friend, no matter he was French . . . and I *honoured*

176

that pledge. *We* honoured, rather, for 'twas *you,* most of the time, who saw to her raisin'. Did she ever dally with anyone? You *ever* suspect Sophie's morals, ever hear or see anything with your own senses that led you to believe she played either of us false?

"Or . . . do ye place complete trust in those damned letters?" he pointedly asked. He didn't *relish* a fight with her, and knew that he had set one off, after months of tippy-toeing, but he was simply tired of being treated like a leper.

Her fierce frown, and the way one slippered foot and shin jiggled, was all the answer she made, and was all he needed to know.

"What, you've gotten another 'un?" he tried to tease. "Darlin', they're all lyin' packets!"

"Oh. Was your Corsican whore, Phoebe Aretino, a made-up fantasy, Alan?" was Caroline's vexed reply. "Or was she real? In Genoa, there was a Claudia something-or-other . . . was *she* spun from thin air? That slutty mort who bore your bastard child, Theoni Kavares Connor . . . I *read* of you and her *long* before seeing them both in Hyde Park! Just fever dreams, were they, you . . . *bastard?*"

"Now, now . . ." Lewrie tried to shush her, setting aside his tea and pushing hands towards her. They'd never lodge at the George Inn again, if she went on like that, and as loudly!

"*Whore*-monger . . . Corinthian . . . *rake-hell!*" Caroline skreeched. "Just like your bloody *father* . . . like *all* your line, most-like! The other letters proved true, so why not the ones about your precious and sordid Sophie, hah? Like the one about that vulgar circus bitch!"

"What?" Lewrie gawped, rowed beyond genteel temperance and volume himself. "Eudoxia Durschenko? You must be joking! Or, somebody must. I *told* you, Caroline, she set her cap for *me,* but I never laid a fing—"

"*Vain* and *prideful* bastard!"

"You got a fresh letter, is that it?" Lewrie demanded. "Let me see it!"

"So you can destroy it, then call me 'tetched'?" she accused.

"I've never *seen* one of 'em," Lewrie explained, getting to his feet. "I've told you and *told* you, 'tis someone who despises me . . . thinks I done him wrong somehow, and is gettin' his own back, through *you!* My father *described* one t'me, just after the Nore Mutiny. Fine bond paper, Spencerian copperplate hand, all that? I'd hoped Mister Twigg could've found out more. I told him of 'em last year, and —"

"*Another* of your circle of whore-mongers?" Caroline scoffed. "Why, does he wish to read them, late at night, Alan? Or, is he ready to swear on a Bible and lie for you . . . convince me that they're all false . . . then laugh with you, at me, behind my back?"

She sprang from the settee and began to pace the room, and the proper "languid" graces bedamned. She was all but stomping.

"Caroline . . . Zachariah Twigg is most certainly no friend of *mine*," Lewrie tried to explain, almost finding some faint amusement in the very idea. "His place at the Foreign Office is that of a *spy*, a meddler and intriguer overseas. Toppled *rajahs* and foreign princes who stood in England's way . . . a cut-throat, an assassin, and probably still is, despite his official retirement. One of the most dangerous men ever I met, but . . . not a real friend to anyone, or me. He knows forgeries, hand-writing, or knows people who do. I thought that he'd be able to 'smoak out' the identity of your anonymous scribbler."

That stopped her in her tracks, wide-eyed in surprise.

"I've been his gun-dog since '84, in the Far East," he went on, sensing an opening. "Dancin' t'Twigg's music in the Med, and the West Indies, too. And, every time Twigg, or one of his agents, shows up with a scheme, I feel rabbits runnin' over my grave. He finds me a . . . useful *asset,* Caroline," Lewrie spat. "*Still* does, else I'd never have gained support from the Abolitionists t'defend me, nor gained such a good attorney. God help whoever it is writin' those letters to you, my girl, if Twigg discovers 'em. He can make an enemy just disappear, on the quiet. All the pain they've caused you . . . wouldn't you desire t'know who's plagued you, and have something done about it?"

"I . . . never knew," Caroline softly replied, looking puzzled; not any less bitter, but it *was* a slight improvement.

"I was never at leave t'tell you, or anyone," Lewrie said. "Now, show me this latest letter. As Twigg and I coach to London together, I can show it to him, and let him have a go at it. Please, Caroline?"

She took a long pause to think that over, her arms snugly tucked under her breasts, hands gripping both elbows, and looking at the floor, before making up her mind, and going to the bedroom to fetch it.

Damme, I think I know *this hand!* Lewrie told himself as he read the first, for Caroline had fetched not one, but two of those letters, both much crumpled in her past rages. *From where, though, or when, I wonder? Still could be a man's hand . . . or a woman's.*

The oldest was about Sophie, full of scurrilous "observations" of her behaviour in London society, perhaps just after the time that she fled Anglesgreen and went for shelter with his father. Sophie was portrayed as frivolous, flighty, and "flibberty-gibbet," openly flirting with the many beaus who sniffed about her, *sporting,* and playing balum-rancum on the sly with impressive bachelors and rich married men who kept her "under their protection" like a mistress or a courtesan, then creeping home to Sir Hugo St. George Willoughby, into his bed where *they* whored together, and regaled each other with minute recollections of their latest conquests!

The anonymous writer included an allegedly overhead conversation 'twixt Sophie and some other infamous young belle, about how she filled her days, and nights, but could not wait 'til her "hero," long out at *sea,* could return, so they could pick up where they'd left off, and continue their long affair . . . right under her Paladin's roof!

"Caroline, this is utter, bloody . . . tripe!" Lewrie gravelled. "All the years Sophie lived with us, sweet and virginal, how *can* you believe she'd act so, or sound so, carnal? What girl, not a penniless waif, but damned-well supported and reared, would *say* such things to *anyone* if she had any hopes of makin' a good match!

"This supposed overheard conversation . . . Sophie might've been heard talkin' 'bout Anthony Langlie . . . comparin' dance partners, and tellin' some other girl why she was so indiff'rent to 'em, that's all. Someone's twisted it all round, and salted it with smut," he told her.

Caroline had moved to the tea table, and had poured herself a cup. She sipped standing up, and looked over the cup's rim at him in faint, mute agreement that his supposition might be correct.

The second about Eudoxia Durschenko was even more scandalous, more lurid. She was portrayed as an amoral Roosian *foreigner,* a jade who didn't own the morals that God promised a *stoat,* a *circus* person who performed nigh unclothed, and thought nothing of it, an *actress!* — which was a bare cut above a street prostitute, if the sum was right.

According to the scribbler, Lewrie and Eudoxia had rogered in his great-cabins, on long country rides, naked as earthworms right out in the open, in her private dressing room before *and* after performing.

Well, he'd *fantasised* such, but nothing like that ever happened . . . more's the pity. *Can't be anyone from the convoys, aboard* Proteus, *who wrote this trash,* he grimly thought; *this is all made up, a fever-dream for certain. Worse'n a novel 'bout a sultan's seraglio!*

And, how had the nameless writer discovered all this?

". . . 'introduced to her following a performance of Wigmore's New Peripatetic Extravaganza,' " Lewrie read aloud, his scorn and sarcasm positively dripping on the threadbare carpets, "cross the Thames in Southwark, and, after complimenting her upon the heroism she and the circus performers had shown when assailed by a French frigate in the same South Atlantic battle in which her paramour won his latest fame, she thanked me prettily, but then began to regale me with tales of how she had emulated her Navy lover. Then, to my astonishment, told me of their lovemaking, as if it was the most natural thing in the world, or so it might be to such a trull, who may not even be strictly allowed to be considered a Christian!'

"Damme, Caroline," Lewrie spluttered, "she and her father were Roosian Orthodox! Arslan Artimovich slept with one eye open to keep her a virgin, with a dagger in one hand, and his bullwhip in t'other, and there wasn't a man in their troupe who'd dare even let his *glance* linger! For someone t'know details . . . all of 'em false, mind! . . . he had t'be close t'me this last year past, and . . . ," he paused to compare the handwriting of both letters, "and these letters are both done in the same hand. The one time . . . *once,* I tell ye, that Dan Wigmore invited me back-stage after the show in Recife, *none* of the performers had a dressin' room t'roger *in.* Rickety foldin' mirror tables, with a thin curtain t'dress behind, that was all! Eudoxia was *never* guested aboard *Proteus,* and you go aboard *Savage* tomorrow morning, you ask of anybody, from wardroom to gun-deck, they'll tell you *that!* Can't you see that someone *is* spinnin' tales 'bout Sophie, and Eudoxia, out of thin air?

That this is all spite?"

"Though she behaved so *fond* of you, when I met her during the circus parade, right here in Portsmouth, Alan," Caroline coolly said, seemingly intent on her tea as she slowly paced the rooms, slowly and more gracefully. "Rode right up onto the sidewalk, bent down to *kiss* you, in a most intimate fashion from horseback, did she not?"

"I was in all the papers after we anchored and paid off, *she* was famous, and saw a way to increase the audience by a public show," he countered, managing to sound relatively reasonable about it. "And I introduced you and the children to her, did I not? Would a guilty man do that?"

"The slyest ones would, yes," Caroline said, "and could. She *flung* herself upon you, you said, Alan. How *much* did she fling, hah?"

"We met aboard the circus ship, the time the dancin' bear tried t'eat my hat and shins," Lewrie replied, "I told you o' that, and she found me amusin' . . . what happened t'me, amusin'. Didn't see her at all 'til we anchored at Recife, and I went to the circus, and Wigmore invited me back-stage. I talked to a *lot* of circus people. He wanted me t'use what influence he thought I had with Captain Treghues to let Navy sailors have shore liberty, so they could attend his shows, makin' him even more 'tin.' Faint chance o' that, *you* remember Treghues. We sailed for

Saint Helena, they put on the circus, and the comedies and dramas there, and I sat in the front row one night, and after the curtain call, she hopped off the stage and plopped herself in my lap, just as I told you . . . for a jape on her father, for the audience, 'cause it was *funny!*"

"Ha . . . ha," Caroline mocked.

"At Cape Town, I barely saw her," Lewrie pressed on, going over old news of his innocence. "She stayed in Cape Town when others from the circus went inland t'hunt new beasts for their menagerie, and we were down at Simon's Town, salvagin' a new rudder. She rode out the mornin' we set off, for target practice with her bow and her guns, and met us on the road . . . in front of a dozen sailors, and a dozen more drovers . . . and we talked for a bit as we rode along . . . Pennsylvania rifles and Fergusons, the Red Indian moccasin boots she got in Savannah, Georgia . . . a shootin' contest, perhaps, then she galloped off to exercise that white trick stallion o' hers, and that was all, dear."

"Uhm-hm." One brow was up, high, and her eyes were squinted.

"Your own brother met her," Lewrie stanchly soldiered on with his protestation of innocence. "The mornin' we were loadin' the new rudder into a barge, she came down to the docks t'sight-see, Burgess came ashore off one o' the home-bound Indiamen, and I

185

had t'introduce her, or give her the 'cut-direct.' And, when I named him as my brother-in-law, she called me a slew o' names, like I'd led her on false . . . *tarakan* . . . *sikkim siyn* . . . *peesa* . . . cockroach, son of a bitch, and well, ah . . . *prick,* if ye must know . . . pardons."

"How discerning of her," Caroline said quite brightly, faintly amused; though not *that* much. "My estimation of her, foreign or no, rises. *Peesa,* hmm. And, *sikkim . . . siyn,* is it? How apt."

"One o' my Black hands had run away with the circus hunters," Lewrie contined, wondering if Caroline would go buy herself a stack of foreign lexicons, to find new ways to say what she couldn't in public. "Mauled by a lion. Some of her fellow circus people had been killed, too, she'd come t'ask of her father, and she helped t'get my sailor to their own surgeon, who knew more of animal wounds than ours, and that was the absolute last time I saw or spoke to her 'til that parade here in Portsmouth back in the spring, Caroline, and haven't since."

"A *plausible* tale, Alan," she coolly replied, after finishing her tea and pacing back to the settee, where she arranged herself most primly, her back erect, her gaze level and un-revealing, and her hands in her lap. "Even if nothing did pass 'twixt you and that barely clad . . . creature, even if she was then, and still is, a naïve and feckless young virgin in deluded 'cream-pot love' with you, I suspect it wasn't for want of *trying* on your part. 'Twas lack of opportunity."

Knows me too damned well, she does! he sorrowfully thought.

"Caroline, we'd begun writing each other again," Lewrie said in a soft and pleading tone. "God's my witness, I'll admit I was tempted sore, but . . . I . . . *didn't!* And, *not* for lack of opportunity, for I'd hopes we might, you and me . . . all this about Sophie, or Eudoxia, are vicious, sordid lies. And that's the truth."

She looked down at her hands and considered that for a long bit. She then looked up, the simmering of anger back in her amber eyes, and with a most odd expression, as if she *wished* to believe him, but found past betrayals just too massive.

"Perhaps that is so, Alan," she said, "and my nameless torturer has overreached, at last, but . . . there are still so many others to explain. Do you deny your taking that Phoebe Aretino as a mistress?"

"Ah . . . ," Lewrie dithered, feeling like wincing, if he could get away with it and not doom himself and all his recent pleadings. "Six, eight months, and thousands of miles away from home, Caroline, and . . . a man has . . . well, I ain't a saint, nor a tonsured monk."

"Oh, how well I know that of you," Caroline said with a bitter little chuckle. "Your Italian mort in Genoa?" she asked, nigh-gayly.

"Twigg . . . he *ordered* me to, and it was just the once," Lewrie told her, chin tucked into his collars, and realising how lame that sounded, even as he said it. "S'truth! Claudia was a French spy, and go-between 'twixt the Frogs and the cabal that wanted France to seize power! She got set on me, thinkin' I was gullible enough t'blab just what they needed t'know, and Twigg *used* that . . . used *me* . . . t'feed her what *he* wanted 'em to know, so we could lay a trap for their best . . . ye recall what I told ye of Guillaume Choundas?"

"Why, for King and Country, Alan?" Caroline sweetly said with a very false smile. "How patriotic of you! I may still be but a North Carolina country girl, but do not imagine that I am a *total* fool!"

"But it's true, I *swear* it!" Lewrie protested. "Ask Twigg!"

"Hah!" was her opinion of that. Calming, she continued, as if she were the cat, and he the cornered mouse. "And what of the mother of your bastard, Alan? Theoni . . . Kavares . . . Connor," she intoned as if savouring each scornful syllable. "After you rescued her, and her natural child, from those Serbian pirates, was *she* so enthralled, was *she* so grateful that she simply *had* to fling herself upon your manliness, and your *sterling* and heroic character?"

"It was, it . . . ," Lewrie stammered, totally dis-armed. This had simmered like an acrid pot between them, and finally, finally, there it was, served up like manure soup. "It happened, aye, no denyin' it. In the Adriatic, after. I was wounded and groggy with laudanum, there wasn't enough room aboard for all our British refugees 'fore the Frogs took Venice, so . . ."

"And, in Sheerness, too, Alan?" Caroline remorselessly reminded him, as if he had need of reminding. "Before you sailed for the West Indies, the last time . . . a whole *week* with her, you spent. Sharing a lodging for all the world to see."

"Aye," he had to confess, sitting down in his wing-back chair again, too limp with guilt to protest. "After you'd stormed off home."

To Hell with more tea, for by now he was starkly sober, more in need of brandy, or Yankee corn whisky, could he find any. "After you threw me away, and wrote t'tell me I would never be welcome under the same roof with you, again, well . . ."

There; it was said, at long last. Out in the open.

"Port in a storm . . . ," he lamely tried to expound.

"Damn you!" his wife blurted. "Damn you

to Hell, Alan!"

"Caroline . . . what d'ye expect a man to *be?* How much time have we had together since the war began? Two months, three, out o' seven bloody *years?* Even before *then,* . . . swaddles and spit-ups . . . pantries and still-rooms, flower gardens . . . 'not this time o' month,' you said. 'Three children were enough,' you said . . . *'Perhaps,'* you said, if I'd employ protections, and Charlotte an accident, and nigh six months for nursin' and celibacy after, and you blamin' me for riskin' your life t'child-bed fever one more time, and . . . !"

She flounced off the settee halfway through that, stamping the bounds of their lodgings, arms stiff at her sides and her small fists balled.

"Me, more like a burden than a loved husband," Lewrie went on, spilling all his pent-up recriminations on how such a loving marriage, with so much spectacularly exciting intimacy, had become so drab and lacklustre. "Right, I'll never be a farmer or a herdsman, we know it, but . . . you're so complete to yourself and the children, and I —"

"Go!" she snapped at last, pausing by the one window, her arms across her chest once more, looking *out,* not at him. "Go up to London, to your damned ship, to your *lovers!* Go to the *Devil,* why don't you?"

190

"Look, Caroline, Twigg'll discover who's been bedevilling you with these letters, and . . ."

"What bedevils me is *you*, you faithless, amoral bastard!" she shouted, turning about to face him. "I shall make your excuses to your poor children. God knows I've gained practice at doing so, these many years with you *never* at home . . . and day-dreaming about all your doxies when you *were!*"

"That's not true, Caroline!" Lewrie insisted. "When I was home, and *you* were there for me, *with* me, I *never . . . !*"

"Do *not* try to beguile me, Alan," she spat, fighting the tears that blinded her, striving not to lose her voice as her breath caught in hitches in her chest. "Just go! Go be your Navy's hero, a hero to the anti-slavery people, preen all you wish . . . but you will do all of that without *me!* Go be *tried* without me . . . or *hung* without me!"

"Dearest . . . !"

"Hah!"

She picked up the first thing that came to hand, a cheap Toby Jug in honour of some ancient sea-victory of some kind, and hurled it blindly. It came within a bare inch of breaking his nose, and making his "bung sport claret," had he not shied at the last moment.

Caroline darted for her bedroom door, flung it open, then shut it with a titanic bang. Bed-ropes creaked as she flung herself cross

191

the coverlet and mattress.

Lewrie shut his eyes in pain, and utter defeat. He felt pain, because he'd caused *her* pain, but . . . oddly (*perversely, more-like,* he chid himself) he felt nothing much beyond that, at that moment; just a *faint* twinge of conscience. A touch of shame that he had brought it upon himself? Of a certainty, a tad of that. There was nothing more he could do; the woes in Pandora's Box had already fluttered away, and there was no point in shutting it. Putrid old wine had been spilled, and there was no re-bottling it.

Perhaps there never *had* been a hope of reconciliation; the whole thing had felt forced and sham-ful anyway, a stiff and un-natural show for friends, family, and children, for Navy and Society. But there had been no warmth in it, not even a hint of the old intimacy, or the trust or the forgiveness, or . . .

Lewrie heaved a deep, resigned, and shrugging sigh. It was over, sure as Fate. He redressed in uniform, cocked hat, and sword, trying to compose his face as neatly as he could his clothes, looking round the set of rooms as if to discover a single thing that held even a *jot* of warmth, of comfortable familiarity . . . of *Lewrie-hood,* either his, or hers, and found nothing, for it was as empty and impartial as the yawning, gun-less gun-deck of a hulked warship.

Nothin' for it, he grimly decided, snatching

up those damning letters and cramming them into a side pocket. Perhaps Twigg *could* do him proud. The identity of the mysterious writer would never bring his wife round, but . . . there was always his *own* vengeance to wreak. That might prove satisfying.

He'd coach to London to try to save his life and honour. She would coach to Anglesgreen, and erase him from her life, and there was likely an end to it.

"Give ye joy o' the day," Lewrie sadly whispered as he stepped out into the hall and softly shut the door. "For ev'ry weddin' day is a time for good cheer."

■ ■ ■ ■

Book II

■ ■ ■ ■

It is hard to say, whether the Doctors of Law or Divinity have made the greater Advances in the lucrative Business of Mystery.
Edmund Burke (1729–1797),
A Vindication of Natural Society (1756)

CHAPTER FOURTEEN

When Zachariah Twigg had said "my coach," Lewrie had pictured a typical six-passenger equipage, drawn by four horses, the sensible sort of carriage that most people of means owned. Come dawn, however, there before the Black Spread Eagle stood the twin to the commercial "dilly," the diligence, or balloon coach, big enough for nigh a dozen, if they were fairly intimate dwarves, and with even more seating atop.

Twigg was there already, in top-boots, old tricorne hat, and the voluminous double-caped greatcoat that Lewrie remembered from the harum-scarum ride that Twigg had given him the year before in his "sporting" two-horse chariot from his Hampstead retreat, Spyglass Bungalow, to London at a terrifying rate of knots, with Twigg cracking his whip and howling maniacally, with the wind blowing back into their faces with a breath-stopping force!

"You'll, ah . . . not be takin' the reins, will

you?" Lewrie asked in trepidation as an assistant coachee took his valise and carpet bag to stow in the boot.

"Oh, I thought at least one stage," Twigg said, eyes twinkling in evil glee and anticipation, "once on the flat."

"Oh, Christ," Lewrie muttered.

"And, your father, Sir Hugo, may take a leg, as well."

"Oh, no!" Lewrie gawped.

I'd known this, I'd've hunted out a priest for last rites! he grimly told himself, feeling like he should cross himself.

"Ah, there's me slug-a-bed." Sir Hugo chuckled as he came round the lead pair of the six-horse team, after checking harness, admiring the quality of the beasts, as well. "Breakfasted? Been t'the jakes?"

"Aye. But, hearing that you and Mister Twigg'll be driving, I feel a sudden, new need," Lewrie chaffered.

"And, well-armed, too, I see. Good lad," his father haw-hawed.

Sir Hugo looked positively piratical, sporting a pair of double-barreled pistols in his waist-sash, and the pockets of his ornate general's coat sagging with another pair of lighter single-shot "barkers." He'd traded his *rajah's tulwar* for the plainer small-sword that Lewrie recalled from earlier days.

Come to think on it, Twigg's greatcoat showed similar bulges and lumpiness, and

198

the drag of a sword scabbard could be seen under its hem . . . knowing Twigg, Lewrie strongly suspected that there were even more blades in hidden places — slim poignards, *krees* daggers from the Far East jammed into his boots, and God knew what else.

Might have grenadoes up his rectum, Lewrie decided.

Ajit Roy and Trilochan Singh came out of the inn carrying final articles of luggage, and both of them positively clanked with weaponry, chattering away in Hindi or Urdu as gay as magpies. Compared to them, Lewrie thought his hands, Cox'n Desmond, Landsman Furfy, and Landsman Jones Nelson, looked fairly naked, outfitted with but a cutlass each, clumsy Sea Pattern single-shot pistols, and their personal knives, which served for everything from work to dining.

"Like it?" Twigg asked, gesturing towards his coach. "Hired it on from a fellow who refurbishes 'dillys.' Usually damned comfortable when travelling with only four or so," he went on, whether Lewrie made a good or bad opinion, or none, as was his wont. "Time is precious . . . the sun will soon rise, and we must be off. Board, sirs, board if you please."

There were two additional bodies up in the box, the driver and an assistant, wearing subdued burgundy livery under their greatcoats. Two more held open the doors and lowered the folding metal steps, wearing the

199

same livery, and, as Lewrie got aboard, he took note that the fellow who held the door with a blank-faced servant's expression for him, but, with darting, sly eyes for everything beyond, wore the most cunning set of holsters sewn inside his greatcoat. The briefest look at the fellow's overall appearance, and his taut and wary face, before he was seated inside, convinced Lewrie that the man had been a soldier at one time, and not a timid rear-ranker, either.

The coach swayed on its leather suspension straps as Desmond and his party clambered up onto the roof seats, poor Patrick Furfy awkward and heavy, as usual; it'd be a rare day that anyone sent Furfy aloft!

There came a clatter of hooves as four mounted men, all dressed in the same great-coats, hats, and livery, paced up from a stable down the street. The leader leaned close to Twigg's lowered window, muttering a reply to Twigg's whispered instructions, and touched the brim of his hat before touching spurs and cantering away. Lewrie got a glimpse of a brass-hilted Heavy Cavalry Pattern sabre in a scabbard mounted on the saddle, a saddle-holstered pistol forward of his right knee, and a scabbarded musketoon's wooden butt peeking above the horse's rump.

"Out-riders, just in case," Mr. Twigg confided with a hiss, and the look of a scrapper just spoiling for a battle; the way hungry men might look forward to toast and jam. "Four, altogether. Once it gets warm enough, they'll doff the greatcoats . . . just so anyone contemplating ambush will be daunted, or . . . eliminated," he added, with savage relish.

"The coachees and the footmen just as well armed?" Lewrie asked.

"Oh, yes!" Twigg said, smiling broadly as the coach lurched, and began to roll forward. "A most useful party of men, altogether. Not always so overt in their purpose, but, in this instance, not only our showy appearance, but a show of *force,* I thought them necessary."

"Rode down before us," Sir Hugo casually imparted, yawning like an hippopotamus. "Zachariah whistled 'em up, soon as he discovered the Beaumans' arrival. Lurked 'bout the piers, the church, and the wedding breakfast, and I'll wager ye never even noticed."

"Didn't think *t'look* for such at a wedding," Lewrie said with a snort. "Disguised as ushers and acolytes, were they?"

"Most useful men, indeed," Twigg told them all. "Disguises *do,* now and again, play a part in their line of work. Hard as it is to believe in time of war, there are some nefarious sorts who will play spy for our foes . . . *Britons,* in the pay of the French or Spanish, who are in need of . . . convincing," he said with a leer. "Foreign agents who covert themselves in our nation, and operate traitorous bands of native-born informers, who must be 'smoked out,' exposed, and hung, or simply drop off the face of the earth, to the utter confoundment of their spymasters in Paris or Madrid, or . . . certain other foreign capitals," he said with a sage tap aside his nose.

"Skulkers for the Foreign Office, ye mean," Lewrie said. "Who work for you. I thought you were retired, Mister Twigg."

"Years of service overseas has made my face and name much too well known to our opposition," Twigg told him. "I now merely keep my hand in with consultations, and . . . some few tasks closer to home. My fellows here, well . . ." He leaned over the top of his walking-stick towards Lewrie, on the rear-facing bench. "My in-town residence, on Baker Street, among other locations, is the most convenient place for discreet comings and goings, so . . . I call my fellows the 'Baker Street Irregulars,' though private armies are no longer allowed in Britain."

He had himself a little simper of amusement.

"You forget, Zachariah," Sir Hugo reminded his odd choice for a friend, "that some Scottish lairds still maintain private regiments . . . 'Lord Thinggummy's Own Highland Foot,' or 'Lord Sheep-Thief's Border Reivers,' haw haw!"

"Fortunately, all on temporary loan to His

Majesty, though, old son," Twigg quickly rejoined in like good humour, "and part of Great Britain's army . . . 'til they feel an urge for rebellion and independence once more, God save us. In point of fact, a fair number of my fellows come from such private regiments . . . easier to second from any regular British unit, whose soldiers took the 'King's Shilling' for long enlistments. Though there are *ways* . . . should a fellow be promising, ha!"

"Mercenaries, in essence," Lewrie asked with a worried frown.

"Trust Twigg, my boy," Sir Hugo assured him. "I do b'lieve our side pays better than our foes, so with such lads about, you're as safe as a babe in his mother's arms."

Even as light as the balloon coach was, with such a light load aboard, all of them had to get out and push to help the horse team get to the crest of Portdown Hill. Fortunately, the road was new-gravelled and dry, so they didn't end looking like Thames River mudlarks. And six horses made it bowl along quite nicely and swiftly under the reins of the regular coachee, a tad faster when Twigg took his turn upon the box, or when Sir Hugo tried his hand at emulating Jehu, the Biblical charioteer. As the sun rose and the summer warmth gathered, the greatcoats were shrugged off, baring livery and uniforms, and the oddness of their Indians' garb. Twigg was right; they *did* make a raree show! And, every twenty-odd miles or so, when the horse team had to be changed for fresh beasts, they received a variety of greetings.

"Run, lads, run an' raise th' Yeomanry!" one myopic twit cried as they clattered into Petersfield. "The fookin' French are 'ere!" As loosely organised as the local volunteer soldiery were, the travellers were long gone by the time a sergeant turned up with half a dozen men, all still struggling into uniform. At least their coach's stop had given those poor fellows a good excuse for leaving work, and angrily chivvying free beer for their troubles from the weak-eyed old fool.

"Huzzah! Th' circus is a'comin'!" a young stableyard hand yelled in glee when they stopped at Guildford, and *that* brought out a mob of gawkers, who, though disappointed that their party wasn't the circus, at least took joy from such an *outré* batch of travellers.

"Crikey, ye ain't th' King isself, is ye?" the publican at the last stage stop wondered aloud as their coach rolled to a halt at his tavern and posting-house on the outskirts of Kingston, near the south bank of the Thames. His customers and help tumbled out to witness the arrival, ready to curtsy, doff their hats, or tug their forelocks, 'til Twigg and Sir Hugo alit, not looking all *that* royal, and slunk back to their labours or their drinks.

Lewrie stretched his legs, rolled his shoulders, and eased his aching fundament in the shade of a large oak just outside the doors to the tavern, sitting on a wooden bench with his legs at last stretched out instead of awkwardly pinched up crabwise. Desmond and Lewrie's two other hands got down from the coach-top seats, and stood licking their lips in expectation.

"The team need changing, d'ye think?" Lewrie asked his father, who was, with Twigg, seeing to the horses' watering, and stroking them over. It wasn't that much further to London proper; from where he sat Lewrie could espy the city's taller steeples already.

"They seem sound enough to make it to the Elephant and Castle," Sir Hugo told him, and Twigg shrugged, then nodded his agreement.

"Half-pints, then, Desmond," Lewrie said, digging for his coin purse and handing his Cox'n a crown piece. "One for me, too."

"Aye, sor!" A half-pint sounded good to Desmond, though Furfy rolled his eyes and heaved a sad sigh of disappointment that they had no time for a full'un.

So many stops had taken a toll upon Lewrie's purse; beer with hard-boiled eggs to tide them over at Petersfield; beer, roast beef, and currant duff at the posting-house in Guildford . . . at the paying passengers' rate, not the price of a two-penny ordinary; and one stop midway 'twixt Guildford and here for cheese, apples, and more beer . . . !

His sailors came out of the tavern with their half-pints, and a rather pretty serving girl fetched Lewrie his, returning his change as she gave him a fair curtsy and smile, and Lewrie returned it, allowing her the last few pence for a tip, which earned him a second smile and bob. He took a sip, appreciating the brew, probably unknown to other towns beyond a long walk, and laid up in the tavern's cellar.

What a dead bust! Lewrie thought; *all this way, and I could've ridden it alone, for all the danger we've seen.*

He wasn't exactly sure just how long the Beaumans had been here in England, but began to doubt that they could have enlisted thugs for out-of-court revenge *this* quickly. Wouldn't know their way about, nor know whom to approach . . .

"Hoy, there," one of the out-riders called. All four of them had come to the watering troughs to freshen their mounts at the same time; all were now dismounted, but one of them — the taciturn leader — had kept his wits about him. Twigg and Sir Hugo snapped their heads about in the direction he was chin-pointing.

Up the London road near a thick stand of trees and shrubbery, a lone man stood by the head of his horse, stroking its nostrils to keep it silent, and half-hidden waist-deep in the bushes. Lewrie got an impresion, a quick'un, of dark clothing, a wide-brimmed and flat black farmer's hat. About an hundred yards or so away, Lewrie estimated, as the fellow, now aware that he was being stared at, sprang up onto his saddle, urgently sawed his horse's reins, and spurred away before any of their out-riders could even think to saddle up. Within moments the strange rider was out of sight round a bend, leaving small dust-puffs of dry dirt road that hung like a tan mist where shafts of sun dapples filtered through the trees!

"Uh-oh" was his father's sour comment. "Trouble at last, ha! Skirmishers, out. You concur, Zachariah? Your men . . . your call."

"Scout for an ambush, Perkins, there's a good fellow," Twigg said with a harsh snap. "Damme! Just, damme!"

"Might've been a highwayman," Lewrie supposed aloud, finishing his beer, setting the mug on the bench, and walking to the head of the horse team for a better look, as their unofficial cavalry vedette hastily mounted and cantered away in pursuit. "Make a try for a rich coach but thought we looked too daunting, so he . . ."

"Not a bit of it, sir!" Twigg countered, slashing the air with his walking-stick like a cutlass. He peered at Lewrie with a pitying expression, as if he were the most naïve fool in the world, or as blind as a bat. "No one *innocent* spurs off in such fashion. A highwayman . . . perhaps, but . . . in whose *pay*, Lewrie, and the leader, or sentinel, of how large a band? I *thought* our luck had been a tad too good. But it does make eminent sense to wait and watch nearer London than try their hand closer to Portsmouth. Where you must go, after all, hmm?" Twigg said with an arch leer. "Too many roads to watch, else, but . . ."

"Trouble, sor?" Cox'n Desmond asked his captain.

"Might very well turn out t'be, Desmond, aye," Lewrie answered. "Do you have the lads see t'their arms."

"Rush on," Sir Hugo suggested. "Is an ambush laid, better that we gallop through it. Your lads press the bastards hot, they *cannot* take the time t'choose a second lay-by, if flushed from their first. Doubt they're sharpshooters good enough t'strike swift-movin' targets."

"Take the initiative, yes," Twigg said after thinking it over a bit. "Put them wrong-footed."

"Worked often enough in India," Burgess Chiswick seconded. "Not a tactic they'd expect, even were they ex-soldiers themselves. And I know for a fact that most shooters never get enough practice to hit a blessed thing that isn't standing stock-still, and no more than thirty yards off! Right, Sir Hugo?"

"Mount up and be at 'em, instanter!" Sir Hugo urged. "Get everyone aboard the coach, and let's get crackin'!"

"And weapons ready on either beam," Lewrie added as they trotted back to the coach doors. "Back up top, lads! We're off!"

"Simple robbers, or hired *badmashes*, no matter," Sir Hugo, short of breath but full of vinegar, said as their coach quickly clattered to a swaying, rocking pace. "They try us on, we'll give 'em Hell. Scatter the bastards, if nothin' else, and leave 'em in our dust! Once past 'em I doubt they've the 'nutmegs' for pursuit."

"The shortest route into London, though, just in case," Twigg suggested, now with a brace of pistols in his hands, one laid atop his left arm ready to fire from his window. "On the widest streets, so any others cannot assault us."

"Right," Sir Hugo heartily agreed, "Westminster Bridge, and into Whitehall. Up Charing Cross to Oxford Street, thence to either my own gentlemen's hotel, or your house in Baker Street, Zachariah."

"My house," Twigg quickly decided, his full attention out his window. "More secure even than your Madeira Club. Once there, we may send a runner to Mister MacDougall and let him put his plans afoot for Lewrie's defence and court appearance."

"We gallop past whoever they are, Mister

Twigg," Burgess piped up, "and we'll be ahead of them passing word to their other associates. Best they can do is send two or three to skulk behind us, to discover where we're bound."

"True enough, Major Chiswick. Thankee," Twigg replied.

"The Beaumans . . . ," Lewrie said, trying to be helpful. "Even if this fellow's one of theirs, they don't know a bloody thing about who the rest of you are. An Army general, but who? They don't know about my father, what little time I ever spent with 'em, I never said a thing 'bout him, and we don't have the same last name, so . . . there is you as well, Mister Twigg. They won't know *your* connexions, or how dangerous you can be, either! Don't know *my* connexions, my in-laws, so they'll not recognise, or bother t'watch out for Burgess, here.

"And . . . ," Lewrie went on, sneering, "the Beaumans, for all their money back in Jamaica, are a *cheap* set o' bastards. Thousands for show, but penny-pinchin' at all else. Hugh Beauman, the senior now, is used to *slaves,* d'ye see? T'stay covert and innocent-lookin' behind a pack o' bully-bucks, he can't hire a *lot* of 'em, lest they blab too wide in their cups, and most-like'd weep over the expense of more than a whole dozen. So new to England, to London — *he's* never been here before! — he wouldn't know his way round

Cheapside, Seven Dials, or any of the stews where the *real* cut-throats can be had. Like Wapping . . ."

"And, need a city map, a lanthorn, and four hands t'figure his way about, ha!" Sir Hugo chimed in.

Zachariah Twigg turned away from gazing out his window over his pistol barrels so intently, and might have said something in reply to that; his expression seemed almost inspired with some new thought (and a tinge of surprise to hear something sensible coming from Lewrie) but the faint sound of faraway gunshots ended that!

The coachee blew a long, straight horn in the "tara-tara" octet of notes usually heard when the dogs have flushed a fox, signal for the hunt to be on, and Desmond, Furfy, and Nelson shouted almost as one and in naval parlance, "Enemy in sight! Two points off th' starboard bow!"

Twigg's private cavalry out-riders *had* flushed an ambush, forcing four or five armed men out of hiding on the right-hand side of the road, stampeding some of their horses and leaving a few of their armed foes to dart about on foot, out of the bushes onto the verge of the road. Twigg's horsemen were whooping and hollering, sabres in hand after discharging their pieces, and slashing their way through thick foliage.

"On the right! Take close aim!" Sir Hugo

bellowed loud enough for the coachee and his assistant in the box, and Lewrie's sailors on the coach-top to hear. Lewrie tried to find a window on the far side, but Burgess filled one, and his father the other, and Twigg nigh-back-handed Lewrie out of the way as he took post in the door window. Shots rang out, powder smoke filled the coach's interior in an instant, and muffled return shots *thunked* into the body of the coach and one of their wheel horses, making it scream with shock, surprise, and pain!

"Got 'im!" Sir Hugo crowed in old battle-lust. "Take that, ye bastard!"

"One t'larboard! 'Ware, larboard!" Desmond shouted down, and Lewrie swivelled awkwardly about to level a pistol in that direction before their coach galloped past the threat. He got off one shot but missed by a wide margin, with the mad swaying and rocking of the coach. The foeman ducked, turned, and darted away into the woods on the far side of the road, abandoning his musket and pistols in his wake so he could run faster . . . or pop up innocent as anything later on and feign mere curiosity . . . "Shootin'? *Wot* shootin', an' where?"

Lewrie dared stick his head and shoulders out the left-side window just in time to see one of their out-riders dash cross the road and into the woods in pursuit of that escaping highwayman, sabre held ready for a pursuit slash that could remove a fleeing foe's head from his shoulders, or slice his back open from the nape of his neck to his waist. A faint "View, halloo!" and he disappeared into the forest.

Twigg was thumping his walking-stick on the roof, and the coach slowed and came to a stop, so they could all spring down with loaded weapons or swords out. Back behind them, there were bodies staining the gravel and dirt with blood, sprawled like heaps of cast-off clothes. Perkins, the leader of their out-riders, knelt over one man who gasped and twitched his death-throes. To Twigg's tacit query, Perkins heaved a shrug and shook his head; the fellow was gone.

The out-rider Lewrie had seen gallop into the woods returned to the road as well, all smiles, and with his sabre blade bloodied right to the hilt.

"Got 'em all, sir!" Perkins yelled. "Half a dozen, all told . . . and all dead," he confirmed as all his men returned whole.

"Fetch 'em all out, Sergeant Perkins," Twigg sourly ordered as he sheathed his un-used small-sword. "And search their bodies for any letters or large sums of money that might point to the one who paid them. Usual drill, hmm? Damn! I'd have wished for *one* witness for a magistrate to attest to!"

A few minutes later, and six dead men were laid out in a line together, pockets turned out and belongings being sorted through for clues. Pipes, plugs of tobacco, pocket knives, hanks of twine, tokens from taverns for free drinks or doxies . . . which, in coin-starved England in time of war could almost be passed as easily as Crown coinage! . . . and, what seemed a rather suspicious amount of the new, much-hated paper currency; too much for the hobble-de-hoy griminess and cast-off finery that their late assailants sported.

"Too much 'chink' for needy highwaymen," Burgess Chiswick said as he counted the loose, crumpled stack of bills. "If they'd stolen this much earlier, I'd think they'd be off celebrating . . . spending it like water . . . not staging another robbery. Somebody paid them to do a job, certain," he firmly decided.

"It would appear so, sir," Mr. Twigg agreed, pacing among those rumpled bodies and poking them with his walking-stick as if attempting to make at least one of them "blab" his secret in a death-croak. "But no sign of *who,* or written-down instructions to explain why ours, and Lewrie's, coach was their specific target. The attack on us might as well have been instigated by some disgruntled Liverpool slave traders, businessmen involved in sugar, rum, and molasses trading. Bah!" Twigg snarled, kicking one of the dead highwaymen in the rib cage.

"So, how did they *know* who to shoot at?"

Lewrie fretted.

"Whom," Twigg primly corrected.

"At whom t'shoot," said Sir Hugo. "Tsk, tsk."

"Bugger" was Lewrie's frustrated comment.

"We must take these curs to the nearest magistrate, no matter," Twigg directed. "The attack upon us points the finger at *someone,* at any rate, for it most certainly was not random. Nor may I recall all that many highwaymen working in broad daylight, nor in such numbers. I am certain that a magistrate will find this crime unusual, as well . . . unusual enough to raise dire suspicions . . . in the right quarters," he said with an enigmatic grin.

"Too bad their leader, there, didn't carry one o' those damned Abolitionist tracts, with Alan's 'saintly' features illustrated," Sir Hugo snickered. "So he'd know his quarry."

"Does anyone happen to *have* any of them?" Twigg asked. "Pity. I would suppose any that you kept are aboard your ship in Portsmouth, Lewrie?"

"I don't keep 'em," Lewrie groused. "They went right into the quarter-gallery for bum-fodder, long since."

"Sounds a bit sacreligious, that," Burgess japed. "Wiping your fundament with pictures of 'Saint Alan the Liberator.' "

"Only banned in Catholic countries," Lewrie shot back.

"Ahem!" Mr. Twigg loudly harrumphed to stifle their low levity. "As I was *saying,* gentlemen . . . we must convince the local magistrate that this assault was *not* a random event, then . . . tracts, yayss," he drawled. "Reverend Wilberforce and his associates in the anti-slavery crowd can turn this into a positive *flood* of new tracts, whether the Beaumans were the instigators, or not. The attempted murder of their champion, their Paladin, by person or persons unknown?

"Combine that sensational news with hints of slaver, or sugar, interests, *and* the merest mention of how the Beaumans' arrival barely a week before coincides so mysteriously, ah? Nothing libellous, to be certain, *but . . . !*"

"Newspapers," Sir Hugo suggested, though he despised them.

"Just so, Sir Hugo," Twigg said, almost twinkling with delight. "The latest editions have featured rumours of Lewrie's impending trial, so news of *this* will make quite the uproar. Newspaper owners, editors, and newswriters are, in the main, a sad and scurrilous lot of ne'er-do-wells, drunks, whores, and gossip-mongers. Five pounds in the proper ink-stained hand will buy you favourable words in *any* publication, and, one *can* skirt libel in a printed letter signed with a pseudonym, such as 'Elia' of the strong opinions, who is really Charles Lamb. For all the London papers to be *inundated* with a slew of anonymous letters . . . speaking in Lewrie's favour, and *subtly* linking this attack to the Beaumans, well . . . even the most cursory reader might make the hinted connexion, ha ha!"

Good Lord, more *press!* Lewrie thought with a groan.

"My field," Twigg smugly allowed. "I shall see to it. In the meantime, we'll dis-arm ourselves and our people. I doubt there will be a second ambush awaiting us today. I'll send Perkins and his men on ahead, separately. There will be covert work for them in London, before our arrival. Now, when we wake the nearest dozing magistrate, let us agree that we had no out-riders, and that I, Sir Hugo, Lewrie, and Major Chiswick were the only ones of our party who bore weapons. I see no need to involve Ajit Roy or ex-*Havildar* Singh, or your sailors, Lewrie. We were suspicious, d'ye see, of the lurking rider who stood watch for us, *then* armed ourselves, a bare minute before these felons burst from the woods and began firing at us.

"No 'stand and deliver' demand for us to stop and hand over any valuables," Twigg intently schemed, "but, an attempt on all our lives."

"Got it," Sir Hugo said with a quick nod.

"You fellows . . . ," Twigg instructed the coachee and his assistant up on the box. "Hide your weapons, and don't let on that you were armed when it happened, right? Same for you Navy lads. Your Captain Lewrie, his father, Major Chiswick, and I did all the shooting, right?"

"Aye, sor," Cox'n Desmond firmly replied, peering at big Jones Nelson, who grunted his understanding; then at his mate Furfy, who was looking a bit puzzled. "I'll spell it out for ye, Pat. Makes a better tale for th' newspapers, an' helps th' Cap'm."

"Ah, arrah, I git it," Furfy replied with a wide smile.

"We have all the miscreants' horses, Perkins? Capital!" Twigg crowed. "Bind them over their saddles, fetch their weapons into the boot of the coach for evidence, and we'll be on our way."

"At least, Alan," Burgess opined as they stuffed the dead men's small possessions into a draw-string bag, "there's no survivors left, so, no way for the Beaumans to know their ambush failed, and no alert for anyone else hired-on in London. They'll be completely in the dark 'bout where you, or any of us, go."

"And, lads," Sir Hugo added in right good humour as he swung an armful of muskets into the boot, "when word of this gets out among the London *badmashes* that half a dozen o' their stoutest met their Maker, how many'll be willin' t'hire on with the Beaumans *after,* ha?"

"And, with Mister Twigg's watchers and

followers to guard us," Burgess said, taking time to re-load and re-prime one of his pistols in spite of Twigg's assurance that the worst was over, "*and,* seeking out where the Beaumans have lit, there's a good chance we might know how many more we must watch out for . . . perhaps spot them by face."

"The Beaumans, ah!" Sir Hugo said, inspired to "set the scene" even further by drawing his small-sword and bloodying it with the gore of a dead highwayman now slung head-down cross a saddle, then wiping the blade clean on a pocket handkerchief. "Evidence," he snickered as he did so. "A couple of 'em got hacked t'bits, so some of us must own blooded swords, d'ye see? You, Burgess . . . you, son."

"You were sayin' 'bout the Beaumans?" Lewrie asked as he obeyed his father's suggestion.

"With Twigg's men t'smoak out their lodgings, and with a little money t'inspire the local 'Captain Tom o' the Mob' in their parish, the Beaumans might not get a single night o' rest *anywhere* in London! Hue and cry, rocks an' cobblestones through the right windows . . . dung an' mud slung at 'em when they dare go out by a . . . properly outraged Mob o' Londoners, hmm?"

"A capital idea, old friend," Twigg applauded as he rejoined them at the coach door. "The blooded swords and the harassment, both. Let an anonymous letter or two get into the papers, suggesting that a pack of cruel and arrogant slave-holders have no place in a civilised England, in London, and they'll rue the day they took ship! I believe I may be able to arrange that, as well!

"Come, then," Twigg ordered, turning grimmer. "Let us be away. The quicker we're done with the magistrate, the sooner we shall be in London, where we will dine on roast lamb and *tandoori* chicken. Then, our plans may be set afoot!"

CHAPTER FIFTEEN

And, it was a true Far Eastern, Hindi feast, the sort of thing that Lewrie ravenously remembered from his time in Calcutta. All four of them at-table in Twigg's Baker Street house that evening were veterans of India, and each new course was cheered much like the arrival of the Christmas pudding. Genteel and witty conversation, expected of diners at refined English tables, had given way to lip-smacking, slurping, and only occasional sallies in finding new adjectives and adverbs to congratulate Twigg on his chef and his creations.

But, instead of lingering over nuts, sweet biscuits, and port (and entertaining each other with the aforesaid witty conversations to the wee hours), their small party broke up just before ten of the clock, Sir Hugo and Trilochan Singh taking the short walk to his private town-house, and Burgess Chiswick, yawning heavily, off to the Madeira Club, where Sir Hugo had arranged a room, and temporary membership.

"You are surely exhausted by our arduous adventure, today, sir," Twigg imperiously announced, as if the matter was settled, "and by the early hour at which you, and we, were forced to arise for our journey. Ajit Roy will light you up to a spare bedroom for the night. You are sure you brought along your best uniform, your medals, and such? Good. Such a brave show, your barrister assures me, will go a long way with the Lord Justice who will conduct your evidentiary hearing tomorrow. Good night, *bonne nuit . . . achchhaa raat, sonaa t'heek** . . . all that.*"

"Thankee, again, sir," Lewrie replied, loath as he was to give Twigg thanks for much of anything, for he still had his lingering suspicions of the man's motives.

"We breakfast at seven in this house" was Twigg's parting comment as he betook himself to his first-floor study with a lit candle, with no acknowledgement of Lewrie's gratitude, sincere or not.

If Twigg's country estate, Spyglass Bungalow, was Hindi-exotic, a museum and treasure trove of priceless Far East relicts, his London house was the epitome of subtly understated Palladian grandeur, a home furnished and decorated by a rich, but modest, English

* *achchhaa raat, sonaa t'heek = good night, sleep well*

gentleman, from the crown of his head to the tip of his toes. Albeit with rather *more* fire-power available than most. No bejeweled *tul-wars* or valuable Asian matchlock or flintlock *jezzails,* but, here a gun-cabinet, there a gun-cabinet; a brace of rifled duelling pistols in a glass case in the salon, a brace of rare Ferguson rifled breechloading muskets standing in the library, and double-barreled fowling pieces secreted behind almost every open door! Twigg obviously was a fellow who'd spent too long in the field to sleep well without something bang-worthy near to hand. In Lewrie's own spacious, but darkly panelled, bedchamber, his own double-barreled Mantons were set out on the wine-table, much like a house servant might spread out his "housewife" shaving kit ready for the morning. There was a shotgun (presumably loaded and primed for any emergencies) 'twixt the wall corner and the *armoire,* and a brace of infantry hangers crossed on the wall near the door!

Sleep well, mine arse! Lewrie thought as he undressed; *Court in the mornin', gaol right after dinner, and the noose after breakfast o' th' next day? Shit!*

He did give sleep a try, *sans* the silk ankle-length night shirt so thoughtfully laid out for him, for even the mild warmth of a London summer was a tad too hot. The wee decanter of brandy left on the night-stand didn't help much, either; nor did the rumble of wheels, the clops of hooves, or the squeal of axles from the street outside, even if the road had been strewn with straw to dampen the din. Window open and the noise was maddening; window closed, and it was too stuffy to breathe.

He sponged off and dressed in slippers, breeches, and shirt and padded back down to the first floor with a candle in his hand to find a book to read . . . or another decanter of brandy. At the library room's door, though, he heard a suspicious noise. There was a skritching and rustling, sounding as if someone had snuck into the house despite all of Twigg's security, and was rifling through his files. There was also a gurgling, bubbling sound. Someone's throat had been cut, and was now in his final gasps for air? The office door was open, and there was a light inside, so he went on tiptoes to investigate.

But no, it was only Mr. Twigg, sitting cross-legged on a pile of large and garish tasseled pillows with a portable writing desk in his lap, and quill pen in hand . . . now more comfortably dressed in equally garish *pyjammy* trousers and robe, with a long night cap on his head, now and again sucking on the mouthpiece of a "hubble-bubble" pipe, and blowing smoke rings 'tween scribbled thoughts.

"Oh, 'tis you," Twigg snippishly said. "Can't sleep, hey? Oh, come in, then, if you must."

"I thought t'find a book, or . . . ," Lewrie said, excusing his odd-hour ramble. "Was it Doctor Samuel Johnson who said that 'the idea of being hanged concentrates the mind most wondrously'?"

"*Some* scribbler, yayss," Twigg drawled. "Or, it very well might have been Boswell, to make the old grump sound more lively."

"You're up late," Lewrie commented as he found a more conventional seat in a wing-back chair. Looking about for a bottle of something.

"I find that as I age, the need for sleep is less," Twigg said, finishing off whatever he was writing with grand flourish, and a smug sniff of pleasure, before sanding it and setting the paper aside. "Of course, when younger and more active in the Crown's service overseas, I perhaps developed a habit of sleeping with one eye open, in short bouts, and have never really lost it. *You,* I should expect, usually have no difficulty sleeping deep, long, and well."

Insult me more, *why don't you?* Lewrie silently groused.

"Something about all this *has* disturbed my sleep, for the last year or better," Lewrie said.

"And, what is that, Lewrie?" Twigg asked, looking nettled to be interrupted in his thought processes as he prepared a fresh

225

sheet of paper and dipped his quill into the ink-pot.

"Why you, of all people, all of a *sudden,* are so solicitous for me," Lewrie said. "Half the time, I imagine you're saving me for future work upon your behalf, the other half the time I think I'm being used in some scheme you've dreamt up, but for the life o' me, I can't find what advantage there is in it. I can *halfway* believe that you are as opposed to slavery as Wilberforce and his crowd, but . ... knowing you and your ways by now, I'm always haunted by knowing that nothing with you is ever that clear . . . that you always have an ulterior motive, or a whole set o' motives. Am I to hang as your martyr to further some grand scheme o' yours, or . . . ?"

Twigg took a pull on his *hookah* pipe, smiling mysteriously.

"All those damned tracts an' such. Was it you, or the Abolitionists who ran 'em up? Hired *Cruikshank* t'do the art-work?" Lewrie pressed. "They can't afford all *that,* surely."

"Perhaps I merely wish to watch you wiggle," Twigg snickered, " 'twixt honesty and morality, and . . . whatever feels necessary at the time, and pleasureable to you. Following your career can be *very* entertaining, ye know. Well . . . it seems a night for home truths, so I will, this once, mind, explain my motives to you.

"Slavery," Twigg harrumphed, almost rolling his eyes. "As long as there are Hindu *ry-ots* and Irish day-labourers, England has no *need* of slavery, Lewrie. It is a despicable, abhorrent practice, one which all civilised gentlemen must deplore. I, personally, despise slavery, but that is of no matter, any more than your own detestation of it *preceded* your liberation of those dozen Beauman slaves, or is a sudden . . . 'conversion by indictment.' "

He just has t'goad me, even when he's serious! Lewrie thought.

"But, where does slavery principally *thrive*, Lewrie? Here, in England? In France or the Germanies, in Sweden? No. Europe and the *civilised* parts of the world have done away with it, the French abolished slavery even in their West Indies colonies . . . all that *Liberté, Egalité, Fraternité* nonsense taken to the ultimate extreme. For that giddiness, I might almost admire them. The rest of the world . . . ha! What heathen, pagan, backward cultures may do in their benighted lands, of no consequence to Britain or anyone else, bothers me not a fig!"

Lewrie cocked his head over that seeming hypocrisy, which only made Zachariah Twigg snigger in smug amusement.

"Slavery thrives in Spanish and Portuguese dominions, Lewrie," Twigg continued, after a satisfying puff at his hubble-bubble. "One a continual foe, one a doubtful neutral. Their colonial economies, and the wealth that flows to Spain and Portugal from them, could not survive without slave labour in mines and fields. Consider also the United States of America, whose constitution may *claim* that all men are created equal, but restricts full rights to European descendants. A quarter of the inhabitants cross the Atlantic were slaves before their Revolution, and their numbers yearly increase through the further importation of slaves, the fecundity of the Negro race, and the lascivious doings of their masters, who indulge in a sordid practice which, so I am told, is termed 'going through the cabins'; to wit, the rape and impregnation of comely Negresses as a matter-of-fact *right!*

"Now just *when,* d'ye think, Lewrie," Twigg archly posed, "might the enchained and oppressed in the Americas take the uprising of Saint Domingue, or Haiti, or whatever they call it these days, to heart, and fight to free themselves? And . . . what happens to those nations which thrive and grow rich and more powerful on the backs of their slaves?"

"Chaos . . . civil war . . . slaughter and massacre!" Lewrie gasped. "Generations of it, bad as Saint Domingue for certain."

"And, how important, in the scheme of things, will Toussaint L'Ouverture's free and independent Haiti *ever* be, Lewrie?" Twigg asked in triumph. "Too embroiled inside of themselves to ever become a foe to Britain, or a substantial ally to other powers opposed to us, their economies so bankrupt that maintaining a navy to face ours would be impossible, effectively isolating them all in their own regions, unable to affect the expansion of the British Empire beyond the range of some *few* heavy fortress guns, much less affect Europe.

"And . . . ," Twigg concluded with great satisfaction, "ripe for the plucking should we ever wish such hapless, ungovernable snake pits."

"My God, that's . . . Christ!" Lewrie goggled in awe, thinking of the hundreds of thousands, no . . . the *millions* doomed to die in revolts.

"Should they require arms and powder, well . . ." Twigg waved off.

"I don't know whether t'congratulate you, or curse you," Lewrie finally said. "All the Americas up in flames, blood flowin' like rivers . . ."

"Take your Eudoxia Durschenko, she of the long, fine limbs, and firm breasts, Lewrie," Twigg continued.

"Huh . . . what? What does she have t'do with . . . ?"

"Ever been to the Russias, Lewrie?" Twigg almost benignly asked. "I have. Serfdom is the Achilles' heel of the Tsars, as bad an 'institution' as slavery. Once outside the grand palaces and salons of their refined,

French-speaking aristocracy, Russia is as backward and appalling as a trip back to the Dark Ages, all mud, mire, and shite. A serf is a landless tenant so dependent upon the good will of his land owner that he can be flogged to death with great bullwhips . . . *knouts,* they call them . . . for looking at them cross. Turf a serf and his family off the land for some offence, and they become lepers, *pariahs,* unwelcome anywhere, and usually starve to death. The Tsar wishes to fight a war, he has to raise troops, and sends word down to the country aristocracy . . . 'hey ho, each estate must conscript twenty-or-so young men for the army,' and off they go, for twenty years' service . . . marched very far away from home ground, and barracked among strangers . . . so, should they be called out to read the equivalent of the Riot Act, and fire on the locals, they have no compunctions whatsoever.

"Russian peasants are a brutal lot to begin with, so demanding brutal measures from them is an easy matter," Twigg informed him, with a shrug. "Their pretty, unmarried girls are prey for young aristocratic 'blades,' as well, and can be treated as brusquely as one may wish."

"You'd turn all Russia topsy-turvy, *too?*" Lewrie gawped, *really* in need of strong drink by then. This was *appalling* stuff, and more proof of Twigg's cold-bloodedness. "Ye think on a grand scale, damme if ye don't, but . . ."

"A Russia whose serfs rise up, at long last, the veterans still young enough, the youths not yet conscripted along with them . . . and, supplied with arms from *somewhere,*" Twigg said with an evil wee smile, "*cannot* field an army to save *itself,* much less interfere in the rest of Europe . . . as they dearly wish to do. You were in the West Indies, and missed our invasion of the Dutch Batavian Republic in '98. *Horrid* muddle, that, with the Russian Navy and Army as temporary, but prickly, allies. Sent forces from the Black Sea into the Aegean, the Adriatic, and eastern Mediterranean, and dearly wished to remain, in possession of anything they could lay their hands on, 'til the Tsar learned that he would *not* be given Malta, as the new Commander of the Knights of Saint John, and recalled *all* their forces. Impossible for us to invade, possessed of *millions* of military-age men, hence impossible for us to contain, should they put their minds to expanding their empire westward. A rebellion of the serfs could estop that for a long time. Ask your Mistress Eudoxia how her family, barely a cut above serfdom, suffered, should you ever run into her again."

"But what emerges from the ruins, Mister Twigg?" Lewrie asked.

"Most likely, a weak and fractious land wracked by eternal wars 'tween various regions, and warlords," Twigg said with relish. "Could I snap my fingers and turn all France to dust and bones, I would do so, Lewrie. A nation which wishes to survive has no friends, only interests."

"And the United States?" Lewrie wondered.

"Hmmpf! As I recall from the reports sent me by you and Jemmy Peel, that loose federation of sovereign states is already at logger-heads. The southern states distrust the cold natures of the people of New England, the northern states mock the culture, manners, accents, and cuisine of the southern. As early as 1783, northern writers show scorn for southerners, and their institution of slavery, which is dying out in New England . . . even if it is the New Englanders who own, and make their money from, slave ships and Negro importation. If there is more anti-slavery sentiment in the North, we shall capitalise on that. If the southern states feel oppressed, we shall find some way to provide diplomatic and military aid, therefore widening the break in the unity of the 'United' States. That nation is far too young to have a nation-wide ethos, as of yet. Men's loyalites lie within their particular state's borders much more than the federal entity, which is far-distant and as distrusted by most as Englishmen distrust a large army."

"And this is Crown policy? Your ultimate ploy?" Lewrie asked. "But what of our *own* economy, the sugar and all from the West Indies?"

"We ban slavery throughout the British Empire, Lewrie, giving us the moral and ethical 'guinea stamp,' " Twigg schemed, "which will be as valuable as any amount of lost trade. Besides . . . the southern United States are almost completely agricultural. May we, by diplomatic and moral force, make slavery so shameful an institution in America that the federal government bans it . . . at least bans the further *importation* of Africans, they are crippled, in need of imported goods, finance, and . . . 'friends,' d'ye see? Our shipping interests, sugar interests, will go where the products are, will make just as much money as they did before, and will be just as happy. The Navigation Acts will not be violated, for British exports, in British bottoms, will sail to ports in the South, and return with all the timber, tobacco, naval stores, rum, and molasses as before, in addition to the burgeoning sources of flax and hemp for linen and rope, and the newer southern crops, such as sugar cane and cotton.

"If the Liverpool slavers in the 'Triangle Trade' are harmed, if the *few* sugar grandees in the West Indies go out of business, then it is a small price to pay," Twigg happily concluded.

"First, though, we have to abolish slavery

in all British possessions," Lewrie rejoined. "And that involves me. Did I just stumble into this, or . . . ?"

"You were, Lewrie, once I became aware of your plight, the perfect example with which to deepen the average Englishman's detestation of slavery, to make more people aware of the issue, and, in supporting a successful naval hero guilty of stealing Blacks . . . an act of liberation, if you will . . . so Britain will be seen by the entire civilised world *doing* something about it, leading the way, setting a high-minded example for the rest of the world to emulate. Wilberforce, Priestly, Hannah More, and Clarkson *et al.,* perhaps even the Wesley brothers and their too-exuberant 'Leaping Methodism' which has so taken hold of the common folk, even Bentham and his rot, are reforming Britain from the ground up, fostering a stronger religiosity, and the concurrent moral climate which accompanies such, so that our 'Christian Duty' will be, in future, to right the perceived wrongs of a sinful world, ha ha!"

"Even if that means I must hang in the process? Shit!" Lewrie spat, getting to his feet in search of Twigg's study for something wet and spiritous. He found a large-ish cruet sort of bottle, but its contents stank bad as hyena piss, so he re-stoppered it. "Wait a bit . . . ! Did you merely take advantage of me . . . or, did you see to it that my case *had* to go forward, get splashed all over the papers? Could I have been swept under a rug, your powers used t'get me off?"

"To your previous question, Lewrie . . . you *stumbled* into it, as you usually do," Twigg said with what most people might deem a sympathic smile. "*You,* alone, leaped into a dung-hill of your own volition, and the Beaumans followed their typically rapacious wont in pursuing you, though Lord Balcarres, Vice-Admiral Sir Hyde Parker, and your Captain Nicely *did* try to sweep you under the rug, as you say. Once the matter became public, about the same time that I became aware of it, I decided to get involved . . . to get you acquitted, firstly, and force the issue onto the public conscience. And that is the bald truth.

"Oh, for God's sake, Lewrie!" Twigg snapped, mercurially changing tone. "You wish a drink, there's a bottle of brandy sitting right beside my day-lilies . . . the bloody *flowers,* yonder! And, I seriously doubt you will hang."

"How can you be so sure?" Lewrie asked, after a goodly slug and a smaller second, right from the bottle, as he sat back down.

"Your barrister, Mister Andrew MacDougall, sent me a note this evening, in reply to mine," Twigg related, sucking meditatively on the mouthpiece of his *hookah.* "Though many Lord Justices are away on the summer Assizes tour, some few remain in London to dispense justice . . . so much crime these days, so many trials to be held. 'Tis the war, I expect, which so unsettles our society; that, and the remnants of the Spithead and Nore mutinies, the lawless examples of the American, and the French, revolutions, and . . ."

"Ahem?" Lewrie grumpily reminded him, impatiently shifting upon his chair.

"Some Lord Justices who preside at King's Bench are impatient, rash sorts, who give the accused short shrift," Twigg said, lips thin in asperity to be pressed to the point before he had ended his philosophical ramblings. "Perhaps they're paid by their number of convictions and executions? They do not wish to involve themselves with any *complex* cases. Mister MacDougall, though, has managed to have you appear before Lord Justice Oglethorpe, a most cautious, and deliberative, man. A member of one of my clubs, in point of fact, Lewrie . . ."

Damme, is it already rigged, *I wonder?* he thought.

". . . bit of a pedant, really, and a dead, ruminative bore, do you meet him in person," Twigg continued, "so much so that he requires nigh an hour choosing from a chop-house *menu!* But, Oglethorpe's your man when it comes to reading, glooming, and meditating over every jot and tittle. Should have been appointed to Chancery Court, where just crossing all the T's and dotting all the I's could take five years or better, and cases stretch out a *young* lawyer's entire life-time.

"Once MacDougall presents the transcript of your trial *in absentia* on Jamaica . . . no lover of rude colonial concepts of justice is Oglethorpe . . . and sees the flaws in it, you stand a very good chance of being carried forward to Hilary Term, next January."

Oh, joy! Lewrie thought with a groan; *six more months of agony an' fret! Six more months for you, Twigg, t'shout abolition in papers and tracts. Hmmm, though* . . . "Six months o' Hugh Beauman stuck in London, bleedin' pounds sterling out his arse. Lovely!

"Our ambush, too," Lewrie further mused aloud. "Word o' that'd put him out o' sorts, too, I'd expect."

"Word of that, right alongside the announcement of your appearance at King's Bench this morning, will hit the streets in the early editions," Twigg smugly told him. "Mister MacDougall was appalled at the news of it . . . but, also delighted. Pleased as punch, he said in his note, that the Beaumans, or some other interest closely involved with slavery, could have been so infernally stupid and arrogant as to attempt such a clumsy and brutal murder, in broad daylight. Trust to the tract printers, as well, Lewrie, who have been toiling away this night, running off express numbers which condemn the attempt in exclamations of the most florid sort . . . the Kingston magistrate's written conclusions, and eyewitness accounts from among our party, your father and Major Chiswick, principally . . . forgive me if I prefer that my part in the affair remains unmentioned . . . will be quite the sensation, so much so that even an impartial Lord Justice may not be immune."

"Well . . ." Lewrie dithered, bottle resting on one knee, and his limbs sprawled in contemplation. "You won't be there, then?"

"Oh, yes, I shall be," Twigg informed him, frowning as the fire in the upper bowl of his hubble-bubble pipe went out. "Though, not in close proximity to you in the dock, nor with the first rows of attendees. Will that be all, Lewrie? Are you more settled of mind? Drunk enough for sleep at last, pray God? For I still have several more letters that must be distributed about the city just after dawn."

"Aye, I s'pose," Lewrie decided, corking the bottle and rising to stretch and force a yawn, which always helped put his body in touch with his mind and fool it into rest. "With any luck at all, perhaps my trial may get postponed 'til after Easter. Hah! More time for Hugh Beauman t'stew and twiddle his thumbs, away from his precious plantations . . . spendin' money like a drunken sailor."

"He has brought quite the *entourage,* as the

238

French call such a large retinue . . . his witnesses and Jamaican attorney, and . . . his new wife." Twigg sniggered. "A classic young and beautiful 'batter pudding' . . . so I am informed. *And,* their personal Black servants."

"That won't make 'em popular in London," Lewrie scoffed. "Anne died? I'm sorry t'hear *that.* She was the one redeemin' member of the whole damned clan. Damned shame," he said more soberly.

"They have not been in London a fortnight," Twigg continued in a somewhat merry taking, "and I doubt there's a single fashionable shop she has not set foot in, as my 'Irregulars' report. Hugh Beauman dotes on her like the most foolish 'colt's tooth' cully. I doubt that they shall much enjoy their enforced stay. Not if your father and I have anything to say about the matter. The Mob, *indeed,* hmm hmm."

"I'll wish you goodnight, then, Mister Twigg. See you at seven."

"Ajit Roy will wake you at six. *Achchhaa raat,* Lewrie," Twigg coolly bade him. "Now go, shoo . . . bugger off and let me work!"

CHAPTER SIXTEEN

"Another little matter," Lewrie dared say to the taciturn Twigg at breakfast, for he had learned through wretched previous experience that Zachariah Twigg was not a man to speak to before his fourth cup of coffee. "You recall our talk last year, at your country estate in Hampstead . . ."

"I *know* where I reside, sir!" Twigg snapped as if vexed beyond all temperance. "Must you?"

"About those anonymous letters to my wife?" Lewrie dared essay.

"Hmmph! What of them?" Twigg said with a stern warning glare.

"I have two of 'em with me, Mister Twigg," Lewrie said, pulling the two most recent letters from the breast pocket of his best uniform coat, left there and forgotten 'til he had dressed that morning; and, a tad trepidatious, slid them over towards Twigg's breakfast plate. "If ye haven't actually seen one, before, well . . . don't think my father had an example t'show ye, either. You said ye might be able t'smoak out who it was sendin' 'em, so . . ."

"Ah," Twigg said with a put-upon sniff. "Those. Which you once suspected that *I* sent, just to plague you? *Those* damning and anonymous letters, Lewrie?"

"Aye" was Lewrie's daunted reply.

"Well, damme . . . ," Twigg said, issuing forth the sort of sigh that usually preceded a death-sentence from a judge. He laid aside his fork and knife, though, swivelled sideways, and crossed his legs, his coffee cup in one hand, and the first letter in the other. "An expensive bond paper . . . most-like sold in two dozen of the better stationers' shops in the larger cities, besides London. A rather fair, copper-plate hand as well . . . the letters smaller and finer than those done with a quill pen, so I might deduce that your anonymous tormentor owns a fine-point steel-nib pen. Flourishes and un-necessary *serifs* here and there, so I doubt the writer is a military man. Almost . . . prissy, hmm. At one time, I recall that you also suspected one Commander Fillebrowne? Yet, have you run into him since your service in the Adriatic?"

"Neither hide nor hair, sir," Lewrie answered, emboldened by the man's curiosity, which was now piqued.

"And, during your brief association with Fillebrowne, did you gather any impression of . . . fussiness?"

"Idle . . . languid, vain, and arrogant, aye, but not fussy," Lewrie told him before returning his attention to his toast, butter, and jam. After a bite, chew, and swallow, he added, "Came of a rich family, they all did their Grand Tours of the Continent. Art collectors, all that? Thinks damned well of himself. I can't recall we ever corresponded by letter, so I wouldn't know his writing style."

"I shall ask of him at Admiralty, and compare his hand to this," Twigg promised. "Though I very much doubt . . ." Twigg shuffled pages, scowling at what he read. "Did *any* of this bawdiness occur, Lewrie?"

"Absolutely *not!*" Lewrie could say, and with some heat, too. "I swear on my sacred word of honour! Not with Sophie, nor Eudoxia, either!"

"Odd," Twigg said with a smirk; evidently he was now fully awake and back to his usual top-lofty asperity. "No mention is here made of your bastard son, Desmond McGilliveray. Peel wrote me on that head," Twigg said with a sunnily sarcastic smile. "Indeed, a British frigate captain meeting his by-blow, a Midshipman in the *United States Navy,* in the West Indies . . . offspring of a temporary marriage to a Cherokee *Indian* wench, well! Your reputation, and sobriquet of the 'Ram-Cat,' is now widespread in the Fleet, so I do not understand why Fillebrowne . . . is he your tormentor . . . would not have heard of it.

242

Has your wife at any time thrown this *particular* bastard in your face?"

"The only own she seemed aware of was Theoni Connor's," Lewrie told him. *And, damme, that'un was bad enough!* he grimly thought.

"Then it is patently obvious that your unknown scribbler has no knowledge of Desmond McGilliveray's existence, either," Twigg assumed. "Hence . . . *not* a Navy man, nor anyone of *long* acquaintance with you."

"Doesn't narrow the field, much, though," Lewrie said.

"Yayss, there's a *myriad* of people with a grudge against you," Twigg sniggered. "Damme, Lewrie, but I could spend the rest of my entire career, defending you from yourself."

Lewrie winced, and hid behind the rim of his own coffee cup.

"Intriguing, this, though," Twigg muttered, quickly re-reading both letters, and frowning in deep study. "I've a suspicion, but . . . I will say no more, for the nonce." He folded the letters and stuffed them into a side pocket of his sober black coat. A pull on his watch and a peer at its face, and he turned brisk at finishing his last cup of coffee and dabbing his lips before rising and throwing his napkin onto his plate. "Time we should be going. You're to meet MacDougall by eight. My coach is already brought round."

Half a chop, half his eggs, and a fresh-buttered slice of toast remaining; Lewrie had barely made a dent in his own meal, but "grumble you may, but go you must" was the day's motto. Besides, by noon, he could be remanded to gaol in the Old Bailey; which dread thought made what little he had consumed turn to a 12-pounder round-shot.

CHAPTER SEVENTEEN

But for the circumstances, it might have been a hearty reunion in the grim and dour courtroom, so darkly panelled and gloom-making. Lord Peter Rushton was there, all huzzahs, and taking a morning from Parliament (not that he did all that much when he did sit in session!), along with a fancily dressed Clotworthy Chute, another old companion from Harrow, a moon-faced, fubsy "Captain Sharp," who looked as if his career at fleecing new-come "Country-Put" heirs was progressing nicely.

Sir Malcolm Shockley had taken the morning from the House of Commons, along with his wife, Lucy, ironically once Hugh Beauman's sister; still stunningly pretty, blond and fair, with the most amazing aquamarine eyes, bee-stung red lips, short and sweetly rounded figure . . . and the wits of an addled sheep, one discovered after an hour in her company, and *why* Lewrie ever thought her a fine match back in 1781, he could no longer fathom.

Beauman money, and those tits, he decided, thinking back on his early years as a penniless, futureless Midshipman.

His father and Burgess Chiswick were both there in full uniforms of their respective services, Burgess attending Miss Theodora Trencher and her parents from the Abolitionist Society, so it appeared that he'd made good progress in his suit . . . as was the Rev. Clarkson, whom Lewrie had met at the Trenchers' home to gain the Abolitionists' support, and, by God, so were the Rev. William Wilberforce, Mistress Hannah More, and a platoon of the leading lights in the Clapham Sect and reform-minded!

His barrister, Mr. MacDougall, made the introductions to a very well-dressed youngish man as Sir Samuel Whitbread, he of the vast brewery fortune, who led a pack of like-minded younger progressives in both Commons and Lords, all of whom had to pump Lewrie's paw and tell him that he was "the very Devil of a fellow"! The greetings and introductions took so long that Lewrie could imagine that he was at "Old Boys' Week" at one of the many public schools he had (briefly) attended, *and* the captain of the champion cricket team, to boot!

"Your wife and family, Captain Lewrie," MacDougall fretted in a whisper as they finally neared the defence table, "they do not attend? T'would have been better, were they to be seen in support."

"Don't even ask, Mister MacDougall," Lewrie muttered back, with a forced smile plastered on his phyz, and a cynical roll of his eyes. "Now we're here, what exactly am I to do?"

"Look innocent, of course," MacDougall softly instructed, wryly grinning. "Rise with the others when the Lord Justice is announced . . . hat off . . . and, when called upon, enter the prisoner's dock . . . there," he said, directing Lewrie's attention to a railed square dais, before the judge's higher, and ornate, bench. "Identify yourself when asked, and, when put to the question of guilt or innocence, state firmly that you are *not* guilty . . . it is *pro forma.* Not *too* loudly or emphatically, mind . . . *nil desperando,* hmm? Calm, forthright, perhaps with a *touch* of indignation that you are forced to be here, but not so much of that as to appear arrogant, else you might put off the jury. Once we begin to lay our arguments, you may sit, but you *must* remain erect and attentive, continuing your calm demeanour. No twitches, shivers, tics, or pulling faces. The Lord Justice will note such as signs of guilt, as would a jury, once empanelled, though I firmly doubt we shall get that far today. You may even evince surprise or disagreement with what Sir George Norman, the prosecutor, may use in his statement, *but* you must

247

not cry out in protest."

"Like playin' whist, is it? Stone-faced?" Lewrie asked, ascowl.

"Very like, Captain Lewrie," MacDougall said. "Ah, here comes our opposition."

"Can I glower at 'em?"

"Glowering, to a *point,* is allowed," Mac-Dougall told him, indicating that he should take a seat behind the accused's table for a bit.

Glower, Lewrie did, developing an instant and instinctive abhorrence for the prosecuting attorney, Sir George Norman, for that worthy was a very sleek and elegant fellow in his early thirties with perfect wavy blond hair underneath his side-curled court peruke, and strutting languid as a peacock in his black silk robe, attended by a pair of law clerks who carried his files and such for him.

Glower even hotter, for right behind him came Hugh Beauman, the stout bastard, glaring angrily at one and all. Hugh Beauman had come as grandly dressed as anyone could wish; his hat was a sleek and fat beaver planter's hat, pinned up on one side, adrip with egret plumes, and trimmed at the brims with silver lace over light blue ribbon, his coat an older frock style richly embroidered in almost a paisley swirl of turquoise, light blue, and light grey satin; under that his waist-coat was a longer old-style, figured and embroidered pale gold silk or some other shimmery stuff. His breeches were the same pale gold colour, but thankfully plain silk or satin, with white silk stockings, and his clunky-heeled black shoes bore real gold buckles inlaid with diamond chips! He slowly paced, employing a long ebony walking-stick with its gold ferrule and a large gold knob atop . . .

A clompin' breedin' bull, tarted up for auction! Lewrie thought; *tryin' for languid an' graceful, too. And, a wig like that? Powdered? Haven't seen such a "Macaroni" in twenty years! Height o' fashion, my arse! Who found his tailor, Clotworthy Chute?*

Hugh Beauman's face was set in a porcine, full-chinned, high-nosed look of royal boredom, surely an affected sham taught him far in the past by out-dated tutors . . . though he *did* let it slip a bit when he finally deigned to let his slow gaze turn far enough to espy Lewrie at the accused's table, *S'prised I'm still alive, are ye?* Lewrie sarcastically thought. Or, perhaps Beauman's arrogant demeanour had been shaken more by the rustle of titters and snide whispers that those who attended the court made when they saw his garish suitings.

The snickers among the ladies present certainly nettled the arch woman on Beauman's arm! Whoever *she* was, or had been before, Beauman's new wife had not been exposed to London fashion, or the harsh judgement of the "fashionable." For she was tricked out like a bookend to her husband, *too*-elegantly gowned in the same embroidered and figured pale gold material as Hugh Beauman's waist-coat, her wide straw bonnet ribboned with cloth that matched his coat, and bound under her chin with a pale blue ribbon. Over her shoulders she wore a gauzy and diaphanous blue shawl figured in silver lace, and Lewrie just knew that her shoes held real gold buckles with diamond chips, too.

She was tall for a woman, about five inches shy of six feet in her heeled shoes, slim and willowy, coolly ash blond, and with eyes of the most disconcerting and icy pale green. She *was* strikingly lovely, Lewrie thought her, but with the air of an unimpressed empress forced to appear among the lowly; imperious, cold, but very aware of the power of her looks. *Deserve each other, I swear they do!* Lewrie thought, and speculated who had selected their attire, Hugh Beauman, or her; and, at the end of the day, who would get scathed for it in the privacy of their lodgings! *That'd* put a chill on Beauman's new "domestic bliss"!

Then, to the further embarrassment of the Beaumans, there came in their wake a brace of Blacks in livery grander and more gilt-laced than any admiral or general, both very dark-skinned and young teenagers in pure white wigs, just far enough behind the Beaumans to appear as if they could bear the hems of long royal trains, if required. Another brace of female slave servants, quite comely young girls in a matching livery, also entered, ready to see to Mrs. Beauman's every whim, and the titters and snickers from the onlookers turned to hisses and cat-calls. "Fie! For shame! Boo!" rippled through the audience, abashing the wife, whose cheeks turned crimson, but only serving to anger Hugh Beauman further.

"Make ye pay, Lewrie!" he growled across the room, shaking one fist in Lewrie's direction. "Hang, damn yer eyes!" Which utterance set off a wave of outright revulsion, and winces from Sir George Norman and the Jamaican attorney, who had been gawping about in bumpkin-ish fashion to enter a real English court of law.

For a fleeting moment, Lewrie could almost feel sorry for the prosecuting barrister, Sir George Norman, K.C., as he tried to silence his troublesome client, for that worthy looked about "fed up to here" with Beauman and his crudities. Just for a *wee* bit, though; after all, does one lie down with dogs, one rises with fleas!

The grim thud of a mace and a cry of "Oyez, oyez, oyez!" drew everyone to their feet to honour the majestic entry of Lord Justice Oglethorpe, the chief bailiff intoning the ancient opening ritual to awe them with the power and solemnity of justice: ". . . all who have business before this honourable court, draw forward, and be heard!"

"Should I keep my sword on, or . . . ?" Lewrie muttered, unsure of a sudden. At naval courts-martial, it would lay on the judges' table.

"God Alm . . . wear it. Now, *hist!*" Mac-Dougall whispered back.

"The accused will enter the dock," the bailiff announced, and Lewrie stepped into it, standing right by the rail with his arms at his side at attention, bare headed. "State your name and occupation, sir," he bade, as if there was any doubt of Lewrie's "line."

"Captain Alan Lewrie . . . Royal Navy," he stated.

"Captain Lewrie, I charge you now," began Lord Justice Oglethorpe, up behind the *banc* and seated upon a high-backed chair resembling the throne of a minor kingdom. "You stand accused of a heinous crime, the theft of twelve Black slaves from a plantation on the Crown colony of Jamaica . . . three years past, and, the offer of armed violence in the perpetration of that act. How do you respond to these charges, sir?"

"*Not* . . . guilty, my lord," Lewrie firmly answered in a voice close to a quarterdeck call.

"Counsellor MacDougall, you are ready to

proceed, sir?"

"I am in all respects, my lord," MacDougall responded.

"Sir George for the prosecution, are you ready to proceed, sir?"

"I am, milud" came the nasal Oxonian drawl.

"You may sit, Captain Lewrie," Oglethorpe instructed. "Begin, if you will, Sir George."

"Milud, gentlemen, and ladies, we are come today to present to this honourable court the results of a capital trial *already* concluded . . . one held in a court of law in Kingston, Jamaica, which resulted in a guilty verdict against Captain Lewrie, *and,* a sentence of death by hanging . . . a proceeding conducted *in absentia* due to the fact that Captain Lewrie had, upon learning of his impending trial, fled the jurisdiction . . . surely, the act of a man who acknowledges his guilt, and fears the consequences of his crimes . . ."

Lewrie sat stiff-backed, head up, but fuming as the worst sort of calumny was poured out against him. When the vilest sort of lies were trotted out in Norman's opening statements, lies "guinea-stamped" by the presence of the trial transcript, which the prosecutor took for granted as Gospel Truth, Lewrie just *had* to frown and scowl, to gawp in astonishment and look to MacDougall for help, wondering why he was sitting slouched and silent, merely rolling his head at the worst of the accusations, even pretending to study his fingernails and speculate did they need a cleaning with his pen-knife!

". . . ask you, milud, to uphold the verdict found against Captain Lewrie, as well as the sentence, and remand him to prison so that the sentence may be carried out. I thank you for your attendance upon my presentation, milud, and feel certain that you will find for the prosecution, so that Mister Hugh Beauman, Esquire, may find justice at last, and the return of his property, before this honourable court."

His presentation completed, Sir George Norman turned about with his robe flaring and solemnly paced back to the prosecutor's table, to sweep his robe forward so he could sit in his chair with an exhausted, but smugly satisfied, sigh, fold his hands together atop the table, and sit stiff-backed and chin high; slightly smiling as if he had passed orals at Oxford, and was just waiting to be awarded a well-earned Blue.

"Counsellor MacDougall?" Justice Oglethorpe solemnly prompted.

Andrew MacDougall leaped to his feet, quick as a striking cobra, took several impatient steps to a post before the bench, and stamped to a stop (doubtless waking every nodder in the courtroom after hearing Sir George's sonorous declamations) and cried, "All that has gone before, milord, is a perversity . . . a total sham!" Which declaration aroused several in the audience to shout "Hear, hear!" like back-benchers in the Commons.

"Aye, milord, there is the transcript of Captain Lewrie's trial on Jamaica," MacDougall went on in the same heated tone, "to which we do not object, for its introduction before this honourable court cuts both ways, like a dual-bladed knife. On its face, it *seems* legitimate, but upon a closer reading . . . *and* with more information anent the background which led to its conduct . . . one may surely discover that such a trial, conducted *in absentia,* was held at such short notice that no one in Crown government, no officer senior to Captain Lewrie in the Royal Navy, and certainly no friends or allies of his, were even aware that it was on the docket before these sham proceedings were done! Note as well, milord, as you closely peruse the transcript, the complete, utter absence of *any* defence witnesses called, not even one to attest as to Captain Lewrie's character.

"For the very good reason, milord, that the barrister for Captain Lewrie's defence was found cooling his heels and scraping for cases at a *tavern* close by to the courthouse in Kingston, was given but half an hour to familiarise himself with the particulars by the local justice, then was ordered to proceed before said defence attorney could at any odds say who exactly it was he was *defending,* much less *discover* a witness for the defendant!" MacDougall quickly accused.

That created a mighty stir of displeasure among Lewrie's allies, and the idle curious who had wandered in to witness a "raree show," as well, which Lord Justice Oglethorpe had to gavel down.

"I would now wish to humbly submit as evidence to such, a change, milord, a deposition, properly witnessed by several gentlemen from the offices of Lord Balcarres, the Crown Governor of Jamaica . . . upon that worthy's stationery, milord may note . . . obtained from the defending attorney, one Mister Herbert Pruett, Esquire, who . . . and here I quote him from memory . . . 'thought the matter extremely odd, but was night the easiest twenty pounds and eight pence ever I have earned.' Mister Pruett's deposition will shew that he himself was not aware that a trial would be held that day, milord, and was in search of future proceedings when he was found, *in his cups,* he freely admits, and given the brief."

"Do you then plead incompetent counsel, sir?" Oglethorpe asked, looking a tad queasy with that revelation.

"Indeed *not,* milord!" MacDougall said as he handed over the affidavit to a clerk. "Given the circumstances, I doubt the ablest barrister in Great Britain could have done any better. You will also note, milord, that Mister Pruett *attempted* to plead a delay so that he might discover witnesses, but was *denied,* and told to proceed at once by the presiding Justice. Why, milord," MacDougall said with an impish grin as he turned to face the back of the courtroom, "under such pressure, even *I* might have failed!" Which made everyone (the Beaumans and their *entourage* excepted, of course) enjoy a good laugh.

"Secondly, milord, I would also to submit for your information a roster of the seated jurymen, along with their occupations, and their kinship to the Beauman family, their financial or business dependence upon, or their direct employment *by,* the plaintiff, or their employment in the despicable slave-trading *industry,* as evidence that the jurymen were most carefully selected *beforehand* to render a conviction and the sentence most desired by the plaintiffs . . . namely, the hanging of the man who participated in a duel as second to Leftenent-Colonel Christopher Cashman, formerly commanding officer of the local regiment raised by the Beaumans, which duel resulted in the death of former-Colonel of the regiment *Ledyard* Beauman *and* his cousin Charles Sellers, both of whom cheated in the most *egregious* manner requiring Captain Lewrie *and* the judges to shoot him down, as well!

"Milord will note that there is a man named

Sellers listed as a gentleman of the *jury,*" Mac-Dougall further accused, "and if this whole affair is not an act of personal revenge with the very majesty and dignity of the Law perverted as revenge's *implement,* then I do not know what *else* to call it!"

"Silence!" Lord Justice Oglethorpe had to thunder above the baying and cat-calls of the audience. "I will have silence in the court!"

"If milord pleases," MacDougall went on once the crowd had done with their booing. "I have also obtained, and would lay before you as further evidence of previous grudges, affidavits from the gentlemen at the duel, and their official findings . . . one of whom is a very well-respected retired magistrate, detailing how it all fell out, resulting in the wound in the *back* suffered by Leftenant-Colonel Cashman, and the most necessary deaths of both Ledyard Beauman and Charles Sellers, and their dishonourable conduct upon the field."

"Murderer!" Hugh Beauman bellowed, leaping to his feet and just about beside himself with rage, his face mottled nigh-purple. "They were murdered! That bastard, Lewrie . . . !"

"Silence, I said!" Oglethorpe roared right back, banging away with his gavel, and turning a choleric shade himself. "Sir George, I conjure you to control your party's outbursts."

"Bloody lies!" Beauman went on despite Sir George Norman's urgings and tuggings. Beauman shrugged him off like a street beggar's hand. "Slave stealer, he is! Convicted! Want him hanged! Hear me?"

Like all the Beaumans, even when in calm takings, Hugh Beauman pared his words to the bare minimum necessary; and, like all the clan, anything that went against his instant wishes had to be crushed. They had made *themselves,* after all, but, despite the wealth and finery, at bottom were tenant-tramplin', shootin', huntin', dog-kissin', slave-whippin' "John Bull" squires of the most brutish sort; "Chaw-Bacons," for all their money. There had been times, even when head-over-heels in lust for Lucy Beauman, that Lewrie hadn't been too sure of *her!*

"Can you not manage yourself, sir, I will have you removed from my courtroom!" Oglethorpe threatened. If Beauman thought the boos he got before were insufferable, they were nothing to the new chorus that rose up, and continued despite the Justice's hammering.

When at last the din subsided, and Beauman had at last listened to reason from his hired barrister and his icy young wife, MacDougall presented his last affidavits to the clerks, and held up a newspaper.

"*Murder,* is it, milord?" MacDougall said with an indignant tone. "Do we look for murder, or its attempt, we need look no further for it than the south bank of the Thames, just outside Kingston . . . no further in the past than yesterday, for in the early afternoon, six well-armed men, *ostensibly* highwaymen, lay in ambuscade within sight of the spires of our great city, and opened fire upon Captain Lewrie's coach! Fortunately for Captain Lewrie, he was travelling with his father, Major-General Sir Hugo Saint George Willoughby, and his brother-in-law and former Major Burgess Chiswick, late of the East India Company Army, and a comrade with Captain Lewrie at the siege of Yorktown, from which they escaped . . . due principally to then-Midshipman Alan Lewrie's abilities both with firearms and boats, I might add . . . who gave better than they got, Whilst none of these alleged highwaymen survived to testify as to their motives . . . or, *who hired them!* . . . a rather *large* amount of money was found upon their persons, leading one to believe that, *were* they in the highwayman trade, had, at that moment, no *need* to perpetrate a bold, *daylight* robbery, *or* . . . ," he slyly paused, "*someone* deeply engaged with the slave trade, slave *shipping* interests, *or* . . . someone unsure that a conviction and sentence of death could be obtained in an *English* court of law, thought to eliminate the cause of their grief, frustration, and *vengeance* by hiring on a pack of toughs to do it for them . . . or him!"

It was a good thing that orange-selling wenches, fruiterers, or greengrocers were not allowed to do business in a law court, as some of them did at the theatres, else Hugh Beauman, his elegant wife, his witnesses, and his barrister might have been buried under an avalanche of rotting goods. Even the most bored and cursory attendees found such a deed most heinous and foul, and let loose a cacophony of abuse once more. It just wasn't . . . *English!*

Hugh Beauman leaped to his feet once more, beet-red, and shaking fists at one and all, baying something that was lost in the din, and no amount of urging by Sir George Norman could sit him back down this time. It took a full three minutes before the court was quieted.

"Milord," MacDougall said in the most reasonable of voices, as loud as before upon the ear, but that was due to the utter silence of the audience, as if no one wished to miss his closing arguments. "In light of this event, I would also wish to submit to you the depositions of Captain Lewrie and his travelling companions, as well as the affidavit from the magistrate at Kingston anent this sordid affair.

"Captain Lewrie has been subjected to a Star Chamber proceeding, as arbitrary, as capricious, as corrupt and premeditated as any suffered by gentlemen falsely accused and *executed* in less than an hour by that past body, in late and un-lamented times, that blight upon our history, our traditional sense of fairness, justice, and honour," Mr. Mac-Dougall solemnly intoned. "*Grant* Law, which obtains on Jamaica, is not *English* Common Law! There, *injustice* may be sanctified by wigs and robes, and false solemnity. This so-called trial *in absentia* which condemned Captain Lewrie, a man of exemplary courage, bravery, sagacity, and honour, to death by hanging would *never* be countenanced in *England,* milord. I appeal to your common sense and your own sagacity, your long experience upon the bench, after reading all the pertinent evidence placed before you, to set aside the verdict and sentence as a sham, a fraud, and the travesty of the very *word* Justice that it is."

"Hear, hear! Huzzah! Hear him! Boo!" from Lewrie's supporters, who, by then, included just about everyone in the court-room.

"Should you find that the initial charges have merit, milord," MacDougall further pled, "a trial conducted in an *English* court of law must ensue . . . a trial to which Captain Lewrie looks forward with all eagerness, so that he may clear his escutcheon of such sordid charges, and, certain of his innocence, also eagerly expects his aquittal. But . . . *this* hook-or-by-crook Jamaican proceeding, I

262

humbly ask you to set aside.

"Further, milord," MacDougall said with a hand upon his breast. "In the interim, Captain Lewrie is just completing the rigging, arming, and commissioning of a new ship, soon to be despatched by Admiralty 'gainst England's foes. *Must* Britain be deprived of Captain Lewrie's extraordinary skills and talent for battle by ordering him to remain ashore awaiting milord's decision? Or, may he post a money bond with the court, and agree, upon his sacred honour, to give up his command and return to England should you deem an *honest* trial necessary?"

"No! By God, no!" Hugh Beauman shouted. "Mine, I tell ye, he's mine!" His barrister, Sir George Norman, didn't even try to contain the man this time, but lowered his head and bit at his lip, sagging in defeat even before a decision was forthcoming. "*Can't* slip away!"

"Silence, sir!" Oglethorpe roared, the objectivity and dignity of the Law bedamned, at last. "Bailiffs, *remove* that man! Shame on you, Sir George. Fie upon your *client!*" Which might have been a worse slur, for barristers — gentlemen who didn't engage in *trade* or handle *money* — didn't *have* clients, only "briefs."

"Given the circumstances, and the wealth of contrary evidence presented," Lord Justice Oglethorpe solemnly said once Beauman and his party had been herded out in dire huffs, "I find myself forced to take some considerable time to weigh the various aspects of the aforesaid proceedings conducted on Jamaica . . . proceedings which, upon their face, begin to sound . . . colourable."

MacDougall swivelled about on his chair to grin at Lewrie, and then at those supporters from the Abolitionist Society seated behind him. He even tipped Lewrie the wink!

"Until such time as I come to a firm conclusion, I will not, as you, Counsellor MacDougall, request, declare the result of the Jamaican trial null and void, but . . . since such deep perusal and contemplation in search of the truth shall surely expand beyond this Law Term, and in fact far into the Michaelmas Term, I do find that there is no plausible reason why the accused may not be allowed his freedom after money bond is posted. Captain Lewrie?"

"Sir? Milord?" Lewrie piped up, rising to attention in the dock.

"Do you solemnly swear upon your honour as an English gentleman, and a Sea Officer of the King, to return to appear before this court at such time as I order?" Oglethorpe posed to him.

"I so swear, milord," Lewrie firmly answered.

"Then you are, sir, for the moment, free to go, about your business on the King's Service," Lord Justice Oglethorpe announced with a final rap of his gavel, "and these proceedings are, for the nonce, at a conclusion."

"Huzzah!" Burgess Chiswick howled, setting off the crowd once more, coming to embrace Lewrie and pound him on the back the second he left the confines of the prisoner's dock. A great many people came to do the same, clapping him on the back, shaking his hand vigourously, or even embracing him. And, from the ladies came enthusiastic curtsies and hand clasps, even some fervent, but chaste, kisses upon his cheeks. By the time his party reached the outer halls, Lewrie had amassed a rather cumbrous pile of posies and nosegays, as well.

"Free to go? Really?" Lewrie breathlessly asked his attorney.

"For now, yes, Captain Lewrie," MacDougall happily assured him. "Best we could expect, and thank God for Beauman behaving so de-witted! Doubt old Oglethorpe'll uphold the Jamaica trial, so . . . pardon me, my dear lady . . . a complete new trial will be necessary, and we both know that the Beaumans will press the matter hotly. Believe me when I tell you, though, Captain Lewrie, that I am more than ready for that, ha ha!"

Christ, does it ever *end?* Lewrie glumly thought, all joy of the moment dashed; *all this is but a temporary reprieve? Niggles aside,*

I did *steal 'em, and they'll be the first t'confess that I did, so . . .*

Then the Rev. William Wilberforce was there, along with Hannah More, the Trenchers and their daughter Theodora, nigh-giddy with lady-like thrills over the court's decision; *or,* to have a handsome suitor such as Burgess Chiswick at her side, who had shot it out with hired assassins, and won, in support of the Noble Cause. Sir Malcolm and Lady Lucy Shockley were next up, Sir Malcolm sternly, but warmly, in approval, and even Lucy acting delighted.

"Let us celebrate!" MacDougall cried, once they were outside, ready to descend the steps to the street, and their waiting coaches.

"Hang, ye will!" Hugh Beauman swore from the window of his own departing coach, shaking a fist and walking-stick at them. "Get ye yet, I will, ye vile sonofabitch! Bastard!" Which cries only thickened the shower of horse turds, rotten vegetables, curses, and paving stones that followed him.

"My treat, and gladly . . . ," Lewrie began to say, quite enjoying the sight, and reaching for his wash-leather money bag, but . . . "My God! My money's gone! My pocket's been picked!" Frantically, Lewrie felt over his possessions, and found his watch and fob gone, too.

"What? In a court of law?" His father Sir

266

Hugo gawped, unsure whether it was funny or not.

"Hallo, old son, and joy o' the day to ye!" Lord Peter Rushton cried as he and Clotworthy Chute came to congratulate him. "What? Yer pockets picked? Ain't *that* damned gall!"

" 'Three-handed Jenny,' I'd wager," Clotworthy stated with a grim and knowing nod. "Never misses a sensational gathering. Pretty light-brown-haired wench, with big blue eyes? Recall a kiss or touch from a girl o' that description, Alan? I'll see to her. Grand at the 'liftin' lay,' Jenny is. Could filch a violin an' leave the music playin,' she can, but damme if she'll get away with it this time. Not from one o' *my* friends, she won't. Know where she lodges, haw haw!"

"Damme if there wasn't a money bond I was t'post, too," Lewrie realised. "Mister MacDougall, what of that matter, if I haven't . . . ?"

"A note-of-hand 'pon your solicitor or banker will serve just as well," MacDougall told him. "Damme! Right in the law court! I *warned* you law's a foul business, *but* I *say!*"

"Celebratin', were ye?" Lord Peter queried. "Think nothing of money, Alan, for you'll not pay ha'pence. Allow me to treat . . . should you gentlemen allow me, and Clotworthy here, to spur good cheer along."

"Know the very place!" MacDougall quickly agreed, making Lewrie sure that wherever they lit, it would be grander and more expensive an establishment than any he had had to pay for with MacDougall before!

"Alan, might ye oblige me?" Sir Hugo asked.

"Oh! Remiss o' me," Lewrie said, ready to slap his forehead. "Father, allow me to name to you Lord Peter Rushton and Mister Clotworthy Chute, old friends of mine from Harrow. Expelled the same time as me, unfortunately. Lord Peter, Clotworthy . . . my father, Sir Hugo Saint George Willoughby."

"Lord Peter . . . Mister Chute," Sir Hugo replied, shaking hands with them in turn. "Of the school governor's coach-house fire, I take it, haw haw? Harrow men, hey?"

"Briefly" came from Lord Peter, from Clotworthy, from Lewrie, and, finally, an echo of "briefly" from Sir Hugo as well.

"Never would've taken, anyway, Sir Hugo," Lord Peter haw-hawed right back. "Education's rather over-rated, don't ye know. Not quite necessary in Lords, I've noted."

"Mister Chute, sir," Sir Hugo said with a wicked gleam in his eyes. "You are familiar with London's underclass, I take it?"

"Enough to warn those who come to the city and request my services, yes, Sir Hugo," Clotworthy replied with a greasy smile. "Guard 'em, their purses, and . . . morals. All that," Chute simpered.

"Excellent! We must speak, sir! Hugh Beauman, hmm?" Sir Hugo said with a wink, knowing a rogue or a pimp by sight.

"Oh, deuced wicked, yes!" Chute quickly agreed, hopeful of huge profits from such an under-handed commission; which sort was right up his alley. "Where are we to celebrate, sirs? So that I may find you, once I retrieve Alan's possessions from 'Three-handed Jenny.' "

"Why, it'll be just like old times, won't it, Alan, old son!" Peter Rushton crowed as they went down the steps to the waiting equipages. "Merriment, mirth, and glee . . . with wine freely flowing!"

That's what I should be feared of! Lewrie thought with a wince.

■ ■ ■ ■

BOOK III

■ ■ ■ ■

In Fame's temple there is always a niche to be found for rich dunces, importunate scoundrels, or successful butchers of the human race.

Johann Georg von Zimmerman,
Swiss physician, writer (1728–1795)

CHAPTER EIGHTEEN

HMS *Savage* bowled along Sutherly with the prevailing winds from the West on her starboard beam, slightly hobby-horsing over long swells in the Bay of Biscay. It was now nigh High Summer, so the fierce gales that could drive ships ashore to their ruin on the rocky, and hostile, western coast of France lay in the future — God willing — when the seasons turned to a brisk Autumn, then to a bitter and boisterous Winter, and one storm following the last for months on end . . . all determined to batter and dis-mast and wreck the weary ships of the British blockading squadrons, which kept remorseless watch over enemy seaports for a sally by their foe, or to interdict all trade that might comfort, arm, or feed the French.

For now, though, it was paint-brushed, high wisps of clouds upon beautiful cerulean skies, the sort one might wish for when "summering" in some exotic locale, and the seas tossed less than three to four feet, in long, marching wave-sets flicked with only the faintest foamy surges at their crests, and the colour of the Bay of Biscay ranging from steel blue to blue-silver.

"Deck, there!" the main-mast lookout cried from high above in the top-mast cross-trees. "Sails, ho! Ten . . . *twelve* sail! Three points off th' larboard bows! T'gallants an' tops'ls, in line-ahead!"

"Our line-of-battle ships, one'd think, sir?" Lt. Urquhart said as he turned to face his captain on the quarterdeck.

"Either that, or the French are out, and better managed than we expect, sir," Lewrie replied with a snicker. Picking up a brass speaking trumpet, he called aloft, "What course do they steer?"

After a moment, the lookout howled back down, "In line-ahead, due *North!*"

"Thankee!" Lewrie bellowed back, then returned the trumpet to a slot in the compass binnacle cabinet. "Ours, most-like. Were they the French, they'd be scuttlin' seaward, as far from our liners as ever they could, Mister Urquhart. That, or bound Sou'west t'clear Cape Ferrol to join the Dons again, or pick up the Nor'east Trades off Portugal, and stir up some mischief in the West Indies."

"Are they really capable of that, sir?" Lt. Urquhart said with a derisive sneer. "So far this war, they've not shown *that* much skill at sea. Comes from sitting idle in the ports we blockade, with very little time on the open seas."

"True, there's only so much trainin' conscript sailors may do in port, sir, but someday some Frog Admiral will get lucky, and put to sea in *halfway* decent shape. Slip by us, get a fortnight, a month or more, of real working-up, and they just might give us a bloody nose," Lewrie mused aloud. To Lt. Urquhart's cocked eyebrow and dubious expression, he added, "Not *that* much a bloody nose, but . . . more a nasty surprise. I've met *some* Frogs who knew how to put up a good fight, and they made my bung 'sport claret' a time or two, before we settled 'em."

"Never under-estimate, you're saying, sir?" Urquhart asked.

"Exactly so, Mister Urquhart," Lewrie agreed. "Now we're nigh t'comin' up on our squadron, sir. Have a turn about the ship to search out anything that'd make *Savage* look like a dowdy, unkempt whore under the flag's eyes, and put it right before we come up alongside."

"Aye aye, sir," Urquhart responded, tapping the brim of his hat with two extended fingers, a salute more casual than doffing it.

"And I'll go change," Lewrie said on, which made Lt. Urquhart fight a small grin, for Capt. Lewrie, RN, had come up from below in his dowdy and faded old coat, no neck-stock or waist-coat or sword belt. And that coat! Three years before, when first returned to the West Indies, Lewrie had had the bright idea to have a tailor run up some coats in cotton, not wool, so to better survive the heat . . . never expecting that dark blue-dyed cotton would not hold its colour. A sweaty supper aboard another officer's ship, and he'd come back aboard his own with Royal Navy blue sweat rings and giant stains upon his shirt, waist-coat, and snowy breeches. A few wearings more, a day-long shower or two, and those two coats had ended up the same pale blue as this day's sky, with the gilt-lace trim of buttonholes, pocket seams, and collars turned the *oddest,* sick-making, gangrenous green shade; the colour of deathly pus (fortified by the verdigris green that all gilt lace turned after long exposure to salt water and sea airs) and so repulsive that one expected them to reek like a corpse's armpit.

Lewrie stubbornly kept them, for they *were* cooler than the usual wool uniform coats, and at this stage could look no *worse* when washed, which one could not do with wool. They could be stuffed into a mesh bag and drug astern, with the bed linens, and by then, had bled all the dye they were ever going to, hence no threat to his other apparel.

Oh yes! Lt. Edward Urquhart was finding his new captain to be a *most* unusual bird!

"Deck, there!" the lookout called again. "*Courses* now in sight! Private signal from a *three*-decker!"

"Mister . . . Grisdale," Lewrie said to one of the Midshipmen on the quarterdeck, "hoist the flag, and send up our number, quickly now."

Get his damned name right? Lewrie wondered: *Too bloody many new-comes aboard.*

He had already had a fair bit of fame (or notoriety) before the last battle against the French *L'Uranie* frigate, and after the papers got through with it, one might have thought he'd become Admiral Nelson . . . or his new replacement arm. Letters had come aboard *Savage* as she was just being manned from hopeful Midshipmen without a post at present, or from hopeful parents looking for advancement, or a first place, for their second or third sons. Not knowing any of them from Adam, though, and with very little aid from other captains in Portsmouth, Lewrie had pretty much been reduced to writing their names on stiff card stock and tossing them, blindfolded, into his upturned hat, for all the chance to pick through the aspirants he'd had.

Savage, a 36-gunned frigate of the Fifth Rate, of nearly 950 tons burthen, and with a larger crew of 240 men, required one Midshipman for each fifty hands; or so Admiralty said. That had meant five new-comes, with the well-seasoned Mr. Grace to make up the necessary six. Three, *including* Grace, might . . . *might,* mind! . . . have the wits and abilities that God had merely *promised* geese!

There was this Grisdale . . . if that, indeed, was his name, for Lewrie was still sorting them out . . . who'd come passably recommended, whose father was a Rear-Admiral of the Blue. When watched closely, he could keep his mind to his duties . . . so far, it seemed. But if not, Mr. Grisdale could be a lazy sprog. So much akin to Lewrie at that age that one could almost take a liking to him!

There was a Midshipman Locke, whose father was in the Commons, and one of those "steam engine" men who'd made a fortune off the war. He, at least, was sixteen, and had had some experience at sea. Stern, and a bit of a martinet with the ship's people, but not a *complete* tyrant, and Lewrie and Lt. Urquhart could chide that flaw from him.

There was a Mr. Mayhall, son of another rich and influential man, landed in the *huge* way, and aristocratic in both speech and airs. Oddly, the crew seemed to take to him, for though he was only fifteen, he "knew the ropes" already, and projected the aura of a lad who would be a proper Sea Officer someday, should he survive the process.

Then there was Midshipman, the Honourable, Carrington, and so far he was proving the truth of the old naval adage that titled families sent the family fool to sea. He was sixteen, and supposedly "salted" by a three-year stint aboard a two-decker — but Good Lord! — was as dense as round-shot, and nearly as inert! And, when prodded into motion, was as dangerous as an 18-pounder ball rolling cross the deck. Daddy *was* in Lords, though, one of Wilberforce's fondest followers, detested the slave trade, and was *very* influential.

And, lastly, there was Midshipman Dry, a King's Letter Boy from that miserable excuse for a naval academy at Dartmouth; he had entered at twelve, son of a widower second mate off a merchant vessel who needed a berth for the lad. Dry had grown up aboard merchant ships and boats, so he'd been utterly bored to tears by more than a year of "training" at the academy, knots, ropes, rigging, and such, with only the reading, French, and navigation interesting. A year more of harbour scut-work for a port admiral (another admirer of Lewrie's, thank God!) who also sat in Commons, and here he was at fourteen, so much like poor little Midshipman Larkin, HMS *Proteus*'s bastard Irish by-blow in shabby cast-off uniforms, all elbows and knees, but impish and cheerful despite a humble beginning. Hmm, perhaps *too* impish?

"Our number's received, sir!" Grisdale announced. "New hoist . . . from *Chatham,* the flag. 'Come Under My Lee,' sir!"

"Very well, Mister Grisdale," Lewrie replied. "Pass word for the Cox'n to muster my boat crew, and get her spanking ready."

"Aye aye, sir!"

And, which Midshipmen would be on watch when *Savage* came alongside HMS *Chatham* in an hour or so? Lewrie had to fret. He'd prefer to have Mr. Grace in charge of his launch, but such favouritism would not do, and would dispirit the others. He checked his pocket-watch, which Clotworthy Chute had recovered from that "Three-handed Jenny" back in London. Hour and a half, say, and the watch would still be Grisdale and Midshipman . . . Oh God, the only other choice was Carrington!

"When Desmond arrives, Mister Grisdale, he is to see the boat, and its crew, turned out in their best," Lewrie added, before leaving the quarterdeck for his great-cabins.

With his fingers crossed!

"Ease helm, Mister Carrington!" Lewrie's Cox'n, Liam Desmond, harshly whispered as the neatly painted launch neared the main-chains of the towering HMS *Chatham,* which was still under way, and generating a substantial flurry of parted waters down its massive sides. "Don't wanta git et by 'er wake, now, so . . . Jesus an' Mary!, ease . . . !"

The launch rose up on the out-thrust curl of the three-decker's wake. "In oars larb'd!"

Desmond barked as the launch, at too acute an angle, crossed the curl, tilted to larboard, rather precipitously in point of fact, and met the *suck* of the hull's turning, being *drawn* alongside. "Bow man, hook on!" Desmond snapped, and the sailor kneeling right in the eyes of the launch's bow swung his long gaff at dead-eyes and blocks atop the chain platform, barely snagging its hook round a stout standing-rigging cable. A second later, the launch went *Bonk!* against *Chatham's* side, sucked in like iron filings to a magnet, and the bow man cried something much akin to "Holy shite!" followed by "Eeh!" as he tumbled off the bows to larboard, waist-deep in the ocean, and getting dragged at a rate of knots, a panicky death-grip upon the gaff's pole, and the snagged hook his only salvation.

The launch *Bonked!* again against *Chatham*, and both Jones Nelson and Patrick Furfy leaped to seize the fellow, one by the collar of his waist-length coat, the other by the waist-band of his slop-trousers, before the launch, with only one bank of oars free to pull, began to fall astern for another try.

Cruel laughter could be heard from the quarterdeck, high above.

" 'Ang on, Grisham, 'ang on, now!" Furfy urged.

"Yer pullin' me *trousers* arf, ye daft . . . !"

"Shin up de pole, Grisham!" Jones Nelson

said with a grunt.

"Draggin' th' 'ole bloody *launch,* ye . . . ?" Grisham howled.

"Boat grapnel," Desmond snapped, digging under the after-most thwart by the counter. "Might ye please shift yer legs, Mister Carrington? *Now,* sir?" Desmond tumbled forward with the grapnel and a line, bounding from shoulder to shoulder, took Grisham's place in the bows, let out a dozen feet of line, swirled the grapnel over his head, and heaved, snagging another dead-eye. Furfy and Nelson shifted grips off Grisham to the rope, and pulled the boat back up near the main chains, making fast to a small wood-armed bollard atop the bow. Free of holding the weight of the launch, and with a second assist from Furfy upon the seat of his pants (a mighty heave and toss, that!), Grisham scrambled onto the chain platform, freed his gaff from the shrouds, and pulled the launch to *him,* instead of the other way round.

"Oh, *well* done, Mister Carrington!" Lewrie snarled as he rose to totter amidships of the launch's larboard side. "You and the Bosun must have a little discussion of your seamanship once we've returned aboard, hmm? In fact, I shall insist upon it."

"Aye, sir," the dejected and red-faced Midshipman replied, for a "discussion" with the Bosun would mean a dozen mighty whacks across his upturned bottom with a

282

stiffened rope starter, his body bent over a cannon . . . Midshipman, the Honourable, Royce Carrington would "kiss the gunner's daughter" for his ineptness, and his embarrassment to his ship, and his captain's dignity.

Waiting for the proper moment of the launch's lurches, and the ponderous slow roll of the flagship, Lewrie made a leap of his own for the boarding battens and man-ropes abaft the chains, scored his perch on the first try, and slowly scaled the long ascent to HMS *Chatham's* upper decks, past the closed lower gun-deck entry-port to the proper one, high above. After a deep, restoring breath, and a jerk upon the man-ropes, Lewrie sprang inboard, *trying* to look spry and unabashed.

"Welcome aboard, sir," *Chatham's* First Lieutenant said, hiding his smirk damned well, as did the other officers gathered on the gangway; but it was only the stone-faced sailors of the side-party and the Marines presenting arms in full kit who didn't look highly amused.

"Lewrie . . . HMS *Savage,* come to join the squadron, sir," Lewrie gruffly replied, doffing his hat to the national flag and the Admiral's broad pendant, then the deck officers. "I've despatches and mail with me, some of which I assume will be welcome. If you'll drop a line . . ."

"Indeed, Captain Lewrie," the First Officer brightened, snapping fingers to summon one of the flagship's eighteen Midshipmen to see to it. "My pardons, Captain Lewrie, but . . . though we have not met, your name is familiar to me."

"L'Uranie," another officer prompted from the side of his mouth.

"But, of course, sir! A gallant action!" the First Officer said with a grin; though it did appear as if he might have made another connexion, had his junior not steered him away.

"Quite an arrival, sir! *Most* unconventional!" came a loud, and "plummy," upper-class voice, and a stout older man in the full dress uniform of a Rear-Admiral came plodding up, all smiles. With him was an older Post-Captain, most-like *Chatham's*, and a young Flag-Lieutenant. "Lewrie, are you? Saw your appointment into *Savage* listed in the *Marine Chronicle.* Good God, sir! That one of those Cuffies of yours?" he said, pointing overside at Jones Nelson. "I can see why you, ah . . . obtained him. Strong as an ox, is he? Decorative addition to your boat crew, as well, I should think. Weren't you to stand trial, or be sued, or something? Last news from the London papers were simply full of it, haw haw!"

Oh, that Lewrie! was the expression on many nearby faces.

"King's Bench found the Jamaica trial colourable, milord, and put off the proceedings 'til all evidence is reviewed," Lewrie had to say with a straight face, though fuming at such abrupt treatment from a senior officer. He *should* have been used to such, after his years serving under an host of insulting fools, and a fair number of people who might have had good cause to abuse him now and again, but by God it still irked!

Eat his shite, an' think it plum duff, aye! he grimly thought.

"The particulars are most-like featured in the latest papers I brought from England, milord," Lewrie said with a seemingly uncaring, and unaffected, shrug and smile. "Perhaps by Hilary, or Easter, Term."

"Walk with me, Captain Lewrie," the Rear-Admiral said, turning more business-like. "A glass of something?"

"Nothing for me, milord."

Lewrie's orders from Admiral Lord Bridport, commander of Channel Fleet, had told him to report himself and his frigate to Rear-Admiral Arthur Iredell, Baron Boxham, so he knew with whom he was strolling; even if that august worthy had yet to name himself, which was insulting enough, but to be walked up and down the quarterdeck instead of being welcomed into the great-cabins under the poop deck was even worse!

"We shall soon be coming about, so I will not keep you long," Lord Boxham explained. "Yonder to our lee lies France, at present not six leagues off, sir. My brief, for this particular squadron, is from forty-six degrees latitude, or the north tip of the Ile d'Oléron, all the way down to the latitude of Arcachon, to blockade a coastline that runs roughly one hundred and twenty sea-miles, and 'tis rare that all the liners of this squadron are together in one place, as you find us today.

"Not quite as bad an area to cover as the squadron buried deep in the sack near Bayonne, where Spain and France meet, should a storm roll in from the West, as they usually do, hereabouts," Lord Boxham said with a visible wince. "Navigation is also tricky, I warn you now. From Rochefort Suth'rd to Biarritz and the Spanish border, this coast is very shoal, the land quite flat, with few notable headlands by which to estimate position. Should fog arise, one may cast ashore before one knows what has happened."

"Aye, sir," Lewrie said as they reached the aft end of the deck by the poop cabins, and turned to pace back towards the hammock netting overlooking *Chatham*'s waist; that reply was usually safest. "Though I have the latest London chartmakers' works, perhaps your Flag-Captain is in possession of more current soundings, and such, which I might obtain or copy, milord?" he went on, trying to sound energetic and thoughtful.

"Your senior in the Inshore Squadron will have better, no doubt, Captain Lewrie," Lord Boxham said, rather dismissively, as if he resented having his lecture interrupted. "*Savage,* so I note, is of the Fifth Rate, which means that she has a draught of seventeen or eighteen feet, Lewrie? Good. That will serve nicely.

"Now as I was saying," the Rear-Admiral went on, and yes, he *had* felt interrupted, and was irked by such from a mere frigate captain. "There is another squadron keeping an eye on Rochefort, the small ports of the Vendée region, Saint Nazaire, and the mouth of the Loire up North, whilst *my* duties principally encompass the river Gironde, and what the French possess in the way of warships built or building, fitting out, or readying for sea from the port of Bordeaux, up-river."

"I see, milord," Lewrie replied with his best stern phyz on.

"Once on-station, a perusal of the charts will shew you, Lewrie, that the Gironde, below the last of the *aits,* is actually a very wide *ria,* thirty miles or so long, and over six miles wide as it approaches its mouth. Rather a lot of places for French warships to find a safe mooring."

"And, for French merchantmen as well, I should expect, milord."

"You demm'd frigate captains!" Rear-Admiral Iredell, Lord Boxham, barked in disgust. "All prize-money and loot, with not a *thought* for anything else!"

"Your pardons, milord," Lewrie countered,

"but starvin' our foes o' food and naval stores, both, keeps 'em tied up alongside the piers, and eases our duties, I should think."

" 'Thout the proper battle that stops their demm'd business for good an' all?" Lord Boxham said with an outraged snort. "God forbid! Well, you'll be in good company, Captain Lewrie. All I may spare for the close blockade are *light* frigates, some over-aged sloops of war, some newer brig-sloops, and eight-gun cutters under mere Lieutenants . . . all of whom dream of *money!*" he gravelled, in a huff.

"Very well, sir," Lewrie flatly replied.

"You're to seek out and report to Commodore Ayscough, in HMS *Chesterfield* . . . ," Lord Boxham said.

"The one with the bagpipers, milord?" Lewrie could not help but blurt out, for then-Captain Ayscough had been his superior in the Far East 'tween the wars, in *Telesto.*

"Yess, him!" Lord Boxham barked, as if rowed beyond all temperance to be interrupted a third time, or that the sound of bagpipes set him howling mad.

"Delightful, milord!" Lewrie happily said, sure of a better welcome.

"Deserve each other, more-like," the Admiral spat. "Well, off with you, Captain Lewrie. Now your mail and despatches are aboard, I shall not keep you. Ayscough *should* lie to the Sou'east of the river mouth today."

"Thank you for receiving me, milord. *Adieu*," Lewrie said with a doff of his hat, and a sketchy bow in *congé*.

"Try not to *drown* yourself, sir!"

"Can't afford to, milord," Lewrie rejoined. "I've not yet *been* to France!"

Rias? Lewrie fumed on his way back down the battens to his boat; *rias and aits? A ria's a narrow estuary, and the Gironde's as broad as the Straits of Dover. And what's wrong with river islands, not* aits? *Good old Ayscough a Commodore, though! Even if he still has his damned bagpipers!*

Lewrie sat himself down on a thwart near the launch's tiller to contemplate whether Commodore Ayscough would go so far with his fondness for all things Scottish as to dine him aboard on a *haggis,* cock-a-leekie soup, and turnips! And, on a happier note, Lewrie also considered whether he should send Midshipman Carrington aloft to spend the night perched on the cross-trees, or hang him from the main-mast truck with a line round his balls!

CHAPTER NINETEEN

HMS *Chesterfield* was an older two-decker 64, bluff and beamy, but, with a more pronounced tumblehome from waterline to her gangways and bulwarks, was much easier for Lewrie to board — this time with Midshipman Grace in charge of his launch. *Savage* had run across her in late afternoon, in company with one of the few large 44-gun Fifth Rate frigates, HMS *Lyme*. As soon as numbers and private signals had been exchanged, *Chesterfield* had made two more short hoists; "First Dog," followed by "Captain(s) Repair Onboard," as sure an invitation to supper as a hand-delivered note, or a butler's china bell. Still in full dress, Lewrie gladly paced 'til near Seven Bells of the Day Watch, then called his boat and crew away once more. Just at the last strokes of *Chesterfield's* bell chiming Eight Bells, he was at the foot of her boarding battens, and scrambling up. As the dog's vane atop his cocked hat crested the lip of the entry-port, a drum rolled, Bosuns' calls began to shrill; Marine boots on oak decks, Marine palms on polished muskets stamped or slapped, and . . . God, there was the dreadful preliminary drone of single bagpipe, before the piper launched himself into a lively rendition of "Campbell's Farewell to Red Castle," one of Ayscough's very favourites, as Lewrie could attest after three long years serving under him; hearing it, and being told its title, every bloody day!

"Lewrie, you young scamp, sir!" Commodore Ayscough bellowed with glee as he came up to doff hats with him, then seize his paw and shake vigourously. "Look at the laddie, will ye all . . . a Post-Captain on his own bottom, just clanking with medals for bravery, ha ha!"

" 'Tis good to see you again, too, sir," Lewrie rejoined. "And, you a Commodore. Had Admiralty a *parcel* o' wit, you should've hoisted a broad pendant *years* ago."

"Aye, and if more cripples and wheezers meet their Maker, I'll make Rear-Admiral as they fall off Navy List," Ayscough whooped. "You are delivering orders, or are you to join my motley crowd, Lewrie?"

"To join, sir, and see if we may have a merry time with the foe over yonder," Lewrie told him, vaguely pointing off to the East, where the French Biscay coast could almost be made out in the quickly dying sunset. "As we did in the Far East."

"*Toppin'* news!" Ayscough exclaimed. "The Frog shore is crawlin' with smugglers, spy boats, and all sorts of shippin', and too many of *them* still manage to get past us, thin as we are in these waters. How many guns is your *Savage,* and what's your weight of metal?"

When told that she mounted twenty-six 18-pounders, with a pair of 12-pounders for chase guns, and mounted eight 9-pounders and eight 32-pounder carronades, Ayscough was delighted.

"*Chesterfield* is a stout old barge, Lewrie, but a slow-coach," Ayscough grumbled as the music died, the side-party and Marines were dismissed, and they paced the length of the gangway. "Good for commanding a squadron, but not for helping at close inshore work, either. Rather have me a frigate like yours . . . keep me hand in, partake of a hot action now and then, but . . . ," he said with a resigned sigh. "Now *Lyme,* there, is fine for the open sea, too, but a fourty-four-gun frigate can't pursue runners close enough ashore any more than can I. Her captain is already come aboard . . . solid fellow, is Captain Charlton."

"Captain *Thomas* Charlton, sir?" Lewrie gawped in surprise, and further pleasure. "I served under him in the Adriatic, sir, when he had *Lionheart,* back in '96! This really *is* an 'old boys' reunion."

" 'Deed it is," Ayscough chearly agreed.

"Recall young Hogue, do you? Made Commander last year, and I made sure to request him when I got sailing orders. He's here into a brig-sloop, the *Mischief*. And a damned good choice o' name, too, for he's energetic and full of it . . . *mischief*, that is, ha ha!"

"I'd be delighted to see him again, too, sir," Lewrie declared. "I read of his posting, but haven't seen him since *Telesto* paid off in '84."

"See him soon enough," Ayscough promised, "soon as I despatch you and your fine frigate closer to the coast. Know how the Royal Navy works, Lewrie," Commodore Ayscough said with a wry scowl. "Decades of swallowin' ninny's shite, and only findin' a few truly good'uns here and there, so . . . when one finally has the seniority, and the active commission, one seeks out as many good'uns as one can get away with. What place and influence is worth, that . . . employ the best one discovered, and make fond daddies happy, to boot! Ah, here's Captain Charlton. I think you know our third guest, Charlton?"

"Good God above," Captain Charlton said, almost gasping in surprise as he strode up from aft and below to the gangway. "The last that I heard, Lewrie, weren't you to be hung?"

"Decided t'steal away with a frigate and turn pirate out here, sir," Lewrie japed as they performed the same ritual; first a doff of their hats in formal salute, then a hearty handshake.

"He'd have made a good one, as I recall from the Adriatic, sir," Charlton told Ayscough. "You must reveal all to me, to us, Lewrie. As we dine upon Commodore Ayscough's generosity."

"Speaking of, let us repair below, shall we, gentlemen? I promise you an excellent supper," Ayscough, as host, bade them.

And a most excellent supper it was, for Commodore Ayscough had always set a fine table, and was partial to his "tucker"; though how Ayscough could provide crisply fresh leafy greens for the salad course, and crisp-crusted, piping-hot bread — not maggoty and hard biscuit — after so long on-blockade, Lewrie could not fathom. Nothing fresh could survive the long voyage from England, even stowed aboard the swiftest packet.

There was a mincemeat pie, the inevitable "reconstituted" soup, of course, but the main course, instead of salt beef, salt pork, or a chicken from the forecastle manger, was *lobster,* served up surrounded by boiled shrimp, and even the clarified butter was *fresh,* not rancid from the tub on the orlop, and each diner got a small dish of a horseradish sauce vaguely reminiscent of the French-style *à la mayonnaise,* or a *rémoulade!* And the wines . . . ! The bottles set out on the sideboard all bore distinguished French vineyards' names and varieties not seen in England since the war had begun in 1793, but for a few cases brought in by Channel coast smugglers every now and then, and priced so dear that even the wealthy might take pause before purchasing some.

"How do you *do* it, sir?" Lewrie marvelled between bites, and a deep, appreciative sniff of his fresh-poured wine. "One'd think that, by the time you arrived on-station, such victuals'd have long ago run out."

"Get the bulk of it from the Frogs, Captain Lewrie," Ayscough gleefully told him. "S'truth! God, the look on your face!"

"French fishermen put out every morning to earn their livings," Capt. Charlton was glad to expound. "Does one of our cutters or brigs close them, these days, they've learned that their boats are too tiny for us to take as prize, so they no longer run in fear of us. British silver . . . a little British silver . . . goes a long way."

"For wine, fresh food, some of their catch, or . . . information," Commodore Ayscough cryptically said. "Give the Frogs this much . . . They still manage to mint solid coin after seven years of war, whilst we've had to resort to paper bank notes. Not great *value* to their coinage by this time, of course, what with all the . . . what do they call it, Captain Charlton?"

"Inflation, sir," Charlton supplied with a grin.

"And what a pot-mess their coinage is," Ayscough derisively grumbled. "God knows what a *denier* is made of. Soft iron? But, three of them make a *liard,* or twelve *deniers* make one *sol,* but you're still in the range o' ha'pence. Four *liards* make one *sou,* twenty *sous* make one *livre,* six *livres* make one *écu,* and you *begin* to talk of something in silver . . . four *écus* makes what once was called a *louis d'or,* before they chopped poor King Louis's head off, that is, and you finally get to gold . . . 'bout the same as our guinea. All a jumble left over from the royal days, along with local-minted tripe, and how the Devil even the French keep track of values is a mystery to me! More bread, sirs?"

Ayscough's cabin servant made a quick tour round the table with the bread barge, and Lewrie took another thick slab. Now that he knew what he was dealing with, he could put a name to it; a *boule* loaf.

"Would the French fishermen run from a *frigate,* sir?" he asked.

"Not any longer," Charlton informed him. "No dread of us taking them for spare hands, nor of seizing their boats. Fetch-to within two miles of the shore, and they will most-like swarm you like bumboats in a British harbour. Mind the spirit smuggling, though. Our sailors are not that fond of wine, when they can get rum for free, and most French beers are simply ghastly, but the fishermen will have small flasks of brandy or *arrack* aboard. Not *good* brandy, mind," Capt. Charlton said with a wry expression.

"Pearls before swine," Ayscough snickered.

"Though the *arrack,* a rather fiery equivalent to rum, *is* desirable," Charlton continued. "Probably stolen from French naval stores."

"No American whisky, I s'pose," Lewrie said with a downcast expression of his own. "Grew rather fond of it in the West Indies, the Kentucky sort, which is aged several years in oak barrels. Bourbon, I think they're beginning t'call it."

"Dear Lord!" Charlton softly exclaimed, rather in awe of anyone who would prefer such a strong drink.

"I do have two five-gallon barricoes aboard, but God only knows how long we'll be on-station here," Lewrie said. "You've never tried it, sirs? Might I decant a gallon each for you to sample?" he teased.

"A quart, perhaps, for me, Lewrie," Ayscough replied, grinning impishly. "For I doubt a Yankee Doodle bourbon can measure up to my Highland Scottish whisky. *Usquebaugh,* by God . . . the 'water of life'!"

"I am set down amid fur-coated barbarians." Charlton pretended to shiver. "Vikings with the palates of Philistines!"

Oh, it was grand to be in company with such fine men, officers he had long before learned to trust and rely upon, Lewrie deemed during their supper. Ayscough, that burly fellow with salt-and-pepper hair, clubbed back into an old-fashioned sailor's long queue, his cheerful weathered face, and piercing grey eyes! Charlton, still the tall, lean, and wiry epitome of the genial and articulate, soft-spoken English gentleman — off his quarterdeck, of course — and possessed of a droll and dry wit. Charlton's mild brown eyes and regular, unremarkable features had many times crinkled in amusement in their private moments. And both of them were sailors' sailors, as experienced and canny as any rough "tarpaulin" man, right down to their toenails.

Away went the last plates and the white wine, and out came their dessert and its accompanying drink; ripe Anjou pears amid crumbled sweet biscuit, drenched in a sweetened brandy, with large blobs of stiffened and whipped cream atop! And with it, a rich, dark Madeira port.

"Magnificent!" Lewrie pronounced it.

"Rather succulent, aye" was Capt. Charlton's restrained praise.

"Bit off," Ayscough commented, though he was spooning it up like a starved hound.

"Haven't laid hands on any, as of yet, but I've heard there is an orange-flavoured brandy of French distillery, and I cannot help but think that the rob of oranges, combined with a fine and aged brandy, would be even better."

"I could ask, once inshore, sir," Lewrie offered, intrigued by the novelty of such a liquour.

"Inshore, aye," Ayscough said as the dishes were removed, the tablecloth was whipped away, leaving only a bowl of nuts and the port. "To business, if I may, gentlemen? Droop, kindly fetch me the charts, now the table's cleared, then leave us be for an hour or so."

"Aye, sir," Ayscough's cabin servant replied.

"We've three actual groupings of small ships standing blockade, the numbers varying due to refits, recalls, and new arrivals, such as your *Savage,* Lewrie." Ayscough sketched out on the chart, tapping one finger near Rochefort and the Ile d'Oléron. "Charlton here commands an assortment of brigs and cutters in this area, whilst down South, Captain Percy Lockyear keeps watch off Arcachon and its large basin. He has but a twenty-gunned older Sloop of War, *Arundel,* to support *his* smaller clutch of ships, suitable to the shoal conditions obtaining there. A *nice* fellow, is Lockyear. You're sure to like him, do you ever meet.

"And I, 'til your timely arrival, do the best I can keeping an eye on the mouth of the Gironde, that leads to Bordeaux," Ayscough said with a self-disparaging tone. "Very wide entrance to the estuary, and sufficient depth of water rather far up, so *Chesterfield* can sail most of it, but for several forts sited on the tops of the headlands, which out-gun all of us, both in number of artillery pieces, and their weight of metal. Dammit, though . . . that's not what I am to do with my ship," Ayscough groused. "I am *promised* a second sixty-four to join me here, so I may employ two middlin' ships to re-enforce our lighter ships if they run into trouble . . . even if *both* of us would still be too slow to really catch anything incoming or outgoing."

"Should the French come out in force, Lewrie," Capt. Charlton said with dry wit, "our brief is to harass if we may, or fall back upon Lord Boxham's line-of-battle ships and alert him, if we cannot."

"Aye," Ayscough added with a guffaw. "Run screaming out to sea, like a pack of hysterical women!"

"Well, perhaps not *run,* sir," Charlton rejoined with a twinkle. "Nor scream, either. It would be more of a purposeful *lope,* along with loud shouts of hue and cry, or 'tally-ho,' hmm?"

"Oh, o' course, sir!" Ayscough chuckled. "Stout hearts, strong legs, and lusty voices.

What I mean t'say, Lewrie, is that I can't exercise overall command of this coast, *and* have any fun at all, anymore.

"That is why I will place you in command of the river mouth."

"Me?" Lewrie gawped in surprise.

Me? Are you daft? he thought, a tad dizzy at the prospect; *wee little me, in command o' me own . . . squadron? Ye'd have t'be* barkin' *mad t'turn* me *loose!*

To that very instant, the most he expected to control was his frigate, his crew, and his penchant for strange and nubile quim! To acquire more responsibility than that, he had always supposed that he'd have to attain Ayscough's age, and that would be years in the future, but . . . well, he *was* a Post-Captain of More Than Three Years' Seniority, and times were hard. Even if he was less than a year in that rate.

Could he have physically turned his head and gone cross-eyed to look at his pair of gilt-fringed epaulets denoting his rank, he would have, if only to confirm that he was, indeed, the Lewrie that Ayscough was talking about. He almost snickered out loud at how ludicrous such a posting sounded!

"Hear, hear!" Charlton congratulated, taking the port bottle to top Lewrie up for the coming toast. "After all you did with independent action in the Adriatic, I can think of no one more suited to driving the French demented, and stopping the Gironde like a beer keg bung."

"Well, I *knew* the Navy's short-handed these days, but, Lord!" Lewrie responded. "What do the French have, up in Bordeaux, then?"

"I'll get to that," Ayscough told him, pouring himself a fresh glass, as well. "What you have to work with, first. There are five smaller vessels you will command, Lewrie. First are a pair of new-ish brig-sloops . . . our old compatriot Hogue's *Mischief,* of sixteen six-pounders, and *Erato,* with much the same armament. Then, there are the cutters . . . *Argosy* and *Penguin* mount eight guns, and *Banshee,* which is a hired merchant brig, and a little larger, mounts ten. Of course, all mount eighteen-pounder carronades in addition to their long pieces. If you think it best, further divide your forces into pairs, or two groups of three, should you deem such necessary. Daily stations, and patrolling areas, will be up to you, but . . . ," Ayscough all but wheexed with amusement, "knowing you, I am certain that your penchant for cunning will harass the French to no end, and I may rest easy at night with you out there with your eyes wide open."

"Whilst, pray God, the French do not get a *wink* of sleep, wondering what new devilment will befall them," Charlton seconded.

"Hogue is senior, then?" Lewrie asked, knowing that even large one-masted, fore-and-aft rigged cutters were usually Lieutenants' commands.

"Ah, no." Ayscough sobered, even looking a shade evasive for a second. "Commander James Kenyon in *Erato* is senior by a year."

Lewrie's lips half-parted, and his face took on a stunned look.

"Know him, do you?" Ayscough off-handedly enquired.

"Second Lieutenant of my first ship in 1780, old *Ariadne,* sixty-four," Lewrie found wit to reply. *That back-gammoning bastard's here?* he thought, stupefied.

"Took him long enough," Charlton said with a shrug at the fickle nature of Navy politics. "Must not have had a single decent patron for 'interest' or influence 'pon his career."

"God pity you!" Ayscough commented with false sympathy. "First ship a doddering old sixty-four, and as feeble a sailer as *this* barge!"

"Became the stores ship at Antigua, did she not?" Capt. Charlton asked, faintly frowning to recollect. "Seem to recall . . . no matter. Did I not have to hunt about and use up half *my* 'interest' and patronage, I'd gladly let *Lyme* become a stores ship or troopship, like the few of her sort still in commission, and trade up to a Third Rate."

"And, toss *Chesterfield* into that pot, too,

303

God willing," Commodore Ayscough quickly seconded. "Well, then! Here's a double toast, sirs. Success to Captain Lewrie . . . and confusion to the French!"

"Hear, hear!" Charlton cried as they tipped their glasses back to "heel-taps."

"We need a bowl of punch, by God!" Ayscough decided. "Droop! Fetch us the bowl and makin's for a good, stout punch!"

"Come all ye bold heroes, give an ear to my
    song,
and we'll sing in the praise of good brandy
    and rum.
'Tis a clear crystal fountain good England
    con-trols.
Give me the punch ladle, I'll fath-om the
    bowl!"

Lewrie and Charlton sang along to Ayscough's rough, raspy lead, twice through all verses before the ladle was first dipped, and cups were filled. *Kenyon, my God!* Lewrie grimly thought, no matter the good cheer; *how am I t'deal with him, after all these years?*

CHAPTER
TWENTY

Dawn came hazy, with a light fog up the estuary of the Gironde. The sea was slack and glassy, and the winds from out of the West were light, though steady. Right after breakfast and a shave, Lewrie bent *Savage's* course inshore, the frigate enjoying the tops'l breeze, with her main course twice-reefed, and t'gallants and royals brailed up to the upper yards, but all stays'ls and jibs hoisted for quicker manoeuvring.

It was second-best uniform for Lewrie this morning, his plainer cocked hat on his head, without all the formal folderol of the previous evening's supper. Though it was a cool morning, a touch shy of nippy, the breeze on *Savage's* starboard quarters felt too humid to savour.

"Showers by the middle of the Day Watch, I would wager, sir," the Sailing Master, Mr. Winwood, gloomily pronounced as he peered, bird-quick, from each headland or sea mark to the next with his pocket compass, one of his new charts spread atop the binnacle cabinet. Though he did not pencil bearings on his chart, Winwood did mumble to himself as if memorising reciprocal courses. "Were I a wagering man, of course."

Lewrie glanced astern to scan the skies for weather signs, but could not discover any cause for Winwood's prediction. For the man's nervousness, Lewrie could determine good cause; slap Winwood up against a strange new coast, hostile or no, and he would turn as skittery as a whore in church, for he had not yet *known* it, had the proper seaman's distrust in twenty-year-old re-drawn and re-printed charts, and was just as responsible as his captain for the safe navigation of the ship. Miss just one shoal or rock that *was* marked on the charts, hit one that *wasn't;* either way, his career was on the line, and, until Winwood was as conversant with their new area of operations as he was of his own palm lines, there would be no living with him, no cheer in his body.

Not that ponderous and cautious Mr. Winwood had ever been much for good cheer.

"Mister Mayhall reports six and a quarter knots, Captain," Lt. Urquhart stiffly reported, doffing his hat by Lewrie's side. "A light breeze, sir, even if it is on the quarter."

"Good enough for now, Mister Urquhart," Lewrie said. "No sense chargin' in like a Spanish fightin' bull. Sooner or later, they get stabbed by the *matador's* sword. Today's a get-acquainted day, get the feel o' things . . . meet up with the lighter ships, and their captains, anyway. And," he quipped in a softer voice, inclining his head towards Mr. Winwood, "we must allow the Sailing Master t'get his feel for ev'ry wee pitfall. He'll not sleep a wink 'til he does."

"Aye, sir," Lt. Urquhart replied, with a brief, but shy, grin, as if he had to think about it before reacting.

Two of a kind, really, Lewrie thought as he took a sip of his coffee, then strolled over to the starboard mizen shrouds. Urquhart might as well have been Winwood's bastard son, for all his humourlessness. *Comes o' tryin' too hard?* Lewrie speculated; *or, is he just a sober-side from birth?*

In their few weeks at sea, Lt. Urquhart so far had appeared as taciturn and serious as a Scottish Calvinist preacher. The man *never* slouched, never allowed himself more than four glasses of wine in the wardroom (so his cabin servant and personal cook, Aspinall, had heard from the officers' mess servants), never took part in any of the high-cockalorum antics his fellow Lieutenants might stage, appeared to need no more than four hours sleep a night, and could always be found fully dressed and on the quarterdeck, sometimes for as little cause as when the nanny goat farted.

Was he competent? Yes, immensely so, and Lewrie could find no fault with how, during his London absences, Urquhart had seen to the ship's fitting-out, storing, and re-arming. Was Urquhart the complete sailorman, a tarry-handed "tarpaulin man" with the addition of a gentlemanly education, manners, and dignity? Aye, he was. He just was not . . . Anthony Langlie, Lewrie could resignedly bemoan. Langlie, during their three years in *Proteus* . . . Lt. Knolles, his First Officer aboard HMS *Jester* . . . even Arthur Ballard when he had had the converted bomb-ketch *Alacrity* in the Bahamas. All of those officers had been young, though able, possessed of quick wit and good humour. Ballard, well . . . he had *his* ponderous moments, but *sly* and *dry,* and a good friend, as well.

Been spoiled, I s'pose, Lewrie thought with a sigh. All of his First Lieutenants since his first commands had felt more like helpful and supportive *friends!* Urquhart, though . . .

Lewrie supposed he could put his moodiness down to all of that punch, port, claret, and rhenish that he'd sloshed down with Ayscough and Charlton. It had been past eleven when he'd reeled his way aboard *Savage,* and barely managed to undress before sprawling into his swinging bed-cot, and falling asleep as if pole-axed, and had been roused, drooling onto his pillows, both by the Bosuns' calls for "All Hands," and the chimes of Eight Bells as the Middle Watch ended at 4 a.m. Well, all that, and the cats. Stocky Toulon, the black'un with white markings, and Chalky, the youngest with white fur and grey splotches, had pawed, leaped upon him with all four paws as close together as a quartet of coins abutted on a publican's bar counter, with *loud* and raspy "We're Starving!" squawls, and urgent digging at the bed linens right by his nose!

Toulon had been "refugeed" from the port of Toulon; Chalky had been found by his bastard son, Desmond, the American Midshipman, aboard a French prize brig in the West Indies, and presented to him as a gift.

They were both, therefore, *French!* Perhaps they knew the smell of their homeland off to loo'rd, and wanted Lewrie to rise and take 'em on deck to share their furry *rencontre!*

And, damned if they weren't poised atop the quarterdeck hammock nettings that very moment, peering forward towards the shore, sniffing the air, tails curling and jittering like they did when they saw a sea bird glide cross the decks, and sharing looks with each other, now and again.

"Not thinkin' o' jumpin' ship, are ye, catlings?" Lewrie teased as he came to the forward end of the quarterdeck to give them a stroke or two. He was rewarded with head butts on his hand, some wee, trillish mews by way of greeting. "I'll brook no desertion, hear me plain?"

"Deck, there!" a lookout atop the main-mast cross-trees called. "Fishin' boat t'larboard! Three points off th' larboard bows!"

Lewrie wandered over to the top of the larboard gangway ladder as Lt. Urquhart and Mr. Winwood raised their telescopes to peer at the fishing boat, which was just beginning to emerge from the haze, and the low-lying skim of fog atop the estuary waters.

"She appears to be un-armed, sir," Urquhart reported. "Only a few men on deck, with nets ready for streaming. Rather good-sized, I do allow, though, sir. 'Bout the length of a Port-Admiral's barge?"

"Your glass, sir," Lewrie bade, and took a squint for himself. He saw a two-masted lug-ger, both her broad gaff-rigged sails and her single jib streaming slackly astern as she came into the wind, probably to lower her fishing nets before coming about to wallow inshore for the first of her morning's trawls. Four, no, only five sailors in sight, and none of them showing any evident signs of alarm at the appearance of a "Bloody's" frigate cruis-ing up to Range of Random Shot.

"Hands to Quarters, Mister Urquhart," Lewrie ordered, lowering the borrowed glass and handing it back over. "Carronades, quarterdeck nine-pounders, chase guns, and swivels only. No point in manning the eighteen-pounders for such a feeble target. Spare hands, and Mister Devereux's Marines, for a boarding party."

"Aye, sir! Bosun! Pipe 'All Hands' and 'Quarters'!"

"S'pose I must pass the word for the Surgeon," Lewrie chuckled. "I'm told my French is a horror, and Mister Durant was born speakin' Frog."

"Uhm, I am considered quite fluent in French, sir," Urquhart almost timidly put forward, with a throat-clearing harrumph.

"Excellent, Mister Urquhart!" Lewrie cheered. "When closer to, call for them to fetch-to, and prepare t'be boarded. Have her captain come aboard so you can . . . interrogate him."

"Aye aye, sir."

A quarter-hour later, and both *Savage* and the French lugger were fetched-to into the light winds, no more than one hundred yards apart. Though Lewrie's French *was* horrid, he could make out a few phrases of invective . . . "Damn you 'Bloodies,' we're *working* here!" . . . "Death of my life, you put us in *poverty!*" . . . "Go and fuck yourself, you arrogant 'beefsteak' turds!"

They quieted though, and lapsed into surly silence, when cowed by the size of the boarding party, and the Marines with their bayonets and muskets. A brief inspection above and below decks, into the reek of the lugger's hold, half-filled with sea water to preserve any catch 'til they could be landed ashore, then Lt. Urquhart's launch was coming alongside *Savage* with a lone Frenchman amidships, a wiry older man in loose pantaloons, bare feet, a filthy canvas fisherman's smock, and a tasseled "Liberty" stocking cap upon his grizzled head.

"Captain, may I name to you Captain Jules Papin," Lt. Urquhart gravely and punctiliously announced. *"Capitaine Papin, permettez-moi de vous présenter notre Capitaine de Vaisseau, Alan Lewrie, de le frégate Sauvage."*

"Capitaine Papin," Lewrie said, doffing his hat. *"Bon matin, m'sieur."*

"Hawh!" the Frenchman growled back, scratching at his unshaven grey week's worth of stubble. *"Bon, mon cul! Où est le rum?* Have rum?"

"Ah, hum" was Urquhart's stricken comment, his face reddening.

"Aspinall," Lewrie called over his shoulder. "A bottle o' rum and glasses for our guest. "You speak a little *Anglais, Capitaine?"*

"Un peu, mais oui," the grizzled, fish-scale-speckled old man gravelled back. "Mus' *parler* tongue of thief an' invader, if I cannot *bataille* . . . fight, *hein?* 'Ow you t'ink ze *pauvre*

312

homme make living if keep from ze fish, *hein?* Firs', cutter *nous arrête* . . . stop us, jus' in river, zat damn' *Argosy.* Zen, *mort de ma view,* is *Erato* brig, zen, *et voilà, maintenant* you' damn' *frégate! Zut alors,* I be *full* ze fish by now!"

"Rum's up, sir," Aspinall said, appearing with a new bottle of Jamaica's best, and a pair of glasses. He poured for Papin first, and began to pour for Lewrie, but the Frenchman eagerly tossed the contents of his glass back like the experienced toper he looked to be, and gulped it all down his gullet in one swallow, making Papin wheeze, wince, then grin and shake his head in appreciation of raw, un-watered rum. And he thrust his glass out for a refill!

"I am delighted to hear that my . . . our other ships are alert and doing their proper duty, *Capitaine,*" Lewrie told the Frenchman as he took a cautious sip of his own rum, stifling a wince and a belch as the fiery spirit slid down his throat and hit his already-unsettled innards. *Hair o' the dog mine arse!* Lewrie thought.

"What you wish?" Papin impatiently snapped, after his glass was replenished. "Fish? *Quel dommage, M'sieur Capitaine,* I have none, for you' *pirates* do not give me *peace* to fish! *Langoustes et crevettes?* A lobster or . . . shrimp? *Small* boats close inshore have zose, not *moi!* Champagne,

wine, *eau-de-vie,* ze brandy? *Argosy* an' *Erato.*
Zey buy all I had, *avant vous. Damn* you'
language! *Before* you, I say! You wish? Take
you' damn' big *frégate* to shoal waters, run
agroun', an' break you' *back!*"

"Wouldn't dream of it, *mon vieux,*" Lewrie
casually shrugged off. "Mister Urquhart, his
boat clean of arms and contraband?"

"Completely, sir," Urquhart gravely replied.
"Nothing but clasp knives for sailors' work
aboard, and no goods beyond their dinners
and such, either, sir."

"Very well, then," Lewrie said, turning back
to Papin. "Sir, I will trouble you no longer.
You are free to go about your fishing."

"No good zat do, now, zis late in morning,
pawh!" Papin growled, looking at Aspinall
and the rum bottle, and his newly emptied
glass in expectation of a "stirrup cup," and
licking his lips.

"Sorry 'bout that," Lewrie allowed. "Con-
vey *Capitaine* Papin to his boat, um . . .
l'appilation des votre bateau, Capitaine?" he
asked, making Papin wince again, this time
over Lewrie's lack of grammar, and his
outlandish accent. "The *Marie Doux,* is it?
Sweet Marie? Thankee. I shall know you and
your boat in future. Perhaps . . ."

Lewrie gave the man a sly look, nodded to
Aspinall to pour him a third glass of rum,
and posed the question.

"I *would* appreciate an occasional bottle or

two of good wine . . . perhaps a case at a time, as would my wardroom officers, I'm certain, *Capitaine* Papin," he posed. "And, as you say, lobsters and shrimp, a parcel of mussels or clams, are not your normal catch, but you could, are you reasonable, *obtain* such from the smaller boats to sell me. A decent brandy, hmm? American corn whisky, if you could get it, haw!" Lewrie concluded with a scoffing laugh at such an out-of-the-ordinary wish, as if asking for a slice of cheese off the moon.

"Ze 'Merican whisky, ze . . . bourbon, *m'sieur?*" Papin said with almost a wink, slyly scratching at his week's worth of grey stubble as if considering such a request, and what he might charge for it. "*Mais oui, Capitaine* Le . . . Luur . . . *m'sieur.* Ze 'Merican ships still come to Bordeaux . . . get pas' you' blockade, all ze *time,* hawn! You wish ze whisky, *peut-être* ze 'Mericans sell *à moi.* Ze res', is *très* easy to sell you. Non ze bank *note!* Mus' 'ave silver coin."

"Uhm . . . chickens?" Midshipman Mayhall muttered nearby. "Eggs?"

"Ze lad wish ze fresh *omelette, oui?*" Papin asked with a greasy laugh of his own. "*Difficile, m'sieurs,* for ze *gendarmerie* punish ze smuggler 'oo trade with you 'Bloodies.' See ze livestock be loaded on boat, *et voilà,* I am lose my boat, and be in ze prison. *Peut-être,* ze small parcels, *hein? Non* ze cow and sheep,

315

hawn hawn hawn!"

"Lots of American ships up-river, are there, sir?" Lewrie asked, trying to sound off-handed and not *too* interested.

"Ze few, *Capitaine*," Papin replied, a sly smile on his face, and a brow cocked as if they were getting to the main trading points. "You wishing to know when zey sail, *hein? Ze . . . information?*" he added in a much softer, conspiratorial voice. "*Peut-être* you wish to know of ze forts, ze *navire de guerre?* War-ships?"

"Hmm," Lewrie replied in like voice, daring another sip of his rum, finding it easier on his stomach this time, and taking another. "That might prove . . . useful. For such, of course, one must expect to be rewarded."

"Oh, *mais oui, Capitaine* Lurr . . . *m'sieur,* hawn hawn!" Papin chuckled, in the fashion of a pimp or tout who'd just landed a customer to enter his brothel. "I 'ave nozzing to tell you now, but . . . !"

"Oh, but surely our ships will meet again, *Capitaine* Papin . . . soon," Lewrie said to that, a smug and satisfied grin on his face as they all but clasped hands and shook on the bargain. "Care for another glass of rum, sir?"

"Give me ze bottle," Papin insisted. "I curse you."

"Eh, what?" Lewrie asked, suddenly befuddled.

"*Mes hommes* see us," Papin said with a

shrug as he accepted the re-corked bottle and tucked it into the large cross-wise pocket of his rough smock. *"Zut alors,* I curse you, I look like patriot. Zey will *non* mind I sell food an' drink, but ze information? *Non!"*

"Ah," Lewrie said with a nod. That was all he had time for, for Papin suddenly went into a ranting screech, like to pull his hair out, stamping about the quarterdeck, hocking up a glob of spit as he cried *"Jamais!"* or "Never!" . . . along with a rich store of invective about the English, poverty, Lewrie's doubtful ancestry, the piratical Royal Navy, syphilitic kings and queens, the Battles of Agincourt and Crécy, the burning of Joan of Arc at the stake, that thieving *foutre* Henry the Fifth, the English language, Anglican Protestant heretics, invaders and chicken thieves, and the filthy English habit of bathing too often! He concluded with a dramatic, arms-akimbo, aggressive stance so he could hock up another large glob of spit, and shout "Pawh!"

"Does this mean we won't get any fresh cheese?" Mayhall asked in a wee voice, which quite destroyed the spirit of the thing.

"Cheese, *oui . . . plus tard.* Later," Papin rasped from a corner of his mouth, looking like an actor whose grand soliloquy had been interrupted and ruined by an unruly drunk in the cheap seats.

"Au revoir, Capitaine Papin," Lewrie said,

not sure whether to applaud, or laugh. " 'Til we meet again. *A tout à l'heure.*"

With a final, broad obscene gesture, Papin went to the entry-port and scampered down the battens and man-ropes as agile as an ape.

"See him back to his boat, Mister Urquhart, and recall our men," Lewrie ordered. "And have someone swab . . . that, up."

"Secure from Quarters, sir?" Lt. Adair, the Second Officer, asked.

"Half the quarterdeck nine-pounders, and the carronades, aye," Lewrie decided. "I don't see any boats as large as Papin's out this morning, so the swivels, and muskets, would suit just as well."

"There do seem to be a fair number in the offing, Captain," Lt. Adair pointed out.

"Christ, we stop and search 'em all, we'll be at this 'til sundown," Lewrie said with a scowl. "No, we'll not waste our time on 'em. We'll hunt up *Argosy* and *Erato* first, and get the lay of the land from their captains, before we try on anything else. After all," he said with a chuckle, "they're the ones t'do the stopping and searching. We are here t'back *them* up."

"Odd fellow, this Papin, sir," Lt. Adair commented, as close as he could come to initiate a discussion of what had just transpired. "I . . . pardons, sir, but I would not trust him with much. He's French!"

"Well, as Commodore Ayscough and Cap-

318

tain Charlton told me last night, Mister Adair," Lewrie responded, quite pleased with his initial dealings with the French fishermen, "a great deal of useful information is had from the locals, once cordial relations are established by dint of paying good prices for their catches, then for their smuggled goods. The old Directory of Five in Paris, now Bonaparte, are bankrupting the country with their endless wars upon the rest of Europe. Their trade with the rest of the world is cut to the bone . . . our doin', that . . . and, I doubt *ev'ry* Frog is in love with the Revolution. This Papin, some of his fellow captains, may prove extremely informative."

Some shillings here, a guinea or so there, and these impoverished Frogs'll most-like sell their dead mothers' hair! Lewrie cynically thought; *fed up with war and shortages . . . sons conscripted, or already dead or crippled on battlefields from here to the Alps . . . why* wouldn't *they play spy, if there's some money in it, and get a bit o' their own back on the damned fools in Paris?*

He was quite pleased with himself, all but rocking on the balls of his feet and whistling a merry tune. Oh, perhaps Papin couldn't deliver the *best* information, but surely he could come through on the wine, cheese, eggs, fresh-baked *baguettes* and *boules* . . . the bourbon whisky? If not Papin, some other of these fishermen, in almost daily contact with British warships, could. A cornucopia of fresh seafood, surely!

Newspapers! Lewrie thought of a sudden, feeling remiss that he had not mentioned them. French newspapers, half lies though they might be, could still provide a treasure trove of information; mostly unintentinally, for not *every* paper could he pored over by government censors.

"Uhm, sir . . . ," Lt. Adair spoke up again, all but muttering confidentially, "I noted that, whilst that Papin fellow was doing his rant and dance, he, well . . . from the first moment he came aboard, he kept darting rather shrewd eyes about our ship. Counting our guns and such? And, we haven't seen a single other fishing boat as large as his quite *this* far out near the mouth of the Gironde. Perhaps there are others, but . . . why *would* this fellow dare the blockade, sir? Might Papin be spying for his own Navy, sir? Or, passing information to us as quick as he passes observations to shore? Playing both ends against the middle?"

"Oh, fu . . . !" Lewrie began to blurt with a yelp of dismay, but quickly substituted "Mine arse on a band-box!" instead. *The son of a bitch was spyin' on* me? he had to recognise.

"Didn't notice his demeanour," Lewrie huffed, "and thankee for keepin' your own eyes on him, Mister Adair. And, for your suspicions. Papin may be only the first middlin'-sized boat we've come across. It may be that others sail out this far on a regular basis. We're so new t'these waters, we've no idea, at present. We find *Erato* or *Mischief*, one of the cutters or sloops, and speak their captains, we'll have a better idea of what t'look out for . . . and who . . . Whom, rather."

"Well, there is that, sir," Adair replied, unsure whether to be eased of his suspicion, or not.

"Rather like Mister Winwood and his fear of where the driftwood logs lurk on the tides hereabouts, Mister Adair," Lewrie tried to make a jest of it. " 'Til he's secure in his mind, he'll spend all night on deck, lookin' out-board for ship-killin' trees."

Adair doffed his hat and returned to his duties, leaving Lewrie to pace the length of the quarterdeck nettings and railings, hands in the small of his back, head down, and his neck burning in embarrassment.

Spied on? he chid himself; *just* let *the bastard aboard t'see any thing he wished? Gawd, which o' these Frogs* can *ye trust? This whole endeavour could turn out t'be a* rare *shitten business!*

CHAPTER
TWENTY-ONE

The safe, and navigable, outermost reaches of the Gironde river estuary measured about twelve miles across on a line drawn from Pointe de la Coubre, the tip of a narrow, hook-shaped peninsula on the north shore, an appendage to a clenched-fist larger peninsula whose Atlantic face was labelled the Côte Sauvage — which Lewrie took as auspicious — to a seaside village south of Pointe de Grave on the southern Atlantic coast named Soulac sur Mer.

The south shore peninsula narrowed and bent back to the nor'east at Pointe de Grave, near another coastal village called Le Verdon sur Mer, which actually lay on the inner river bank. From Pointe de Grave to the north shore, and the small town of St. Georges de Didonne just a mile or so south of the larger town of Royan, lay the narrows of the Gironde, which was only about three miles across; a short row for a determined boat crew, or an even shorter sail.

Temptingly beyond those narrows, the Gironde widened considerably, remaining deep and six miles across, only narrowing slightly until it reached the long and skinny river *aits* that Rear-Admiral Lord Boxham had mentioned, near Pauillac and Blaye. Any number of French warships or merchant vessels could be moored below those Pointe de Grave narrows, but as to the getting *to* them, or even sneaking a ship's boat up the river to spy them out, it just didn't look like it was doable . . .

"Now in King Louis the Fourteenth's day, sir," Mr. Winwood said in his usual bleak manner, "the key fort guarding the river was on the eastern bank, 'bout twelve or thirteen miles up-river, ah . . . here, at Saint Fort sur Gironde. One might suppose they deemed fortifications by Le Verdon sur Mer, the tip of Pointe de Grave, and Saint Georges de Didonne too vulnerable to armed landings. Now, though . . . my word!"

Keeping a chaste three miles offshore as they cruised down the north bank, past La Grande Côte, St. Palais sur Mer, and to within sight of Royan in case some monstrous 42-pounder coastal guns might lurk in the forests and bleak fields, they had not seen all *that* much sign of military preparations. They had not been fired upon . . . yet . . . Though, as they neared St. Georges de Didonne, they could finally espy a stout pile of stonework sited about halfway between the village and the town of Royan. It appeared to be no more than one hundred yards long overall, a place formed in a shallow, three-sided U, with the crenellations that served as gun-ports no more than sixteen or twenty feet above the shoreline; but, with an even lower water battery mounting lighter guns to deter an assault by boats at the foot of its centre face.

"I count only four openings atop the walls for heavy guns along the walls . . . well, four per face, sir," Lt. Urquhart pointed out. "It might be open on its land face."

"But, a landing-party would have to go ashore *west* of Royan," Lewrie replied, peering intently through his day glass, "then stumble their way to the fort, and, is Royan garrisoned, they might run into a stiff fight before they ever got to musket range of their objective."

It didn't help Lewrie's lingering hang-over, or his wariness of what might lay hidden, that the Sailing Master's glum prediction had come true; just past One Bell of the Day Watch, the wind had slackened and a sullen, steady rain had begun to fall, blurring the coastline so that, at a cautious three miles offshore, vital details they wished to see now lay partially veiled.

As they watched, a bright and fresh French Tricolour flag was run up the flagpole of the fort, and tiny blue-and-white uniformed figures could be seen scurrying like a disturbed ant hill.

"We'll come about, Mister Gamble," Lewrie told the officer of the watch. "Make course Sou-west by West . . . Half West, if she will allow. Full-and-by on starboard tack."

"Aye aye, sir. Mister Thomlin, pipe hands to stations to come about," Lt. Gamble ordered.

"Does that fort possess forty-two-pounders, it could hurl shot as far as Pointe de Grave all by itself," Lewrie surmised aloud as the scurry of hands drummed upon his frigate's timbers. "Heated shot, as well, do they have enough warning."

"Even twenty-four-pounders, or eighteen-pounders, would serve, Captain," Mr. Winwood commented. "Is there a matching battery near the Pointe de Grave, the cross fire would effecively close the narrows."

"I'd wager on the lighter guns," Lewrie reluctantly had to agree. "Hell, even *twelve-pounders* could do the job . . . fire and be reloaded quicker, and engage even rowboats. I don't see the French investing all that many *expensive* guns in a place like that, Old King Louie was right . . . a determined fleet of Third Rates, with the equivalent of a regiment or two of foot, could open the narrows in one day. Take Royan and Saint Georges, *and* all of Pointe de Grave right down to this Soulac 'By The Sea'.

"And, why in Heaven does a French town honour Saint George?" he concluded.

"Eleanor of Aquitaine, sir," Lt. Urquhart piped up. "All this once was English territory, when Henry Plantagenet, our good old King Henry the Second, married her, 'stead of King Louis the Seventh! We owned it 'til the 1450s. Where we get our best clarets. I believe, ah . . . ," Urquhart said, beginning almost whimsically amused, but ending stiff-backed and ready to cough into his fist for slipping from his usual grim demeanour. "The city of Bordeaux was our capital of the province."

"I see," Lewrie said with a wry twinkle. "Source of claret, indeed. The Médocs, Haut-Médocs, and Saint Emilions, the white Graves, and the sweet, white Sauternes, as well, Mister Urquhart?" he teased.

"All do come from here, sir," Urquhart gravely intoned, lifting his telescope as if it was his prime duty to peer at the southern shore by Pointe de Grave.

Poor, sober-sided bastard was Lewrie's thought; *still and all, I could've gotten a "Merry Andrew" for a First Officer, who'd run us ashore some dark night, and try t'make a jape of it.*

He looked forward as *Savage*'s bows were swung up into the wind . . . what there was of it. Besides the odd Lt. Urquhart and his wary ways, there were several more new faces aboard, despite the majority of *Proteus*'s people turning over into *Savage.* Men holding Admiralty Warrant, once appointed into a warship, usually remained with her all their careers, unless they asked for transfer, even when their ships were laid up in-ordinary.

There was Bosun George Thomlin, for instance, a burly, balding older fellow who had come with *Savage,* as had his Mate, John Ellison, and the ship's Carpenter, Thomas Fisher. Along with them had come some replacement hands, strangers to one and all in the beginning, to fill the shoes of dead or crippled *Proteus* men.

There was a new Marine Corporal Dudley, a sour, taciturn, and so far thoroughly unpleasant ass. There were two new Surgeon's Mates now that Mr. Durant had finally gotten his long-delayed promotion; Arthur Ford, who had been seasick nearly half the time since they'd left Portsmouth, and a dark and heavyset "grump" by name of Harold Gaines. There was a new Gunner's Mate named Foster, a new Quartermaster by name of Raymund; a very gloomy new-come Yeoman of the Sheets named Orwell; an entirely new Purser's Assistant, the "Jack in the Breadroom," who was, wonder of wonders, both scrupulously honest (so far) and energetically aspiring. Well, he was *very* young! The Midshipmen, of course, and at least a dozen fresh hands, most of them dredged up by the Shire Quotas Act, all rated Landsmen, and as clumsy as drunken steers, and Lewrie was still sorting them all out for strengths and weaknesses, and he and Lt. Urquhart had spent many hours going over the muster book and watch lists to sort out the chaff, and re-enforce the weak with better help.

" 'Ware, the point, sir!" Lt. Urquhart called out. "There *is* a fort of some kind on Pointe de Grave. Just there, sir . . . this side of the village. Le Verd . . . what the Devil it's named."

Lewrie raised his own glass and put it to his eye, trying not to look urgent or concerned, as a captain must; nothing good ever came of instilling panic. "Ah-ha, yes," he said instead as the place became steady in his ocular.

Can't sail closer t'the wind, inside two miles o' shore, we're in their range, *and they'll shoot the* shit *out of us if we dawdle along on this next-t'nothin' wind!* Lewrie thought, though; *watched us sailin' in, the last* hour! *Heated shot? Fourty-two-pounders? Christ!*

"It looks to be just where a small stream splits and runs down to the sea in three rivulets, sir," Lt. Urquhart said with the proper amount of stoicism; perhaps the dull note to his voice came from a lack of Lewrie's fervid, dread-filled imagination. "No flag, though. Quite a lot of *activity,* but . . ."

"Well, damn my eyes, Mister Urquhart,"

Lewrie said with what a casual and objective observer might have called a giggle of relief. "I do b'lieve the place is still being built!"

I know I'm not livin' right t'earn such luck, but just thankee, Jesus! he thought.

The fortification near Le Verdon sur Mer indeed was unfinished. There were no crenellations atop its low wall for guns, yet; in fact, it appeared that the sloped stone walls were still being erected, and were barely above the height of a tall man, so far. There *were* Frenchmen in uniform, but very few of them, all now engaged in using their telescopes to peer at *Savage,* waving their arms, and most-like blathering agitated Frog, with much use of *"Sacré Bleu," "Mort de Ma Vie," "Zut Alors,"* and *"Nom d'un Pipe!"* Almost everyone else over there, now scuttling to the rear and into the shelter of the village, seemed to be *civilian* Frogs, and workmen!

"Make a note, Mister Winwood," Lewrie said, lowering his glass. " 'Til we know their weight of metal, once they get their fort completed we go no closer than three miles to the Pointe de Grave peninsula, either."

"I will see to it, sir," Winwood replied with a grunting moo.

"Deck, there!" a lookout called. "Brig t'larboard! Three mile off, an' fetched-to! She's runnin' up 'er flag, an' makin' a hoist!"

"Midshipman of the watch?" Lewrie demanded, though still unsure of which of his new-comes would respond.

"Aye, sir!" Midshipman Dry, their youngest, piped up.

"Make our number to the brig, and conjure me who she is," Lewrie ordered. "And decypher her signal hoist from this month's book."

Midshipman Dry quickly referred to his loose bundle of private signals, and the Navy's list of ship names and numbers, then crisply announced, "She is the brig-sloop *Erato,* sir. Commander James Kenyon."

"Aha," Lewrie said, tensing up a little, for he had hoped that she would be *Mischief,* that he and Hogue could share a glass or two as they conferred, and re-lived old times. "And her hoist?"

"Her number and this month's recognition code, sir," Dry said.

"Very well," Lewrie said with resignation. "Any idea of how long 't will be before we crawl up abeam of her, Mister Gamble?"

"Half an hour, sir?" Gamble replied with a cock of his head and a shrug.

"Once we *do* stagger up abeam of her, Mister Gamble, we'll come about and fetch-to. Mister Dry, assumin' it doesn't take so long that the watch changes, be ready to hoist 'Captain Repair Onboard' to her. Just now, though, young sir, I'd admire did you pass word for my cabin servant, and inform Aspinall we'll have a guest, aft. Perhaps even two for supper."

"Aye aye, sir!" Dry chirped.

Assumin' I don't kill the bastard 'fore the soup!
Lewrie thought.

CHAPTER
TWENTY-TWO

One could usually tell a lot about a sea-captain by how well his ship was kept, despite the ravages of sun, storm, or the inevitable depletion of Bosun's stores after a long voyage, or, in this case, a long time on-station. HMS *Erato* seemed at first to prove that truism, once *Savage* had fetched-to to seaward of her, about a cable to windward.

She was a trim little ship, perhaps 110 feet on the range of the deck, maybe 135 to 140 overall from taffrails to the tip of her bowsprit, about 30 feet abeam, and might draw no more than 12 feet. Lewrie could count eight gun-ports along the beam facing him, and pick out the light 18-pounder carronades she mounted in place of chase guns on her fo'c'sle and flush quarterdeck. Her masts were well painted, her spars oiled, but . . . her sails were the colour of ancient parchments. The running and standing rigging was geometrically taut, the standing well tarred, and the running looked fat and amply slushed with fats skimmed off the cauldrons as salt-meat rations were boiled up.

So far, so good, for no matter his dislike of Kenyon, the man had always been a proper sailor. Yet, it was the little things that made Lewrie wonder.

Erato's figurehead was not an approximation of a Grecian legend, but a simple, rather crudely chopped crowned lion torso, the sort that got churned out by indifferent wood-workers by the dozen, and bore not a single flake of gilt paint trim. The same went for *Erato*'s beakhead rails, entry-port, quarter-deck bulwarks, and counter. Lewrie had not kept track of Kenyon's career, but could only conclude that he either didn't care about the niggling details of decoration, or had no money beyond his naval pay, and could not afford such niceties.

A brig-sloop could not store much more than three months of victuals, rum, beer, or water, so she could not have been standing guard over the Gironde much longer than that, yet . . . her gunwale hull stripe paint was fading, flaking, and peeling, the original blue colour now so pale that she looked as if she hadn't seen a lick of Admiralty-issued paint in over a year, and had gone through several whole gales to boot!

In reply to his hoist of "Captain Repair On-board," a twenty-five-foot cutter was being rowed over from *Erato* to *Savage*, with

Kenyon in the stern-sheets, sitting upright in a boat cloak against the sullen rain.

The cutter, in comparison, was a pristine thing of beauty, with a shiny white hull and royal blue gunn'ls, and the oars being plied by her crew were painted white, with bright blue blades, and the shafts where sailors' horny hands gripped had been turned-down at least a foot with ropework.

The boat's crew and Cox'n were equally rigged out, dressed in a uniform manner as clean and natty as Sunday Divisions. Slop-trousers that had never seen slush or tar, so white they might have been pipe-clayed like Marines' kit; bright red solid-colour shirts under the typical short blue jackets with white tape or piping on every seam, and glittering brass buttons. As the boat came alongside, oars aloft and dripping, Lewrie could see that every man aboard her wore white cotton stockings and fresh-blacked shoes with newly polished brass buckles.

"They'd do an Admiral proud, sir," Lt. Gamble commented.

"Indeed," Lewrie drawled back. "Though I dare say *Savage* makes a much better impression, compared to *her* shabbiness."

"Erm . . . they're awfully . . . *handsome* lads," Midshipman Dry said in an aside to Midshipman Grisdale.

"Indeed," Grisdale agreed in his top-lofty, nasal voice.

Lewrie raised a handy telescope and quickly scanned *Erato*'s bulwarks and gangways. Those sailors yonder were nowhere near as natty as the boat crew, their slop-clothing the usual stained, patched, and ragged motley, their shirts mismatched from several baled lots of calico or gingham, and from appearances, stripped from dead beggars and turned down by rag-pickers. The most slovenly of *Savage*'s people looked like footmen at a formal supper by comparison.

Captain's "pets"? Lewrie silently sneered as he stowed the telescope back in the binnacle cabinet; *Kenyon's hareem? Well, a captain is second next to God at sea, and sets the rules.*

He returned to the head of the starboard gangway ladder just as the Bosun's calls began to shrill, the officer of the watch, Lt. Gamble, presented his sword, and the Marines stamped and slapped their boots and palms. Commander James Kenyon's hat had just loomed over the lip of the entry-port, and the ritual was on.

Damn, he's got old! was Lewrie's first impression. In 1780 he had been a trim and lean figure of a man, a fellow who certainly could have been considered handsome and fetching, but now . . . !

As Kenyon doffed his hat in return salute, he revealed heavily salt-and-pepper hair, more salt than anything else, greatly receded at his temples, thin atop, and worn long and combed straight across like seaweed . . . *pomaded* to stay in place to cover his advancing baldness in strands!

Kenyon's features, once so regular and dashing-handsome, had a sad old hound's thick and flaccid droopiness, heavily lined and just a touch pale, too. His body looked to be as lean as Lewrie dimly recalled; perhaps a touch too lean, for his uniform seemed to hang upon his frame, as if he was ill with something.

"Welcome aboard *Savage,* sir," Lt. Gamble said.

"Thank you, sir," Kenyon replied, though looking aft at Lewrie with what could be taken for a wry, secret smile.

"Commander Kenyon, welcome aboard," Lewrie was forced to say as he walked up to him, lifting a hand to his hat.

"Captain Lewrie," Kenyon responded, doffing his hat again. He sounded a bit bemused, and still wore that taut, wry expression as if he found the situation funny, which immediately raised Lewrie's hackles. "I am glad to see that the French did not put a ball or two through yer hull when you swanned into their range. Didn't anyone warn you of the fort on the north shore?"

No, yer not! Lewrie thought, irked at once; *you'd've adored it!*

"Well, perhaps we should go aft to my cabins, then, Commander," Lewrie all but snarled, though keeping a smile on his own phyz whilst he said it, "so you may impart t'me your vast store o' knowledge about the Gironde defences . . . and save me from myself!"

Lt. Gamble, and Midshipmen Dry and Grisdale, all winced or made *moues* over that retort, sure that their captain would put this fellow in his place, right smart, though it didn't seem to have any effect on Kenyon, whose face still bore that bemused look.

"But, of course, Captain Lewrie," Kenyon said, allowing himself a broad, tooth-baring grin.

Damn my eyes, is he drunk? Lewrie thought as he caught a whiff of wine on the man's breath; *and, teeth so grey, it looks as if he's been on the fifteen shillin' Mercury Cure for the Pox!*

"This way . . . Commander," Lewrie offered.

"A glass of something, sir?" Lewrie asked once they were seated at their ease in the great-cabins, at the collapsible settee and matching chairs. "Claret? Brandy? American bourbon whisky? Cold tea?"

"*Cold* tea?" Kenyon asked with a brow up, seemingly appalled.

"Quite refreshing in summer," Lewrie told him, "as I discovered in the West Indies. With an admixture of sugar and lemon."

"Brandy, I s'pose," Kenyon allowed, then, as Aspinall fetched a brandy for him, and a glass of white wine for Lewrie, swivelled about to look at the cabins' furnishings, that brow still up in nigh-mocking appreciation; just one more thing that raised Lewrie's dander. Maybe Kenyon liked the wine-cabinet and the desk in the day-cabin, the table and chairs, and the side-board in the dining-coach, or Caroline's portrait hung on the bulkhead . . . the wide-enough-for-two hanging cot?

"*Heard* you married," Kenyon said after a deep sip. "Your wife, there? Handsome woman."

"Aye," Lewrie said. "And you?"

"No . . . not yet," Kenyon said with the same sort of easy smile that Lewrie could recall. "What's the old saying, 'marry in haste, repent at leisure'? Besides," he simpered, crossing his legs and shifting rather uneasily in his chair, "between the Navy, and merchant service, *and* long spells of half-pay ashore, I never seemed to be able to amass the wherewithal to set up a proper household, and it always felt wrong to me to force a trusting lass to share my poverty, hah hah!"

Same old Kenyon, Lewrie thought whilst keeping a straight face; *still playin' the upright, rugged sort o' man, knowin' just the right dissemblin' blather t'say.*

"You, though, Lewrie," Kenyon continued

in a jovial manner, "I must imagine you're *rolling* in prize-money by now, and have got right famous, to boot, so maintaining a household for wife and kiddies is no bother. Pocket change, what? Though, your recent *legal* matter is . . ."

"Tell me all you know of the fort by Saint Georges de Didonne, Commander Kenyon," Lewrie coldly rejoined. *Damme, does he imagine I'm still his raw "Johnny New-come" Midshipman?* "And, tell me all you know of a French fisherman name of Jules Papin . . . or any others of his ilk. Who you think are spyin' on us, who you think are dis-affected, and a reliable source of information. Give me all the cautions."

It was as if he'd reached over and slapped the man in the face! Kenyon recoiled, and for a revealing second, allowed his face to slip from that taut, self-controlled bemused expression to one of hot, slit-eyed hate! Which was as quickly erased; with a step between anger, and the requisite subordinate's blandness, that came across as stunned and blank as that worn by someone head-butted and concussed!

"I see," Kenyon at last said, nodding slowly in recognition of his place in the universe, as if he'd expected better, but Lewrie (the top-lofty, lucky bastard!) would always be a disappointment. "Papin, well . . . he and four or five others dare to fish almost out of sight of

339

land, sir. Most are to be distrusted, really, for anything beyond wines, or fresh victuals from shore. I've attempted to vary my routes about the estuary, the times I appear, and the boats I stop, so, are any of them passing information to our opposition in the French Navy . . . to a merchantman wishing to slip past the blockade, *Erato,* and the cutters, are unpredictable.

"It may make no difference, though," Kenyon continued, shaking his head in the negative, "for any fool with a telescope may lurk atop the dunes, back in the shadows of the pine forests, up in any church's bell tower, and take our daily measure. For all the famous vineyards, and the great *châteaux* up-river, this portion of Médoc, or Aquitaine, is a bleak and grim place, near the sea. Rather boring, I expect, in peacetime, for blockading it is boring enough now."

"My first impression of this coast *does* put me in mind of the American Carolinas, aye," Lewrie cautiously allowed, squelching anger at the recent lack of respect and proper deference; but, ready to slap Kenyon down sharply if he presumed again. "Pine forests, settlements miles apart, and barrens between . . . salt pans and salt works?

"What of the small-boat fishermen, then?" he asked. "Any o' them t'be trusted?"

There were a few, Kenyon informed him, but they knew little and did not come far out to sea; one had to go to them, sometimes in one's jolly boat, launch, or oared cutter, and even then, they didn't venture far from their seaside villages, and rarely went up-river, so they had little of value to impart.

The fort by St. Georges de Didonne? It had only been completed the year before, and was reputed to be thinly garrisoned, with only the French equivalent of British 18-pounders and 24-pounders, perhaps no more than nine guns altogether atop the main ramparts, with about half a dozen 6-pounders and swivels in the sea-level water battery. Kenyon had heard rumours that the French had re-enforced the place with a *few* 32-pounders so they could close the narrows, but no one really knew if that was true, or what the French *wished* the British to think.

The smaller fort on Pointe de Grave, less a fort than a battery, really, had been under construction only a few months before *Erato* had come to the Gironde, and the work seemed to be going slowly. Certainly the French were even more months away before any artillery was put in place, or its magazines filled with powder.

"Saint Fort sur Gironde," Lewrie speculated over a second glass of Rhenish, "up where the river isles split the channel, and force any ship into close range . . . might they be stripping it of guns and shot, Commander Kenyon? After all, it's not all that likely that our Fleet'd barge that deep towards Bordeaux, and surely the Frogs can see that it doesn't serve 'em any use. Move its guns and garrison up here to the bay, instead . . . shift some warships up from Bordeaux to . . . what the Devil's its name? Talmont, that's it. Cutters, gunboats, or galleys into the shelter of the cove in the lee of Le Verdon sur Mer? That'd provide a quicker response. You ever see any Frog warships this far down-river, sir?"

"Very rarely, Captain Lewrie," Kenyon replied, almost wincing as if using the younger, but senior, officer's rank galled him. "And, if a merchantman is trying to thread through the blockade, they, or so I have been told by local fishermen . . . so you may put as much stock as you may in the truth of it . . . anchor under the battlements of Saint Fort sur Gironde itself, and let slip round ten o'clock of an evening . . . and only on nights when it's as black as a boot, sir."

"Do we get all that many 'runners,' Commander Kenyon?"

"Not really, sir," Kenyon told him, musing nose-deep over what had to be his third glass of brandy since coming aboard. "The French need so much of their own produce or manufacture to support their wars that they cannot spare much to export, beyond their wines and brandies. The bulk of the ships we've seen and made prize . . . or frightened off . . .

342

have been so-called neutrals trying to get *in*."

And, so Kenyon informed him, while the French still built ships of war at the Bordeaux yards, and refitted and maintained a substantial number of older and lighter frigates, *corvettes* (the French term for sloops of war) and gunboats for local defence, there didn't seem to be good odds for that glorious yardarm-to-yardarm battle of which Admiral Lord Boxham had spoken so longingly.

"Not a promising place to reap a pot of prize-money, here, sir," Kenyon said with a sullen sigh. "One hopes . . . ," he trailed off, deep in his cups of a sudden, as if the brandy had snuck up upon him like a pick-pocket. "The outer squadrons catch most. We're nigh pointless."

"Well, if the French won't amuse us, we'll just have to amuse ourselves," Lewrie determined with a chuckle, and thanking his stars that Kenyon was sinking so fast that it would be *impossible* to offer him supper, else he'd be charged with *drowning* the bastard in the aforementioned soup course, as he went face-down in it, and utterly comatose. "Raise some mischief . . . keep our hands in, hey? What operations have we conducted against them, since you've been on-station, Commander?"

"Huh? Oh, we . . . keep our eyes peeled," Kenyon replied with a sleepy slur, "stop fishing boats and do inspections, don't ye know . . . ask questions of 'em, and confiscate any contraband. Things like that."

"*That's* about t'change," Lewrie declared. "Now I've been put in command of the close blockade, hereabouts, we'll come up with *some* devilment for the Frogs."

"*You* in charge?" Kenyon blurted out, sounding stunned, again; or sarcastic, it was hard to discern which. "Thought Lord Boxham or Commodore Ayscough'd sent you in to . . . snoop about, make a report . . . ?"

"Yes, Commander. I am in charge," Lewrie took great delight in telling the man.

"Always *were* a lucky bastard," Kenyon could barely be heard to mutter under his breath.

"I will call for your boat, Kenyon," Lewrie snapped, getting to his feet, and if that wasn't a bald hint for Kenyon to stir himself as well, he didn't know what it was. Kenyon slurped down the last of his current brandy to heel-taps, throwing his head far back to get it all, then shambled to his own feet, reeling on the gentle scend and roll of the frigate as she drifted. "*Look* at me, sir! In the *eyes*, sir!"

Kenyon tried, though his own gaze wandered rather wide-about.

"Do *not* make the mistake of familiarity with me again, hear me? Do *not* appear before me reeking of spirits again, either, Commander!" Lewrie barked, and, truth be told, greatly enjoying himself. "You are *supposed* t'be an experienced Commission Sea Officer, entrusted with the command of a King's ship, but believe me, Kenyon, that can be subject to change, do ye cross me, again! Un-der-*stood, sir?*" Lewrie shouted, so loud that anyone on the quarterdeck could hear him. "Aspinall," he said in a much calmer taking. "Pass the word for my Cox'n, that he is to help the Commander to the deck, and see that the Commander's boat is called alongside to bear him back to *Erato.*"

"Aye aye, sir," Aspinall meekly replied, and sped out of the cabins, for he had never heard his usually genial captain in such a rage directed at anyone, other than England's enemies.

"Yer supper'll be ready in half an hour, sir," Aspinall told him after *Erato's* boat had come and gone, and Kenyon had been seen over the side in a Bosun's sling, and into the cutter where his "pretty" sailors had received him with what might be called "fond and loyal" care.

Whatever Hell Lewrie had boasted he might deal the French, there was a lingering dread in him that, when the time came, he could not rely on Kenyon or *Erato.* Kenyon's jealousy, that long-ago detestation that he'd shown when down with Yellow Jack, and it had fallen to Lewrie as a Midshipman, the only "officer" aboard the *Parrot* schooner about to be taken by a French privateer. To

Kenyon's lights, he had done a most dishonourable thing . . . pretend to strike colours
'til the French were close-aboard, then fire
every weapon weak HMS *Parrot* possessed,
employing *dards de feu* — fire arrows — to
set the privateer's sails afire, and make their
escape as the privateer burned to the waterline. There had been no French survivors,
well . . . with half his own crew down with
fever, and quickly succumbing himself, Lewrie hadn't bothered much with plucking
enemies from the sea. There had been their
important passengers, Lord and Lady Cant-
ner, to consider, and keep from any more risk.

Kenyon had gone all huffy about it, once
he'd recovered to the point that he could
listen to the tale, and had gone all prim and
outraged at such a breach of gentlemanly
conduct, even to their foes. He had bought
Lewrie his first hanger, icily writing that he
would surely need it the next time Lewrie
was faced with an ethical dilemma, which
dilemma he would fail, and be called to account on the field of honour!

Spite aside, jealousy aside, Kenyon had had
a *miserable* career, might have spent *years* on
miserly half-pay, and too proud to stoop to
just *any* employment, while still a so-called
prestigious Sea Officer of the King. Only a
new war had put him back in the uniform he
loved.

He said *he did time in merchant service,*

Lewrie recalled; *and that might not've paid that well, either. Proud, priggish . . . punctilious over his precious honour, so . . . where did it all go, I wonder? How'd he reconcile all that with his secret life o' buggery?*

Lewrie considered a note to Ayscough questioning Kenyon's fitness, a request that *Erato* be transferred, but, at the moment, Lewrie had no real evidence against him . . . other than he was as drunk as a fiddler's bitch in mid-afternoon, and the sight of Kenyon and one of his long-ago friends kissing passionately a long, long time before.

No. Leery as he was concerning Kenyon, he would have to accept the notion that, for now, he'd put him in his place, and on warning to straighten up and serve . . . soberly, competently, and chearly.

Lewrie crossed his fingers over that hope as Lt. Urquhart got *Savage* under way, and out to sea for the night.

Damme, though, Lewrie also thought; *if blessing him out wasn't hellish-great fun!*

CHAPTER
TWENTY-THREE

Over the next few weeks, Lewrie could almost agree with Kenyon that blockade duty was boresome, indeed. If there *were* merchant ships attempting to enter the Gironde, they were caught further out to sea by the larger frigates that served with the line-of-battle ships. And if any vessel *was* prepared to depart Bordeaux, then the sight of Royal Navy ships, hull-up and prowling the river's mouth, put the wind up its master.

Given the tides, *Savage* could only spend a few hours deep in the estuary, and then only on fair-weather days, for the continual Westerly winds off the Bay of Biscay could gust up to half a gale without warning, pinning *Savage* on a lee shore, and, able to "beat" only sixty-six degrees off the eye of the wind, she could end up wrecked on either the north or south shores.

Such a "sack" limited the usefulness of the two brig-sloops of his small squadron, too, for, square-rigged as they were, they suffered the same limitations on how close they could go "full and by" should a blow arise. If the weather got really bad, they had two bad choices; attempt to work their way further out to sea, abandoning the blockade, or try to anchor in the estuary and ride it out, with both bowers down and dragging through the unfirm, sandy sea-bed.

It was the fore-and-aft rigged cutters — Lt. Umphries's eight-gunned *Argosy*, Lt. Bartoe's *Penguin*, and Lt. Shalcross's slightly larger ten-gunned *Banshee* — that could dare operate inside the invisible dividing line 'twixt Pointe de la Coubre and Soulac sur Mer on a regular basis.

After meeting and dining-in those three worthies, Lewrie could at least feel secure in his mind that his cutters were in good hands. Lt. Umphries was only twenty-two, and *some* Admiral's favourite, a lad with lots of "interest," and secure enough in his prospects to show a lot of sauce and high spirits. Lt. Bartoe, on the other hand, was in his mid-thirties, had little official favour, and *Penguin* was his very first independent command. He was, therefore, more hard-bitten and taciturn, but just as eager to get at the foe and prove himself, at last. Lt. Shalcross might as well have been a swash-buckling pirate from the first decades of the eighteenth century, from the days of Blackbeard, Stede Bonnet, and Captain Kidd; a very clever and aspiring fellow, with the most engaging and exuberant personality.

All three were growing tired of stopping the same fishing boats each day, of snooping within gun-range of the middling-sized fort near St. Georges de Didonne to draw fire, and nimbly tack about to frustrate the Frogs . . . or of taking a few pot-shots at the battery being built near Pointe de Grave to panic the local workers and slow progress.

Lt. Bartoe was eldest, the more senior by date of commission, so Lewrie gave him charge of all three cutters' daily operations, hinting that he would be highly pleased did the cutters make even more nuisances of themselves.

As for HMS *Mischief* and HMS *Erato,* Lewrie assigned them to work only slightly across the "dividing line," with *Erato* to stand sentry-go from Pointe de la Coubre to St. Palais sur Mer, and sometimes taunt the St. Georges fort, and for Hogue in *Mischief* to pace back and forth from the barren beach point below Soulac sur Mer to Pointe de Grave, and, if the wind allowed, get close enough to take the battery under fire along with the cutters, every now and then.

For himself and *Savage,* though, he could not risk her across the "line" he had drawn except for the rarest circumstance. Lewrie began to feel Commodore Ayscough's frustration with blockade duty, of commanding from a distance, no matter how short; of being there to protect all his smaller and weaker vessels should the French get so tired of them that they sortied to try to drive them off.

He "poached" a little instead, venturing north into Charlton's bailiwick, as far as the northern end of the Côte Sauvage peninsula, to the southern tip of Ile d'Oléron and the Pertuis de Maumusson, the channel that led into the sheltered bay that lay behind the isle, and the maze of waterways near the towns of Marennes and La Tremblade.

To the south, *Savage* might cruise into Capt. Lockyear's territory as far as the north end of the Etang d'Hourtin-Carcans, a shallow "lake" back of the barren beaches 'twixt Hourtin and Maubuisson, just to keep the French honest. And to relieve the boredom of tacking at the stroke of every second watch bell from one bank of the estuary to the other, as predictably as a pendulum clock.

And, to make things even more boresome, Médoc and Aquitaine were unremarkable, with very flat land, no significant hills or headlands by which to navigate or take bearings. The pine forests were immense and dark, and from Soulac sur Mer south to Cap Ferret by Arcachon and its large basin, the dunes and beach were unbroken. When scouting outside his proper area, and going alongside Capt. Lockyear's 20-gun *Arundel* for a relatively merry "get to know each other" dinner, Lewrie learned that the coast Lockyear watched was much the same sameness, all the way to Biarritz and Bayonne in the Golfe de Gascogne. In yawning point of fact, Capt. Lockyear and his tiny squadron of cutters and schooners saw as little activity as Lewrie's, and, frankly, were beginning to make a few forays onto the beaches, just to break the monotony! At least in Lockyear's area of operations, there were several thin rivers, or wide creeks, that fed directly to the sea below Arcachon, where they watered without opposition!

Just Lewrie's luck, though . . . the only freshwater streams he'd spotted so far were near the tip of Pointe de Grave, that split into three rills by Le Verdon sur Mer, right by that bloody a'building gun-battery, and the closest freshwater lake, 'twixt Hourtin and Maubuisson, lay more than two miles behind the beach, the dunes, and the sea! But, the idea of armed landing-parties *was* tempting.

"Have you ever heard an estimate of how many French troops there are in Médoc, or cross the river in Saintonge, sir?" Lewrie asked one day over dinner when Commodore Ayscough, as weary of offshore plodding as he, had brought HMS *Chesterfield* to within five leagues of the shore, and had stumbled upon *Savage* first.

"Can't say that I have, sir," Ayscough had

to admit, frowning. "Your cutters do you proud, by the by, and I am grateful for your kind offer of all this fresh butter. Goes well with the equally fresh rolls. Though, I'd adore did you fetch off a sheep. Why do you ask, Lewrie?"

"Sheer, jaw-cracking boredom, sir," Lewrie said, chuckling. "I spoke Captain Lockyear, and —"

"*Told* you you'd like him!" Ayscough jovially interrupted. "Got on like a house afire, I'd wager?"

"Aye, sir, we did, indeed, but . . . ," Lewrie began again, explaining the watering and shooting parties that Lockyear was performing upon his own beaches and streams, supplying his crews with fresh game meat as well as potable water. "He reported very little opposition, almost next to nothing, sir. Surely, there's more we might be doing than just . . . swanning about and stopping the odd fishing smack. There is that battery being built on Pointe de Grave, for one. I'd dearly love to have a go at it before it's completed. Several kegs of powder, all of my Marines, and a boat or two of armed seamen from each brig or cutter to run off the few French troops we've seen, and we could blow it sky-high.

"But, there's no peeking round the point into the two shallow bays east of Le Verdon sur Mer," Lewrie complained, "not with t'other fort cross the river able to fire completely across the Gironde."

Pointe de Grave tapered to the nor'east; immediately to the east was a wide, sweeping, but small bay where all sorts of shipping, or gunboats, might lurk. In fact, after peering over the charts for hours on end, Lewrie had come to think of Pointe de Grave as a dragon's head . . . the point itself was an erect crest, the shallow bay below it on the river was the slope of its snout, and, below that, he could imagine the mouth and fangs, for a very narrow small peninsula dashed due south as a natural breakwater very much like a long fang to protect the harbour of Le Verdon sur Mer, which looked like an opened mouth, with another equally narrow peninsula or breakwater jutting East like a thin lower jaw. Below that, where a stout neck would meet an upper torso, lay one more cove, which the charts indicated had sufficient depth for lighter coastal shipping . . . and all of it as unknown as the blank swathes of an unexplored continent; *terra incognita,* indeed.

"We've not learned all that much about the fort by Saint Georges de Didonne, either, sir, the weight of its artillery, or the strength of its garrison," Lewrie explained, "whether there's a rampart on the land face, or whether it's an open, three-faced *lunette.* Before hostilities commenced, the French guarded the Gironde with Saint Fort sur Gironde, far

354

up-river, and most-like maintained a substantial garrison at Bordeaux, but now . . . who knows? That they're building these two forts or batteries may indicate they've stripped Saint Fort of troops, powder, shot, and heavy artillery, and have elected to defend closer to the sea."

"Doubtful we'd ever muster sufficient forces to raid that deep up the Gironde, really," Ayscough mused aloud, knife poised ready for a thick smear of mustard on his mutton chop, "not after the debacle of the Vendée landings. Trusted Royalist Frogs to raise their commoners, what, and spring to arms with Great Britain? Thank God we didn't lose all *that* much when it failed . . . prestige notwithstanding."

He took a bite of his mustardy mutton, chewed blissfully for a moment, then took a sip of wine. "Aye, it is possible that the French *have* shifted troops and guns nearer the estuary. The risk to our own side in sending Third Rates and frigates up-river, with the Westerly winds square in their teeth in a narrowing stream should they be deterred, would be too great. Take whole *regiments* . . . perhaps an entire *brigade* of Army troops, as well. And, you and I know for certain that such an undertaking would have to be schemed and planned in London at Horse Guards, which might take two *years* before a decision was reached, *then* shuffled over to

Admiralty, where *another* two years of muddling would be necessary. Hmmpf! Wish we could do something active, though. Your French fishermen . . . they've related nothing of value?"

"Some of the larger boats, and some middling-sized, do venture out past Pointe de Grave or Pointe de la Coubre, sir, and they've come to accept *Savage*'s presence as a minor nuisance, not a threat to their livelihoods or boats . . . and, a source of coin for whatever they might smuggle out. All our vessels hereabouts are reckoned good customers."

"As I told you, ha ha!" Ayscough rejoined as he buttered a new roll. "A few silver shillings go a long way."

"They're locals, though, sir," Lewrie bemoaned, "and never get up-river, so they know nothing of note about Bordeaux, or the condition of the old fortress. They've no reason to enter the local forts . . . or, the French Army won't let 'em, for fear of what they'd see. A *few* of the captains *sound* like they'd sell information, if the reward was big enough, but . . . I'm still not sure which of 'em I can trust."

"Well, there is that," Ayscough said with a wry rolling of his eyes over the perverse slyness of the French. "Damme, though, Lewrie . . . wouldn't it be fine to put together an expedition to both of these pesky fortifications! Recall our assault on the pirate lair and fort in the Spratly Islands, or our two-pronged attack on Balabac, in the Spanish Philippines, where we ran that fiend, Guillaume Choundas, to earth, at last, ha ha! What grand times those were!

"What sort of force might you muster for the landing?" Ayscough suddenly demanded, intrigued, and savoury mutton chops bedamned.

"My own Marine complement would amount to forty-three, and off the brig-sloops, another fifty-six, sir," Lewrie told him, having done some preliminary scribblings over the last few days of *ennui*. "About ninety to an hundred armed sailors off all six vessels, before our artillery and sail-tending suffer. Not nearly enough, sorry t'say."

"No Marines aboard your cutters and such, aye," the Commodore grumped. "*But!* Should you smoak out the particulars anent what force the French own, and does it sound feasible, I have seventy-odd Marines aboard *Chesterfield*. Perhaps in a month or two, the second sixty-four I requested *may* turn up, with a matching number of Marines available, and, with two sixty-fours, I might be able to assemble about an hundred and fifty sailors to go ashore with them. *And,* bring both liners inside the estuary to take the *lunette* fort by Saint Georges under my fire, to boot. My God! Charlton!"

"Sir?"

"I'd wager a *rouleau* of gold guineas Charlton would leap at the chance, and be heartbroken to be left out!" Ayscough hooted. "That'd add another fourty Marines and perhaps fifty sailors to the endeavour. And, does your plan seem intriguing to Lord Boxham, I might be able to convince him to close the coast with two or three of his Third Rates, and add his own Marines and tars to the landings. Lewrie, you dog! A man after mine own heart! A glass with you, sir, and success to you in discovering all needful facts."

Cabin stewards refilled their glasses from a bottle of Château d'Issan Bordeaux, a splendid little wine from a local seventeenth-century vineyard little known beyond the Médoc region so far, but one that both Ayscough and Lewrie thought a treasure that went well with the mutton.

While it was more than pleasant to have Commodore Ayscough toast him, and declare him an aggressive and active fellow possessed of such uncanny wit and wile, Lewrie thought there was one niggling hitch to such praise . . . he would now have to *deliver.*

It was one thing to speculate idly, and quite another to enter into a thorough investigation, which would require long hours questioning French fishermen; cajoling, getting drunk, bribing, and playing a spy's game to determine whether he was being told the truth, the half-truth, or having his leg pulled, and two out of three could prove fatal.

Then, perhaps gulled like one of Clotworthy Chute's newly come heirs, or haying the entire French defensive plan laid before him like Moses' first peek at the Commandments, he would actually have to *plan* a complicated operation . . . with *his* head on the chopping block did it go awry!

Oh, won't this *be just* bags *o' fun!* he sarcastically thought as he clinked glasses with Ayscough; *should've kept me bloody gob stopped! What* was *I thinkin'? This is more Twigg's game than mine. Sortin' fact from fiction. Christ. Don't know if I'm* bright *enough for it!*

Another realisation struck him, right after that doubt. Well, two realisations, really. The first was that, whenever in his life, be it in his personal life or his naval career, he had felt sly-boots and clever, Dame Fortune usually woke from her nap and came down from Mount Olympus to kick him firmly in the fundament.

The second was that he would have to make nice of a sudden with *Capitaine* Jules Papin, and that might be just too horrid to contemplate.

CHAPTER
TWENTY-FOUR

"D'ye trust any of the fishermen ye run across?" Lewrie asked of Commander Nathaniel Hogue some days later, and finding it remiss of him to have served with the younger man in the Far East, yet never learned his Christian name 'til then. "This Papin fellow, for instance?"

"Oh, him!" Hogue said with a wry chuckle. "Frankly, sir, I am surprised he hasn't crammed a dozen local whores aboard his boat, and pimped them out to us on a day-rate. Papin is a thorough rogue, in my humble opinion. Rogue enough to sell information, at any rate. And . . . so far, what little he's grudgingly related to me, or the cutters, has proven true. Mind now, Captain Lewrie," Hogue cautioned, "I only speak of *shilling* revelations, not gold. Lieutenants Bartoe, Shalcross, and Umphries and I hold much the same opinion of *M'sieur* Papin, and where his loyalties lie . . . which is in personal profit."

Such a confident young man, Lewrie

thought, recalling the last time he'd served with Hogue, when the lad had been a somewhat shy and diffident cully, a tad naïve of the ways of the world, and straight as a die. Now, though, after years of service, and "on his own bottom,' Hogue was as chirpy as a magpie, and just about as sure of himself. In those days, when Hogue had contracted the Pox from some Chinese whore, he'd blushed and stammered and skulked in shame like a pregnant nun . . . *Damme, was I a bad influence on him, back then?* Lewrie asked himself; *most-like, aye.*

"I've something in mind, sir," Lewrie told him over glasses of cold tea in *Savage's* great-cabins; late summer in the Bay of Biscay was warm days and muggy seaside nights, just enough so to make the cold tea refreshing. "Do we gather enough information to improve our odds, we might have a chance to reduce the battery on Pointe de Grave, and may even convince Lord Boxham to bring some of his 'liners' inshore to help take the fort cross the river, too. The biggest snag, o' course, will be what forces the French maintain hereabouts, and where; what weight of artillery we really face, and how quickly the local garrison could march to counter us. May not come off, but . . ."

"Oh, finally, sir!" Hogue crowed, rocking boyishly on his chair with a hand clasping a raised knee. "We've spent weeks and weeks just staring at that new battery as it is being erected, at last being allowed to *fire* upon it . . . well, to land, take it, and slight it would just be delightful."

"Just watching it being built?" Lewrie asked, puzzled. "How so?"

"Well, sir . . ." Hogue reddened slightly, and lost his buoyant airs. "Far be it from me to say anything uncomplimentary, or insubordinately, of a senior officer, but . . ."

"Don't know why not," Lewrie cynically scoffed, " 'tis usually a hellish-good relief."

"Uhm, in that case, sir, since you put it that way," Hogue said in a soft voice, all but peering squint-a-pipes in the dark corners of Lewrie's quarters to see if there might be a witness to his disloyalty, "Commander Kenyon said our chiefest role was stopping commerce entering or departing the Gironde, sir. That we were not to risk our vessels by entering the possible gun-range of the Saint George fort, or dare to go East of Point Grave. We could stop and search as many fishing boats as we wished, and *ask* of doings ashore, but that was to convince the French of the impossibility of any imports or exports, and, by not confronting their guns, or giving them any chance to do us harm, foment in French minds a notion of our . . . invincibility, and inevitability."

"Ahum . . . I see," Lewrie slowly drawled, a dark frown forming on his face. "Well, such *might* be decent goals, but . . . once the battery on the point is finished, such orders and cautions would force us to give *it* a wide berth, too. Convincing the Frogs that, do they build a set of batteries up the north shore, we could be frightened out beyond Pointe de la Coubre, or three miles to seaward of Soulac sur Mer!"

"Assuming, as we have, sir, that the French possess fourty-two-pounder guns in sufficient number," Hogue pointed out. "The Commander may have decided that the few men we have aboard our ships could make no impression on the Saint George fort, for certain, and could only delay the completion of the one on Point Grave . . . and, were we repulsed with casualties, fill the French with confidence."

"Defeats tend t'do that," Lewrie mused aloud. "If I thought the Frogs had four or five thousand troops they could whistle up on short notice, I'd be much of the same mind. But, so far we don't know just *how* dangerous a landing could be. And, we must find out."

"Just like the old days, isn't it, Captain Lewrie?" Hogue asked with a cheerful grin. "Chasing the French and Lanun Rovers from the Malacca Straits to Canton, and back . . . and but *slowly* knitting all of the clues together?"

"Very *much* like, aye," Lewrie agreed. "I

will speak *Erato* sometime this afternoon. For the nonce, I'd like you to pass word to our cutter captains, and tell them to begin pressing, cajoling, and bribing the fishermen even sharper. And, I would very much like for them to discover for me just what lies behind Le Verdon sur Mer. The port, the bay by the point, and that cove below the village."

"Uhm, if I may make a suggestion, sir," Hogue said. "But, we've come to name places more Anglicised, to avoid confusion. We say Point Grave, 'stead of Pointe de Grave, and say it like a churchyard *grave.* Verd'n . . . Saint George, 'stead of all that de Didonne flummery. Soo-Lack; Mashers, 'stead of Meschers sur Gironde, Point Coober, 'stead of de la Coubre, and Royan . . . well, that'un needs no change, but . . ."

"I *see,*" Lewrie said. "Well, thank God for't, for my French is next to nonexistent, and I mangle enough already. So, it'isn't the Côte Sauvage, it's the 'Savage Coast,' is it? *My* coast, perhaps? Or, might well be by the time I'm done with it, ha ha! Capital idea. Just 'cause the Frogs own 'em is no reason we have to go all nasal and 'hawn hawn' t'say 'em."

"Uhm, there will be another matter, Captain Lewrie," Hogue said in a more serious tone, "so far we purchase wine, foodstuffs, and *news* with shillings, half-crowns, and crown pieces, in silver, and, with the shortage of *specie* aboard our ships at present, and the shortage of it at home, we might need an infusion of *coin,* and how *that* may be found, or from whom, I've not the slightest hope. I seriously doubt that Admiralty would ship us out a keg or two o' guineas."

I'm suddenly so responsible for it I have to pay *for it, too?* Lewrie gawped to himself; *this could get as expensive as* lawyers!

"I'll sail out and speak to Commodore Ayscough again," Lewrie somewhat reluctantly vowed. "Who knows? Maybe his Scottish clan is richer than Midas. Maybe he could arrange a whip-round of his wardroom for *donations!* God knows, if Ayscough has to submit it to Lord Boxham, they both have to refer it to Admiralty, we'll still be spectators off this coast 'til *next* Epiphany."

"If Lord Boxham thinks it valuable, sir, he *might* give us some of his contingency funds," Hogue rather wistfully suggested.

"He wants what fleet the Frogs might have up by Bordeaux to come out, so he can crush 'em, Commander Hogue," Lewrie gravelled. "Ruining their forts, spikin' guns and all, might scare them out of the idea."

"There is that, sir, sad t'say," said Hogue, deflated.

"Perhaps we could bribe these fishermen in other ways, Hogue," Lewrie mused. "Bosun stores, lumber, spare canvas and such? With *rum?* Ragged as most of 'em dress, *slop-*

clothing might move 'em! Tell our cutter captains we must do it 'on the cheap,' but done it must be. If the French prove t'be too strong t'take on, then we won't become debtors and beggars. If the endeavour *does* prove practicable, then we've bought ourselves a victory for ha'pence."

"I shall be on my way, then, sir," Hogue declared after he had finished his cold tea, "and thank you for a most refreshing beverage. I must obtain some lemons from shore, do they grow them here, and emulate you."

"God speed, young sir, and it was *damned* good t'see you, after all these years. My congratulations 'pon your promotion, and command, and aye . . . now we work together again, as we did in the Far East, we may raise a *parcel* o' Mischief on the French, hey?" Lewrie said as he walked him to the quarter-deck.

"I await such with *all* avidity, Captain Lewrie!" Hogue assured him.

CHAPTER
TWENTY-FIVE

Another day, another disappointment, Lewrie glumly decided, as HMS *Savage* sidled up alongside yet another French fishing boat, nearly five miles off Soulac sur Mer, now better known as "Soo-Lack." He had met up with *Capitaine* Jules Papin and his *Marie Doux* several days past, but *rencontre* with that fish-smelly rogue had not exactly been all that productive in the way of information.

In other ways, Papin had proved true to his word, for his boat had produced nearly a sling-load of goodies from shore. Papin had promised cheeses and eggs, and he had come through, to the delight of the Midshipmen's mess, and the officers' wardroom, who had vowed to chip in and go shares. Navy-issue cheese came in two varieties; a Cheddar and something else unidentifiable, hard, and crumbly, both of which sprouted mould and simply *oozed* wormlets after a month or so at sea. These, though, were fresh, and as creamy, sweet, and soft on the tongue as pats of butter.

The eggs, several dozen of them, had probably not been candled to determine whether the shells hid tasty yolks or un-hatched chicks, but a quick inspection in front of a strong lanthorn could decide that, and, with luck, the broody hens already roosting in *Savage*'s forecastle manger would accept a few extras and keep them warm 'til they hatched . . . resulting in a few more roast chicken suppers for the fortunates.

Papin had come through with several straw baskets of fruit, as well; apples, pears, and such. There had been middling sacks of sugar and flour, baskets of table grapes, and bags of raisins. Three young suckling pigs, two smallish turkeys, and a kid goat . . .

"And a par-tri-idge in a pear tree!" Midshipman Mayhall had caroled, to the amusement of all, as he seized a bag of fresh cherries.

Small baskets of peas and beans, for *fresh* soups, not the reconstituted "portable" soup the Navy issued in gangrenous-looking slabs; salad greens, carrots, cabbages, and onions, oh my, it was a Godsend!

And for Lewrie, along with some foodstuffs, had come a case of wine, a mix of Médocs, Sauternes, and white Graves, along with the reds of the region from Château Margaux, Château Latour, Brave-Mouton and Lafite.

There were Batailleys, d'Issans, Loudennes, Paulliac and St.-Estèphe, and, wonder of wonders, a one-gallon stone crock of American bourbon whisky, which bore the stencil-painted mark of the Evan Williams distillery in far-off Bardstown, Kentucky!

"*Capitaine* Papin, you are a miracle worker!" Lewrie had told him.

"*Non, m'sieur,* I am ze smuggler, *miraculeux,*" Papin had sourly rejoined. "I am ze smuggler 'oo is to be *paid, n'est-ce pas?* Ze *dry* smuggler, in need of ze *rum,* hawn hawn."

They had repaired below to crack a bottle for Papin, which he'd keep, and a second bottle for his crew, to keep them sweet and silent. Lewrie dug into his coin purse and laid out the reckoning, allowing the Frenchman to see the gold guinea coins that he had placed in it just for that purpose.

"You are successful in prize-money, *Capitaine, hein?*" Papin commented as Lewrie laid the purse out of reach . . . but still in sight. Papin licked his lips and gave the wash-leather draw-string purse sly side-of-his-eye glances, and rubbed his *still* unshaven chin.

"Rather well, in fact," Lewrie told him. He thanked Papin for the delivery, striving to not sound *too* profusely grateful, hinting that a working arrangement, once a week or so, would be welcome.

"And . . . there is another matter, one you

raised when we first crossed hawses, *Capitaine* Papin," Lewrie said, striving, too, for off-handedness; idle curiosity, not avidity. "Concerning information?"

"Ah, *oui*, ze information, hawn hawn," Papin said, a hand inside his coarse and filthy smock to scratch his chest. "I do not know zat much, but . . ." He tossed back a deep slug of rum, keeping his eye locked on Lewrie's all the time. "What *m'sieur* wish to know?"

"Well, for one, do the gunners at Saint Georges de Didonne keep the guns manned round the clock? Damme, I must sail into the bay and keep watch, but I dislike being shot at all the time," Lewrie said in a forced chuckle. "*Savage* is a stout ship, but not proof against their fourty-two-pounders."

Papin smiled back, saying nothing; a particularly greasy smile.

"Mean t'say . . . ," Lewrie had gone on, feeling lame, "do they have enough troops t'maintain *three* watches?"

"Give me guinea, *m'sieur*," Papin soberly said, holding out his hand, palm up. "Garrison is small. Non 'ave 'eavy guns. *Dix-huit*, ze eighteens, *et* ze *douze?* Ze . . . twelves? Only ze six six-pounders in water battery, below, an' ze swivels. *Non* as much as you fear. Ze guinea . . . *vite, vite?*" he insisted, snapping his fingers.

Lewrie handed over a guinea coin, still

unsure if he was being twitted and taken for a fool; it sounded too good to be true. "Not as many as I fear, is it? How *many* of the heavier guns, *Capitaine?*"

"I see zem drill, I 'ave count, *Capitaine* Lirr . . . *m'sieur*," Papin growled as he slipped the coin into a slop-trouser pocket. "*Mon Dieu*, keep *Marie Doux* at Royan dock, 'ave home in Royan, an' when zey practice, zey keep *all* awake!

"Each face 'ave ze four openings, *oui?*" Papin explained, leaning forward. "Fort 'ave *two* of ze twelves, only *one* of ze eighteens, each face, *comprendre?* Only 'ave men each gun require, plus ze dozen more for keep watch, *hein?* Old *navire de guerre* at Bordeaux, rotted at piers, zey strip an' bring *ici* by ze barges. Ozzer old ships zat cannot sail, *l'Armée* strip, *aussi*, tak mos' guns to forts on Channel, to *l'Est* . . . on German frontier, *m'sieur.*"

"As they bring the stone for the Pointe de Grave battery walls?" Lewrie asked, pouring Papin another dollop of rum.

"*Oui*," Papin agreed, leaning back in his chair, legs extended. "Stone mus' come from ze Dordogne, zere is *beaucoup trop* sand in zis part of Médoc, an' Saintonge, cross river."

"Many barges?" Lewrie prompted. "Are they ever *escorted?*"

"*Une* more guinea," Papin tantalised, hand out once more.

"When you can tell me how many, and when they come," Lewrie said instead, slyly chuckling. "And, if they're escorted. I assume they put into that wee harbour behind Le Verdon sur Mer?"

"Sometime," Papin slowly allowed, with his own sly laugh.

"What *does* lie behind the point? In the port, bay, and cove?"

"*M'sieur,* you do not pay, I do not remember," Papin replied with an avaricious, oily grin. "Wish to know, I mus' go see. *Zen* you mus' pay me 'nozzer guinea. I do not go to Le Verdon zat often."

"Try this, then," Lewrie wheedled, handing over two shillings. "Where could I land boats and gather firewood and water without a risk of being attacked?" He spread a chart for Papin to look over.

Papin took the silver coins and shoved them into his pocket. "I wish wood an' water, *m'sieur,* I go ashore on La Côte Sauvage. Spend night, sometime, off beach . . . here. Get to fish before ozzers 'oo 'ave sleep in port. Fresh stream, *beaucoup* trees . . . almos' no one live zere, an' no soldier. *Presque jamais,*" he concluded with a shrug.

"*Hardly* ever, hey?" Lewrie translated, aloud, finding it droll. "Very well, then, *Capitaine* Papin. Fair enough. *Merci* for what you have told me so far. And, for all the wine, bread and butter, and the whisky. We must meet again . . . soon. Perhaps then, you will have learned more, and another guinea'd be a fair trade. Perhaps more, if you could learn how many troops there are here, say . . . within twenty miles of Royan or Pointe de Grave?"

"*Bon!*" Papin cynically cried, "I 'ave ze *devoirs,* ze a-sign-e-ment? I am good boy, I win ze prize, *hein? Oui,* I do zis *pour vous* . . . even if you are cursed *Anglais sanglant,* hawn hawn!"

Papin had thrown back the last of his rum, tucked the bottle in the large chest pocket of his smock, grabbed a second to take for his small crew — felt in his trouser pocket to re-count his money for a brief half-hour's work — and had gone on deck for his boat.

"Now who's this'un?" Lewrie asked as they sidled up near another decent-sized boat, out fishing beyond the hook of Point Coober. "Have we seen her before, Mister Urquhart?"

They both peered at a single-masted boat of about thirty feet or so, rigged with a small jib and a gaff-hung mains'l. She was worn and shabby, and held but three crew, none of whom seemed alarmed by a British frigate. She and HMS *Savage* were four miles to seaward of the coast, so there could be no escape for her. Oddly, though, she steered *towards* the frigate, putting Lewrie in mind of a similar boat full of maniacs and powder kegs, who had tried to blow HMS *Proteus* out of the water off St. Domingue's north coast during the British invasion of that gory French possession, and the slave-army's rabid resistance. Lewrie almost felt an urge to steer away, let this one go, just in case the Frogs had gotten so frustrated by the loss of commerce that a screeching, hair-pulling official in Bordeaux had asked for volunteers full of patriotism and hatred who'd take a British warship with them!

By the prickin' o' me thumbs, somethin' wicked this way comes? Lewrie thought.

"I *believe* I've seen her before, sir," Lt. Urquhart carefully ventured. "Something 'bout her sail patches, but . . . much closer down to Soulac than here, I *think* it was."

Lewrie peered at her with his telescope a piece more, then took a look about *Savage*'s decks. The swivel guns were manned and ready in the iron stanchion mounts atop the bulwarks, and at least ten Marines and a Corporal were in full kit and red uniforms, following his standing orders for dealing with so many inspections and searches.

She comes alongside, an 18-pounder ball dropped overside would sink her in a blink, he decided.

"She looks as if she *wants* t'be stopped, Mister Urquhart, so . . . we'll oblige," Lewrie said. "Fetch the ship to, if you please, sir.

Cox'n?" he called out.

"Aye, sor!" Liam Desmond piped up from below the quarterdeck in the waist, where he had been idly chaffering with his mates in Lewrie's boat crew.

"Bring the launch round from towing astern, and be ready to inspect yon fishing boat, Desmond. The usual drill . . . Marines and a Midshipman . . . this morning it's . . . Mister Mayhall," Lewrie ordered.

"Aye, sir!" the Midshipman cried, eager for something to do.

It took only minutes to swing *Savage* up to the wind, haul round the launch to the larboard entry-port, and get Desmond's oarsmen and a quartet of Marines and Midshipman Mayhall aboard. For a minute or so, it looked as if the fishing boat might try to come alongside, but just as soon as they saw the launch being manned, her captain took in sail and let her rock and toss on the ocean's scend to await a boarding.

"Bottle o' rum in my cabins, Aspinall," Lewrie casually ordered. "Same as usual. And lay out my coin purse. You know the drill."

"Aye, sir. I'll have a glass o' tea poured fer you, too. Th' same colour, p'raps this Frenchie won't know th' diff'rence, an' won't be insulted," his shrewd cabin servant replied. "Long as ye just sip at it slow, Cap'm," he cheekily added, "an' don't give the game away."

"Point taken, Aspinall," Lewrie laughed. "Off with you."

Back came the launch, to the starboard entry-port this time, as a sign of "honour" rendered, even to a civilian Frenchman. Four hands and four Marines made the saluting-party, and Bosun's Mate Ellison did a pipe on his silver call worthy of a Post-Captain, though it looked wasted on the fellow who scrambled up the battens and man-ropes.

"*Capitaine . . . bienvenu à bord,*" Lewrie said, going so far as to doff his hat, and receiving a sketchy knuckle to the right brow below the burly Frenchman's knit cap. "*Parlez-vous l'Anglais?*"

"*Oui,* I do," the husky fellow admitted.

"Captain Alan Lewrie, His Brittanic Majesty's Navy."

"Jean Brasseur, *Capitaine,*" the fellow answered. "Long ago, we are nam-ed Brass. You' Commandeur Ho . . . Hogue, *oui?* . . . he speak to me, uhm . . . las' week? Does he mention zis?"

"Not yet, no sir," Lewrie said, mystified. "*Brass,* did ye say your name was?"

"Long ago, *oui,* it was Brass," the fellow said with a chuckle of faint amusement. "Now, we 'ave live here so long in Aquitaine, we are known as Brasseur. Long *ago,* we were English, but now *Français.* You are serving ze rum, ze *arrack,* like ze ozzers, *oui?*"

"Whatever you wish, Captain Brasseur," Lewrie told him, becoming both fascinated and wary. Was the man a French agent who hoped to dispel mistrust with such a tale, so the Frogs could spin him lies?

"I adore ze fine brandy, *Capitaine*," Brasseur suggested, with a broader grin. "*Aussi*, uhm . . . also, I have ze fine fish to sell."

"Then, pray join me below," Lewrie offered, "where you may have an *excellent* aged brandy, and we may discuss what you have to sell."

Like all men who grow from boyhood to middle age in the fishing trade, Jean Brasseur was a weathered man, with exposed flesh seared to a dry, tanned leather. His hands were large and callused by nets and sail-tending lines, by oars and hard labour, his fingers blunt and his nails square-cut, with one or two missing. Like Papin and so many of the other fishermen that *Savage* had come across, Brasseur wore a loose *serge de Nîmes* smock over a plain ecru shirt and faded dark blue slop-trousers.

Unlike the others — perhaps for this meeting? — he was new-shaven, and his long, dark, and curly hair looked fresh-washed, too . . . and he didn't even *half* smell of fish!

"Ver' good brandy, *merci, Capitaine*," Brasseur said with a grin of pleasure. "Zese days, good brandy 'ard to find."

"More than welcome," Lewrie said, playing host and sipping at his tea — slowly, as Aspinall had directed. "You say your kin were once English?"

"All Aquitaine own-ed by *les Anglais*, three century, *Capitaine*," Brasseur explained with a large Gallic shrug, hitching himself upright on his chair. "Is 1400s when France take it back, at last. *Ma famille* come as *Anglais* soldier . . . *John* Brass, *peut-être* around ze 1390s? 'E marry local *jeune fille*, an' reside in Bordeaux for few year, but move to coast when France conquers. Zey change name to be more French, and, were always Catholique. End in ze quiet village, Le Verdon sur Mer, away from trouble? And, even if Médoc an' Aquitaine is French, *les Anglais* come for wines, trade, ze claret, which you *Anglais must* 'ave, *hein?*" Brasseur said with a wry chuckle. "We are trade wiz ships coming an' going, last-minute purchases. *Enfin*, take up ze fishing, *wiz* small trade in Médoc wines, which are ze *bon marché*, not like Bordeaux merchant."

"A quiet little place, indeed," Lewrie carefully began to ask, "at least 'til the war began. And, your army began to build the battery on the point."

"Ah, *mais oui*," Brasseur grumbled, "is no more ze nice, quiet. Noisy worker from Bordeaux, chip-chip-chip on stone, dawn to dark, an' ze mule, 'orse, an' ox make so much stink an' *merde,* oh la!"

"You're quite a way from Le Verdon this morning, though, sir," Lewrie pointed out (rather cagily, he thought to himself). "Do you always fish this far from home waters?"

"Oh, we 'ave more zan enough, before worker and soldier comes," Brasseur breezily dismissed, "ze mussel, s'rimp an' lobster, ze clam? Wiz zo many now 'oo wish, ze beds grow thin, an' I must sail far out for big fish, an' . . . 'ow you call, *poach* ze beds of La Palmyre for ze oyster, lobster, an' mussel. 'Ave you ever had ze *mouclade, Capitaine,* ze fresh mussel in white wine? Mmm, *magnifique!*" Brasseur said, with a kiss of his bunched fingers as he made yummy sounds. "O la, *chats!*" he cried as he espied Toulon and Chalky, who had come to see the new cabin guest, slinking almost to scratching range. *"Bons amis, les chats.* 'Ave some, *moi.* What fisherman does not, *hein? Hawn hawn hawn! Ici, minets . . . ici, venez,"* Brasseur coaxed, puckering his lips and making "kiss-kiss" enticements, even essaying a *meow.* And Toulon and Chalky got up enough courage to sniff at his trousers. After that, it was instant adoration, for the man's clothes did bear a *faint* reek of fish.

"The big black-and-white'un is Toulon. Where I got him," Lewrie told his guest, to answer Brasseur's raised brow. "In '94, at the siege. The littl'un, that's Chalky . . . *Crayeux?* Came off a French brig in the West Indies in '97."

"When young man, I am in West Indies," Brasseur declared with a broad grin of pleased surprise as he stroked both cats, who found the aromas on his fingers as tantalising as his trouser legs. "Was in ze Navy wiz Admiral, Comte de Grasse. Battle of ze Chesapeake . . . zen at Yorktown. *Malheureux* . . . unfortunate, was *aussi* at ze Battle of ze Saintes, where you' Admiral Rodney defeat us."

"*I* was at Yorktown!" Lewrie exclaimed in like enthusiasm to meet a veteran from the opposite side of his early adventures. "We got out the night before the surrender. So, you *were* French Navy," Lewrie said, with an idle thought in the back of his mind that the man might *still* be.

"To end of *Américain* war, *oui, Capitaine.* Come 'ome, sail wiz merchant trade a few year, but . . . I visit Le Verdon, 'ave ze *rencontre* wiz *jeune fille* I know of old, we marry, an' . . . she wish zat I no more go away so long, so . . . give up sea, buy boat, an' fish wiz *mon* father.

"Brother *à moi*," Brasseur said, turning sad, "was Navy, *aussi.* Stay in, make . . . 'ow you call . . . *petty officier? Hélas,* at ze Battle of Nile, *nous a quitté* . . . 'e is gone away from us."

"My condolences for your loss, *m'sieur,*" Lewrie dutifully told Brasseur, topping off the man's brandy.

"Was time I think to go *back* to Navy," Brasseur said, "when ze Revolution just begin, but . . ." He heaved a sigh and stuck his nose in his glass for a deep sip. "Many good people 'ere in Médoc are for ze Assembly, end of King Louis's rule, an' become free *Républicains* like America, but zen . . ."

Brasseur laid out a litany of woe, as the initial high hopes of a reasoned, logical, and bloodless call for change had become a revolution, turning more violent and capriciously murderous with each passing month. Locals in the Médoc, in Saintonge cross the Gironde, were torn 'twixt monarchy or its complete eradication. The provinces of Vendée and Charente, not so far north of Médoc, had risen in counter-rebellion in favour of the King, in defence of the Catholic religion, which the revolutionaries had banned and stripped of its riches, which brought blood, murder, plunder, and no-quarter combat, and the people of Médoc had shivered in dread of their own neighbours as the armies of the Directory marched closer, with their drum-head courts and guillotines in tow like siege-artillery. After King Louis and Queen Marie Antoinette were executed in '93, and the madmen of the Terror had begun to lop the heads off anyone even *slightly* ennobled (or who had worked for the monarchy, even serving girls who had styled the hair of the rich and titled!), the Médoc had turned on its own, and long-term spites, grudges, envies, or debts had turned to accusations of being monarchist reactionaries. True enthusiasm for the Revolution had gone away, replaced by fear for one's own safety, and dread of neighbours!

Then had come conscription to raise the world's first *enormous* army of citizen-soldiers from every class, the *levée en masse,* so the frontiers could be defended against what had felt like all the *rest* of Europe.

The *levée* had swept up Brasseur's eldest son, his younger brother, and both his in-laws' sons. One died in Alsace under Keller-man, one died of the Black Plague near Gaza under Napoleon Bonaparte, one had come home half-blind and crippled from Bona-parte's first Italian Campaign, and . . . Bras-seur had not heard from his son, posted on the Savoian border, in months, and feared the worst.

"May be good, zat zose fools in Paris 'ave been swept aside," Brasseur morosely stated. "All pomp an' silliness, ze men of ze Direc-tory. Revolution, counter-coup, fighting among zemselves? Ze new calendar, which make no sense. Centimetres, metres, an' kilometres, ze gram, centigram, an' kilogram, bah! Still 'ave church in village, still 'ave priest, but, when fort is finish, an' garrison come, will zey allow *notre* church stay open? Or, turn it to Temple of *Reason!*" Brasseur sneered.

He thought it was good that General Napoleon Bonaparte was now First Consul, after *his* successful *coup d'état* that had removed the tyrannical and illogical Directory. *Maybe* Bonaparte would abandon his military career and sue for peace, then concentrate on righting many wrongs to set France to rights. But Brasseur also thought that the crowned heads of Prussia, Austria, and Great Britain could not tolerate revolutionary, Republican, and successfully militant France . . . not for very long, if they wished to keep their own citizens in line and docile. Too many cast-iron Liberty Trees had been set up across Europe. With America, now France, to emulate . . .

"*Peut-être, Capitaine,* what 'as 'appen in France will be good."

"So long as France doesn't feel duty-bound to spread revolution round the globe," Lewrie countered.

"Cork is out of bottle, *peut-être?*" Brasseur rejoined, smiling in a world-weary manner. "An', *peut-être,* France must be beaten, for example, 'ow *not* to become ze Republic."

Here now, that *sounds intriguin'!* Lewrie thought; *what's this man offerin'?*

"How so, *Capitaine* Brasseur?" he asked.

"Do ze Dutch need guillotines to be ze Batavian Republic? Or, ze Piedmontese, Venetians, ze ozzer states in Italy? Zey *depose* ze royalty, but not behead, or purge zeir peoples, *m'sieur.* If France is no more aggressive, if France 'as more care for things at home . . . if France 'as to look West to protect ze coast, *au lieu de* . . . uhm, 'ow you call . . . ?"

"Instead of?" Lewrie supplied, wishing he could cross fingers, for his French was awful.

"Ah, *oui,* instead of, ah . . . looking to expand east, *comprendre?*"

"Perhaps a flea-bite along the Biscay coast, every now and then, a repeat of the Franco-British expedition on the Vendée coast," Lewrie carefully posed, "might keep Bonaparte looking over his shoulder, not looking for new conquests into the Germanies?"

Keep the bastard from plannin' an invasion of England, certain! Lewrie grimly thought.

"Ze . . . flea-bite, *oui, M'sieur Capitaine,*" Brasseur gravely replied, with a slow, sage nod of his head. "Ze many flea-bite, *hein?*"

"Hellish-hard, that," Lewrie told him, " 'less sufficient forces could be scraped t'gether, and a good place discovered to strike, with no intelligence of local sentiments, opposing forces available . . . all that. One would require a great deal of factual information, *m'sieur.*"

384

Brasseur left off petting the cats and leaned forward, elbows atop his knees, and rolling his glass between his hands. "Such facts *could* be found out, *Capitaine,*" he said in a soft, guarded voice, and with a sly glare in his eyes. "All I suffer . . . all neighbours suffer . . . I owe *la Révolution* nozzing, *m'sieur.* Last son *à moi* is sixteen. Revolution take my eldest . . . do zey take *him, aussi?* 'E become gunner at Pointe de Grave fort, or march away to die in faraway *Prussia?* Bah! Peu! *Peut-être,* a flea-bite *'ere, m'sieur!*" Brasseur declared in heat, before calming, and, still hunkered over, sipped at his drink.

"I speak of zis to *votre Commandeur* Hogue," he added. " 'E say 'e must speak to you, or I speak to you myself."

"If," Lewrie cautiously supposed aloud, "if you were to supply the information which made a 'flea-bite' here possible, might you and your family require a means of escape, *M'sieur* Brasseur . . . Jean?"

"It is possible, if ze authorities discover 'oo talk to you," Brasseur cagily allowed, rubbing his chin and shrugging. "But, zere are so many fishermen you stop each day, 'oo is to say which man tell you? What is it you need to know before the flea bites, *hein?*"

"Your village," Lewrie said, daring to trust him, at last. "I can't see round the point, so . . . your little harbour, the bay north of Le Verdon, the cove south of the mole. How far along the construction of the battery, how many troops already there . . . and, how many troops on the south side of the Gironde there are within two hours' march. When you have discovered all I ask of you, stray out to sea again, and . . . hoist a long pendant from your mast-tip. I note you have none now. I shall pay guineas for what you learn, *Capitaine* Brasseur. Say, a guinea now, as well?"

"Non, m'sieur," Brasseur replied. *"Non* ze guinea. Better ze silver shillings. Spend gold coin, an' ze *gendarmerie* take notice of zis, and suspect. Besides, I 'ave not yet sold you my *fish, hein?"* Brasseur said with a wide smile and a laugh.

"Done, and done!" Lewrie declared, reaching for his coin purse.

Lewrie ended up with another basket full of a medley of oysters, clams, mussels, and shrimp, along with Brasseur's wife's recipe for the famous Biscay mussel dish, *mouclade,* which he would serve his officers that very evening. Brasseur had also sold the wardroom and the Midshipmen's cockpit some large fish he had trawled on his way out to sea.

Since Brasseur didn't usually put in on the north shore of the river Gironde, he knew little of the doings at the St. Georges fort or the weight of its guns . . . he had *seen* the artillery barged in over the last year, and *thought* they might have been long eighteens, or twenty-fours, but could not say with certainty.

Yes, barges laden with Dordogne stone put into his home port of Le Verdon sur Mer, and he had never seen an escort, and it was a rare thing to see a sail-driven or galley-style oared gunboat near Pointe de Grave, nor many light warships, either.

And, yes, Brasseur had *sometimes* sailed along "the Savage Coast" to go up to Marennes or La Tremblade on the far side of the peninsula, mostly to trade for salt so he could preserve some of his catch, but he had never overnighted on the windward beaches, so could not confirm the presence of a freshwater stream or pool. Pine trees for firewood? But, of course there were! he had assured Lewrie.

Lewrie could barely contain his rising excitement 'til Papin, or Brasseur, or both, fetched back news from shore. *Newspapers!* Lewrie chid himself again, though he'd all but tied a string round his finger to recall the need for recent French papers, and what they might inadvertantly reveal.

No more, just these two, Lewrie silently decided as HMS *Savage* slowly loafed her way seaward for the night, into the beginnings of a spectacularly fiery sunset. Too many pointed questions of too many of the local fishermen, and suspicions would be roused with the local authorities; too much coin doled out, and just *one* drunken fisherman who had cooperated, and *Savage* would be *swamped* by others eager to earn a golden guinea with just *any* sort of fantasy or moonshine!

If Papin and Brasseur brought back good tidings, he *could* come up with a workable plan to lay before Ayscough, who was always ready for a good scrap; perhaps a good-enough plan to entice Rear-Admiral Lord Boxham to participate, too, before he died of boredom out beyond the horizon, yearning with drawn daggers for the French to sortie.

Jules Papin; could he trust him? So far, he'd proved greedily honest, and what little he had related was true. An amoral man without a jot of patriotism, with his eyes ever on the main chance.

Jean Brasseur? Lewrie wondered. A fellow in need of money, but a *disappointed* patriot, as well. At least Brasseur had not attempted to spin a fool's tale, had freely admitted what he did not know, and could not say with assurance.

Take what both *say with a grain o' salt, aye,* Lewrie speculated; *that'd be safest. They agree, all well and good. Their accounts vary* too *much, then . . . Christ, what'll I do, then? If they* do, *though . . . !*

Lewrie resisted the urge to chew on a thumbnail as he pondered what he wished to

388

accomplish, clapping both hands in the small of his back and rocking on the balls of his booted feet, instead; wondering if he might be aspiring to *too* much.

Not just a landing by the Pointe de Grave battery to drive off the workers and officers, so he could blow it apart, no; there was the completed small *lunette* fort by St. Georges de Didonne, too. With any luck at all, there might be barges in Le Verdon's harbour to take or burn. With enough force devoted to the endeavour — and he'd have to talk a blue streak to see that there was! — a landing *could* be made by Royan. A quick march *behind* the St. Georges fort, an assault from the un-guarded land side (pray God that Papin could tell him for sure!) so he could spike all those guns, as well, lay charges to topple those ramparts, rout *both* garrisons, and sail out with prisoners . . . perhaps — *peut-être!* — even stay ashore long enough to barge the artillery out to sea and scuttle them, or have enough Marines to meet any relief column on the shore road from Talmont and give *them* a bloody nose, to boot?

Hopeless! Bloody daft! Lewrie irritably thought, reining in his galloping imaginings; *yet . . . it beats waitin' t'hear 'bout my legal troubles, or a recall t'face trial! . . . don't it bloody-just!*

There was also a nagging qualm that would not stay tamped down; *am I doin' all this 'cause it needs doin'? Or, am I so desp'rate for glory t'keep me from the hangman?*

CHAPTER
TWENTY-SIX

The task of wooding and watering at Papin's indicated spring required a good part of the day, with *Savage* anchored half a mile off-shore of the lonely and heavily forested Côte Sauvage, parallel to the beaches with the best bower and heaviest stern kedge anchor down, with springs on the cables. The starboard side guns were manned, and, by tightening or loosing the spring-lines, HMS *Savage* could be swung to bring fire against any threat that emerged from the woods.

All the ship's boats were led from towing astern, or hoisted off the boat-tier beams that spanned the breadth of the hull, swung out by employing the main course yard as a crane, then loaded with the oldest water casks, the ones whose contents had gone whisky-tan and so reeky as to make the stored water a punishment to drink, and giving a sickly taste to any rations boiled up in it.

From the first peek of dawn to long after the mid-day meal, the working-parties hewed and chopped wood, gathering dryer deadfall limbs and twigs for kindling, taking down manageable-sized younger trees for cordwood, hacking and splitting them to thigh-long lengths. The inside of each huge water butt was scoured clean of slime with salt water and beach sand, rinsed, then trundled inland to the freshwater creek and a spring that Jules Papin had vaguely pointed to on a chart, filled, and trundled back to the beach, to be rowed out to the frigate, then labouriously hoisted aboard for storage in the bilges, on the orlop, with the cordwood and kindling crammed between to keep them from shifting.

Least the sea's kind, Lewrie thought as he took off his hat and mopped his brow on a shirtsleeve . . . then felt like spitting for luck. Though the skies had clouded over by mid-morning, and the height of the incoming waves breaking on the barren beaches had risen a foot or so, his frigate was not yet pitching, heaving, and rolling, and threatening to pluck her anchors from the sandy bottom and drive aground sideways. The ship's boats, working in *Savage*'s calmer lee, made good time fetching their heavy cargoes back alongside, and the scend that rolled under the keel still allowed the landsmen doing the heavy pulley-hauley work to hoist the refilled butts up and over the side and into the holds.

"Still no sign of trouble, Mister Devereux?" Lewrie asked of his Marine officer.

"The sentries have yet to report any movement along the road, sir," Lt. Devereux replied. He had landed with two files of Marines, twenty men in all, leaving Sgt. Skipwith aboard with the other half of the Marine complement. Cpl. Plymouth, with ten Marines, was posted in a wide arc about two musket shots to the east of the spring, for a close guard over the working-parties. Cpl. Dudley, with another ten Marines, Devereux had posted even deeper into the woods to keep watch over the rough sand and dirt track that lay a mile further east, to alert them to any threat coming along that road. "I must allow, sir, that this is the most amazing thing, to actually be standing on the foes' home ground."

"Pray God, sir, do we land in France again, we meet just as dull a reception," Lewrie joshed. "But, aye . . . it does feel daring, to be here."

A *proper* Post-Captain would have remained aboard, pacing slowly and fretfully about, allowing his junior officers and Midshipmen opportunity for action, and "mention in despatches." A *lazy* Post-Captain most certainly would. By this point in his naval career, though, Alan Lewrie knew himself too well; he despaired of ever being *proper,* and, given his druthers, *would* be lazy, yet . . . the lure of walking on firm soil for an hour or so, the temptation to tread on *French* sand, gravel, pine needle beds, and grass to, in essence, stick his tongue out at the "snail-eatin' bastards" was simply too great to be denied. And, admittedly, the fretting about the rising of wind and sea, the arrival of a French column, a young peasant couple disturbed from their fornication in the shady groves by the spring, who'd leap up and away and raise the hue and cry, had driven him beyond distraction!

So, once most of the water butts, most of the firewood, had been stowed below, he had ordered Lt. Urquhart to take charge of the frigate and had gone ashore himself; armed to the teeth with his pair of twin-barreled Manton pistols, his hanger, his Ferguson breech-loading rifle-musket slung over his shoulder, and an East Asian pirate's *krees* knife and scabbard jammed into one of his Hessian boots.

The "knuckles" of the imagined "clenched fist" which the Côte Sauvage resembled (in Lewrie's mind, at least) ran north to south for seven miles or so, and the charts did not show any settlements at all the whole way. At the bottom of the "fist," inside the hook of Pointe de la Coubre, lay the tiny village of La Palmyre; east of the "thumb" up north lay Ronce les Bains, cross the channel from the Ile d'Oléron, and but one lonely track that squiggled through the forests from one to the other.

"Might be a garrison at Ronce les Bains, d'ye imagine?" Lewrie asked.

"To close the Pertuis de Maumusson channel, sir, I'd think there would be a battery near there, but . . . the closest garrison town would more likely be La Tremblade, or Marennes," Lt. Devereux speculated in a soft voice, his eyes focussed more on the dense woods than Lewrie, on wary guard 'til back aboard the ship. "About five miles from here, as the crow flies, but eight miles by this road, Captain."

"And, are our charts accurate," Lewrie also mused aloud, "about fourteen miles from Royan, unless there are more roads than the one I see that runs from La Tremblade to Saujon, with a secondary road from *that* good road at the crossroads, that turns south to the village of Saint Sulpice de Royan to the coast."

Commander Hogue's *Mischief,* just days after Lewrie's encounter with Papin and Brasseur, had stopped one of *his* regular fishermen, and had finally produced a slew of newspapers, and a rough chart of roads and settlements north of the Gironde, which Lewrie had ordered copied and distributed to all his commanders. How much trust he could put in it was still up in the air, but, at least it was a start. The papers, barely days old, were full of boastful malarkey and gasconade, but of much more evident value when it came to information about the state of things in France, and in the local area.

"Last water butt is ready to roll, sir," Lt. Gamble announced. He looked quite pleased with himself, and a tad excited that they had snuck onto their enemy's shore, and seemed to be getting away unseen.

"Very well, Mister Gamble," Lewrie said with a grin, feeling a sense of relief himself. It was one thing to *dare,* but quite another to linger too long. "Be sure we gather up all the axes and saws as we go. Mister Fisher, the Carpenter, would have our nutmegs off, did we lose a single honing stone."

"I shall call in my sentries from the road, sir," Lt. Devereux said with a casual finger to the brim of his hat in salute.

"I s'pose I should return to the beach," Lewrie told him, with a sigh of resignation. It had felt *so* good to get his boots dusty for a few hours! "You'll find me there, Mister Devereux."

"Aye aye, sir."

But, before Devereux could send a runner to Cpl. Dudley, a Marine private came panting out of the woods *from* the road, his musket unslung and held across his chest, ready for action. "French sodjers on th' road, sir!" he panted as he slammed to attention, lowering his musket to his side. " 'Bout 'alf a comp'ny, Corp'r'l Dudley says, sir! 'E thinks no more'n thirty'r fourty of 'em, sir! *Shamblin'* along, 'e says t'tell ye, sir! From th' south, sir."

"From Royan, most-like," Lewrie muttered. "But, why? Why now, and why here?" *Damme, have we been betrayed?* he furiously thought.

"Do they seem to be looking for our presence, Private Langdon?" Lt. Devereux asked in a harsh rasp as he fiddled with the hilt of his small-sword, and the tightness of his blade in the scabbard.

"Uh . . . *shamblin'*, more-like, sir, like Corp'r'l Dudley said," Private Langdon repeated, bracing to stiffer attention. "Off'cer on a 'orse, coupla mules carryin' tents'r somethin' . . . goin' along at route step, an' gobblin' away in Frog, sir!"

Lt. Devereux turned a wolfish look at Lewrie; Lewrie looked at him with a gleam in his eyes, and unslung his Ferguson. Lt. Devereux was all but wagging his tail and whining to be let loose, to be sicced.

"Mister Gamble, un-armed men to get the water butt back to the beach . . . armed men to come with me," Lewrie growled. "Mister Locke will come with me. Sorry, Mister Gamble, but someone *must* command the others, this once."

"Aye, sir," a let-down Lt. Gamble sighed, whilst Mr. Locke the Midshipman about hopped in joy.

"Let's go and see if we can sting the bastards," Lewrie snapped. "First of the flea-bites, Mister Devereux."

The coast road was a mile inland of the spring from which they had taken their water, and Lewrie's party of Marines and armed sailors were shambling and panting by the time they reached it. Cpl. Dudley rose from a crouch behind a thick clump of bush and waddled, bent over, deeper into the forest to report to Lt. Devereux.

Twenty Privates, one Corporal, one Lieutenant, Mister Locke, if he does *know how t'shoot,* Lewrie toted up as he lingered further back in the woods waiting for Devereux's report; *eight tars with muskets, and no marksmen either, and me. Hmmm. Damme, but all this runnin' . . . !*

"Corporal Dudley, here, spotted them down the road, sir, coming from La Palmyre, it would seem," Lt. Devereux whispered, after he had retreated to Lewrie's side. "The road is clear north of us, and he's seen no traffick other than these French soldiers. They're about half a mile down that way from us, at present, shuffling along slowly, sir."

Lewrie looked about, wondering how the Devil they could hide an ambush, with the Marines kitted out in their red coats and white pipe-clayed crossbelts, his sailors mostly in calico shirts and white slop-trousers. "In your considered military opinion, Mister Devereux, any cover thick enough in which to hide our men 'til they get up to close musket-shot?" *Shit! Was that grammatical? he chid himself; sod it!*

"Hmm," Devereux speculated, going on tiptoe to the verge of the road and peeking up and down its length, then coming back. "There is a copse of secondary growth about two musket-shot to the south, Captain. Quite thick, it looks to be. Do we order the men to lie prone 'til the last moment, it should serve quite well. They would march past us as near as ten yards, sir. Hats off, of course."

"But of *course,* Mister Devereux!" Lewrie agreed with a twinkle. "Let's sneak our people down there whilst we can."

"Prime firelocks, now . . . *carefully,* ye ign'rt maggots," Dudley hissed at his Marines. "Once primed, *slowly* ease yer pieces off cock, an' God 'elp th' man discharges 'fore the Leftenant saysta, for ye'll git no 'elp from me, hear me?"

"Mister Locke, our men are primed?" Lewrie asked.

"Um, I, uh . . . don't know, sir," the eager Midshipman answered.

"Christ!" Lewrie spat. Sailors were trained in the use of muskets and pistols, but were nowhere near as well drilled as the Marines.

"They even *loaded,* ye wonder, Mister Locke?"

The lad turned red as Lewrie went to see for himself. No, not a single piece was loaded, so he saw to supervising loading himself, after they got into cover. "Half-cock . . . good. Prime. Good. Now, close yer frissons. Now, very carefully, or you'll give the game away and we won't get a chance t'kill *any* Frogs . . . firm thumb on the lock, *sneak* the triggers, and *ease* 'em down . . . slow, slowly. Everyone off cock? Thankee, Jesus. Now, don't get the damn' things hung up in the bushes as you lay down, with yer hats off, and lie quiet as the grave."

Lewrie drew both his pistols and placed them on the ground for easy grabbing, took off his cocked hat and lay down with his long-arm by his side. "You must be skilled in weaponry, Mister Locke," Lewrie whispered to the Midshipman, who had come to lie prone by his captain's side, looking miserable. "More than the hands, so you may be the tutor, the master at everything that our sailors must know, d'ye see. It was my fault their muskets weren't loaded, since we were countin' on our Marines to guard us, though I imagined that Mister Gamble had ordered them loaded and safely set aside before they began work. My fault to *assume.* Use me as an object lesson, if you will, young sir, how *not* to fart about," Lewrie concluded with a wry grin.

"Aye aye, sir," Midshipman Locke whispered back, gulping in awe that a Post-Captain, the fearsome "Ram-Cat" Lewrie, would admit to his mistake.

"And, when the time comes, rise up when ordered, pick a target, keep yer eyes open 'stead o' shuttin' 'em, aim for the belly, a little below your fellow's breast plate, or the Vee of his crossbelts, then gently squeeze the trigger, and take the frog-eatin' sonofabitch down," Lewrie instructed, grimly this time. "No false sentiment, no shootin' wide or high 'cause it don't seem Christian t'kill a man, unawares and unready. There's nothin' fair 'bout what we're about t'do, so don't bother looking for 'fair.' Better him than you, what?"

"Aye aye, sir," Locke mumbled, his face now pinched and paler than before, as the enormity of what they were about to do struck home.

"Hist, now, lads. Quiet as mice" was Lewrie's last whisper.

They heard the French coming; the clop of the officer's horse, the dull plopping of the pack animals' hooves, and the shuffle and drum of un-synchronised, out-of-step infantry boots on the soft dirt and sand of the road. It might once have been "planked" by laying trimmed tree trunks either end to end or cross-wise, with soil, sand, and stabilising gravel, but, from what little Lewrie had seen of the road, it had been a long time ago, and the handiest trees beside the planned road had grown back into a tangle of secondary growth and thick bushes not six feet beyond the verges. The pines and mixed hardwoods beyond easy cutting stood nigh an hundred feet tall, with adult boughs interlaced together overhead, so that the road resembled a narrow but deep tunnel through a very *dark* green and gloomy thicket.

Laughter; someone was telling a joke; another Frenchman related his need for a loan 'til the end of the month; one bitched about that whore who'd cheated him at the bordello in Royan. A sergeant was down on the typical ne'er-do-well lack-wit soldier, whose pack straps were chafing him, whose musket showed sign of rust round the fire-lock, and "Bernard, you skin-flint, hand me your tobacco pouch," and "Go *foutre* yourself, Alphonse, you *never* pay me back, you sorry beggar," from the fellow named Bernard.

"Wait . . . wait . . . wait!" Lt. Devereux was mouthing under his breath, rising to one knee, then . . . "Up! Cock yer locks! Aim, and *fire!*"

The range *was* about ten yards, as the Brown Bess muskets levelled in rough aim. The French soldiers froze for a second, their shambling march halted. Lewrie saw one fellow with his shako on the back of his head, his musket borne behind his shoulders, and probably unloaded, to boot. Before he could free a hand to swing it down from behind his neck, a musket ball thrummed dirt and dust from the white facing of his tunic, and replaced it with a bright splash of blood just above the man's brass breast plate and cross-belts!

Lewrie cocked his Ferguson, took aim at an older soldier with a single diagonal chevron on his lower sleeve, fired, and knocked the man off his feet with a ball in his stomach. Kneel! Pick up one of the double-barreled Mantons. Cock! Aim, and fire the right barrel. Down went a hatless soldier who had turned to run into the woods on the far side of the road, and Lewrie took him just below his knapsack. Scream of a horse as it toppled over! The officer with his sword half-drawn, twisting in agony from bullet wounds as it fell on him, pinning him beneath its kicking, thrashing weight!

Left barrel, and a Frenchman trying to load his musket howled in instant pain and terror as Lewrie's ball shredded his lower throat!

Less than five seconds of the initial volley, a few follow-up shots from Lewrie's, Devereux's, and Midshipman Locke's pistols, and it was over in an eye-blink! There were four or five French soldiers still on their feet, haring back down the road to La Palmyre, or all the way to Royan were they terrified enough, their heavy knapsacks stripped off for more speed, and their muskets thrown away.

The rest of the French unit — perhaps as many as twenty men — lay where they had fallen, only a few of them able to writhe as the pain of their wounds forced them to stir. One knelt on splayed knees, puking blood; another tried to crawl away, leaving a gory stream in his wake. The officer was screaming as loud as his horse, and one of the Marines went to him. He took his time reloading, then stuck the muzzle of his musket to the horse's temple and fired. Again, he took his time to bite cartridge, pour powder in the pan, the rest down the barrel; spit the ball down; draw the ramrod to tamp it down; return the ramrod to its brass pipes, then ease the firelock from half-cock to un-cocked, each motion as smart as parade drill. Then the Marine muttered "poor bastid," performed "Right About," and marched away from the dying officer. It was Lt. Devereux who approached him with pistol drawn, and gently spoke to him in French, before leaning down to give the unfortunate fellow the requested *coup de grace*.

Lewrie strolled out into the road, amazed and appalled, but in secret glee that none of his own had even gotten a scratch. Mr. Locke staggered out to look down on one of the Frenchmen who lay on his side but was struggling to roll over onto his back, as dying men will do. Locke turned away and fell to his knees, throwing up.

"You well, Mister Locke?" Lewrie asked as he re-loaded and re-primed his pistol. Brutish as it was, both Marines and sailors pawed over the dead and the dying for tobacco, coins, pipes or clasp knives, breast plates, and shakoes for souvenirs, crowing with triumph.

"My God, sir!" Locke stuttered, "It's . . . horrible!"

"It's war, Mister Locke," Lewrie grimly told him. "You think *this* is bad? Worse things happen at sea, when ships come to 'pistol-shot' range and flail away at each other. Chearly, now, young sir . . . the men are watchin'. You're blooded, you marked your man and lived t'tell of it. Here. Take his shako. The rest of the Midshipmen in the cockpit'll be green with envy, and, after a rum or two, you might feel like braggin' of it."

"Aye aye, sir," Locke said with a gulp and a final retching noise as he got to shaky feet; but he accepted the shako, and even found the courage to pick up an infantry hanger, as well.

"Quite useful in close combat, a hanger, Mister Locke," Lewrie told him as they began to stroll away from their massacre. "I prefer its shorter length, stoutness of blade, and the slight curve, which'll let you get in a slash or drawin' stroke, when a small-sword'll be hung up, and all you have is the point t'work with. Lighter than our brute cutlasses, too, you'll find. Quicker in the hand, and in *riposte.*"

"I . . . I wondered why you wore one, sir, but could not dare to enquire," Midshipman Locke said, trying to play up game in his captain's esteem. He went back to strip the baldric and scabbard from the nearest dead Frenchman, for later.

Why the Devil'd I do this? Lewrie asked himself as they tramped back to the spring, loose-hipped and cocksure, even loaded down with a pile of booty and French weapons. He had had no motive for ambushing those pitifully unprepared French soldiers, beyond the fact that they were there, his people were there, and the opportunity had presented itself. *What t'make of it, then,* he mused as they followed the creek to the beach; *and, what'll the* French *make of it? Have I ruined any chance t'take those forts because of it? Will they re-enforce, now we gave 'em my "flea-bite"? And . . .* where *might they re-enforce?*

Might the French think that it had been Captain Charlton's work, forcing them to send more troops to La Tremblade, Marennes, the Ile d'Oléron, for it had been in his watching squadron's bailiwick, after all. *Well, close to it, anyway; quibble, quibble, quibble,* he scoffed.

Was there a sizable garrison at Royan already, and that unit had been a part of it, the French might despatch company-sized road patrols to the Côte Sauvage peninsula, find the newly felled trees, the signs of a British presence round the spring, and to counter any new landings, might even shift some light guns, a flying battery, to lay an ambush of their own, which would weaken the infantry force that could defend the fort at St. Georges de Didonne!

Might it spur the French to rush the completion of the battery on Pointe de Grave? That would mean more barges loaded with stone or timbers coming to Le Verdon sur Mer . . . *vulnerable* barges, open to a night-time cutting-out expedition by Bartoe, Shalcross, and Umphries.

What would that *do, though?* Lewrie wondered as they reached the beach, and the waiting boats; *result in a whole regiment sent into the area from St. Fort sur Gironde, down-river? From Saintes, or up from Bordeaux, too?*

" 'Ave a bit o' fun, Cap'm sor?" his Cox'n, Liam Desmond, asked as he brought the jolly boat to ground its bows on the beach. "Sure, an' we heard th' shootin'. Furfy, here, sor, was all outta sorts ya went an' danced wi' th' Frogs, an' left us aboard!"

"Niver 'as any fun, does Furfy," Willy Toffett teased, tousling Furfy's hair.

"We'll make it up to him, Desmond . . . soon," Lewrie promised as he swung a leg over the gunn'l. "The last water butt aboard?"

"Aye, sor, it is, 'bung up an' bilge free.' "

Desmond chuckled.

"Then let's be off," Lewrie ordered. "Mister Locke?"

"Sir?" the Midshipman replied from the launch, alongside.

"Everyone present and accounted for, sir?" Lewrie asked.

"Aye, sir," Locke firmly replied, beaming with pleasure as the sailors who had been denied a scrap oohed and ahhed and made much of his prize shako and hanger. "I called my muster list, and all of the hands answered, sir. And, not a scratch on any of our people, sir!"

"*Very* good, Mister Locke!" Lewrie said in exuberant praise, as much for Locke's quick recovery as for his attention to duty. "We'll make a scrapper of you, yet! *And* half a clerk!"

Might not be able t'use that place t'water anymore, Lewrie had to imagine as he discharged his pistols overside, once back aboard HMS *Savage. Pity 'bout that,* he thought, for his one taste from the creek and spring had been marvellously fresh and pure. *Use it or not, I'll send one of the brig-sloops, one of the cutters, cruisin'* close *ashore, and maybe draw French troops there, away from Royan. Let 'em hope to hurt us back!*

Yet, as he returned to his cabins for a well-deserved glass of something wet, there was a thought that troubled him. He had queried only two men about a good place to wood

408

and water; one was Papin, and the other was Brasseur. Perhaps Kenyon, Hogue, or one of the cutters' captains had asked the same, but . . . he could not quite silence the nagging qualm that one of those two Frenchmen had mentioned it to the military commanders charged with the defence of the Gironde mouth. Why *else* would French soldiers he taking the *coast* road, not one of the more direct routes?

One of those two had set him up! Now, which one of them could he trust?

CHAPTER
TWENTY-SEVEN

"Aye, I've known of that spring since *Erato* took station here," Commander James Kenyon said with a frown as he and Lewrie dined aboard Kenyon's brig-sloop, cruising slowly about five miles off the Côte Sauvage. Kenyon paused over his plate with knife and fork poised mid-way 'twixt mouth and meat. "The captain of a departing ship related its existence to me, in his parting briefing."

"Did you ever avail yourself of it?" Lewrie asked.

"I always judged that too risky, sir," Kenyon replied, showing Lewrie that enigmatic, "I know how to do this better than you" smile. "A mile inland of the beach, within a mile of the coast road, and deep in rather thick woods? Or, so I was told, sir. When the stores ships and water hoys arrive from neutral Lisbon, or from England, we humbler ships of the Inshore Squadron usually are summoned seaward for replenishment," he said with a dismissive shrug. "Top up your wine, sir?"

At Lewrie's nod, an extremely handsome, chisel-featured steward of about eighteen or so, too frail to Lewrie's lights for pulley-hauley or sail-tending aloft — almost a *beautiful* young blond fellow! — poured Lewrie's glass of Château Margaux full again.

As Lewrie took an appreciative sip, he let his eyes dart about Kenyon's great-cabins . . . not so *great,* really, aboard a flushed-deck brig-sloop that small, compared to his. And, in keeping with "stoic" Royal Navy suspicion of too much idle luxury (which translated to distrust of *any* comforts!), Kenyon's quarters were Spartan in the extreme.

Dove grey paint over ship-lap panelling, with dove grey canvas and deal partitions as plain as an artist's un-used frames, with nary a stab at attempting to make them look like false moulding or plaster walls. Below the panelling, the inner faces of the hull scantling and timbers were the usual blood-red. There was a scuffed old black-and-white chequer-board canvas nailed to the deck, but no colourful figured carpets in sight. The table at which they sat, the chairs, the wine-cabinet, and desk in the miniscule day-cabin looked as dull and utilitarian as the chart-space cabinets; second- or third-hand cast-offs of a poor chandler's stocks, or built from scrap lumber some Bosun hadn't missed.

The glasses from which they sipped, though, were good quality, and spotless, the dinnerware rather elegant Meissen china from Hamburg, the flatware a particularly showy and heavy sterling silver, not cheap pewter or iron, and even the tablecloth was as white as new-fallen snow with not a single faint smut from previous spills and washings.

Like Erato *herself,* Lewrie thought; *either grand or shabby.*

Lewrie could not fault the care lavished upon the brig-sloop; as he came aboard, the man-ropes were golden-new Manila, served elaborately with Turk's Head knots, the battens fresh-painted and sanded for a firm foothold. The decks were nigh as white as the tablecloth; every gun was new-blacked, and everything involved in sail-tending or gunnery was in Apple-Pie Order. Paint? Kenyon did not seem to care, though.

And the crew . . . either beggars in rags, or fresh as Sunday Divisions, and that seemed to depend on how young and fetching the sailors were. They had mustered to doff hats and welcome Lewrie aboard, but it had been a sullen endeavour, dutiful but lacklustre.

Well, I ain't a famous actress, nor a Nelson, but still . . . ! he had thought at the moment.

And, with so many smugglers eager to sell, and the prices so low on their goods, the dinner was excellent. A French onion soup loaded with fresh cheese and shredded bread bits; de-boned chicken breasts in wine and cream sauce, a fresh, picked-that-day salad to clear the palate, followed by boiled, unshelled shrimp with horseradish sauce, then medallions of veal with haricot beans, upon which they fed, that moment. Lewrie was sure that a pear or apple confection would follow that, and another exquisite choice of wine. Kenyon did not *dine* "Spartan"!

"I'm troubled by the presence of French soldiers, when I landed for wood and water," Lewrie said after a bite or two more of the veal.

"To be expected, though, sir," Kenyon said back. "The presence of a British frigate so close ashore simply *must* have drawn their attention."

"I don't think so," Lewrie countered. "Oh, it *could* have been a company sent out t'shake off the barracks dust and sloth, I do allow, but . . . it happened just days after I *enquired* of our smugglers or our informants of a place to water. Jules Papin . . ."

"That rogue!" Kenyon scoffed, cynically amused.

"Or Jean Brasseur. Know of him, sir?" Lewrie asked.

"We might have come across him and his boat a time or two, sir," Kenyon hesitantly supplied, rubbing his chin as he tried to remember.

"I suspect one of those two passed word to the French army, so they could lay an ambush, Commander," Lewrie told him, setting aside his knife and fork for a while. "Too few men to spare . . . doubts that his information was true . . . for whatever reason, *something* put a half-company of infantry on the coast road. And, I *could* not have alerted them to my intentions, for I closed the coast from the North, so no one watchin' for us on the South shore would have seen our approach, like I was from Captain Charlton's flotilla, come t'poach on *my* area. Thank God our sentries along the coast road spotted 'em *before* they were up level with the spring, and we could lay *our* ambush well short of where they might have been put on the *qui vive* by their officer.

"Try to recall what impression this Jean Brasseur made on you, sir," Lewrie pressed. "Or, whether you think Papin is the culprit."

"Well, I still think it mere coincidence, sir, but . . . ," Kenyon said, wiping his mouth with his napkin, and taking another deep drink from his glass. "Brasseur, hmm . . . Brasseur, oh! Fellow who *claimed* his family was once English?"

"That's the one," Lewrie answered as Kenyon summoned his cabin steward for another refill of wine. Kenyon this day had a close shave, had taken pains with his appearance, but could not hide his thirst for very long, making Lewrie wonder how long the meal, and their conversation, would continue before he went face-down in the apple pie.

"Didn't really make much of an impression on me, at *all,* sir," Kenyon said, after smacking his lips. "Just another hulking, ignorant Frog fisherman . . . all brawn and 'beef to the heel.' "

Didn't ask d'ye find him fetchin'; Lewrie thought, but kept his face neutral.

"Gloomy sort . . . sort of hang-dog," Kenyon went on, waving his glass about slowly. "Eager enough when it came to selling us something, but . . . he made no impression, sorry."

"Didn't offer you any information, then?" Lewrie enquired.

"Can't recall, sir. But then, I don't remember asking for any."

"No sad tale about suff'rin' under the Terror? No fears expressed 'bout his sons conscripted into their Army?" Lewrie prodded.

"Don't think he did, no," Kenyon said. "Sir," he added.

"Well, for a thinly populated piece of coast, I don't think it coincidental that troops were there the very day that we were, sir," Lewrie objected. "And, to smoak them out, here's what I wish you to do tomorrow . . . or, weather allowing, Commander Kenyon," Lewrie told him.

Mr. Winwood, his ever-cautious Sailing Master, had expressed doubts of how closely they could lurk off a lee shore, now that the seasons were changing, and a more boisterous Autumn was advancing. "The next clear and calm-ish day, I wish *Erato* to close the coast, 'bout four miles to the South of the Maumusson Channel 'twixt 'the Savage Coast' and the Ile d'Oléron . . . 'bout where we anchored . . . and *pretend* to go ashore for a few kegs of water, and a cord or two of firewood."

"Pretend," Kenyon said, blankly goggling at him.

Lewrie went back to his veal and beans for a bite or two, then a sip of wine. "If the French now guard the spring, and that stretch of beach and forest, I wish to know it," he told Kenyon. "So far, I don't know the strength of the local garrisons, but I *do* desire to discover whether the local commanders have posted troops and guns there to prevent future landings, and a *rough* idea of in what strength, d'ye see."

"Uh, aye, sir," Kenyon replied.

"Close the coast," Lewrie instructed. "*Savage* and I will stand off a mile or so further out. Come to anchor, or fetch-to, whichever you deem the weather will admit of, put down all your boats, and *act* as if you're sending an armed party ashore for wood and water. This side of the estuary is yours, and *Erato*'s movements are, by now, mostly taken for granted by the Frogs. Do you make your approach from the North, as I did, and there is no response, then I may assume there aren't any Argus-eyed watchers lurkin' in the woods . . . clingin' t'tree tops like Red Indians?" he japed, after another sip of wine. "Do you provoke a response, though, then we'll know for certain that the French now have a guard over the creek and the spring, and that that half-company was sent out there a'purpose, after one of 'em, or *both* Papin or Brasseur, played us false."

"But, Lew . . . but, sir . . . after you massacred those soldiers t'other day, of *course* they'd be guarding the springs," Kenyon pointed out, much like a tutor exasperated with a particularly dull student. "Revenge . . . 'once bitten, twice shy' . . . call it what you will. They see an opportunity to get their own back, assuming we're silly enough to try it on again, well . . . I don't think their presence now will be enough to prove your assumption of betrayal."

"Humour me, Commander Kenyon," Lewrie told him with a wink and a nod. "*Do* they shift troops and guns there, that's a few *less* round Royan, the Saint Georges fort, and Pointe de Grave. Fifteen miles of hard, quick march from where they *should* be, when the time comes, hmm?"

"I should see whether the French are there . . . and what their strength is," Kenyon grumbled, not quite finished chewing on a clump of fresh, buttered shore bread. "Because you envision an assault upon the forts, eventually?" He looked slightly aghast.

"Exactly so, sir," Lewrie gladly told him. "If the Frogs *don't* shift troops, I'd be very much surprised . . . but we must know. And . . . I still hold that they had no business being there in the first place, unless I *was* directed to the spring on purpose, and set up for killing."

"Uhm . . . how much of a charade must I play, then, sir," Kenyon asked, sounding loath to even go through the motions, and looking sick. "Should I actually land on the beach? March inland a ways, sir? And, how far? All the way to the spring? How close to shore do you wish?"

"There's enough depth for a brig-sloop to come-to within a half-mile offshore. *Savage* fetched-to that close, certainly. A short row for your boat crews, and an even quicker return aboard should the Frogs be tempted to fire upon you. If they're there, of course. Lay on yer oars within musket-shot of the beach, if you wish, as if you were wary, and lookin' the place over right-sharp, before committing. I surely do *not* wish you to really land, unless, in your considered opinion at the moment, the French *aren't* there. Your judgement, completely, sir."

"Trail my skirts . . . serve as 'bait'!" Kenyon gravelled sourly, and all but spat "bait" like a piece of gristle. He shot Lewrie a dubious and bleak look for an unguarded second, before passing a hand over his face, which had broken out in a sickly sweat.

"I'll have *Savage* within a half-mile of you, and will swoop down to cover your withdrawal," Lewrie assured him. "Your own six-pounders can engage, shootin' over the heads of your landing-party as they row out. Who knows? With any luck at all, our guns will slaughter a few more o' the bastards! Our seeming attempt, and its repulse, may lead the French to re-enforce their 'success,' luring even *more* troops away from the narrows."

"Or, result in them sending a brigade up from Bordeaux to garrison every point, sir," Kenyon gloomily supposed aloud.

"Then we tried, at the least," Lewrie told him, "and will have to content ourselves in cruising off this miserable place 'til the next Epiphany. At least the victuals and wines'll be tasty!"

"The next calm day, then, sir?" Kenyon resignedly said.

"The next calm day, aye."

Suitable conditions did not come, though, until nearly a week later, for with the arrival of Autumn came more boisterous seas, with gusting winds, now and again round-the-clock showers, and tall curlers breaking on the beaches of Sou'west France so hard the sands thudded.

Savage, perforce, had to stand further out

from the coast, and tack sentry-go North and South under reduced sail, with the shore lost in the mists and swirling rain. The brig-sloops and cutters attempted to maintain their vigils on the Gironde, but the weather, now and again, drove them out beyond the "invisible line" 'twixt Pointe de la Coubre and Pointe de Grave, and even several more miles to seaward, to avoid the risks of grounding on a lee, and hostile, shore should a real storm howl in from the open Atlantic.

Finally, the skies cleared, the violence of the wind-whipped sea subsided, and the tiny squadron could stand in to take up their guard positions once more.

"*Erato* signals 'Affirmative,' sir," Midshipman Grisdale eagerly reported.

"Very well, Mister Grisdale. Lower the hoist," Lewrie ordered. "A point more to loo'rd, Mister Urquhart. Follow *Erato* shoreward."

"Aye, sir," the First Officer glumly replied, then relayed that to the Quartermasters on the helm.

Is he still *sulkin'?* Lewrie thought, part amused, part put out.

Lt. Urquhart's nose was out of joint over missing the opportunity for notice and glory by participating in the ambush. The sight of souvenir shakoes, hangers, and such nigh-made him growl and grind his teeth! He was

420

even "pettish" over Lt. Gamble's small part in the action, even if all that worthy had done was trundle water kegs back from the woods to the beach without losing a single sailor to sprained fingers, loading the boats, and merely standing by . . . most-like anxiously and enviously himself!

Wasn't my *fault I wanted t'walk on solid ground,* Lewrie thought with a weary groan; *wasn't like I* knew *the Frogs'd turn up just then,* and *I gave him credit in my report to Ayscough, for re-stowin' so damn' quick.* Told *him so, damn my eyes! But* no, *he's peeved as a drunk bear!*

"A fine morning for it, eh, Mister Urquhart?" Lewrie assayed.

"S'pose so, sir, aye," Urquhart dutifully replied.

"Winds light enough to fetch-to, 'thout any risk of drifting on the beach," Lewrie commented once more, hoping for a better response. "A mile off, and North of *Erato,* so our guns aren't masked by her, and ready to get back under way, quick as a wink. Think the French really have set themselves up yonder, sir? A fine morning for killing, have they done so."

"Aye, sir, a fine morning for that," Urquhart answered, sounding a *tad* perkier. "Our larboard battery's ready for it, sir."

I'm babblin' like a ninny! Lewrie chid himself;

and who the Hell cares *how he feels? Only one set o' feelin's aboard this barge.* Mine!

Lewrie put those niggling, petty details away and lifted a telescope to his right eye as *Erato* began to round up into the wind, hands aloft to reduce sail even further. All her rowing boats, already off the cross-deck boat-tier beams and towed astern, were being hauled up close astern, to be led round to the entry-port. Kenyon would not let go anchors, but fetch-to, *Erato*'s stern angled towards the beach. One great spin of her helm and she could fall off her precarious balancing act, and bare her own larboard 6-pounder cannon to the foe . . . assuming the French were there.

He pulled out his pocket-watch, opened the cover with his thumb, and took a look at the time; ten minutes, and the boats were yet to be loaded and sent off.

"Takin' his own sweet time, ain't he?" Lewrie muttered under his breath. "Come on, damn yer eyes, get a move on!"

"Off Point Coober, sir . . . the good weather's brought out some of the local fishermen," Lt. Urquhart pointed out from the starboard side of the quarterdeck. "About six miles off, just outside the 'hook,' " he said, using the colloquial slang pronunciation the squadron had adopted.

"Thankee, Mister Urquhart," Lewrie replied. "Time, I think, to round up and take in sail, though. Spanish Reef courses and tops'ls, let fly jibs and spanker, as we planned."

"Aye aye, sir!"

Finally, all three of *Erato*'s boats were loaded with oarsmen and other hands armed to protect them. A few middling kegs were visible amidships all three, not the great butts usually stored on lower tiers, but the sort spotted on the weather deck and mess deck for the crew to dip into to slake their thirst.

"Lovely day, really," Lt. Adair could be heard to comment to one of the Midshipmen. And it was, Lewrie thought. The sea was mostly calm, rippling with a myriad of wavelets of silvery blue, most artfully so, more like a lake stroked by gentle winds than a salt sea. The beaches were broad and inviting, with waves raling in and out almost sleepily, with light froth where they broke. A myriad of sea birds were a'wing, too, and flocks of gulls wheeled and gyred round the fetched-to ships. It was only the forests behind the beach, beyond the overwash dunes or scraggly salt grasses, that looked deep, dark, and foreboding.

"Coming? So is Christmas," Lewrie griped as *Erato*'s boats, now within musket-shot of the beach, rocked and heaved slightly on the incoming waves, the sailors resting on their oars, and Coxswains and the Midshipmen commanding each boat peering intently through their telescopes at the woods. Lewrie raised his own glass to peer at them, then swivelled about to look at *Erato*'s quarterdeck. Even at half a mile's separation, he could espy Commander Kenyon pacing the lee side of his ship, his own telescope to his eye, and now and then slamming a fist on the cap-rails of the bulwarks in frustration and fret.

"A hoist from *Erato,* sir!" Midshipman Grisdale piped up, breaking the hushed, anxious silence. "It's . . . not for us, sir. It's . . ." He fumbled with his code book, for it was one rarely used and unfamiliar to him. "To his boats, it would appear, sir . . . 'Proceed.' "

The lead boat, *Erato*'s cutter, began to stroke shoreward; slow, to be sure, with the brig-sloop's First Officer standing in the stern. A moment later, and the other two, the gig and launch, started to follow.

"Didn't order him t'do *that!*" Lewrie all but yelped in worry. "What the Devil's he playin' at? Be ready to get a way on, sir," he called over his shoulder to Lt. Urquhart.

The cutter was almost up to the gentle surf line, a musket-shot from the edge of the dense forest, a *pistol-shot* from the dunes, with the two other boats still following on either quarter of the leader's boat in a deep V.

"Frogs!" came a howl from the main-mast tops.

"*Damn* my eyes!" Lt. Urquhart cried, one hand leaping to seize the hilt of his small-sword, no matter how useless the gesture was.

"Get under way, sir, this instant!" Lewrie barked. "Open ports, and run out the larboard battery, Mister Adair. To your stations for action, gentlemen."

A two-deep line of French soldiers sprang from the earth, just back of the overwash dunes where they had hidden themselves from view in the shallow, natural ditches. *Erato*'s cutter was frantically backing starboard oars, thrashing ahead with larboard oars, to try to turn her in her own length, the boat's Cox'n throwing his whole body on the tiller! The rest of the boats were wheeling about, too, but a massed volley of musketry spurted from the muzzles of at least three companies of infantrymen's musket barrels, and the shallows about each boat got churned by a torrent of lead ball.

"*Three* bloody companies, d'ye make it, Mister Devereux?" Lewrie asked of his Marine officer, more experienced with such matters.

"Aye, sir . . . but, note their spacing," Devereux urgently said. "There must be fifty or sixty yards 'tween each company. I'd suspect an artillery piece in each gap, so they may fire upon *Erato,* without risking their own men."

"Two gaps . . . say, another pair on the ends

of the line," Lewrie quickly surmised, stunned by the suddenness of the French ambush. "Four guns, together. Mister Adair! Solid shot *and* grape, and order gun-captains and quarter-gunners to concentrate on the gaps *between* their troops, and on the woods at either end, as well. Might be guns . . . !"

There *were* guns . . . great gouts of yellow-grey gunpowder smoke belched from the gaps, from the flanks. A second or two later, there came the sounds of the explosions, terrier-bark-sharp, and tinny with distance.

"Six-pounders, perhaps," Lt. Devereux spat. "Perhaps as light as old regimental four-pounders, Captain. Four pieces would be right, and fit what little we know of current French Army practice."

Savage was moving again, falling off alee, parallel to the seashore, her clumsy-looking clewed-up sails billowing and starting to fill with wind, her fore-and-aft stays'ls, jibs, and spanker filling with rustles and cracks.

"A touch more to larboard, Mister Urquhart," Lewrie demanded. "Let her fall off to about a half-mile offshore before coming back to abeam the wind."

Christ, what a pot-mess! Lewrie groaned to himself, peering at *Erato*'s boats. They were now come about, and were being rowed madly out to sea, the gig and launch weaving from one beam to the other to make themselves unpredictable targets, but still followed by a veritable hailstorm of bullet splashes, and the occasional cannon shot.

The cutter, though . . . she'd taken the full brunt of that first mass volley, and, while her oarsmen were *bending* their ash oars, going almost flat on their backs and panting like dogs at each stroke, there were casualties among them. In the ocular of his telescope, he could see panicky sailors stumbling over each other to haul wounded men into the soles of the boat, a dead man or two being heaved overside to make room for the living to replace them. In the stern-sheets, the officer and a pair of tars were firing back, the Cox'n bent low over the tiller, almost hidden under the gunn'ls.

Lewrie's view was blotted out by a white sheet of water as one of the cleverly hidden artillery pieces pounded a round-shot near the boat, thankfully an "over" 'twixt the cutter and *Savage,* which raised a tall feather of spray that slowly collapsed upon itself.

The second cannon ball was much nearer, a half-minute after the first. And, suddenly, the gig on the left-hand side of the reversed V took a ball so close that half of the oars on its starboard side were shattered, and it slewed about as if hulled, heeling over so far for a moment that it surely must capsize!

Closer to, *Erato*'s 6-pounders were barking at last, their round-shot and grape clusters bowling through the centre company of

French infantry, scattering them like a cat's paws would a boy's toy soldiers, forcing the survivors to stumble back into the woods for cover, leaving their dead and wounded where they fell. And, seeing the appalling ease with which their fellow soldiers had been butchered, the officers of the two wing companies ordered their own men to retire into shelter among the forest, too. Their smoothbore muskets were almost out of practical range beyond seventy or so yards anyway, and they had drawn their enemy's blood. A few stalwarts did continue to shoot, fingers-crossed-hopeful, but there were no more massed volleys of an hundred or so muskets going off at once. They left the rest of the fight to their artillery, which was still banging away rapidly.

"Pardon, Captain Lewrie, but . . . were I in their shoes, I'd not count on the woods for shelter," Lt. Devereux said, his face looking feral and eager. "Better they'd return to the depressions behind the dunes, which would just soak up both round-shot and grape. What our eighteen-pounders can do to them . . . !"

"They'll discover, to their sorrow," Lewrie completed for him. "Mister Winwood, the last time we were here, can you asssure me of the depth, do we stand in a little *closer* than half a mile?"

"Uhm . . . ah," the Sailing Master flummoxed, looking stunned by the suggestion. " 'Tis a making tide, sir, and there *should* be thirty feet or better, *perhaps,* but, ah . . . I can offer no assurances, Captain."

"Half a mile it is, then," Lewrie growled in frustration. "Pray place leadsman in the fore-chains, Mister Urquhart, directly."

"Aye aye, sir!"

"You mark those guns, Mister Adair?" Lewrie called down to the waist. "*Very* good. Do you direct at least two guns on each of 'em, and scour the woods with the rest."

"Oh, dear Lord," Mr. Winwood moaned, drawing his attention back shoreward. The cutter, slowest and most crippled of the three boats, had been bracketed by two round-shot, rocking her onto her beam ends to larboard, then to starboard, the feathers of spray so close that their collapse came down in a deluge that nearly swamped the boat!

Erato was still firing, quick as individual guns could be served, Kenyon no longer waiting for controlled broadsides. Six-pounder shot and grape lashed the trees and raised clouds of dirt and sand from the overwash dunes. Commander Kenyon had reduced sail almost to nothing; he'd not sail away and abandon his sailors. The French response, when it came, was to lift their aim from the rowing boats to *Erato* herself, and shot splashes began to blossom round her, now.

"Stout fellow," Mr. Winwood congratulated.

If ye only knew, Lewrie sarcastically told himself.

Erato's gig and launch had finally reached her sides, though it was no longer a place of safety with the French artillery banging away at her. After a close shot splash, the boats hastily ducked round her bow and stern to the unengaged side, so they could get back aboard at the starboard entry-ports.

The cutter still struggled, crawling snail-slow even though she was no longer a target, still a heartbreaking two hundred yards short of salvation, with the remaining armed men lending their strength upon the oars to spell those who were utterly exhausted, their bodies most-like shaking, palsied with panic and weakness.

"About another quarter-mile, before we may open upon the left-most artillery, Captain," Lt. Urquhart adjudged. "I make the beach to be about half a mile off. Should we come up to the wind, sir?"

"Aye, make it so, Mister Urquhart. Course Due South, and wait for it," Lewrie agreed. "Mister Grisdale? Signal to *Erato* for her to 'Make Sail,' then, 'Windward,' else we'll either run right up her arse, or she'll lay there, blockin' our guns."

"Oh, dear Lord," Mr. Winwood commented again, sounding like some badly milked cow. "It would appear the French have found the range to her, sir."

Sure enough, *Erato*'s slack sails twitched to round-shot passing low over her decks, and she shivered to a hit on her larboard side that raised a sudden cloud of engrained dirt, peeling paint flakes, and the usual small eruption of splinters.

Still, her hoist in reply was "Unable."

"Cock your locks!" Lt. Adair instructed his gun-captains. "Wait for it . . . wait for it! Ready, at your orders, sir!"

"By *your* best judgement, Mister Adair," Lewrie called back.

"Very well, sir. On the up-roll . . . *fire!*"

Smashing, lung-flattening, heart-skipping thunder-cracks! Huge gouts of powder smoke, jets of flame, and firefly swarms of hot embers shot from the muzzles of the great-guns! HMS *Savage* stuttered in her stately-slow progress, hull groaning and reverberating to the slamming of the explosions, shuddering again as the brutally heavy 18-pounders surged back from the port-sills to be checked by breeching ropes bound round the guns' cascabels, through the bulwarks' ring bolts!

"*That's* the way, you Savages!" Lewrie yelled, the battle-fever come over him at the first whiff of gunsmoke and the first crashing roars. "That's the way, my *bully* lads!"

Thirteen of her 18-pounders on the larboard beam, four of her quarterdeck 9-pounders, hurled a blizzard of iron into the dark woods, and even stout old trees swayed and thrashed like saplings assailed by the gusts of a West Indies hurricane! Shattered limbs came whirling down, pines with trunks as thick as a young woman's waist burst twelve or fifteen feet from the ground, and came lancing down among a cloud of splinters. That first crushing broadside bracketed the left-flank gun position and the place where the left-hand company of infantry had gone to ground!

"Swab out! Up, powder boys!" Lt. Adair chanted, pacing behind the recoiled guns, now and then cautioning crewmen to overhaul the run-out and recoil tackles, and watch where they placed their feet, else a man could be crippled for life in a twinkling. "*Shot* your guns . . . !"

"Bloody *grand,* Mister Adair!" Lewrie shouted down, making their young Scot beam with pleasure. "Serve the snail-eatin' shits again!"

Spikes and crow-levers came out so the men could shift aim for the centre positions. Wood quoins beneath the gun breeches were carefully adjusted for elevation. Adair looked up and down the deck, and found every gun re-loaded. "Run *out* your guns! Clear away the tackle! *Prime!*"

"Four fathom! Four fathom t'this line!" the larboard leadsman shouted from the forechains.

"Half point t'windward, Mister Urquhart," Lewrie cautioned.

"Take careful aim, let's not waste 'em!" Lt. Adair was yelling. "The finer your eye, the more Frogs we get to kill."

"Jus' like ol' Mister Catterall, 'e is," a quarter-gunner cried with a laugh, referring to their former Second Officer, who had died the year before in the South Atlantic. " 'Orrid mad for fried Frogs!"

"Waste your fire, Pulteney, and I'll curse like Catterall, too!" Lt. Adair promised, japing back. Gun-captains' arms rose into the air to signal readiness. *"Cock* your *locks!"* The final step done, the arms went back up, the gun-captains' other hands drawing the lock cords taut as bow-strings. "On the up-roll . . . *fire!"*

Titanic roars, more heavy shudders, great clouds of powder smoke blotting out everything to leeward, and only slowly drifting away, and thinning, but Lewrie, now perched atop the larboard bulwarks with a hand to shield his eyes, could relish the avalanche of grape, and round-shot that *harvested* trees like a farmer's scythe for a joyous second before the smoke cloud took his view away!

"Uhm . . . should he be *doing* that, Mister Winwood, sir?" Midshipman Grisdale timidly asked the Sailing Master.

"Oh, this is nothing, Mister Grisdale," Winwood replied in his usual phlegmatic way. "You should see the way he acts in a *real* scrap. Our Captain is a man *born* to combat."

HMS *Savage* served the French positions yet another heavy broadside as she slowly cruised down the coast, passing in front of *Erato,* which Kenyon had at last gotten under her own slow way, going up to windward just far enough for *Savage* to shave by down her larboard side. And, with the guns levered round 'til the muzzles, hot enough to scorch wood by then, pointed as far aft as they could bear for yet another, a parting broadside. And, there was not a single shot fired in reply by the French. Their light artillery might not have been smashed, crews who served them might not have been slaughtered to a man, but . . . they had all been buried under enough fallen trees and scrap lumber to make a good start at building a *small* Sixth Rate!

"Secure the guns, Mister Adair," Lewrie finally ordered as he hopped down from his perch atop the bulwarks. "Damned fine work, men! Damned fine shooting, by every Man-Jack! When the Bosun pipes 'Clear Decks and Up Spirits,' we shall 'Splice the Main-Brace'!"

"Stand out to sea, sir?" Lt. Urquhart enquired, looking a lot perkier than he had an hour before; action agreed with him, it seemed.

"If ye'd be so kind, Mister Urquhart," Lewrie told him, smiling back. "Sorry we could gather no souvenirs this time."

"Well, a bucket of what's left yonder, sir, is hardly what one might take home to boast of!" Urquhart rejoined with a chortle.

Lewrie gave him another grin and a reassuring nod, then went aft down the larboard side, past the quarterdeck 9-pounders and the gun crews who were now sponging out, to the taffrails and larboard lanthorn at the stern to survey the beach. With telescope extended to its uttermost, he could discern movement ashore; a *few* French soldiers in white trousers and blue coats staggering about amid the man-high reef of tree limbs, digging for their comrades, and dragging free the stunned living and the wounded.

Astern . . . *Erato* had fetched-to once more as her cutter limped alongside at last. Men swarmed over her larboard side to the boat to help their wounded aboard, and rope slings and a quickly rigged Bosun's chair were going over the side, as well. The Lieutenant in the cutter's stern-sheets seemed to have survived his ordeal, which was a glad sight to Lewrie; had the man been killed or wounded, and were Lewrie to do the "charitable thing," he might have had to give up one of his Commission Officers into her. *Charity?* Lewrie queasily thought; *or guilt?* For it had been by his orders that *Erato* and her crew had been placed in jeopardy, and . . . he'd made an error.

Didn't expect that *sized French presence,* he gloomed; *infantry, yes, maybe* one *gun, or* two, *but . . . I told Kenyon* t'pretend *t'land, not go*

435

all the way! His cutter's bow was almost t'dry sand! Well, close enough ashore that the sailors could've stepped out and not gotten wet above their knees. Drab as Kenyon's career's been so far, perhaps he needed t'exceed his orders, and get a line or two in the newspapers.

And, Lewrie could savour *one* good that had come from the action; the French had reacted to his recent ambush and the slaughter of their soldiers . . . *over-reacted*, really, and had committed about a half of a regiment and, what Lt. Deveroux told him was the entire artillery complement of that regiment. What little joy the French might have taken from their clever ambuscade, he had dashed by decimating the soldiers and artillery pieces assigned to it!

So, what'll they do, next? Lewrie asked himself, his lips curling up in a secret smile; *after they're done with cursin' and pullin' their hair out? Call for more troops, aye, but . . . where'll they* put *'em, I wonder?*

Lewrie could fantasise a host of barges coming down-river from Bordeaux, the Frogs in a fury to complete the Pointe de Grave battery, and transport another company of troops to guard it, faster than they could march. Another company to the St. Georges fort, perhaps? With another taut grin, he could imagine a whole string of hidden batteries down the Côte Sauvage; by the tip of the Maumusson Channel, the one by the creek and spring re-established, this time with even more troops and guns, guns heavy enough to deal with a frigate. And, might they also try to defend *every* point? St. Palais sur Mer, Soulac, Royan, and the "hook" of Pointe de la Coubre? Might they also fear that a British expedition might sneak past the guns of St. Georges and go for Meschers sur Gironde, or even Talmont, where the blockade runners supposedly put in, in hopes of a dark, moonless night?

God A'mighty! Lewrie suddenly thought; *Papin told me the fort by Saint Georges has 12- and 18-pounders, nothing heavier, so . . . right now, they can't span the river narrows, not 'til the battery at Pointe de Grave's finished! Oh, scurry, scurry, scurry, Froggie! And, who tries t'defend ev'rything, ends defendin' nothing!*

Why, a few more of those "flea-bites" of his, and they might end up transferring an entire brigade to the mouth of the Gironde, robbing Peter to pay Paul.

Lewrie turned to pace back to the forrud end of the quarterdeck, hands behind his back, yet with a spring to his step. He knew he had two things to do, immediately; one would be to speak to Kenyon and ask of his losses, try to atone for them, *without* admitting that he'd been wrong. The second would be to run down Papin and Brasseur, some other fishermen, and get a sense of what the local reaction was, and . . . shell out a guinea or two for what information those two had gathered.

No, a third thing to do; compare what Papin said to Brasseur's version, and determine which of the bastards was telling the truth!

CHAPTER
TWENTY-EIGHT

"Welcome aboard, Captain Lewrie," HMS *Chesterfield*'s First Lieutenant bade him with a smile as Lewrie doffed his cocked hat. "Commodore Ayscough awaits you."

"Thankee, sir. Who's the new arrival?" Lewrie asked, pointing with his chin towards the strange new 64-gunner that cruised astern of the flagship.

"Oh, that's the *Jersey*, sir," the First Officer confided as he walked Lewrie aft towards the poop himself. "Captain Edward Cheatham. She joined us only three days ago."

"And most welcome, I'm bound," Lewrie said, "after the Commodore has requested, begged, and God knows what else to get her."

"She brought *mail*, sir," *Chesterfield*'s First Officer said with glee. "First we've received, the last two months. Commodore Ayscough's clerk is holding yours, and your other vessels'."

"I'd admire did you sack it all up and hand it to my Cox'n for delivery aboard *Savage*, if ye'd be so kind, sir," Lewrie asked, partly delighted, and partly fearful of what dire news from his barrister the mail might contain.

"I shall see to it directly, Captain Lewrie."

A Marine in full kit guarding Ayscough's great-cabins under the poop deck raised his musket in salute, then returned it to his side to slam the butt on the oak deck with a loud cry of "Cap'm Lewrie . . . SAH!"

"Enter . . . but he'd best have a sheep with him!" came a muffled shout from within.

"A prime sheep, aye, sir!" Lewrie called back before he entered, "bleatin' on the starboard gangway!" Commodore Ayscough, being a Scot, was hellish-fond of roast mutton or lamb, and obtaining one from French smugglers was a standing request of any warship coming off the blockade.

"Captain Lewrie, give ye joy, sir!" Ayscough beamed as he rose from one of his collapsible leather-covered chairs in his day-cabin. "Ye'll stay aboard to dine upon it with us, I vow." His hand was out, and a glad smile was on his face. "I *swear,* you're a terror, Lewrie. Went at 'em like a 'Ram-Cat,' hey? Take a pew, sir, and accept a glass of this lovely claret. Captain Cheatham, may I name to you one of my most energetic officers, Captain Alan Lewrie of the *Savage* frigate . . . leads our close watch of the Gironde mouth. Lewrie, this is Captain Edward Cheatham of the

Jersey, sixty-four, recently come to join."

"Your servant, sir," Lewrie said with a bow of his head.

"Delighted to make your acquaintance, Captain Lewrie," Cheatham replied. He was an older fellow, approaching fifty, grey-haired, and one who still wore his hair in a mid-shoulder long queue, rather than the neat, wee sprig just barely atop the uniform coat collar that most officers now sported, or the younger ones, who eschewed the queue altogether. Cheatham was lean, leather-faced, and tanned the colour of golden walnut. "The Commodore has imparted to me the inner squadron's most recent exploits, for which I offer my congratulations, Lewrie."

"Thankee kindly, sir," Lewrie replied, feeling the need to go "modest" and self-deprecating. "Just keepin' Monsoor Frog on the hop?"

"One does wish to be a frigate man again," Cheatham wistfully said. "They seem to have *all* the fun."

"Perhaps we may yet have some fun of our own." Ayscough grinned as he summoned a cabin servant, so Lewrie could get a glass, and the others could get a top-up. "Depending on what Lewrie here has gleaned from his sources 'mongst the French fishermen, that is." Ayscough tapped the side of his nose, as if to preface great revelations, looking at Lewrie like a tutor at his best scholar, about to do his Latin recitations before the rest of the faculty.

"Well sir, what I've been *told* since our raid is contradictory," Lewrie had to admit, after a sip of wine, wondering if it was a Lafite or Brave-Mouton. His time off the Gironde had done wonders for his palate, and thank God for clever smugglers. "What we've *seen,* sirs, is quite another matter. After our second raid upon the Savage Coast . . . Côte Sauvage, rather . . . the French have begun some new emplacements along it. There's one at the base of Point Coober . . . pardons, again, sirs. The lesser ships have simplified local place names, for their ease of understanding. As I said, at the base of the 'hook' . . ."

"Chart," Ayscough impatiently ordered, and they ended leaning in over a chart laid atop the table 'twixt the chairs and the settee.

"One here, to close the Maumusson Channel to Rochefort, Marennes, and La Tremblade," Lewrie pointed out. "One by the creek and the spring where we watered, and one here, where the Pointe de la Coubre peninsula begins, right where the coast road curves sou'east to Royan, sirs."

"Captain Charlton told me of this'un," Ayscough said of the one furthest north. "Pity he can't get to grips with it as you did, Lewrie. The fort cross the Channel on Ile d'Oléron prevents him. Else, he'd give it a daily bombardment, as I expect you treat these others."

"I *don't,* sir," Lewrie confessed. "I *want* the French shiftin' men and artillery to the Savage Coast. It's sixteen miles o' march from there to Royan, and Fort Saint Georges de Didonne, so . . . should the French *think* we're planning a large assault here," he said with a stab at the lonely, almost uninhabited forest, with its road that led to La Tremblade and Marennes, threatening the naval base of Rochefort, "then that's fewer guns and soldiers to defend the completed fort here, and the one they're buildin' *here,*" he said, shifting his finger to St. Georges, then Pointe de Grave, which guarded the Gironde narrows.

"Ye don't wish . . . ?" a deflated Commodore Ayscough all but babbled.

"The Pointe de Grave battery is still unfinished, and, of late, we've seen fewer workers, not more, as I'd expect," Lewrie continued. "We can't see far up the Gironde, but what little we've been able to spy out reveals more barge traffick comin' down from Bordeaux. Were the French intent upon finishin' the Pointe de Grave battery quicker, it'd make sense for them t'hug the south bank of the river and put in at Le Verdon sur Mer, here," he said, indicating the bay, harbour, and cove, "and some *have,* sirs, but the bulk of what we've seen with our *own* eyes is barges hug-gin' the *north* bank, runnin' close ashore 'tween Meschers sur Gironde and Saint Georges. Frog-built roads," he scoffed, and the other two senior officers shrugged and rolled their eyes. And, it was a given that a brace, a dozen, sailing barges could carry more cargo than an hundred supply waggons, even if they had to employ sweeps to make headway into the wind and tides, at times, and bear everything an army needed much faster than heavy guns and waggons could trundle along bad roads.

"What we've been able to see of the French emplacements on the Savage Coast, sirs, what artillery they're entrenchin', seem heavier than the six-pounder regimental pieces we encountered. It's possible that the twelve- and eighteen-pounders meant for Pointe de Grave have been commandeered to prevent the feared landing on the Savage Coast.

"Lots of French warships incomplete at Bordeaux," he speculated. "Lots of artillery sittin' idle, as well. They *will* finish the Pointe de Grave battery eventually, sirs, but not any time *too* soon, and . . . ," Lewrie tantalised with a sly, bright-eyed smile, "for the nonce, Fort Saint Georges's twelve- and eighteen-pounders cannot close the narrows. They haven't the range, and there's a mile or better of deep, navigable river on the south bank, by Pointe de Grave and Le Verdon sur Mer, sirs. That's where I *really* mean to strike.

444

"Oh," he quibbled, "I have *Erato* and *Argosy* maintainin' a presence off the Savage Coast, sirs, with my frigate further out to sea to provide support . . . cruisin' slow, and as close ashore as they dare go . . . taking *soundings,* sirs?"

"As if preparing the ground for ships of the line, and deeper-draught transports, aha!" Capt. Cheatham exclaimed, "twigging" to his scheme.

"I trust you've included *us* in this plan o' yours, Lewrie," the Commodore demanded with a pout.

"Oh, indeed, sir!" Lewrie told him. "*Savage,* and all the rest of the innermost blockaders, land on Pointe de Grave to demolish the unfinished battery, with as many Marines and armed sailors available from the ships of the line. It was my intention that *you,* sir, with *Chesterfield,* now with the welcome addition of *Jersey,* perhaps with Captain Charlton's *Lyme* to re-enforce you, sail in and engage the Saint Georges fort . . . with additional re-enforcements of more Marines and armed sailors from the line-of-battle ships, which, I hope, will make a grand diversion, a . . . demonstration, on the new French batteries near the spring, and the base of the 'hook' of Point Coubre . . . so the French will be distracted long enough for us to destroy both emplacements on the narrows, sirs."

Capt. Cheatham was all ears to hear the

nature of the various fortifications, nodding eagerly as an old cavalry mount might when the bugle notes of "Form Ranks by Squadrons" sounded.

"Just as well Lord Boxham's seventy-four gunners will only make a noisy demonstration, Captain Lewrie," Cheatham finally said. "Sand, earth, and log ramparts, built low, with gun embrasures protected with gabions, 'til ready to be run out, are almost impossible to defeat. As the palmetto log and sand fortification at Charleston, South Carolina, defeated us . . . Fort Moultrie, aye. When I was a lad, a lowly Lieutenant 'board a Third Rate, in the first year of the American Revolution, we sailed in, expecting to sweep all aside and take the city, one of the richest ports in America, but Fort Moultrie, constructed as it was, simply swallowed everything we fired at it for most of a day, and was mostly undamaged when we'd run out of shot and powder, and had to sail away with our tails 'tween our legs. When may we begin, sir?"

"Well . . . ," Lewrie hedged. "That'd be up to Rear-Admiral Lord Boxham, sir, for he's not seen a bit of this yet, Captain Cheatham."

"I'll see to that, no fear," Ayscough assured them, eager for a chance to do something other than cruise and plod.

"He'll surely ask what gems of intelligence

446

lead me to assume it'll work, Commodore Ayscough," Lewrie had to impart. "And . . . I still don't possess *solid* information. As I said in the beginning of our meeting, what I've been *told* is contradictory, sir."

"Ahem," Ayscough soured. "Indeed," he added, frowning; giving Lewrie the sort of look a drunken, blank-minded student who'd flubbed his walking-out recitations might get from the aforesaid hopeful tutor.

"I'm told encouraging things by one of my principal informants, sir, bleaker tidings by the other, and frankly, I'm not sure which of 'em to believe," Lewrie had to admit. "After the wooding, watering, and massacre, most of the fishermen have turned surly on us. After the second incident, surly turned to hatred, and even our ships longest on-station . . . Commanders Kenyon and Hogue, and our Lieutenants' commands, can't get a kind word from the Frogs who seemed the friendliest, and most informative.

"They've become uncooperative, even when it comes to selling us victuals and wines, sirs," Lewrie bemoaned. "Nothing is available, of a sudden, or if it is, the price has climbed higher than that fellow's, Montgolfier's, hot-air balloon. Best make the best of your sheep, sir, for I fear we'll not see its like anytime soon."

"And, 'til you discover which of them is truthful, your planned operation cannot be advanced, Captain Lewrie?" Capt. Cheatham asked.

"No sir, it can't," Lewrie confessed. Going even further, he also said, "Now, were one of our Foreign Office agents here, one experienced at sifting truth from fiction, and able to see through the duplicity of the French, well . . . frankly, I feel a tad out of my depth, Captain Cheatham."

"Well, damme," Ayscough gravelled, slumping in his chair, and profoundly disappointed by the situation; looking askance at his "star pupil," too, as if profoundly let down by him, as well.

CHAPTER
TWENTY-NINE

Mine arse on a band-box, Lewrie grimly thought, all but wringing his hands in frustration; *who'd trust* me *t'scheme this out?*

After dining aboard HMS *Chesterfield,* Commodore Ayscough said in parting that he should go ahead and sketch out his plans for presentation to Rear-Admiral Lord Boxham, on the off chance that he could find a way to discern which of the fishermen was telling the truth, which to trust. For the moment, though, he didn't even know where to begin!

Lewrie sat at his desk in his day-cabin as HMS *Savage* groaned, creaked, and gently shuffled along under reduced sail for the night. Before him on his desk lay tide tables, ephemeris, and personal charts, now much doodled-upon, which agreed with the Sailing Master's. A pair of metal lanthorns, hung from an overhead deck beam, slowly swept back and forth, as regular as metronomes, throwing meagre pools of light on the problem before him.

Pre-dawn was always the preferred choice for attacks; that, or the wee hours of the night, was there enough of a moon to prevent confusion and dread among one's own forces. Low tide for a firm beach on which to ground, or high tide, so the ships' boats had a shorter row, less time for the enemy to react, and fetch the supporting warships' guns into closer range? Which, which, *which?* Tides, the stage of the moon, time of sunrise, nothing seemed to concur to guarantee success.

And damn Kenyon's blood! Lewrie found himself fuming, which was a grand distraction from his *contretemps,* almost a welcome one.

"A last matter, Lewrie," Commodore Ayscough had imparted, after Capt. Cheatham had departed for his own ship. "Commander Kenyon sent me report of your most recent action, and I must tell you that he is . . . *wroth* with you. He does not *quite* accuse, but I gather from his tone that he feels you forced him to trail his coat to draw fire from the French, which resulted in the loss of three hands killed, five men wounded, and minor damage to his vessel. I gathered he thought you'd done it from spite . . . to work off some long-standing grudge."

"I *told* him he was bait, sir," Lewrie had angrily countered, "I surely did. Was Hogue

450

and *Mischief* the brig appointed to watch over the northern approaches to the Gironde, I'd have used him and his ship instead! Kenyon's instructions were to demonstrate, not make an actual landing, sir. His boats were all but in the *surf* before the foe opened upon us."

"But, was there some incident in your past with him, Lewrie?"

"He thought me dishonourable, once," Lewrie had weaseled. "Lured a Frog privateer close aboard by pretending to strike, then firing upon them, and setting them on fire with fire arrows. Kenyon was down with the Yellow Jack, as was half our crew, and it was our only chance. We re-hoisted colours a second before we opened, sir, burned her to her waterline, and saved our important passengers, secret despatches, and our lives. I s'pose he's resented me since, though I've quite put it out of my mind *years* ago. I've also made 'Post,' whilst Kenyon's still commanding below the Rates, so . . . is there any spite involved, sir, I suggest it is *he* who holds the grudge."

"Plausible," Ayscough decided, stroking his chin while they stood on the starboard gangway, waiting for Lewrie's boat to arrive. "I must confess, I've had my doubts of the man ever since he arrived on-station, Lewrie. Drinks far too much . . . slovenly in his personal habits. Uhm . . . the one time I was aboard *Erato,* I *was* struck by the, ah . . .

451

strange aura about her, the mood of her crew, and the lack of uniformity in how they were accoutred, as if Kenyon plays favourites."

"Well, perhaps some of his killed or wounded were better-dressed, sir," Lewrie suggested with a bland face, "his favourites."

"Good God, you're not suggesting . . . !" Ayscough had blanched.

"Have no idea, sir," Lewrie had told him, hoping that Ayscough might figure it out on his own, without having to recount what he had witnessed all those years ago, . . . which *would* sound like spite. There they had left it.

Lewrie rolled his shoulders and leaned his head far back to ease the onset of a crick, before forcing his attention back to the charts and tables.

"Don't have a bloody *clue!*" he whispered. "They'll find me out at last. 'Oh, that bloody Lewrie, what a *fool* he was,' they'll say." Ever since being all but "Pressed" by his own father in 1780, he'd had a mortal fear of making a monumental cock-up, sooner or later, as if he had spent all his career, not one of his choosing, playing the *role* of a competent Commission Sea Officer, but was at base a mere dilettante, a sham, a "cack-handed, cunny-thumbed" fraud. And now that he had the rank and seniority, the *responsibility,* he would be found out.

Chalky, the younger cat, half-opened his eyes and raised up his head from a tail-tucked, paw-tucked drowse on one corner of the desk, and Toulon, sprawled cross his lap, looked up hopefully, giving Lewrie a loving head swipe upon his waist-coat.

"At least *you* two still respect me," Lewrie muttered to them as he gave each some stroking. "Christ!" He leaned back in his chair again, running both hands over his hair, looking up at the slowly swaying lanthorns and the deck beams for inspiration. "Should've stayed a Lieutenant . . . a *Midshipman!* Or, stayed ashore on half-pay and become a buttock-brokerin' pimp, after the Revolution!"

It was one thing for him to spin moonbeam fantasies of blood and mayhem over the wine-table, but quite another to set a plan on paper, with a dozen copies saved for later revelation, a plan that could get a lot of good men killed or wounded if it was a half-baked shambles, ending in an egregious failure. The Country's, the Navy's, and Capt. Alan Lewrie's repute could go smash like Humpty-Dumpty, and its author cashiered for hen-headed incompetence.

Think . . . think, ye bloody half-wit! he chid himself; *what is it ye wish t'do? More t'the point, what d'ye wish the* Frogs *t'do? Smash those forts on the narrows, that's what, but . . . how? I need a few o' Lord Boxham's "liners," Marines, and sailors, hmmm . . .*

He considered that, like the sketchy plan he'd formed a year or more ago to seize New Orleans, and Louisiana, from the Spanish . . . one now most-like mouldering in an occasionally flooded basement at Admiralty, or Horse Guards, this one might *never* be implemented, thankee Jesus! Lord Boxham might look at this one and reject it out of hand. But, if he *liked* it, and it turned out to be a farce . . . !

The local tides, he considered. The deep-draught ships of the line had to get within practical gun-range, close enough to the shore to frighten the French into *thinking* that a massive invasion force was going to be landed. Deep-draught ships would have to back up his own light ships in the Gironde, too, *close* ashore.

He shifted tables, books, and such on the desk, and his personal mail, still bound in twine and unopened, fell off the desk to hit the deck with a loud thud. "Ow!" he yelped as Chalky sprang off the desk, as Toulon abandoned his lap in a prodigious leap to larboard, and his claws dug in deep into his thighs for a *sure* launch, right through his breeches, and damned close to his "wedding tackle"!

"Say somethin', sir?" Aspinall asked, drawn from his pantry as he was getting ready to hang up his apron. "Oh, the wee poltroons got a scare on, poor darlin's."

"Ow," Lewrie sarcastically reiterated as he checked his thighs for blood. The cats landed with legs wide-spread, low to the deck with tails bottled up and whisking rapidly, looking at each other as if to ask, "What the bloody Hell was *that?*" before stalking on stiffened legs to sniff noses with each other, then sniff each other's arses.

"Was about t'say, sir, 'tis nigh on Two Bells," Aspinall reminded him. "Will ya be needin' anythin' more this ev'nin', sir?"

Two Bells of the Evening Watch, 9 p.m., was the time for all lights belowdecks to be extinguished, every lanthorn and every glim, so no accidental fire could break out, the worst danger for a wooden ship chock-full of pitch, tar, resin, gunpowder, and sailcloth. Soon, the Master-at-Arms, Mr. Neale, and his Ship's Corporals, Burton and Ragster, would start their rounds.

"No, nothing more, Aspinall. You go turn in," Lewrie told him. "Leave the coffee warming on the candle, d'ye please. I'll work a bit longer. Tell Mister Neale I'll try *not* t'burn us to the waterline."

"Aye aye, sir, and g'night," Aspinall replied, and departed . . . after a last, reassuring set of "wubbies" for the cats.

"Start of the flood-tide," Lewrie muttered to the empty cabins, once Aspinall was gone. "Dawn's always the best time, but . . ."

No, according to the local tide tables, the

flood-tide would be strongly making *after* the time of dawn shown in the ephemeris, and the top of high tide, and the slack, would not come 'til 9:55 a.m., or thereabouts, depending on Lord Boxham's iffy approval, the weather, and the state of the moon's tug. A week from then, the slack would not arrive 'til 10:03 off the Côte Sauvage, and probably ten or twelve minutes later off Royan!

Worse yet, line-of-battle ships, on a decent Westerly wind, had fifteen sea-miles to sail from the tip of Pointe de la Coubre to Royan; three hours or better before they could take up bombardment positions facing Fort St. Georges, and even if the French came down with a *serious* case of *la chiasse* — "the runs" — and scurried to the Côte Sauvage like a whole flock of beheaded chickens, they'd still have three hours to see right through the ruse.

"Unless . . . ," Lewrie grumbled, "we turn it round on 'em. Like a 'Three-handed Jenny,' yes! Watch *this* hand!"

He set all his sources aside, fetched a blank sheet of paper from a drawer, opened his inkwell, and wetted a captured French steel-nib pen. "To Rear-Admiral Lord Boxham, aboard HMS *Chatham* (he wrote) . . . My Lord, allow me to lay before you a plan for an operation against the French in the Gironde, the object of which will be to reduce both Fort St. Georges, and the presently unfinished battery on —"

Slam! went the Marine sentry's musket butt on the main deck oak.

"Master-at-Arms . . . SAH!"

"What?" Lewrie barked impatiently.

"Yer lights, sir?" Mr. Neale ventured through the closed door. " 'Tis just been struck Two Bells, sir, and . . ."

"Workin' late, Mister Neale. I'll be careful," Lewrie promised.

"Aye aye, sir," Neale replied, sounding daunted but dubious, and Lewrie could imagine him shrugging and rolling his eyes at Burton and Ragster, and the Marine private.

"Now, bugger off," Lewrie whispered as he began to lay out his scheme. He laid the start of the letter aside for a moment, to sketch out a drawing of the plan, and begin a rough draft, on separate pages from his desk drawer. It would be a long night, so he rose and poured himself a cup of that sour and bitter, too-long-on-the-heat coffee to prompt his wits, and wishing that there was any sweet goat's milk, or that he'd kept Aspinall a bit longer. There wasn't even time to unlock his sugar, tea, and coffee caddy, so he drank it black.

Hours later, he leaned back, eyes burning and his buttocks numb. He flexed the fingers of his writing hand. Lewrie yawned widely, just as Seven Bells of the watch chimed, spaced in three quick pairs, with a short pause between each set, then a final *ding* that echoed on and on.

Half-past eleven? he marvelled; *bugger it, I'm too tired t'read it now. Do the final draft in the mornin', and let* Padgett's *fingers cramp for a change. What captains' clerks are* good *for, damn 'em.*

The coffee pot had simmered itself dry long ago, and he feared that Aspinall would have a real chore to scour it fresh, come morning. Lewrie fetched a cheap pewter candle holder from the pantry and lit a taper off the warming candle, then snuffed it. The swaying lanthorns over his desk were snuffed, as well, then he lit his stumbling way to the sleeping space as *Savage* gently rolled and bowled along.

Might not even make a lick o' sense in the *mornin',* he thought as he tugged off his Hessian boots, breeches, and shirt, flinging all atop his sea-chest. He pinched the candle at last, and rolled naked into the cool, damp hanging-cot's box, setting it swaying wildly for a minute or two. The upper halves of the sash windows in the transom were open, and the night was almost nippish. To get under the sheet and coverlet, though, involved displacing the cats, who had snuggled up into a ball with each other. Awakened, Toulon and Chalky assumed that it was time for a bit more adoration from a human, and even after he had rolled over on one side and punched his pillow into shape, they were damned persistent. Whose bed *was* it, after all?

Sleep on it, Lewrie thought, once they had settled down in the lee of his knees, and the nape of his neck, and Eight Bells, signal for the change of watch, and the start of the Middle, peacefully chimed.

CHAPTER
THIRTY

"Zut alors, Capitaine La . . . *m'sieur,* but you mak ze *grand emmerdement,"* Jules Papin chortled over his first tall glass of rum, *"mon cul* eef you do, hawn hawn! *Officiers de l'Armee,* you give *la chiasse,* 'ow you say, ze 'runs'? All Médoc, all Saintonge, is be like ze 'eadless chicken, an' *soldats* be march *de long en large,* uhm . . . ze backward an' forwards?"

Papin gleefully related that a demi-brigade, perhaps two thousand men, was rumoured to be on the way to re-enforce Rochefort, Marennes, and La Tremblade. More troops, about three or four companies, had come up from Bordeaux by barge, at least as far as Meschers sur Gironde, and heavy guns with them, at least six pieces that he'd seen himself, and judged to be 12-pounders. They had all gone down the coast, afoot or upon extemporised gun-carriages, though, for he'd seen them on the coast road, a bit west of St. Palais sur Mer when he'd run a trawl near the shore; perhaps, Papin speculated idly, to set up their guns by the site of his murderous ambush, and his humiliatingly sprung trap.

There was some anger and sadness among the locals over the death of so many soldiers, no matter they weren't local boys themselves, he related; too much a reminder of what had happened, could happen to their own husbands, fathers, sons, and kinsfolk conscripted into the Army, and now very far away.

"More barges, *Capitaine? Mais oui,*" Papin went on, eying that fresh rum bottle jealously. *"Nord* bank of river, to Pointe de Grave not so much, *hein?* Some say guns for zere are . . . *détourner.* Diverted? An' *beaucoup de travailleurs* . . . many workers ze *Armée* hire to make fort on ze point, I see go in boats *do* Le Verdon to Royan. I do not *go* to Le Verdon, *moi,* for people 'oo live zere are *tous les fumiers,* an' ze *régime des hautains salauds dégueulasses!"*

All of them were shits, and a bunch of stuck-up, disgusting bastards, Papin meant; Lewrie's time off the Gironde was doing wonders for his command of colloquial French, if not the drawing-room variety!

"And, what about Fort Saint Georges, *M'sieur* Papin?" Lewrie said as he poured the man's glass full with his own hand.

"Is open at rear, as I say before," Papin said with a sly look. "Wiz *l'arsenal* hid-ed in woods, an' zere is a furnace for heat ze shot in centre. T'ree wall, t'ree eighteen-pounder. Two each ze twelves on each wall, *aussi* . . . make six twelve-pounder. Six of ze six-pounder down in beach battery at foot, *n'est-ce pas?*"

Seven . . . let's say nine *gunners per 12-pounder,* Lewrie hurriedly speculated to himself, all but counting on his fingers for a bit; *eleven for each 18-pounder, and eighteen French equivalents for powder-monkeys runnin' cartridge from their magazine. Five men on each 6-pounder, another dozen boys . . . say, four Lieutenants, two Captains, and a Major, and that's, uh . . . 'bout 150, all told.*

He named that figure to Papin, who frowned over it, shrugged in the Gallic manner, and guessed a lower number, perhaps only 125. "An', *M'sieur* Law . . . uhm, ze 'alf *compagnie infanterie* zey 'ad to guard zem, you 'ave already massacre, an' I see no more come, *encore* . . . still. *Peut-être,* no more zan eight or nine remain of zem, *hein?*"

Well, that's *encouragin',* Lewrie thought, leaning back to take a sip of his cold tea, his "mock rum."

"*Un autre, m'sieur,*" Papin idly said, sipping deep and scratching his unruly hair at the same time. "Ze ozzer t'ing. Before you massacre, before you bombard . . . rumour say *beaucoup de soldats, beaucoup d'artillerie* are to go *nord, au* Channel coast, but now? *Non.*"

462

And, that's . . . int'restin', Lewrie thought. Could their new Consul, Napoleon Bonaparte, so fear a British invasion cross the Dover Straits that he was fortifying Artois and Picardy against such? Or, was Bonaparte amassing an invasion army of his own against England? In either case, whatever pin-prick or "flea-bite" launched here off the Gironde could disrupt either of Bonaparte's plans.

"*Merci, merci beaucoup, Capitaine* Papin, for all your tidings," Lewrie warmly told him.

"T'anks, *mon cul!*" Papin growled. "T'anks be damn, *m'sieur.* I pass you' 'school assign-e-ment,' better ze rum, ze *gold,* be ze reward, *hein? Aussi, non* to expect you buy from me ze *bon marché* . . . ze cheap, no more, *non. Gendarmerie* 'ave spies, are now anger-ed, an' are now *soupçonneux,* uhm . . . ze suspicious? Cannot bring you much, an' risk mus' be *repaid, hein?* I curse zose *fumiers,* bad as I mus' curse you, *comprendre?*"

Two hours later, as *Savage* made her daily rounds of the estuary, the lookouts espied Jean Brasseur's boat, just as shabby and dowdy as she ever was, but, this time flying a much-faded pale blue long pendant from her mast-tip, the agreed-upon sign that Brasseur had information to sell, along with fish.

"Fetch-to, Mister Urquhart," Lewrie ordered. "We shall let our fisherman come to us. Nine-pounders and swivels to be manned and loaded, just in case. Pass the word for Desmond, and he is to ferry an inspection party over to his boat. Mister Devereux, do you oblige me to send four Marines and a Corporal with my Cox'n."

"Directly, sir," Lt. Devereux crisply replied. "Though I fear they must be de-loused once back aboard. She's a filthy thing."

"Permission to mount the quarterdeck, sir?" Mr. Maurice Durant, their émigré French Surgeon, asked from the foot of the larboard ladder from the waist.

"Aye, Mister Durant," the watch officer, Lt. Gamble, allowed.

"Ah, Captain," Durant said, once near the binnacle cabinet. "I hear we will fetch-to, *oui?* Might I enquire how long this stillness may last, sir? Able Seaman Brough, 'is teeth are very bad, and I must extract three of zem, all at once, *quel dommage.* I wish to do this on deck, sir, not in ze cockpit or my sick bay."

And Brough had put off the Surgeon's suggestions that he suffer those teeth to be removed several times, 'til the pain was blinding, and Brough could not even take his daily rum ration without groaning. Lewrie strongly suspected that Brough's mates, and more than a few of the crew who served under the Quarter-Gunner, wished to see him howl.

During her conversion from a French frigate to a British ship, *Savage* had, at Mr. Durant's urgings, re-made the starboard half of the deck under the foc's'le into a most modern sort of sick bay, near the galley for warmth, but fairly open and airy, which all the authorities deemed healthier than a lower-deck compartment. There just wasn't as much room for *spectators* as was the frigate's waist!

"Very well, Mister Durant," Lewrie decided. "Carry on, sir."

"*Merci,* Captain!"

Brasseur came almost empty-handed this time, apologising over the quality and quantity of his smuggled goods, the indifference of the assorted bottles of wine, the day-old loaves, and the paucity of fresh cheese.

Even the tightly woven straw basket of oysters, clams, mussels, shrimp, and crabs — along with a few gasping and weakly flopping fish, caught that morning — was only half full.

Brasseur took his ease in Lewrie's great-cabins, silently accepting two bottles of rum and one of Spanish brandy from Lewrie's stores, and a glass of a better brandy, a cognac from Normandy smuggled to England by *British* scofflaws. The cats, of course, once Brasseur was seated, made their usual great fuss over him . . . damn 'em.

"You fly your pendant, *Capitaine* Brasseur," Lewrie said by way of a beginning. "You have news for me?"

"*Oui, Capitaine* Lewrie," Brasseur replied, rolling his glass in his hands after a couple of sips. "*Pardon,* but time mus' be short . . . ze *gendarmerie, n'est-ce pas?* Zey watch us now, and to spend much time togezzer will be suspect, so . . ."

"Say on, quick as ye must, sir," Lewrie urged.

Barges, yes; more barges were coming down-river from Bordeaux. Artillery was rumoured aboard them, hastily stripped from idle ships of the line along the city piers, and troops were being moved by barge or roads to the Côte Sauvage, and the banks of the Gironde; all of which confirmed what Jules Papin had told Lewrie not an hour earlier.

It was the *details* that were contradictory . . . disturbingly so.

Lewrie pretended to nod, grin a bit, and utter "Aha!" here and there during Brasseur's rushed description of French preparations for repelling a British "flea-bite"; he even bothered to make notes of the salient portions of the tale, but . . .

Jean Brasseur laid out a strong reaction to his ambush and his bombardment, with little mention of how his fellow locals felt, which Lewrie thought odd; but, perhaps because the French people had no say in the matter, and no one was asking their opinion, anyway.

A demi-brigade was rumoured moved to Rochefort and the Côte Sauvage, and a *sec-*

ond demi-brigade, gathered from Bordeaux and the provincial capital of Saintes in Saintonge, was to come to Royan and Talmont, to St. Palais sur Mer to erect new fortifications, supposed to be armed with proper 24-pounder and 32-pounder guns. The fort at St. Georges would give up its 12-pounders and 18-pounders for heavier pieces, and those lighter pieces would be sent cross the Gironde to the unfinished battery at Pointe de Grave. With his own eyes, Brasseur swore that he had seen the stone blocks meant to raise the ramparts higher being laid flat for gun platforms, and some blocks of the low walls would be removed to make embrasures for firing.

"I fear, *m'sieur,* zat a half-*bataillon* of *soldats* will come to my poor village," Brasseur moodily told him, "an' take over 'ouses of our people. *Officiers* 'ave mark-ed doors wiz chalk. So many *soldats* of which *compagnie* to each, an' *my* 'ouse zey will take, an' *we* mus' *feed* zem, *hein?*" he bemoaned, looking frantic for a second. "*Mon Dieu, Capitaine* Lewrie, zey stay long, *ma famille* will *starve!* An, if zey suspect anyone of disloyalty, of consort wiz enemy . . . if false accusations are made, ze arrests, ze massacres in ze Vendée, may 'appen all over again. You see why I mus' not be suspect by dealing wiz you?"

"Might you wish to be taken aboard and taken elsewhere, sir?" Lewrie asked; he didn't want the fellow "scragged"! "If you are in danger, an escape for you and your family can be arranged."

"*Mon Dieu, Capitaine* Lewrie," Brasseur said as he set his cognac aside and wrung his hands. "Leave *La Belle* France? We mus' be curs-ed, our *famille*. Long ago *Anglais* outcasts, now, *toujours* outcast from new country. But . . . it may be zat, or face ze guillotine. *Merci, m'sieur, merci beaucoup!* Per'aps I *mus'* ask you for zis."

"Well, then," Lewrie said, reaching for his coin purse to shake out three guineas. "I'll not keep you so long that your police become suspicious, *Capitaine* Brasseur. Daunting as the information you bring is, putting yourself to further risk will not be necessary."

"No 'flea-bite,' *Capitaine* Lewrie?" Brasseur asked. "A pity. But wiz ze re-enforcements 'oo come. . . . ?" He heaved a deep, negative shrug.

"Don't see how we could accomplish anything, now," Lewrie found himself saying. Disgruntlement, perhaps, or a faint, peevish suspicion of his own, but he added, "Nice idea, but no future in it. Not anywhere near where *you* live, *m'sieur*. There are better places . . . no matter." He cryptically cut himself off, still wondering which to take as Gospel . . . Papin's version, or Brasseur's.

"Ah, *j'ai oublié!*" Brasseur cried, all but slapping his head. "Forgetful of me. I 'ave ze newspapers you ask for." He traded coins for a wad of papers kept in the chest pocket of his fisherman's smock. "Zey mention ze raids on Côte Sauvage, an' ze re-enforcements . . . to assure our *citoyens* . . . ze local people."

"At last! Thankee kindly, sir," Lewrie enthused, even though he knew that most French papers lied like a rug — as the Frogs said, "Lied like a bulletin from Paris" — and he would need help from Devereux and Durant and Lt. Urquhart to get a proper translation.

Brasseur gulped down the last of his cognac, stated a sum for his goods, and pocketed his money. Lewrie walked him back to the deck, then up the larboard ladderway to the gangway and entry-port.

Both men stopped, though, for a large crowd of sailors were now gathered round Mr. Durant and his patient, Quarter-Gunner Brough, who sat atop a sea-chest just aft of the main-mast trunk.

"This'll be good," Lewrie told the Frenchman.

Durant, now in rolled-up shirtsleeves and stained leather apron, was reaching into Brough's gaping mouth with pliers. He twisted, and even Lewrie could hear the sickly crunch of rotten roots. Mr. Durant jerked hard, and the sailors whooped, clapped, and shouted "Fire One!" as Durant held up the tooth like a conjurer who'd just

469

pulled a dove from someone's nostril. It was a large molar, worthy of a dray horse, stained brown with a lifetime of "chaw-baccy," and black with corruption. Brough put a hand to his jaw, spat blood, but made no sound.

"Ge' on wi' ith!" he shouted, to show his "bottom."

"Oil of cloves, Brough?" Durant offered, but Brough had surely been dosed with a double tot of rum, already; to which offer the poor fellow shook his head side to side . . . *tentatively,* it must be said. "No fankee, thir!" Brough insisted, glowering at the Surgeon as fiercely as he thought he could get away with, this side of insubordination; the thought that his pay would be docked for his treatment, *paying* for his own agony, might have had something to do with it.

"Care t'make a wager, sir?" Lewrie asked Brasseur. "Two to go, and the odds favour him squeakin' by the third." Fears of lingering too long aboard an enemy warship or no, Brasseur looked bloodthirstily intrigued, with that "better you than me, mate" smirk on his face.

"Go fer t'other'uns!" Willy Toffett urged. "Sure'z Christmas comin', he'll squeal like a shoat. Got money on't, hey, lads?"

Out came the second tooth, as rotten as the first, and with it a spurt of greyish blood and yellow pus which Brough spat into a wood pail, demanding again that Durant get it over with. "Yer *borin'* me, Mister Durant, sir!" he made himself cackle, to the gloomier, quieting crowd of onlookers, some of whom were now regretting their wagers.

Out came the last, and after swigging his mouth clean with sea water, Brough leaped to his feet, arms aloft, and dancing like a successful boxer fresh enough to gloat over his win.

"Huzzah, Mister Durant!" Lewrie called down. "Most neatly done, I vow! And, Brough . . . 'nother tot o' rum and light duties for a day, for ye stood it manful!"

"*Merci,* Captain," Durant called back, bowing at the waist after his pair of loblolly boys had taken charge of his pliers, pail, and apron. *"Ah hé, m'sieur . . . vous êtes Capitaine Brasseur, oui?"* Durant all but skipped up the ladderway to the gangway, and began a palaver in rapid Frog. His chances to speak his native-born tongue were lacking aboard *Savage,* but for the hour a day he tutored the Midshipmen and a few of the Master's Mates who might aspire to Commission, someday; the rest of his waking, on-duty hours were conducted in English, at which Durant had become more than proficient, but . . . when a chance arose he would gladly seize it, if only for a few minutes with another Frenchman, no matter his class or station, and "slang" away. Brasseur on his part seemed to enoy it, too, after making a torturous way with Lewrie and a nearly total lack of a common language between them.

"I offer him my medical services, for him or his crew, sir," Durant said with chuckle. "For *some* reason, *Capitaine* Brasseur *refuses* my kind offer, you see."

"He should not be delayed too long, Mister Durant," Lewrie told the Surgeon. "*Gendarmes,* spies, and the guillotine, hmm?"

"Oh, *mais oui!*" Durant replied, wincing. *Au revoir*s were said in haste, *faites attention* said for Brasseur to take care, and even more *merci beaucoup*s, along with *bonne chance* and good luck before the fellow went down the man-ropes and boarding battens to a waiting boat.

Lewrie stood by the open entry-port, his cocked hat held high in salute, with a smile plastered on his phyz, though fuming that both his informants had given him diametrically opposed observations, and he *still* couldn't fathom which to believe. Bastards! he snarled; *vous menteurs fumiers* . . . lyin' shits! Or, is it *fumiers menteurs?* Tow *an adjective . . . le waggon green, by God.*

"Anything of note aboard his boat, Mister Devereux?" he asked the Marine officer.

"The usual trash, and nothing more, according to Corporal Skipwith, sir," Devereux said with a faint smirk. "Hardly any catch this morning, either, he told me."

"Mister Urquhart? Soon as Desmond secures the launch, pray do get us under way," Lewrie instructed. "We shall continue our little jog down towards Point Grave, and see if there are any changes to the battery there. Might take a pot-shot at it, do I feel surly. And I do."

Lt. Urquhart acknowledged his orders, touched his hat, and went to the quarterdeck. Lewrie thought a stroll to the forecastle and a turn down the starboard side might settle breakfast, but . . .

"Your pardons, Captain," Mr. Durant said, a quizzical look upon his face. "There is something I must mention. I do not know if it is important, but . . . ," he said with one of *his* deep, Gallic shrugs.

"Walk with me, sir," Lewrie offered, and they set off forrud.

"That fellow, sir . . . Jean Brasseur," Durant began, raising an eyebrow in query. "He sells us *more* than fish and wine?"

"He does, Mister Durant," Lewrie admitted, tight-lipped, hands clasped behind his back. "None good, really."

"And he says he is from one of the seaside villages, yes?"

"From Le Verdon, down yonder, aye," Lewrie said, his attention fixed more on the neatness of the flemished piles of running rigging, how lines were coiled over the pins in the rails, and giving the taut stays a thump

473

with his fist.

"Then that is very odd, Captain," Durant said with a frown on his face, "for in conversing with him, I do not hear the accent of the Médoc, nor the Saintonge or Aquitaine, either."

"Hmm?" Lewrie gawped, coming to a full stop to face Mr. Durant. "He's *not* a local, d'ye say, sir?"

"When I study in Paris to be physician, sir, I meet many young men from many provinces," Durant worriedly explained. "If one cannot speak perfect Parisian, well . . . one is teased, yes? My own accent of Picardy resulted in . . . no matter. Yet, because of this, I may swear that this *M'sieur* Brasseur has the accent I recall of fellows who come from Provence. This is very odd, *n'est-ce pas,* Captain?"

"Yet he claims his family's lived by the Gironde since the time of Queen Eleanor and one of our King Henrys!" Lewrie exclaimed. "His multiple granther's s'posed to've been an English archer! Damn my *eyes,* if he's . . . !" *Said* he'd been in the French Navy during the American Revolution."

And what was in Provence? Lewrie furiously recalled; *Marseilles, Toulon, Nice, . . . all of 'em French naval bases! Christ, I've been led round like a prize sheep! He's been lyin' from the start.*

"You couldn't be in error, could ye, Mister

Durant? All these years since. . . . ?" Lewrie pressed.

"At medical college, sir, I was known as quite the witty mimic," Durant told him, smiling in reverie for a moment, almost preening over his old skill. "We *all* made poor provincials the butt of our japes . . . for I received my share, as well, you see? It is not an idle boast on my part to aver that I still possess my . . . ear for accents. He is surely from Provence, sir. Perhaps long-removed, but this Brasseur fellow sprang from there . . . grew up there . . . spent a good part of his life on the Mediterranean coast.

"Another niggle, sir, which just now strikes me," Durant posed before Lewrie could begin to splutter. "Pardons, Captain, but yours is a name which you have surely noted that people you have met, overseas, is difficult for them to pronounce. The closest a Frenchman may come would be something like 'Luray,' yes?"

"Lah . . . Lur . . . Luh, I've heard a slew, aye. Go on, sir."

"Yet, this *Capitaine* Brasseur says 'Lew-ree' as easily as, what is the English phrase? As easily as 'kiss my hand,' yes? As if this fellow knows about you *d'avance,* uhm . . . beforehand, sir?"

"Mine arse on a *band-box!*" Lewrie spluttered; now that he, had something *worth* spluttering about. "Damn my eyes, but that

475

foreign son of a bitch's diddled me! *Thinks* he has, damn 'is blood. But o' course the French sicced Navy officers out here, posing as fishermen, to spy out our doings. Our intentions, too, by God!

"Well, Jean 'Crapaud' Brasseur's got another think comin', sir," Lewrie vowed, in some heat. "And, thankee, Mister Durant. I'd not've tumbled to him, were it not for your keen ear, and keener wit."

"It was nothing, sir," Durant preened in false modesty. "Just an odd . . . niggle in my 'noodle,' hawn hawn!"

"*Keep* nigglin', sir," Lewrie told him, "niggle away! Now we're warned, though . . . we're *on!*" he crowed, to Mr. Durant's mystification. "Now I know which of 'em to believe, and who'd imagine Jules Papin an honest man? Well, mostly so, no matter. As a friend, no — an *acquaintance,* for I'll not call him 'friend' *this* side of Hell — says, 'The game's afoot'!"

■ ■ ■ ■

Book IV

■ ■ ■ ■

. . . wherefore with thee,
Came not all Hell broke loose?
John Milton (1608–1674),
Paradise Lost, Book IV, 917–918

CHAPTER
THIRTY-ONE

A spate of rough weather had forced several days' delay, after an anxious week more before Rear-Admiral Iredell, Lord Boxham, had made up his mind, and had summoned Lewrie from the close blockade, fetching Commodore Ayscough in *Chesterfield,* as well, to thrash the *minutiae* of the plan to a dubious hash, and a mere semblance of Lewrie's original scheme, then re-assemble its various pieces into a cogent whole. That process had required *two* councils of war, a fortnight's worth of dithering, carping, and fault-finding, along with some flushed and angry faces, a great deal of swallowed pride, and here and there some gnawing of finger nails, before Lord Boxham had given his grudging approval . . . depending upon the weather, of course, and the veracity of the information, which Lewrie had to vouch for.

Then had come another full day far offshore for the Marines and landing parties of armed sailors to be transferred from their own ships to HMS *Chesterfield,* HMS *Lyme,* a brace of Third Rate 74s, to HMS *Savage* . . . from which they would be parcelled out to the brigs and cutters.

Another council of war had to be held aboard *Savage* to brief the new-comes' officers, Midshipmen, and petty officers, to assign duties to Bartoe, Shalcross, and Umphries, to Kenyon and Hogue. That one was conducted on a day of curling iron grey seas and greenish white spume, and a sullen, cold rain that lashed down from low, grey clouds, making them all think the idea half-daft, with winter gales expected by the end of the month, and a bootless endeavour best left for the Spring of 1801.

The sash windows in the transom of Lewrie's great-cabins had to be left half-open at the tops, the hinged glass-paned windows along the coach-top were propped partially open, yet the air in the cabins was a frowsty, warm, and almost-airless fug, despite the coolness of the day, and stank of foul bilge water, unwashed bodies and hair, of hot candles and lamp oil, and damp wool uniforms. So many officers puffed away on clay pipes that a pall of smoke clung to the overhead like the greasy cloud spewed from a Muskogee Indian firepit in a clan's winter *huti,* and no amount of wind cross the decks could suck it out, as if Lewrie's entire quarters had turned into a badly drawing chimney.

". . . fetch-to here, just off the tip of Pointe de Grave, as the brig-sloops round the point, and come-to on the up-river side," Lewrie said, using tiny slivers of wood to represent ships, atop the chart he had spread on his dining table. "*Savage* will land Lieutenant Ford and his Marine complement here . . . whilst Commanders Kenyon and Hogue will put Lieutenant Noble's Marines *there,* simultaneously, it is t'be hoped," he added with a brief, rueful smile. "All our boats, along with those borrowed from those officers' respective ships of the line, are to be towed astern, ready to go, and speed of landing will be crucial.

"At the same time as we all sail in together, in line-ahead with the brig-sloops leading and my frigate astern of all, and with all the cutters in a short column a bit North of us, *Penguin, Banshee,* and *Argosy* shall proceed *beyond* Point Grave, as we call it," Lewrie further explained, looking round to continue eye contact with all the officers crammed elbow to elbow about the dining table, "look into the shallow bay East of the point, to see what shipping may be anchored there. We have conflicting reports of barge traffick, so there may be some, or there may not be.

"In either case, Lieutenant Bartoe, the senior into *Penguin,* is to capture or burn whatever he discovers, or continue on another two miles to what we term the 'dragon's muzzle,' just off the Northern arm of the breakwater of the harbour of Le Verdon sur Mer, then wait for support from Commander Kenyon's *Erato* and Commander Hogue's *Mischief*."

"Might I ask why that is, sir?" a Lt. Aubrey, whose Marines and sailors would be aboard the cutters, asked. "I would have sixty men of mine own, plus another thirty off the cutters, all told. We could land on the breakwater, and march on the village, taking the French from the rear, as well."

"It's more than a mile from the place you suggest, Lieutenant, and more than two miles' march from the battery on Point Grave. Were the Frogs garrisoned in the village in strength, we could not take the battery and slight it, *then* march that far quick enough to assist you," Lewrie explained. "Both landing parties would just arrive tired. It's better that you and the cutters wait for *Erato* and *Mischief* to get the landing-parties ashore at Point Grave, *then* sail round to back you up before taking further action. Once they *do* arrive, though, all ships are free to sail right into the harbour, if the pickings look promising, and take a peek into the cove below the 'dragon's jaws.' "

"Unfortunately, sirs," Lt. Devereux wryly commented, "we ain't as spry as our Army brethren, as stout of leg and lung, from marching, trotting, and charging for practice

482

almost weekly, what?"

"And, our main objective is the reduction of the Pointe de Grave battery, and we don't know how long that will require," Lewrie further said, "nor how many kegs of powder must be landed to flatten it, so . . . any attack on Le Verdon must be up to Commander Kenyon's judgement as best he sees it, once he joins the cutters, which, 'til that happens, will be under Lieutenant Bartoe's command. Shipping is primary, if it is there, with assistance from Marine and naval boarding parties, *then* the village and harbour, if it appears that we are not out-numbered.

"Besides, sir," Lewrie said with a shrug and a twinkle, "going ashore on the village docks, if such is practicable, is a much shorter *stroll*," which slight jape raised a collegial chuckle.

Lewrie could not help casting a chary eye on Kenyon, who would bear a great deal of responsibility for the coming landings. Kenyon did not look all that well; his face was waxy pale, and he slumped in his chair, hemmed in closely with officers hanging over his shoulders, and peered blankly at the chart, as though the closeness of the cabins did not give enough air to breathe. His mouth hung slightly open, and the flickering of his tongue over dry lips gave Lewrie the impression that Kenyon would dearly wish a glass of something both wet and intoxicating, no matter the import of the moment.

God, he's a slender reed! Lewrie bemoaned; *why couldn't* Hogue *be senior, his active commission but a* day *older than Kenyon's!*

"*Savage* will remain off the point, and will see that the powder kegs are landed, once Lieutenant Ford's and Lieutenant Noble's people are firmly ashore, and will cover the main landings with our guns. If *substantial* opposition is detected up-river of the point, which might require my re-enforcing, Commander Kenyon will fire off a signal rocket, right, sir?" he prompted, hoping to fetch the man back from catatonia.

Kenyon snapped his head up to look at Lewrie, had to gulp before speaking from a dry mouth, and said, "Of course, sir," by rote, yet . . . "We *know* that we may rely upon your support, Captain Lewrie." And that came with one of Kenyon's slyly snide looks, though the others, with no knowledge of the recent action off the Côte Sauvage, nor the grudge that Kenyon bore for his losses, took as a companionable affirmation of mutual trust!

Goddamn yer blood, you . . . ! Lewrie wished to shout aloud; *can't I relieve him for* drunkeness, *at least? He'll bugger this up, certain! Drunk as Davy's Sow, or from spite for gettin' some o' his Molly Boys knackered!* For better or worse, though, unfortunately, he was stuck with him. *Oh, but if you turn this into a shambles, Jemmy, I'll see ye stomped on like a worm!*

"Believe me, sir," Hogue drolly commented, "are there Frog warships lurking down at Talmont, you'll see a royal *fireworks* of rockets in the air, so you can come join the hunting!"

"Uhm, no . . . ," Lewrie said after the laughter died away. "Let's take signals into account, separated as we are. If you discover Frog opposition, Lieutenant Bartoe, send up *two* rockets, and continue firing, in *pairs,* 'til *I* fire a pair in reply, then limit your advance into the river to the shallow bay North of Le Verdon. Same goes for you, Commander Kenyon, if enemy ships turn up after you sail round the point to support the cutters, and I shall reply the same, to signal my arrival to support *you!*

"Mister Bartoe," Lewrie continued, "if no opposition is found afloat, launch *one* rocket after you are off the 'dragon's muzzle' . . . here," he said, tapping the chart with a fat lead pencil, "to which I shall reply in like manner. Do you espy large numbers of French troops in Le Verdon, launch *four* rockets in a single salvo to alert us that we may expect opposition marching to confront our landing-parties busy at the battery. Again, same goes for you, Commander Kenyon, once you've joined the cutters, and have had a good look of the village and small port. Then, is an attack upon the harbour either

485

practicable or necessary, and, knowing that you have left the beaches at the point, send up only *one* rocket to let me know that you're going in. Anyone takin' notes?" he asked suddenly, peering about.

"I am, sir," his clerk, Padgett, spoke up from a far corner by the chart-space.

"Copies of the rocket signals for each captain, and every officer of Marines, before we adjourn, do ye please, Mister Padgett," Lewrie instructed. "Well, gentlemen, if no one has any questions . . . no? How about comments?"

"Wish we were cross the river, sir, with the asault on the fort, and all," Lt. Noble wistfully said in the sudden silence. "Theirs the greater honour, what?"

"I trust there will be enough honour and glory available to all, sir," Lewrie replied with a grin. "Speaking of . . . might be best, does Commodore Ayscough know our signals, so, should the French have armed vessels up-river, *Chesterfield, Lyme,* and the 'liners' can come to our assistance with their guns, once they've silenced Fort Saint Georges."

"I shall see to it, sir," Padgett told him, reaching into the chart-space for a fresh sheet of paper, but recoiling quickly, as soon as he'd gotten hold of it, for Toulon and Chalky, shy of such a noisy gathering, had taken shelter in the shelves 'tween books, and were of a territorial mood, ready to claw and hiss at anything that threatened to enter their refuge.

"See to it, Captain," Lt. Urquhart also promised, though it was going to be a foul and wet row over to Ayscough's flagship; perhaps he would send a Midshipman, and save his clothing. At any rate, Urquhart looked restless and pleased, for he would be leading *Savage*'s armed seamen onto the beach, with Marine Lieutenant Devereux his second.

"Uhm, I *do* find a bit of oddness to this, though, Captain Lewrie . . . the timing of our assault, in broad daylight," Lt. Ford commented as he shifted uncomfortably from one foot to the other, "and our beginning a bit *before* the other operations, sir."

"Marching distances, Mister Ford," Lewrie told him, tipping him a wink. "Dawn, the traditional time for an attack, rises, and our foes see us deep into the estuary, in strength. We're not doing anything to threaten them, anchored as we are. '*Sacré bleu,*' and other such words of consternation, hey? *Then,* word comes by galloper that *more* warships are off the Côte Sauvage, blazin' away like Billy-Oh, puttin' down an armada of rowing boats . . . where *probes* were recently made, French soldiers were killed, and guns smashed, and their defences *still* aren't sufficient. From those beaches, perhaps a brigade, perhaps an entire *division,* could march on La Tremblade,

Marennes, or Rochefort. Hour or so later, after they've committed forces to re-enforce the few troops they have there, . . . at the double-quick with their tongues lollin' out, and the troops from Royan sent off, too, they find out that *we're* the real threat, soon as we up-anchor, and it's too late to march all those fellows back in time to counter us.

"I *thought* of launchin' things t'other way round, but it would take too long for Commodore Ayscough's force to sail in as far as the town of Royan, and what they might have despatched to the coast up here to the Nor'west could have time t'march back," Lewrie explained, with a wave of his hand over the chart towards the Côte Sauvage. "This way, we show them what they *expect* t'see, and get their pockets picked . . . as I did in London by a girl by name of 'Three-handed Jenny.' "

"So, all that's wanting is a spell of good weather, sir?" Hogue asked, looking as if he wanted to go back aboard *Mischief,* now that the plan had been thoroughly laid out.

"Yes, and pray God that's soon, before we roll our guts out on this half-gale," Lewrie agreed. "So, gentlemen . . . as my Cox'n and my cabin servant serve out glasses, I'd like to propose a toast to success to our landings . . . and, confusion to the French, of course, for this will be the last get-together before Lord Boxham deems the weather suitable.

"And, since I cannot dine you all in as I most certainly should, given the size of my cabins . . . and the state of my purse," Lewrie went on, tongue in cheek, "which a barrister in London seems to have seized . . . allow me to offer you all a *stand-up* meal . . . such as you would see at a drum or rout at home . . . minus the musicians, sorry t'say . . . 'less I could borrow Commodore Ayscough's bagpipers . . . ? We have the makings for hearty sandwiches, though . . . or, as my man, Aspinall, always tells me, should be called 'Shrewsburys,' since it seems *that* worthy called for sliced tongue and bread, whilst Lord Sandwich was too intent on a losing hand to *enjoy* eating?"

Each statement brought a slightly bigger chuckle, then a laugh.

"Do *not,* though, sirs, be entreated into slipping my cats a bit on the sly," Lewrie cautioned, "for the little buggers are already well fed, as fat as badgers, and, as my clerk, Mister Padgett yonder, may attest, they'll only go for yer fingers, after."

The charts were rolled up, the slivers of wood discarded, and a brace of seamen from Lewrie's boat crew brought in heaping platters of sliced roast beef or ham, pots of mustard or fresh-whipped *sauce à la mayonnaise,* with a large stone jar of gherkins in vinegar, roasted potatoes sliced in half and sprinkled with bacon and cheese, and day-old loaves of bread, fat *baguettes* already quartered and ready for piling on ingredients. Jams, jellies, and apple turnovers occupied another platter, and, for the abstemious after the toast, Aspinall's blackened gallon pot of coffee.

"To us, sirs," Lewrie said, raising high his glass of Pomerol, "none *like* us, in the whole wide world. Success when the day comes."

"And, confusion to the French!" Commander Hogue completed, and, with fierce growls of agreement and a "Huzzah" or two, they tipped the wine back and drank it down to "heel-taps."

Those few officers who been seated round the dining table were forced to rise and queue up, by seniority, to get at the food laid upon it, Kenyon included. With a loud scraping of his chair on the canvas deck chequer, and a ponderous old man's shuffling, he slipped back, his buttocks brushing hard on the sideboard, almost stumbling. His face was no ruddier that it had appeared when he was seated, and his long, thin, combed-across hair looked even wispier and more pathetic. Kenyon made his way to Cox'n Desmond, who was refreshing glasses, poured one down his gullet, and demanded a top-up before he wandered away from the victuals.

Kenyon stopped and peered at Lewrie, who had retreated aft to his day-cabin's desk for a moment to stow the charts away, and Lewrie saw his slit-set eyes, and the nigh-lipless hardness of his expression, as if Kenyon had bit into a sour citron.

"Sorry I could not seat a round dozen, but . . . ," Lewrie said with a shrug of apology; he *meant* to be civil.

"It is of no matter to me, Lewrie," Kenyon grumbled.

"Come aft, sir," Lewrie replied, making it a firm and whispered order. "There's fresher air by the transom windows. You are firm in your understanding of your role, Commander Kenyon? When the time comes, that is?"

"Of *course* I am . . . sir," Kenyon remembered to add. "I must hope that *you* will play *your* part . . . as you did before."

There it was again, that slightly lop-sided, mocking half-smile, which was so irksome! *Why can't I just knock him silly?* Lewrie thought.

"Bright-eyed and bushy-tailed on the day," Lewrie tried to jape off, "as our Yankee Doodle cousins say of eager readiness. Your part is most important, 'til I may land the powder kegs for demolition, and cover the landing-parties with fire."

"As you did for me, sir? Well, I'm sure you will fulfill that task . . . elegantly!" Kenyon answered with a soft voice for only them, but his mouth screwing up his smirk into a sour and resentful *rictus*.

"Your First Officer didn't *have* t'go right

into the *surf,* and I ordered a *play* at landing on the beach, . . . sir!" Lewrie snapped back at him in an equally soft, but harsh, tone. "The Frogs waited us out too long, and you lost some hands, and for that I'm sorry, but, was I given the task again, I'd do it the same way . . . with you, *or* Hogue, Bartoe, or whoever was handy! Despite your long-standing grudge with me, that is, or should be, put aside so we may do our *duty. Sober* . . . flinty-eyed . . . *duty,* sir!" Lewrie pointed out, noting that Kenyon's glass was suddenly empty, and could not recall him sipping at it *that* quickly.

At last, Kenyon's face took on a healthy colour, though it was more suffused with stifled rage than a sudden healing. He puffed up, almost a'tiptoe, as if he wished to strike out with his fists.

"Those *men* you cost me, Lewrie . . . !" he gravelled in a rasping rattle in his throat, "my brave, *fine* lads . . . you . . . !" And he almost teared up, making Lewrie feel embarrassed to see such a display of emotion; like watching a proud steed expire on a fence post, one wished to look away, but it was too lurid *not* to watch. "Been with me for *years,* some of them, so promising, so *lively* and . . . and . . ."

"Pretty?" Lewrie snapped, and Kenyon recoiled, deflating into his loose uniform coat as if he was a petty thief nabbed in the taking of a silk handkerchief.

"How dare you, Lewrie, I . . . !"

"I-will-not-warn-you-again, *Commander* Kenyon," Lewrie measured out in heat, "you say *Captain* Lewrie, or *sir* when you address me. And-you-will-do-so-with-the-proper-deference. Hear me, sir? I have *never* made mention of your particular . . . proclivities, but . . . ! Do ye fail me in your part of our coming assault, by God I will! You've already sent the Commodore a letter of complaint, *you* were the one who said a grudge lay between us . . . that I sent you inshore to *spite* you, and I do believe that Ayscough . . . or a board of five Post-Captains, may see who it is acted from spite."

Five Post-Captains was the minimum number required for a court-martial on a foreign station, or at sea in foreign waters.

"All I ask of you is to do your duty, Commander," Lewrie hissed, suddenly weary of the fellow. "Chearly, promptly, and whole-heartedly as an Able-rated man o' war's man. I hold no grudge, or spite, against *you.* I put you out of mind, *years* ago. But, do you continue in your obstreperous, uncooperative, and sulky fashion . . . ," Lewrie warned.

Enough was said, and Kenyon, once again, realised that he'd gone too far; the first time months before when he was in drink, and now in anger. "I will take my leave, sir," Kenyon said 'tween gritted teeth, pointedly setting aside his empty glass.

"I will see that Lieutenant Noble and your First Officer — Mister Cottle, is it? — are provided a boat back to *Erato*. No need to deprive them of a meal, is there, Commander Kenyon?"

"Course not, sir," Kenyon said with a grunting sound. He bobbed a short bow from the waist, turned, and went to look for his hat, boat cloak, and sword, waving off Lt. Cottle in passing the dining table.

"Forgive me if I do not escort you to the gangway, sir," Lewrie said in parting; wasted on the truculent Kenyon. Once the man was past the door to the main deck and gone, Lewrie heaved a bitter sigh, going to Desmond to get a first glass of wine since his toast.

Damn my eyes, what's wrong *with that man?* he wondered silently; *doesn't he know how close he is to losing his career?*

"Sure, an' this Pomerol whativer's right-tasty, sor," Desmond said with a snicker as he poured Lewrie a full bumper. "An' so'z them sammidges, too, Cap'm."

"Took a sample, did you?" Lewrie wryly asked.

"Well, sor . . . Furfy helped me tote it all in, like," Desmond answered. "An' faith, who'd pass up a nip'r two, here an' there."

"God help us," Lewrie chuckled, picturing Patrick Furfy and his two large hands snatching up tasties like a street urchin who had just come upon an abandoned pieman's cart.

"Be trouble wi' that'un, sor . . . that Commander Kenyon, beggin' yer pardons fer sayin', Cap'n," Desmond said in a soft whisper, inclining his head towards the sad-looking Lt. Cottle. "There's a young'un jist dyin' t'tell a tale o' woe 'board 'is ship, arrah. Don't ken th' meat of it, but there's *something'* odd 'bout that *Erato,* sor. Not that it's any o' *my* 'nivver-mind,' sure."

"You have no *idea,* Desmond, how odd *Erato* is," Lewrie muttered. "And, aye . . . I'll speak with him. Mine arse on a band-box, but you've become quite the busybody since I made you Cox'n," he quipped.

"Me Cap'm's best int'rests're me own best int'rests, sor," the fellow said, turning blank-faced and deferent. "Else Oi'll nivver be in sich a foin p'sition, begorra."

Like Sophie de Maubeuge sounding more French when she went all coy, Liam Desmond could put on "the brogue" when he worked a "fiddle," or was in a spot where whey-faced "Paddy" innocence might suit.

Lewrie strolled among the officers, sharing brief comments and gathering impressions of their capabilities, or enthusiasm, for the impending landings. At last, he got to Lt. Cottle.

"Your captain left early," Lewrie began.

"Uhm . . . aye, sir," Cottle replied with a shy gulp, unable to look him in the eyes.

"Knew each other long ago, in the West Indies," Lewrie prompted. "Ended not liking each other very much."

"So . . . so Commander Kenyon has mentioned to me, sir, but . . . ," the young man stuttered in nervousness.

"Loudly and often, I take, it, sir?" Lewrie said, half in jest.

"Uhm, aye sir," Cottle admitted, with a brief, rueful wince.

"Anything you wish to tell me about your ship, Mister Cottle?" Lewrie posed in a soft voice, smiling, so casual observers might think they were merely yarning. "Anything which might endanger the success of the coming landings? A problem of . . . morale, perhaps?"

"Don't wish to speak ill of . . . the hands, they don't," Cottle stammered, "they haven't come together as shipmates, as crews do in my experience, and . . . there's bad blood, Captain Lewrie."

"Because your captain plays favourites most shamefully, and cannot master himself?" Lewrie pressed.

Lt. Cottle winced again, so hard his eyes shut, then could only nod and blush in shame. "They could be a *fine* crew, sir, were some of them weeded out. *Erato* could be a taut ship, yet . . ."

"Under a new captain, who doesn't cosset the 'pretty lads,' and treat them like a private harem, d'ye mean, sir?" Lewrie asked.

"You *know*, sir?" Cottle gasped.

"Suspected," Lewrie countered. "Is he healthy enough to carry out his orders, sir? Of a *mind* to do so, despite his grudge, and his . . . peculiarity?"

"I *think* so, sir," Lt. Cottle stated. "He's a thorough seaman, and can't be faulted at ship-handling, yet . . . he *will* rant at times in nonsense words, just blurt out whatever springs to mind that had nought to do with . . . he's cautious, and conservative, mostly, sir. Not one to dare *too* much. *I* took the boats in so close to the beach, sir."

"And I am glad t'see you survived, sir," Lewrie congratulated. "I imagine he tore a strip off your hide, yes? You say he . . . rants? He don't *look* well, that's for certain, but, is his *mind* sound?"

"I . . . sometimes am forced to wonder, sir," Cottle confessed, now he had a welcoming ear. "At first, he *seemed* sound, but lately . . . *Erato's* his first decent command, sir, and I cannot think that he would *take* such risks to lose it, and his career, but . . . there is nought I can do to amend things aboard, short of . . . ," Cottle whispered, edging round the word "mutiny," which a court-martial would call his attempt to usurp a senior officer's place. Unsaid was the fact that Kenyon's ruin would be Cottle's, too, his career forever blighted by connexion to such a scandal. "I *know* it's 'gainst the Articles of War, sir, and the Good Book, and a mortal sin, but there's little I may *do!* Yet, if *something* isn't done, soon, the bulk of our people will . . ."

Sling a few "handsome" boys over the side? Lewrie thought, finishing Cottle's dread for him; *maybe Kenyon, to boot? Purge* Erato *like the* Hermione *mutineers did?*

"As First Officer, you're there to spur him in the right direction, in *action,* at least," Lewrie told him. "As for his personal life, well . . . hiding what he is all these years is slowly killing him, we can see that. That, and the amount of drink he glugs down."

"We let it *continue,* sir?" Lt. Cottle goggled at him.

"No," Lewrie grimly said. "You brought the matter to a senior officer's attention, at long last. I will see that it is amended just as soon as I am able." *Christ, listen t'me, prosin' like an Admiral!* Lewrie marvelled at himself. "I can't do anything this *instant* since I may need *Erato* tomorrow morning, does the weather moderate. But, were you to write a report on it and send it to me, I'll pass it on to the Commodore . . . who will most-like pass it on to Lord Boxham as if it was a red-hot fire poker, as quick as dammit. Would you do that, sir?"

"Aye, sir, I shall," Lt. Cottle replied, sounding and looking much firmer in his resolves, with what might be called a relieved smile on his face; even a pleased one, in point of fact.

"Enjoy my improvised buffet, Lieutenant Cottle, and pray for a spell of good weather in the offing," Lewrie concluded, giving the man a last smile, and turning away to sample a few tasties himself.

But even a sweet apple turnover could not rid his mouth of the bad taste that lingered. Despite his unwillingness to involve himself in such sordid doings, he now knew that he must. There was no looking the other way in the stern world of the Royal Navy, and ending the illegality against Article the Twenty-Ninth: *"If any Person in the Fleet shall committ the unnatural and detestable Sin of Buggery with Man or Beast, he shall be punished with Death by Sentence of a Court-Martial."* And there was no ameliorating codicil that followed most other of the Articles of War, *". . . or such other Punishment as the Nature and Degree of the Offence shall deserve, and the Court-Martial shall impose."*

No demotion, no cashiering without half-pay . . . death!

Lewrie built himself a ham "Shrewsbury" and stuck with mustard, not too sure if Aspinall had whipped up the eggy-lemony *mayonnaise* the right way, or how long ago. The sauce was like "made dishes," a foreign "kick-shaw," which had carried more than a few trusting souls to join the Great Majority, over the centuries.

Which made him wonder, *Is Kenyon really well enough to continue his command? He looks like Death's Head On A Mop-Stick, and his teeth are chalky-grey. How many times* has *he had a clyster full o' mercury shoved up his prick t'cure the Pox?*

Live with the Pox long enough, and one's brain rotted away, and one's nose collapsed. Was *that* why Kenyon behaved so truculently with him . . . that the Syphilis had destroyed his higher functions to such an extent that he'd just blurt out his inner-most thoughts, was he angry enough? Spiteful and resentful enough? That could explain it.

God help us if that's so, Lewrie gloomed; *I'm not countin' on a slender reed, at all . . . I'm forced t'rely on a raddled, pus-spewin' penis! Directed by a brain turned t'rotten Swiss cheese!*

"God help the French!" Lt. Noble cried, posing a stand-up toast.

"Huzzah, *confusion* to the French!" Lt. Aubrey amended.

"Bugger all, sirs . . . *death* to the French, *I* say!" Lt. Ford proposed, which pleased them all much better.

"Death to the French," Lewrie echoed, and tipped his glass up.

CHAPTER
THIRTY-TWO

"What are they waiting for?" Major Loudenne, commander of Fort St. Georges, and
the 26th Heavy Artillerie, groused, trying not
to look too nervous before his anxious gunners, who lounged beside their pieces with
slow-match burning, and had been on alert
for more than two hours. "Surely, if they
intended to attack, would they have not sailed
in just at dawn, *M'sieur* Lieutenant? Yet they
just *sit* there. And now, they seem to be
signalling to someone ashore . . . so many
signals."

"Those are not signals, Major," *Lieutenant
de Vaisseau* Brasseur said with a telescope to
his eye as they stood atop the ramparts;
partially to hide his smirk at the *Armée* officer's nervousness, and also conceal his
disgust at being dragged away from the first
time of leisure he'd had in weeks. "Nor are
they flags. Those are the Bloodies' *laundry!*
They do their *washing,*" he said of the anchored British warships, squatting about four

miles from either shore, and two miles out of Major Loudenne's heaviest 18-pounders' range.

"That makes no sense, Lieutenant Brasseur," Loudenne spat. "To wash, do they not need fresh water? Even at the low tide, they would have to come up beyond the narrows to dip up water, and that would be brackish, even then."

"They anchor, and do their laundry with water from their own stores, to *taunt* us, Major," Lt. Jean Brasseur replied, collapsing the tubes of his telescope and turning round. "The dossiers which we were sent from Paris told of this *Capitaine* Lewrie's capability to make the grand jest. There are other ships with his, though . . . which tells me that his superiors also possess his sense of humour. This is a feint, a distraction from the *Anglais'* true aim."

"Before you arrived, I sent gallopers to General Fournier, asking for re-enforcement," Major Loudenne said with a grunting sound; he had over-reacted, and *Général de Division* Fournier, and his infantry, would not thank him for a fruitless march of fifteen miles. "But, he still commands three demi-brigades, so, perhaps . . . ?"

The Major of *Artillerie* abruptly waved for his orderly, in desperate need of a calming smoke. The orderly produced two Spanish cigars and a tinder-box. Flint was struck several times 'til the rag caught fire, and both men bit off the ends, spat them over the stone wall of the fort to the stone-flagged "deck" of the water battery below, then bent over to light their cigars.

"Merci," Brasseur said, before turning back seaward and opening his telescope once more, resting it on the parapet, and taking a better look at the anchored British ships. *"Savage,* there, *M'sieur Major* . . . the brigs *Erato* and *Mischief* . . . in our service she would be named the *Espièglerie.* These you know, *hein?* The cutters you see daily, as well. Poor fellows, no 'laundry day' for them, for they still plod back and forth on their usual patrols.

"The larger ships . . . that one is the *Lyme,* which has been seen further North, off the Ile d'Oléron . . . borrowed, no doubt, to make us think the invasion would strike here," Brasseur casually pointed out, "the two next largest are sixty-four-gunned ships, which I do not recognise, neither the two biggest, which are seventy-four-gunned ships of the line. Off-hand, I would say they carry four hundred and fifty Marines, and could muster half-again that number in armed sailors, before reducing their ability to fight and sail their ships."

"You do not reassure me, *Lieutenant* Brasseur," Major Loudenne growled, spitting a loose, wet shred of leaf off his tongue. "I have less than one hundred fifty men here, and my last twelve infantry were taken back into their regiment and sent to the Côte Sauvage."

"But that is where the 'Bloodies' will attempt to strike, Major," Lt. Brasseur cajoled. "After the tale I told their *Capitaine* Lewrie of our fictional readiness here at the narrows, the fool let slip that . . . my family and I in Le Verdon would be safe, and that the blow would be elsewhere . . . on the *coast*. And besides, Major," Lt. Brasseur added as he turned about, to loll against the cool stonework of the parapet and grin, "*part* of my tale is true. There are two companies of soldiers in Le Verdon, and the Pointe de Grave battery, and the artillery *has* come up from Bordeaux, and will be installed as soon as the battery is completed, *oui?* Where *else* might the British land, with the best hopes of success, than the Côte Sauvage, *hein?* Hardly any inhabitants there, *non?* Before their raids, no defences, and no sentinels, either. Once ashore, they could march on La Tremblade by the coast road, and spread smirmishers through the forests to delay our own troops. I suspect we will see *Anglais* warships in the Pertuis de Maumusson to cut General Fournier off, and take Marennes. Then, they isolate your garrison and fortress troops on the Ile d'Oléron, and attempt to take Rochefort."

"Even the stoutest of their ships could not

get past the forts guarding those approaches, *Lieutenant* Brasseur," Major Loudenne scoffed, a bit rankled to hear a *sailor* speculate on military matters. "And we are prepared to meet them if they land on the Côte Sauvage, now that General Fournier has arrived. I only wish that, during the planning, a regiment might have been posted to Royan."

"Well, Major, you have requested re-enforcements, and, with the presence of 'Bloody' warships offshore, surely you will get them, *oui?*" Lt. Brasseur assured him with a breezy smile. "Even if nothing occurs here today, most likely they will remain, making your position here and over the river even more secure, *n'est-ce pas?* This demonstration they make will only amount to an *al fresco* meal, here on the walls."

"Speaking of . . . Alphonse. The coffee is still hot?" Loudenne asked his orderly. "Then bring us two cups. I must apologise, *m'sieur* . . . for calling you from your well-deserved rest, but I needed the experience of our Navy in this matter."

"*And,* the bounciest wench I've met in months, Major." Brasseur drolly leered. "It feels so good to be back in proper uniform, but it is also good to be *out* of it, hawn hawn!"

Delicate bone china cups and saucers were given them, the fresh-brewed Arabic coffee that Major Loudenne's brother had brought back to France from the Egyptian debacle as he had escaped on the same warship that had fetched the new First Consul, Napoleon Bonaparte, was poured from a matching china pot. The sugar was from Spanish Louisiana, off a neutral Danish merchant-man. The spoons, though, were humble brass, the same sort Bonaparte was reputed to use, and both Major Loudenne and Lieutenant Brasseur approved of their plebeian, Republican presence.

Brasseur admired the cup and saucer in his hands. In the old Royal French Navy, he had risen no higher than *quartier-maître en second,* and would never be promoted beyond Quartermaster. The Revolution had changed all that; he enjoyed becoming an officer, and the genteel life that came with it, as comfortable and clean as a minor "aristo" in the old days. If his recent covert work was not as pleasing as he wished, promises had been made that he could return to his native Marseilles, and serve at sea, haunting the sea lanes of the Mediterranean.

"You have had your breakfast, Lieutenant?" Loudenne enquired.

"A hurried one, *M'sieur Major,*" he replied.

"Please, allow me to offer a second, more substantial one. As you said, we will set up a table here on the battlements, *alfresco,* as you also said, and enjoy this fine, clear morning."

"I would be . . . ," Lt. Brasseur began to say, but stopped, turning to look west, and cocking his ears. Major Loudenne frowned, and turned his head that way, too. He scanned the sky, looking for a hint that he was mistaking the sound he heard with a storm on the far horizon, but . . . "It begins," the Major softly said.

"Heavy gunfire, *oui,*" Lt. Brasseur agreed, for in his time, he had heard the faint thunder of far-off fleets duelling broadside to broadside. "Look there, *m'sieur* . . . ," he eagerly pointed out, raising his telescope once more. "The colour of the haze above the Pointe de la Coubre, *oui?* It must have begun minutes ago, and the sound is just reaching us."

"More, and heavier, artillery than we possess behind the beaches of the Côte Sauvage, *hein?* Those are British guns," Major Loudenne gruffly commented. "There is little we may do about it now. Let us have our second breakfast, *oui,* Lieutenant? Alphonse, set the table."

The Major thought it would stiffen his anxious-looking gunners' nerves to see him and the naval officer enjoying themselves, as phlegmatic as artillerymen were supposed to be.

Before they could sip their second cups of coffee, and before a fresh tablecloth could be spread on the collapsible campaign table, a gunner on the western face alerted them to the galloper spurring down the coast road from Royan. "He will kill that horse . . . poor beast," Loudenne said with a sniff.

Within minutes, the galloper, a young officer of General Fournier's staff, rounded the end of the western third of the fort and came into the grassy courtyard between the ramparts, and the buried magazine and forge, reining in dramatically and leaping down to let his exhausted mount stumble on as a gunner took its reins.

The aide dashed up the long ramp to the central wall where the Tricolour flag flew from a tall pole, a white leather despatch case on a matching baldric over one shoulder spanking his hip. He was immaculate in fore-and-aft bicorne hat, natty blue uniform coat with a heavy gilt epaulet; he even wore white gloves! But the young aide's trousers were soaked in horse sweat, and reeked of ammonia. With a youthful sense of importance, though panting in his haste, the aide opened the despatch case with a flourish, and tossed off a salute. "*Général de Division* Fournier sends word, *M'sieur Major* . . . eight British ships of the line came in sight, between the Pertuis de Maumusson, and Pointe de la Coubre . . . two groups of four."

"When *was* this, Lieutenant?" Loudenne gruffly asked.

"Over three hours ago, *M'sieur Major,*" the aide breathlessly related, his chest still heaving. "I was sent with a message immediately, but . . . it is twenty kilometres, so . . ."

"*Bon,*" Loudenne grumbled, reading the despatch quickly. "Four at the north end of the Côte Sauvage, it would seem, another four near the base of the Pointe de la Coubre peninsula, the general says."

"*Pardon,* Major," the young officer interjected, "but the group to the north took our entrenchments and batteries under fire, just as I was sent away."

"Did they anchor?" Lt. Brasseur demanded.

"No, sir," the aide replied, "nor did the second group of four ships near the peninsula, which I saw for myself as I rode along the coast road. They were bombarding the entrenchments there, as well, and that was over two hours ago, by now, *m'sieur!*"

"And which way were they *sailing,* Lieutenant?" Brasseur asked.

"Uhm . . . oh! The northern group was pointing South, and their southern group was sailing North, sir," the aide told him.

"To meet off the beaches where all eight may open fire upon the defences near the creek and the spring, which the 'Bloodies' have already scouted, aha!" Brasseur concluded with a triumphal smile. "They fall into your general's trap, Major Loudenne!"

"Uhm, where did those come from, may I ask, *m'sieurs?*" the aide asked. "And what are they *doing?*" he added, pulling his own telescope from his over-shoulder case.

"Eight ships of the line, eight hundred

Marines," Lt. Brasseur told Loudenne, "and four hundred sailors, against General Fournier and his six thousand? Hah! It will be a slaughter!"

"*Sang-froid, jenne homme.*" Loudenne was chiding the aide to be cool-blooded and cool-headed. "*Toujours le sang-froid.* Such excitement on your part un-nerves others. Always keep your demeanour calm, no matter how urgent the situation."

"*Oui, M'sieur Major,*" the aide-de-camp replied, though thinking that artillerymen were perhaps *too* phlegmatic, like turtles.

"And did you meet any troops coming this way, on your ride?" Major Loudenne queried. "I had requested re-enforcements, as soon as those *Anglais* ships turned up."

"Indeed, Major," the aide reported. "The Fifty-seventh of the Line, all six companies. I met them about five kilometres north of Saint Palais sur Mer, but, I also had orders for them from *mon général* . . . to turn about and march back to the Côte Sauvage. They might have made it back to La Palmyre by now, *M'sieur Major.*"

"Damn!" Loudenne spat, warily eying the anchored warships.

"You return to your general, young fellow?" Brasseur enquired.

"*Oui, M'sieur Lieutenant!* I hope I am not too late to see the battle," the aide told him with a broad, eager grin.

"As little as I am used to horses, I will ride with you, *oui!*" Brasseur instantly decided. "What a grand sight, to see these *Anglais salauds* bayonetted into the surf, and slaughtered by their boats!"

"I will ride fast, I warn you, *m'sieur,*" the aide cautioned. "If you are not a strong horseman . . . but, we will need fresh mounts."

"There are many in Royan," Brasseur told him with a shrug.

"What are they doing here, though?" Loudenne still fretted, concerned about his lack of re-enforcements. "What are they doing?" he snapped, raising his telescope and resting it atop the parapet.

All three officers turned their glasses seaward; all three saw hundred of enemy sailors clambering up the rigging, standing atop the stout oak bulwarks and lining gangways of the anchored warships. Some were lowering . . .

"Mon Dieu!" the aide primly gasped. "They show their *arses* to us? *Les Anglais* . . . the 'Bloodies' are an uncouth people! Swine!"

"They mock us," Brasseur said with a snarl. Even though what the British were shouting could not carry that far, he could imagine what came from those widely opened mouths. "They *think* they have deluded us, and played their part in the charade. *Oui,* let us get fast horses, Lieutenant. We must get to your general, *vite, vite!* These ships hold nearly seven hundred potential fighters, and I think I know what they plan. That regiment you encountered must be alerted."

"M'sieur?" the aide asked with a raised brow; Loudenne was not the only one who thought a sailor spouting land tactics presumptuous.

"Their main landing is on the barren coast, *oui?"* Brasseur impatiently snapped, jutting one arm to the nor'west. "But, if the enemy lands *behind* your general's main line, up the coast from here . . . !"

"There *is* a road from La Palmyre to Arvert, on the northern side of the Côte Sauvage," Major Loudenne all but gasped, and *sang-froid* bedamned. "From there to La Tremblade it is less than four kilometres."

"Your general masses to *contain* them, let half get ashore before his riposte, *hein?* But, if there is a force in his *rear* . . . ? It may not cause our *defeat,* but . . . ," Lt. Brasseur pointed out with another of his iffy shrugs. "And, who knows how many more *Anglais* ships lurk offshore, to follow up on their initial lodgement, *messieurs?"*

"Warn that regiment, Lieutenant, the Fifty-seventh?" Loudenne sternly ordered. "They must keep watch near La Palmyre for movement by these ships. *Vite, vite!* Take my horse, *Capitaine* Dournez's, too! *Go, mes enfants!* By sunset, we can stain the sands red with British blood!"

512

CHAPTER
THIRTY-THREE

"Mister Gamble, we'll have the people's washing taken in now, I think," Capt. Alan Lewrie gleefully told the officer of the watch.

"Hoist from *Chesterfield*, sir," Midshipman Dry called out. "The signal is 'Prepare for Battle,' sir!"

"Once the dirty shirts are below, Mister Gamble, do you order Bosun Thomlin to pipe 'Stations' for hoisting anchor and making sail," Lewrie added, checking the looseness of his hanger in its scabbard. "You are ready, sir?" he asked Lt. Urquhart.

"Completely, sir," Urquhart crisply and firmly replied, nodding his head, as sober and grave as a churchman. If he had been thirsting for action, for significant honour and glory, he had an odd way to show eagerness, Lewrie thought. "As are my seconds," Urquhart added. He'd chosen Midshipman Grace, and, wonder of wonders, Midshipman Carrington, now better-known among the hands as "Mister Foggy," to help him keep good order of the landing-party of armed sailors. Why Lt. Urquhart had chosen the young twit, no one could fathom; sympathy, perhaps, for a sprog whose head was so full of clouds, and not much else; or, as a wag in the wardroom had speculated, a "noble" way to rid themselves of a hen-head more dangerous to *Savage*'s people than the French.

"Should I fall, sir," Urquhart solemnly intoned, "I have left a packet of letters to my kin in my sea-chest."

"Of course, sir," Lewrie said, stifling his own rising excitement and eagerness for a moment to reply in kind.

"All cleared away, sir," Lt. Gamble reported.

"Very well, Mister Gamble. Pipe 'Stations,' and hands to the capstan," Lewrie directed. Fleeting the messenger, binding on nippers, and preparing the decks to receive the thigh-thick anchor cable was, to an uninitiated "lubberly" observer, a form of organised chaos; not even the gigantic three-decked First Rates had enough room on their decks when hundreds of men breasted to the capstan bars and began to walk the contraption round, for "nippers" to rush continually 'twixt hawse-holes and capstan to lash the messenger to the cable, for men with middle mauls to pound the turns of the messenger round the capstan drum upwards so it would not bind upon itself.

Today was not so bad; the river bottom was mostly gritty sand, not so much sucking ooze, and with only the best bower down, the cable came in fairly quickly, the hands at the capstan bars urged on by the Marine boy drummer and the ship's fiddler, who, despite the stricture that only "Portsmouth Lass" was acceptable aboard a Royal Navy warship, played a lively version of "The Jolly Thresher."

"Heave chearly, lads!" Lt. Adair called out. Moments later and it was "Heave and pawl! Get all you can!" After a look over the bows and he changed to "Surge-ho! Heave, and in sight! Up and down, walk away with it, lads!"

"Bosun, pipe hands aloft!" Lt. Gamble ordered from the quarterdeck as the iron ring and the top of the anchor stock became awash and the new-model geared capstan clanked merrily away. "Trice up and lay aloft . . . lead along tops'l sheets, halliards, and jib halliards!"

Lewrie opened the face of his watch as he paced far aft by the taffrails, staying out of the way of men who knew what they were about; a quarter-hour to get the anchor up, catted, and fished, which wasn't bad time for a 950-ton frigate streaming bows-on to wind and tide. Ten more minutes, he judged, would have *Savage* under way off the wind, all hands on deck, the running rigging squared away, and the guns run out and loaded.

"Mister Dry," he told the signals Midshipman of the watch. "It is time to break out 'Form Line of Battle.'"

"Aye aye, sir!" the young fellow answered, almost tail-wagging like a puppy in eagerness. The cutters broke off their patrols, coming out to meet her; *Erato* and *Mischief* came to take station in line-ahead of *Savage,* which idled under loose and flagging sail, having fallen off the wind to face Pointe de Grave. A look to larboard showed the other ships under Commodore Ayscough's command were beginning to sort out in a line-ahead column as well, with the 74-gunned two-deckers in the van, so their heavier guns would be the first to engage Fort St. Georges.

"Not much of a wind, today, sir," Lt. Gamble commented, now that he was satisfied of the frigate being squared away.

"Surprisingly, aye," Lewrie agreed, looking up at the commissioning pendant as it slowly undulated like a boa-constrictor-long, colourful snake. "Seven, eight knots o' breeze, I'd guess. *Perhaps* eight to ten," he amended with a shrug. "Half an hour or better before we come to gun-range of the Point Grave battery. See the people all have a go at the scuttle butts. It'll be dry work, then."

"Aye, sir,"

Erato and *Mischief* were now off their larboard bows, a mile or so off, beginning to haul their wind to steer Sou'west for a time

516

'til they had *Savage* abeam their starboard sides. *Mischief* was hard on the wind, whilst *Erato* was nearer to a close reach to reduce the separation between them to less than a quarter-mile when they hauled wind again, and fell into place in line-ahead.

"And Mister Gamble? I s'pose it's time to let our 'passengers' on deck," Lewrie chuckled. "No point in hidin' 'em below any longer."

"Aye, sir." And Marine Lt. Ford and his hundred men clattered up from the pre-stripped gun deck to join Lt. Devereux's fourty, some of them looking sweaty and red in the face even though the morning had come cool, and the approaching mid-day did not promise much of a rise in temperature. Some fanned themselves with their hats, and some japed and elbowed their mates, but the bulk of them, Devereux's Marines and Lt. Urquhart's landing-party, appeared sobered by what they were to attempt, with the chance to go bayonet-to-bayonet with French infantry.

"We've the depth to go within a cable of the point, in your estimation, Mister Winwood?" Lewrie asked the Sailing Master, who was also looking as if a final prayer might not go amiss.

"*Argosy* skirted the point after dark last week, sir, and by her soundings with the lead, at the peak of high tide, which should be . . . ,"

517

Winwood pulled out his pocket-watch and peered at its face, "just past four minutes ago, we should have five and a half fathoms within a *two* cable range, Captain. I'd not advise going closer, for they did not trawl a grapnel looking for any wrecks which might have gone aground on the point over the years. God knows what lurks below."

"Two cables it will be, then, Mister Winwood," Lewrie decided. *Savage's* 18-pounder great-guns, and their 32-pounder carronades, could hurl solid shot at the stone battery with great effect at such short range, *and* could switch to bags of grape-shot, as well. Beyond musket-range, fifty or sixty yards, grape-shot would scatter rather far, but it could keep any defenders' heads down, and still would have enough force when it struck the unwary (or the unfortunate) to reap lines of opposing infantry in windrows. In Army practice, Lewrie knew from his brother-in-law Burgess Chiswick (the one who would still *talk* to him) defending artillery would switch to grape when a foe's infantry approached within three hundred yards, so he supposed his own pieces, much larger and of greater calibre, would suit.

He strolled to the hammock nettings overlooking the waist, now arseholes and elbows thick with men and weapons. He took another peek at his watch, looked outward to *Erato* and *Mischief,* which were close to within a

518

single point off the larboard bows, about to be occluded by a fluttering mass of inner and outer jibs. It was time.

"Lieutenant Ford . . . Lieutenant Devereux, and Lieutenant Urquhart . . . ," he called down. "Do find a way t'make yourselves thinner and flatter amidships, if ye please. Mister Gamble? Beat to Quarters!"

Major Loudenne's personal mount, and Captain Dournez's horse, were good'uns and goers, and Lt. Brasseur and the aide-de-camp, whose name Brasseur had learned was Carnot, were making good time along the coast road. A spell at the trot, a spell of cantering, a few minutes at the gallop, then checking back to an easier lope, in cavalry fashion — for cavalry could not gallop all the time, no matter how dashing they were — and the lone spire of the church in St. Palais sur Mer was in sight. A newly installed kilometre post by the side of the road — one of First Consul Bonaparte's many vigourous edicts — told them that they were within one kilometre of the town. Carnot felt inspired to put heels to his horse; not to the full gallop, though the image in his mind of "dashing" purposely through the town was pleasing to his martial ego, but a fast enough pace to tell the world that he was on urgent duty, bearing vital despatches, and making the girls of St. Palais turn their heads in admiration.

"The woods thin out, at last, *m'sieur,*" Carnot told his nautical partner, hiding a smile at how clumsily Brasseur rode; like a large sack of turnips. "Ah, there's the beaches again, and the sea."

Jean Brasseur's thighs ached like sin, his breeches were soaked with his own sweat and foul-smelling horse sweat that had seeped into the saddle skirts, whilst his buttocks had gone thankfully numb, after shrieking in dull pain, and *why* he wished to see the coming battle, he could no longer fathom. St. Palais was a small, dull place, but there was rumoured to be a good tavern that served a decent meal, and their wine would be a better-than-average Bordeaux, of course. He was about to beg off, plead a sudden need to return to Royan . . .

He looked seaward as they left the last copses of pines behind, and the left-hand side of the road became blue and open to the horizon, with low, wind-sculpted shrubbery, dune grasses, gritty sands, and the low dunes between beach and overwash barrows.

"What?" he exclaimed, sawing at his reins to bring the brute he bestrode to a merciful halt. "Where the Devil *are* they? They could sail much faster than we could ride."

"Uhm, back there, *m'sieur,*" Carnot pointed out, one arm aimed up-river. "I do not believe they have moved a single metre. No . . ."

Brasseur brought out his telescope, cursing the horse under him as it shifted its shoulders, tried to plod a step or two towards some likely-looking grass along the verge of the road. "*Mon Dieu,* they've made sail, they're under way! God rot and *damn* them!"

"What is it, *m'sieur?*" Lt. Carnot asked. "They are coming?"

"They are *going,* Lieutenant," Brasseur spat. "Going up-river towards the narrows. They were *not* a feint to distract us from an attack on the Côte Sauvage. They were after the forts from the beginning!"

"The Fifty-seventh of the Line!" Carnot exclaimed. "We can get them to turn about and march back. They are the only troops close enough to save Fort Saint Georges. I must ride on."

"And tell your General Fournier that there may not *be* a landing on the Côte Sauvage," Brasseur said with a snarl of impotent rage, for he had been very badly fooled, and the shame of it was just sinking in, strangling his ego. "But . . . something still might be saved. It will take the 'Bloodies' *hours* to get their troops ashore, form up and assault Fort Saint Georges, over-run the battery on Pointe de Grave, and place explosives. Your general has cavalry?"

"*Quel dommage, non, m'sieur,*" Carnot had to confess. "He has only infantry and artillery . . . the closest cavalry is going into winter encampment inland of Rochefort. To feed and rest their horses back to health. Most of our cavalry units are hundreds of kilometres from here, standing ready on the eastern fronti . . ."

"Ride on, dammit!" Brasseur barked. "Do what you can. I will wait for you and that regiment in the town, for there's nothing I can do any longer."

"*Oui, m'sieur!*" Lt. Carnot said with a bright, eager smile, despite his sour surprise, for it meant a gallant and glorious ride. "I am off like a rabbit. *Bonne chance,* Lieutenant Brasseur."

"*Bonne chance, à vous,*" Brasseur echoed, as Lt. Carnot put his spurs to his borrowed horse and galloped away, shod hooves throwing up divots of sand and dirt. "And go to the Devil, you idiot," Brasseur grumbled as he kneed his horse to a walk towards St. Palais. He had no urgency now, but for a satisfying meal, a bottle or two, and a welcome rest for his abused backside and thighs; on the softest pillows the innkeeper had. Lt. Carnot could gallop on to recall that regiment, dash up to his general to announce the deception that the *Anglais* had pulled off . . . Brasseur doubted the lad's arrival would be well received. He would kill a perfectly good horse for nothing; perhaps a second, if he galloped all the way back to Royan or Fort St. Georges.

Lieutenant de Vaisseau Jean Brasseur dismounted at last before the pleasant-looking little seafront eatery, unable to stifle a groan of pain, and a wince. Happily, the weathered wooden signboard boasted *dégustation des variétés de la région,* so Brasseur could sample as many wines as he wished, by the glass, with his dinner.

As he most carefully sat himself down on a large feather pillow, he made a mental note to write the Ministry of Marine in Paris. There was need to add something to Capt. Alan Lewrie's *dossier* that they did not yet know . . . "This man is capable of being a very convincing *liar!*"

CHAPTER
THIRTY-FOUR

"As you bear, Mister Adair . . . you may open!" Lewrie shouted to the waist of the ship.

"*Starb'd* battery!" Adair cried out. "*As* you *bear* . . . fire!"

All of *Savage*'s boats, and the ones borrowed from the same 74-gunned Third Rate that had loaned Lt. Ford's Marines, were in the water and stroking hard for the beach. That was the first flaw that Lewrie had found in his plans; with hundreds of extra men aboard, it would be impossible to take the fort under fire with them crowded behind recoiling pieces. It had been difficult enough to drop a kedge anchor from the stern, take in all sail, and snub the frigate to a stop two cables from the point, with all squares'ls batwinged up snug in the centres in sloppy-looking "Spanish Reefs." He could feel the anchor dragging a little, turn and see the stern cable judder, slacken, then go taut; good enough, though, to place them within very short gun-range, giving the boats a short row to the shore, and, most important, not tiring the rowers to return to the ship and pick up the second half of the invasion force. Now, at least, they could muster the other half of the Marines and armed sailors on the larboard gangway, out of the way, and fire over the heads of the men already on the water.

For long moments, Lewrie's view of the unfinished battery went as opaque as the wintertime coalsmoke fog in London, as quarter-gunners directed gun-captains' aiming points, then allowed them to jerk trigger lanyards on the flintlock strikers, delivering a slow and deliberate series of hammer blows of double-shotted iron. Bow to stern, HMS *Savage* shuddered and groaned to each discharge.

Still un-named, and thankfully unfinished, the small battery's walls bore no artillery with which to return fire. Soil and sand had been piled up in a wide, flat-topped base to support the weight of the completed fortification, and made a shallow berm under the base of the walls. Lewrie doubted the stonework had yet to reach much above a tall man's head, and the top of the uppermost course of stone blocks was yet level and even, with not a sign of an embrasure for guns.

There were *soldiers* in the fort, Lewrie could see after the fog of powder smoke drifted eastward on the moderate wind; shakoes, ashen faces, here and there a bicorne hat worn sideways in the French fashion, at least two senior officers under enormous cocked hats adorned with an even larger egret plume . . . dashing from one of the three walls of the shallow U-shaped *redan* to observe and order their troops about.

"Not much damage done, even with doubled round-shot, Captain," Lt. Gamble pointed out. "A nibble, here and there."

"The base of the wall is stout," Lewrie supposed aloud, "but the uppermost courses of stone are new-laid . . . done so recently the mortar hasn't hardened? They must have finished the parapets, but have yet to raise but the outer-most blocks to support the embrasures. Else, we'd not see heads and shoulders."

"As you bear . . . *fire!*" Lt. Adair shouted after the guns were re-loaded, run out, and the recoil tackles overhauled.

Lewrie looked beyond the point to see *Erato* and *Mischief* come to anchor by their sterns, streaming Sou'east, their own boats rowing hard for the shore, and their 9-pounders barking away. The cutters had run on round the point, and only their mast-tops were visible as they entered the wide, shallow bay above Le Verdon sur Mer. Above the thunderous, ear-splitting roar of cannon, Lewrie fancied he could hear *Bongs!* as round-shot struck stone, and the splintering of shaped rock blocks; each strike raised large clouds of stone shards and showers of sparks like flints in titanic tinder-boxes.

No, it was the four 32-pounder carronades of the starboard battery that were doing the most damage. Their massive round-shot might be slower-flying, and they could not reach out much beyond four hundred yards, but when they hit the battery's walls, they dished out bites the diametre of serving platters, and the depth of soup tureens, shifting stone blocks inwards, and causing miniature avalanches of stone chips to dribble down the face of the walls.

The boats were ashore, bows grinding into the shingle! Sailors were leaping out to steady them, knee deep in the light surf; Marines and armed tars were flooding ashore, and officers with drawn swords, a sergeant or two with their ceremonial half-pikes, were sorting men out into skirmishers and two ragged lines. As quickly as the boats were emptied, their crews were shoving them off, going up to their waists before leaping back aboard even as oarsmen were stroking "back-water" to fend them further off the beach, crabbing them round once in deep water, and returning to the frigate for their next load.

"Frog infantry! There, sir!" Lt. Gamble was pointing.

"See the French, Mister Adair? Serve 'em

grape!" Lewrie yelled.

Second 18-pounder balls were set back in the shot garlands and racks; powder-monkeys scrambled below to the magazine, returning with flannel cartridge bags that held wooden top and bottom discs inside, and inch-round, plum-sized lead balls between. A pause in the firing to ram them down atop round-shot; the strain of running out the heavy artillery pieces, right to the port-sills; some toil with crow-levers to shift aim, some fiddling with elevating quoin-blocks to ensure the spread of grape-shot went over the heads of the shore parties . . . "As you bear, on the *French,* mind! *Fire!*" Lt. Adair bellowed.

An officer was chivvying thirty or fourty shakoed soldiers into a rough line two ranks deep, flooding from the western face of the battery, though clinging nervously close to it.

"Man's bloody *daft,*" Lewrie grumbled. "What does he think he's facin' . . . big damned *muskets?*"

Lt. Ford's Marines were already firing, the first rank kneeling and the second waiting to fire 'til the first rank had discharged their muskets, catching the French soldiers at long range, not doing much to *harm* them, but quite a lot to daunt them and make them shrink back to their rear, and cram themselves elbow-to-elbow, as if that was shelter, even as their officer and their sergeants were shoving and cursing for them to open up their formation.

When the heavy round-shot howled through them, and when a cloud of loose-spaced grape-shot — a thousand or more balls — spattered sand and dirt round them, hammered bodies, smashed musket-butts, tore off limbs and heads, and cut a few of them in two at the waist, they simply melted away . . . dropped to the ground as if they'd never been there! The survivors, a sad few number, dropped their muskets and ran round the western end of the battery and took off in terror, leaving their formerly elegant officer on his knees, his sword broken, and his entrails spread before him as he vomited up blood on his white facings and waist-coat.

Lt. Ford's Marines and sailors gave out a great, jeering roar, and began a quick advance on the battery, muskets held extended, with fresh-ground bayonets winking wicked in the sunlight, at the "Quick." Before the boats had gotten back alongside under the now-silent mouths of the guns, they were in the battery, behind the walls, and into the courtyard, then appearing atop its firing platforms. To the east, Lt. Noble's men appeared atop that wall, too, with British colours waving bravely, even if the flag was only a small boat-jack mounted on a boarding pike.

"Hold fire, hold fire!" Lt. Adair cautioned his gun-captains. "Don't hit our brave fellows, yonder!" Flintlock strikers were taken away from the vents, discharged guns were re-loaded with single solid shot, and the guns were run in and bowsed down securely.

"Well, damme," Lewrie heard a faint, disgusted voice say. Lieutenant Urquhart, Midshipman Grace, and Midshipman Carrington stood on the larboard gangway's after end; looking as downcast as tots who had discovered lumps of coal in their Christmas stockings.

"Lots t'do yet, Mister Urquhart," Lewrie encouraged. "Ford and his lot can stand guard, up the point, whilst you and your lads place the explosive charges, and blow this place to flinders, hey?"

"But of course, sir," Urquhart replied, eyes almost glazed by how quickly the battery had fallen; no glory for him, poor fellow.

"Do you and your party man the boats, sir, and see to the loading of the powder kegs and fuses," Lewrie directed. "Quickly, Mister Urquhart. We must get under way and support the cutters, should they have run into trouble."

Lewrie looked out over the larboard bows, scenting for a threat, but *Erato*'s and *Mischief*'s guns had also ceased firing, and both brigs were shortening their stern cables and preparing to get under way, too. Abeam to larboard, nearly four miles across the Gironde, Commodore Ayscough's two-deckers had come to anchor just off Fort St. Georges, guns pounding by broadsides, deck at a time, and were wreathed in gunpowder smoke. Now and then, a stab of flame revealed a surviving French artillery piece responding . . . almost lost in the hot iron sparkles as the place was being pounded into ruin by heavy, impacting shot. The sound of 24-pounders and 32-pounders bellowing came faint cross the river, an over-the-horizon, stuttering series of thuds and thumps, and the echoey rumble of distant thunder.

Half an hour later, and the kegs of black powder had been slung over the side into the boats, and Lt. Urquhart and Marine Lt. Devereux and their people could at last debark.

"Signal rocket, sir!" Midshipman Dry announced, pointing with an extended telescope cross the point. "A single one, sir . . . no opposition found."

"Very well, Mister Dry. Mister Adair, clear away, the larboard gangway, and reply with *one* signal rocket," Lewrie ordered, extremely pleased that no French warships were in the bay North of Le Verdon . . . but, chiding himself for thoughtlessness. If Lt. Bartoe in HMS *Penguin had* found opposing forces, *Savage's* reply would have been fired whilst the kegs of gunpowder were still on deck, and he winced and sucked his teeth to imagine how large the blast would have been, if only a trickle of powder had caught a spark, for wooden kegs could never be completely spill-proof!

"Ready to proceed, sir," Lt. Gamble told him at last, touching the brim of his hat in salute. "Hands to the after capstan?"

"Suits me right down t'me toes, sir," Lewrie said with a grin.

A half an hour *more* to haul *Savage* to short-stays to her kedge, for Mr. Winwood's worry of obstructions on the bottom had proven true, and one of the anchor's flukes had fouled on something. The tide had gone slack an hour before and was just beginning its long ebb, taking *Savage* sternward, about ready to tuck the cable under her counter, and possibly damaging the rudder. The weakly ebbing tide took the frigate like a folded-paper boat, though, aslant the wind, and quickly hoisting the spanker and the inner and outer jibs gave her just enough way to stand out from the beach into the river and re-orient the anchor cable round so they pulled slantwise, from dead astern to the larboard quarter, and, at last, the fluke was freed, the hands breasting to the capstan bars could almost trot about, and the pawls clacked rapidly, 'til the anchor was up-and-down again, and just coming awash.

"*Now,* get way on her, Mister Gamble," Lewrie said, with an impatient sigh of relief. *Erato* and *Mischief* had rounded the point long before, and only their tops'ls and top-masts were visible above the low land.

HMS *Savage* stood out into the river, wind abeam for a time and pointing her jib-boom and bowsprit at St. Georges de Didonne, making a mile Due East as stays'ls, the forecourse and fore tops'l, and the big main tops'l filled with wind. The continuous gunfire from Commodore Ayscough's two-deckers had subsided to a desultory thumping, the cloud of spent powder smoke had thinned, and, beyond HMS *Lyme's* bows, rowing boats were swarming shoreward like a colony of scuttling cockroaches. For all that Lewrie could see with his day glass, all return fire from the fort had ceased.

"Haul our wind, Mister Gamble," Lewrie said, now they had enough offing from Pointe de Grave. "We shall wear about to Sou'east by South."

"Aye, sir."

"And we shall finally get a good look beyond the river narrows," Lewrie gleefully exulted to one and all on the quarterdeck. "Much like followin' an ancient sea-chart into waters marked 'Here be dragons'!"

"Or, discovering the Land of the Lotus Eaters in a portion that bears the caution *terra incognita,* Captain," Mr. Winwood solemnly said. He *might* be making a quip, but with Winwood it was always hard to tell.

Once worn about, and a mile inside the inner river past Pointe de Grave, the Gironde widened to nearly six miles across, a vast glittering expanse. The small town of Meschers sur Gironde lay two points off their larboard bows, and Talmont, the hidey-hole for ships running the blockade, much on the same bearing, but further away. The shallow bay above Le Verdon was to starboard, and was disappointingly empty of shipping; only some light rowboats were drawn up on the beach by some small huts.

Commander Hogue's *Mischief* was off their larboard side, bearing down on a three-masted merchant ship anchored close ashore just above Talmont, one with no national flag flying at the moment, and the crew huzzahed her, for their frigate was "In Sight," and any money *Mischief* made off her prize, was she "*Good* Prize," that is, they would share, no matter if that resulted in less than a pound apiece.

Kenyon's *Erato* was just off the "dragon's muzzle," about to enter the small harbour of Le Verdon, and the three cutters were further South of her, angling almost Due West in pursuit of *something*. Even as Lewrie eyed them with his telescope, tiny puffs of powder smoke burst from *Penguin*'s bow-chasers, and the sound of her light guns came as a pair of distant dog-barks.

"There's nothing for us to *do*, sir," Lt. Gamble commented, one hand fretting fingers on the hilt of his sword. "No French warships, no prizes in sight to be taken, but for *Mischief's* . . ."

"Success doesn't *always* come with close broadsides, sir," Lewrie told him with a faint smile and a shrug of his shoulders. "Both the fort and the battery will be destroyed, and the French will wear out a thousand pairs o' shoes marching and counter-marching. And, whatever re-enforcements they'll have to send to prevent a *second* beating will be just that many less available to Bonaparte for any future adventures of his, God rot the little bastard. Met him once, ye know."

"Indeed, sir?" Gamble marvelled.

"Toulon, in late '93," Lewrie said, explaining how his temporary command of a *razeed* French two-decker, *Zelé,* fitted with two heavy mortars, had been exploded and sunk by Napoleon Bonaparte's guns, and how he and the survivors had made their way ashore to become Bonaparte's prisoners, 'til rescued by a troop of Spanish cavalry, and how he could not give his parole and keep his sword, not with French Royalist sailors helping man his artillery, and sure to be shot down instanter as traitors to the Revolution, right there on the beach. "The man still has my sword, damn 'is eyes. Besides, it would've cut rough, to live comfortably, waitin' t'be exchanged, while my people would've ended chained up in some French prison-hulk, starvin', and dyin' of sickness. But, I hope t'get it back, someday," Lewrie concluded, rocking on the balls of his feet with his hands in the small of his back. "Go to Paris, once we've beaten 'em, dig round in some palace, and find it."

"Uhm . . . what is he *like,* sir?" Lt. Gamble asked, eyes wide with curiosity, and a certain amount of new admiration for his captain.

"Well, he's a short'un, a minnikin, and a fellow with an eye for gaudy uniforms, as I . . . ," Lewrie began to say, but Midshipman Dry cried out that *Erato* had just fired off four signal rockets; the signal that denoted French opposition in the village of Le Verdon.

"Alter course, Mister Gamble," Lewrie snapped, putting reveries aside, and stalking to the hammock nettings overlooking the waist and gun-deck. "Bring her round to Sou'Sou'west. Mister Adair! It seems we've more 'trade' for you, sir! Re-fit the strikers, and prepare the starboard battery for action."

"Four more rockets, sir!" Midshipman Dry reported, unable to be as stoic as a Sea Officer should be before the hands. "This time, it's from *Penguin,* sir!"

"What was it you said about nothing to *do,* Mister Gamble?"

"Nothing, sir," Gamble replied with an avid smile.

"Be careful what you wish for," Lewrie gently chid him.

Two very large guns erupted in the cove

below the tiny seaport, the sound like the slamming of iron oven doors, followed by the barks and raspy *Woofs!* of the 6-pounders of all *three* of the cutters, as if they had formed line of battle to engage something substantial, powder smoke beginning to wreathe the cove, the British guns stuttering bow-to-stern as they bore. A minute later, *Erato's* 9-pounders bellowed, too, as she penetrated the harbour, A quick look showed her beam-on to the village and piers, a look that forced Lewrie to choose which fight he should support. "Depth in the harbour, Mister Winwood?" he demanded.

"Two fathom or less, sir," the Sailing Master said from memory, after all his months of glooming over his charts.

"*Erato* will have t'deal with things on her own, then," Lewrie muttered, peering intently through his telescope. "Aloft, there! Any French warships in the harbour?"

"*Barges,* sir!" the main-mast lookout shouted down, cupping hands about his mouth. "No warships! They's a *gunboat* South of th' port, firin' on th' cutters . . . three point off th' stah'bd bows! An *oared* gunboat!"

"Stand on into the cove, Mister Gamble. What's the depth *there,* sir?" Lewrie asked Winwood.

"Four fathom within five cables of the shore, sir," Mr. Winwood once more recited from memory, even before he could confirm that from a much-marked-upon chart spread by the binnacle cabinet. "But, it turns *very* shoal very quickly, sir. Even at the top of the tide, there isn't a whole fathom by *three* cables' distance."

"Warn us when you think we're close as we dare, sir. Leadsmen to the fore-chains, and have 'em sing out regular," Lewrie said, eager to get to grips with *something* besides dead stone walls.

But, by the time *Savage* had come to the aid of the cutters, it was apparent that her help was no longer needed. *Penguin, Banshee,* and *Argosy* had closed with a very old-fashioned oared galley, blasting off her sweeps with solid shot and grape, ducked out of the way of a pair of wicked 32-pounder bow guns, and had smashed alongside of her, crushing and splintering the last of her long oars to grapple to her. Men from all three cutters were swarming aboard the river galley, and the French Tricolour had already been hauled down and replaced by a British flag. Far off in the shallows, two small boats full of French sailors were rowing for the beach like the Devil was at their heels, and there were even a few more swimming to escape capture.

"My word, sir . . . an ancient *lateener,*" Mr. Winwood said after a long look with his glass. "Good for going close to the wind in the Gironde, where the winds are mostly Westerlys, but their like has not been seen in real combat since Don John of Austria beat the Turks."

"Worth a penny or two . . . with a museum, perhaps?" Lewrie japed.

"I very much doubt it, sir," Mr. Winwood soberly replied.

"Mister Gamble? Swan us about into the river, again, 'til we may come hard on the wind, and stand in to see what *Erato's* up to," he ordered. "*Sorry,* Mister Adair. Have your gunners stand easy."

Erato no longer needed help, either, for Lt. Aubrey, his loaned Marines, and armed sailors were already ashore on the piers of the seaside village, and her guns had fallen silent. Close off the breakwater Lewrie could see other sailors aboard several large sailing barges near the jetties, and the only resistance seemed to come from within a maze of small shops and houses, and even then the expected, burning-twigs-crackle of musketry had subsided to an occasional *pop*.

Across the river, the tall pall of gunpowder smoke had mostly thinned and blown away up the Gironde, its large, wispy haze drifting over the chimneys and church spire of Meschers sur Gironde, where bells still pealed in alarm. Near "Mashers," HMS *Mischief* was standing out for the narrows, her prize close astern of her, and flying the Royal Navy ensign over a Danish flag. Lewrie pursed his lips, worried that taking a neutral, even one caught red-handed in enemy waters, and full of French export goods, would tie young Commander Hogue up for years in Admiralty Court, and end with the prize restored to her owners, with all expenses of the proceedings, and the years of the owners' loss while the merchantman was tied up in port in custody, on Hogue's shoulders.

I'd've burned her, and called it their *fault,* Lewrie decided; *a drunken mate, an overturned lanthorn . . . woops! But, I doubt Ayscough will let him keep her past sunset, so all may be well.*

If the Commodore didn't say anything, then he would warn Hogue, himself, and strongly suggest he let her go . . . after her cargo was put over the side, of course. No sense in letting blockade runners profit.

"The cutters are coming out, sir," Lt. Gamble pointed out, "with the galley in tow. No value to her, unfortunately. Bless me if *Erato* isn't tied up along the piers, though!"

"Bring us up within five cables of the harbour mouth, and we'll send a boat in to find out what they're up to," Lewrie said, idling his way to the larboard bulwarks. "Fetch-to when in close, sir. It seems all the excitement is over, and there's no need for our services. Do you inform Mister Adair to secure the guns and stand down from Quarters . . . I

540

haven't the heart t'be the one t'tell him it's over."

"Aye aye, sir," Lt. Gamble said with a twinkle in his eyes.

By the time they had fetched-to, though, a rowboat was coming to *them,* with *Erato's* Second Lieutenant of Marines aboard. She had barely touched the main-chains when the young fellow scrambled up the side as agile as a teenaged topman. "Lieutenant Thurston, sir, perhaps you do not remember me," he said, doffing his hat in salute. "Lieutenant Aubrey begs me report, Captain Lewrie, that we shall be ashore a while longer. We've discovered nigh a ton of gunpowder aboard one of those barges we captured, and there's heavy drays in the village, and teams of oxen, so . . . Lieutenant Aubrey wondered if it might be needed at the battery . . . to help blow it up, sir! Take a few hours to load it all up, and take it to the point, sir, but there's no more opposition."

"My brief ends at the beach, Mister Thurston," Lewrie allowed. "But my First Officer is already laying charges, and he might go ahead with the kegs of powder we've already landed."

"No worry on that score, Captain Lewrie," the young fellow said. "Lieutenant Aubrey sent a party of runners to Lieutenant Ford, on the point, and they will delay the demolition until our powder is added to theirs."

"Oh, a *bigger* bang," Lewrie chuckled. "Just at sunset, like a Germanic opera, I take it, sir?"

"Wouldn't know about operas and such, sir," Lt. Thurston said with a briefly furrowed brow and a shrug of indifference. "It will be spectacular, is all I know, Captain Lewrie."

"Much of a fight ashore, sir?" Lewrie asked.

"For a bit, sir, aye," Thurston explained with recalled relish. "Short, sharp, but all in our favour . . . there were about an hundred French infantry in the village, but we routed them right-sharply, and the ship's guns and swivels took the fight out of them." There came a few more faint *pops* from muskets, perhaps a faint, distanced scream as someone saw his death-wound, or got bayonetted, then it was quiet again.

"We've taken *five* barges, sir!" Lt. Thurston happily related. "Four filled with stone and mortar mixings, the last'un loaded with the powder, and the artillery pieces that were to go in the battery. Lieutenant Cottle says he'll scuttle or burn four in the deep river channel, but wishes to tow out the fifth as prize."

"I doubt a sailin' barge'd survive her first deep ocean storm," Lewrie speculated. "But, does *Mischief's* prize prove legitimate, they could be placed aboard her, and sailed to the nearest Prize-Court."

"Oh, goody . . . that would be excellent, mean t'say, sir," Lieutenant Thurston amended, blushing at his youthful slip. "Lieutenant Cottle bade me say that he will sail out with the barges, once we have the waggons on the way out of town, sir, and Lieutenant Aubrey's men to escort them. My Marines and our sailors will be coming back aboard *Erato,* soon as they set off."

"And what does Commander Kenyon say, Mister Thurston?" Lewrie enquired, mystified by the absence of his name in the proceedings. *He join the Great Majority, pray Jesus?* he thought, with imaginary fingers crossed for good luck.

"Uhm . . . Commander Kenyon fell, sir," Thurston reported, going solemn for a *very* brief moment. "Right as he stepped ashore upon the town piers . . . he and several of his boat crew, all at once. A French volley," the Marine officer offered as the cause, though looking a tad cutty-eyed, to Lewrie's lights. "About the only casualties we had, sir."

"I see," Lewrie intoned, with a grave nod of his head, though feeling he'd break out in maniacal cackles and do a little jig of mourning if he didn't get below in private . . . soonest. *Couldn't happen to a nicer fellow,* he thought, biting the lining of his mouth to prevent a broad smile. *And there's* that *problem solved, for good an' all by God!*

"My most utter condolences, Mister Thurston," Lewrie managed to say with a straight face, and a brief semblance of sorrow, himself. "Pray, do you relate to Lieutenant Cottle that I shall take *Savage* to anchor off Pointe de Grave, for the nonce, and wish him to join me as soon as he may be able . . . so we may take all our people off before the battery goes up. And, my congratulatons to Lieutenant Aubrey, and Mister Cottle . . . to you, as well, sir, on your quick victory."

And, just at sunset, after all the surviving sailors and Marines were back aboard their respective ships, the stone-bearing barges had been torched and sunk in mid-river, and all the two-deckers, cutters, and brigs had made their crawling way back into the estuary against the wind, but with a falling tide, there came two spectacular explosions. Fort St. Georges split apart in a titanic, roaring fireball first, and stout stone walls collapsed in a roar as the magazine blew, then kegs of powder at each wall. Heavy artillery pieces, already slighted by having their trunnions sawed off, and their muzzles packed over-full with powder and round-shot, then choked with mud, burst apart as fuses set off by the initial explosions reached the touch-holes, shattering hard iron like *papier-mâché*. And the rubble from the walls came down like an avalanche on the flagstone "deck" of the water battery, just as the charges laid underneath it went off as well, blasting parapet and embrasures into the river, and littering the beach.

Major Loudenne, his two Captains, and four Lieutenants, standing by the bulwarks of HMS *Chesterfield* as prisoners to watch the ending of his fort, all were later reported to be in tears at the sight.

Then . . . just as the sun touched the horizon, the Pointe de Grave battery exploded, too. Rectangular stone blocks went soaring into the sky, silhouetted against the livid blue-white blast of exploding gunpowder smoke, lit from within almost pale yellow for a moment, before turning ruddy amber, and all the waggons, all the construction timbers and scaffolding, all the out-of-town workers' huts piled in the centre of the battery's future courtyard, caught fire . . . helped along by the barrels of lamp oil, resin, turpentine, pitch, and tar that Lt. Urquhart had "borrowed" from bosun's stores to help things along . . . and torched upwards in an instant, volcanic plume of flames that lit up the night, and glowed like a lighthouse long into the evening, visible at sea for over ten miles 'til the wee hours just before dawn.

"Damn' good work, Mister Urquhart," Lewrie told him. "Simply *damned* fine! Pass word to all your people, they did grand work today."

"I suppose I must feel gratified by it, sir, if there was little combat," Urquhart bemoaned.

"Still . . . it does feel some satisfying."

"As I told Mister Gamble, not all victories involve blood and thunder," Lewrie cajoled. "Well, we did make *thunder,* at least, but we accomplished what we came to do, and hardly any of our men were hurt, and none killed, while the French lost hundreds."

"Well, there is that, sir." Lt. Urquhart seemed to brighten as he absorbed that concept. "The greater good, as it were."

"Exactly, so, Mister Urquhart," Lewrie said with a sage nod . . . though, in point of fact, the "greater good" was rather hard for him to swallow, too; especially the part where the more senior he rose, the smaller role he might play when his beloved great-guns roared. Oh, it was all very fine to plan something, then watch as it unfolded successfully, but . . . all he'd done this day was stand round like a fart in a trance and observe the derring-do of *others!*

"You did obtain some rather fine remembrances, sir," Devereux said from the side. Lt. Urquhart had at least come offshore in possession of an elegant French infantry officer's bicorne hat, and that poor fellow's excellently crafted Solingen sabre, scabbard, and snake-clasp belt. Well, he'd had to pay Landsman Newcastle, one of their "volunteer Black" sailors, three shillings for the hat, and Able Seaman Bannister a crown for the sword . . . a fact that would be conveniently forgotten in a year or two, once they were hung on his parents' walls.

"Lord, Cocky, don't nip my boots, ye daft little bugger," Lieutenant Devereux griped as the Marine complement's pet, the champion rat-killing mongoose that had simply turned up after a drunken night ashore in the West Indies, pounced and tried to gnaw on his new-blacked leather. "Private Cocky, M." was distracted from his mischief by Lewrie's cats, which resulted in a three-way tail chase round the quarterdeck.

"You may thank me later, Mister Devereux," Lewrie chuckled as he turned to look out-board to the ruined forts. St. Georges was now but a massive, light-coloured pall of smoke, the broad base of the cloud ruddy with subsiding fires, and the cloud drifting eastward towards Meschers and Talmont like a slowly twisting, towering phantom. Off the larboard quarter, though, the battery they had destroyed still burned as bright as the fabled Egyptian Pharos, with tall flames licking and forking at the sunset sky, turning the waters of the Gironde narrows and the estuary astern to a rippling sheet of brass, or polished copper.

"Commodore Ayscough did well, today, gentlemen," Lewrie drolly said as he stretched and yawned, "no doubt of it, and all credit to him and the ships under his command, but . . ."

He was more than ready to get off his feet, pull his boots off, and delight in what might prove to be his last fresh-fish supper, for the locals would be a long time forgiving the destruction they'd caused along the river's shores; perhaps two bottles of excellent French Bordeaux with it, too . . . the Brave-Mouton would go well.

"Just you look at what we wrought today, sirs," he went on after another yawn. "No matter what anyone says by comparison . . . *our* boom was a whole lot bigger than theirs!"

CHAPTER
THIRTY-FIVE

"What marvellous good fun, ah ha!" Commodore Ayscough chortled as the plates, dishes of removes, and the tablecloth were borne away, and the fruit, nuts, cheeses, and port bottle were placed before them. "Haven't had such a run ashore in years!"

"Took his pipers with him," Captain Charlton dryly added. "Made a fearsome racket. Put the French off, I will gladly allow, though. And, the extra colours proved useful."

"Borrowed a page from young Lewrie, here," Ayscough said as he used a pen-knife to pare an apple. "His father, Sir Hugo Saint George Willoughby, rather. Clean and unused mooring jacks to serve as King's Colours, and a few sheets of our lightest sailcloth painted to represent Regimental Colours, so the French would think we landed *three* regiments, 'stead of the equivalent of one. Just as we did at Balabac in the Far East, so long ago.

"This time," Commodore Ayscough gaily related, "one set daunted a French company, come from Cozes . . . that, and our musketry. Two of them caused the fort to surrender, once we flanked round its open end, and when a French regiment *did* turn up, as we were re-embarking on the beaches, they sat down on their heels, a bit south of Royan, and never advanced another foot."

"Well, covering fire from our ships made that stretch of road a charnel house, and they'd not have charged into *that!*" Capt. Cheatham of HMS *Jersey* added with a merry chuckle. "They'd been marched pillar-to-post already, and were dragging their feet and their musket-butts by the time they arrived, with their tongues lolling out, haw haw!"

"Colours fooled 'em, I grant ye, sir," Ayscough tut-tutted. "I do imagine, though, 'twas the sight and sound of my pipers in full regalia that put 'em off. There's not a Frenchman born who'd tangle with the Highland laddies. Aye, 'twas a grand day, indeed!"

"Wish *I* could have gone ashore," Lewrie faintly complained.

"*You* could not, laddy," Ayscough told him, snickering. "There were five other Post-Captains under me, all competent, and chafing at the bitt to take over should I fall, certain they could do it better! Why else do we toast to 'A Bloody War or a Sickly Season'?

Surest way to promotion! You, however, were, under the circumstances, indispensable to your small squadron, Lewrie. Oh, Hogue *might've* taken charge, he's an energetic lad, but he was round the point with his own duties whilst you and *Savage* were the vital backbone of the entire endeavour, landing the bulk of our forces, the powder . . . it would have taken hours for a small boat to carry word to Hogue, Kenyon, or Bartoe, and hours *more* to accomplish the task and withdraw in good order."

"It just feels that command of distant *others,* not just your *own* deck, is . . . like laggin' back, somehow, sirs," Lewrie told them.

"Comes with seniority," Captain Charlton imparted, giving Lewrie a sympathetic look. "In the Adriatic in '96, I spent most of my time envying you and the others, Lewrie. All I did was despatch you to a chore, then sit back and fret. What senior officers are *paid* to do. Mind, though, gentlemen . . . then-Commander Lewrie kept me up nights, in frets of what mischief he'd been up to lately!"

"I mentioned Commander Kenyon," the Commodore said, turning grave. "Do you gentlemen not object to the discussion of a professional matter or two . . . none? Good. Who should replace the late Commander Kenyon? Lewrie, you worked closer with *Erato* . . . what of her First Officer as a replacement?"

"In an *acting* command, sir, I s'pose he'd do main-well," Lewrie replied, "but Lieutenant Cottle is in his first posting, second in command of *anything*. He's promising, but young and green."

Gawd, you call someone else *young?* Lewrie flinched inside; *poor trustin' bastards, lookin' at* me *like an equal? A* senior *officer, with wit enough t' judge . . . me?*

"Ahem," both Captain Charlton and Captain Cheatham said at the same time, for both men had First Lieutenants aboard their ships whom they thought more than worthy of promotion onto "their own bottom" and independent command. Most such promotions on foreign stations, even if both Lord Boxham's and Commodore Ayscough's ships were officially under the authority of far-off Channel Fleet, were accepted by Admiralty, and were as good as permanent.

Lewrie found the silent interplay amusing, as both turned their eyes to Ayscough, who would have the final say; which of the two prospective Lieutenants had the better record; or, to whom did Ayscough owe more favour, or "interest"? The Royal Navy sailed on a *sea* of "interest" and patronage. Which candidate might earn *him* future favours?

"Damme, and I have a fellow of mine own in mind," Ayscough craftily told them, opening the silent bidding, and teasing them something horrid. "Or, Rear-Admiral Iredell, Lord Boxham, commanding over us all, might wish to put a name forward.

"In point of fact, sirs," Commodore Ayscough went on, carefully cutting a long spiral of apple skin, which was beginning to resemble a very loose red spring, "Lord Boxham is quite taken by Commander Kenyon and his brave, but tragic, end . . . and the capture of the artillery intended for the Pointe de Grave battery. He intends, I believe, for them to go to London for display. Hyde Park or Saint James's was cited, as well as the Strand embankments. In tribute, he said."

"In tribute to *whom*, sir?" Lewrie slyly japed.

"Why, to Kenyon, and *Erato*, Lewrie, of *course*," Ayscough replied, allowing sarcasm free, but subtle, rein. "The 'Kenyon Guns,' the '*Erato* Guns,' something along those lines. Our war with France drags on with so few victories since the Battle of the Nile, and the last time that our Army took a hand, it was a disaster. We shove *mountains* of money at weak and disappointing allies, and are at present *without* any. The people at home need *something* to make the struggle feel worth it.

"Though," Ayscough sourly mused, dancing the coils of his apple peel like a spring atop the table, "given the late Commander Kenyon's, ah . . . peculiarities, '*Erato*'s Guns' might be best."

"Peculiarties, sir?" Capt. Cheatham enquired with a sharp look.

"Health was failing fast," Ayscough almost grunted, "and he was a horrid drunkard, and . . . as Lewrie here gathered from *Erato's* surviving officers, Kenyon favoured . . . 'the windward passage,' " he concluded in a conspiratorial whisper. "Preyed on his most fetching seamen."

"A *'Molly,'* by God?" Capt. Cheatham erupted, looking at Lewrie.

"And poxed to the eyebrows, sir," Lewrie related in a soft voice. "Dyin' of it, most-like, in the final stages of the Pox, when it erodes one's brain matter. That's the only explanation for how he rambled so badly, and the way he was so grudgeful and nigh-insubordinate towards me. I *did* put it down to how much he drank at first, aye, or his spite to find one of his former Mids promoted beyond him, but . . . my Surgeon tells me the disease robbed him of self-control. Think a thing, speak a thing, sir. Put him in his place a time or two, and I *thought* he'd learned his lesson, but . . ."

"Bloody Hell!" Capt. Cheatham spat, writhing in utter disgust; for the topic, for the mortal, bestial sin, for having to hear a word of it, most-like. He waved urgently for the port decanter. "How does a 'back-gammoner' become a Commission Sea Officer, much less gain the command of a King's ship?

Should've been found out *years* ago!"

"He was very careful to play 'Jack, Me Hearty,' sir," Lewrie explained. "When I served under him in the West Indies, one would never have guessed . . . when he had all his wits intact, and could be thoughtful of his Publick Face. The one glimpse I got that roused my suspicions *could* have been explained away, and I was just a Middy, so what did *I* know of things? No *in flagrante delicto,* just . . ."

Capt. Cheatham raised a stiff hand to ward off the rest, and to shush any graphic description; he found restoration in the port.

"Was he extremely discreet, and kept up a stout facade, well . . . ," Ayscough stuck in gloomily. "And, remember, the Navy was very short of competent officers in '94 and '95 as the Fleet expanded. Kenyon was most-like nigh-anonymous, with a mediocre repute round the middle of the Lieutenants' List, just senior enough for promotion."

"The stress of living a life like that, sirs," Lewrie sketched out, impatient for the decanter to pass his way, too. "Then, comes a ship of his own at last, and the strain and loneliness of command atop it? A sense of bein' second but to God at sea, and with his wits goin' fast? and losin' command of *himself,* to boot? We all have known captains who turned . . . eccentric."

"Damme, Lewrie, you *would* bring up my

trained circus of bread-room rats!" Capt. Charlton stuck in, tongue in cheek, to slice through their gloom. It worked; such an *outré* statement stopped them in their tracks and made them *howl* with relieving laughter, declaring Charlton a rare rogue, and starting a period of shared reveries of just *how* eccentric some of their old captains had seemed to them when they were Midshipmen or junior Lieutenants.

"Thank God the poor man's gone, then," Cheatham said with a sad *moue* on his face, pouring himself another topping glass when the port got round to him again. "And, for the good of his family, the Navy, and his repute . . . false though it may have been . . . he fell with his sword in hand, his face to the foe, and his wounds in his front."

"Hear, hear," Ayscough and Charlton chorused.

Do I tell 'em? Lewrie asked himself, unable, to keep a wince off his phyz, for he had conducted the sea-burials for Kenyon and his men, and had seen on which side of his body Kenyon had been pierced, before they had been sewn up in canvas and tipped over the side under a flag.

"How *did* he fall, Captain Lewrie?" Commodore Ayscough enquired, after seeing his pained expression.

Oh, Gawd! Lewrie cringed; *tell the truth, and every Man-Jack in* Erato *is bound for the noose. Lie, and face a court-martial myself!*

"Commander Kenyon, along with a Midshipman and five of his boat crew . . . ," Lewrie began, hesitantly. "They stepped ashore onto the town piers, right after *Erato* came alongside them, facing the town's shops and houses on the waterfront. There was a company of French infantry, sheltered in them, and . . ."

"*Lovely* young fellows, were they?" Capt. Cheatham sneered.

"Ah, in point of fact, I'd s'pose so, sir," Lewrie stumbled at the interruption. "Weapons in hand, all that. Preceding the Marines, who *should've* been first ashore. There were French musket volleys, and return fire . . . swivel guns were fired at the windows and doorways, to drive the Frogs to cover, so the landing-party could join them. There is a *slight* possibility that their deaths were the result of a *combination* of fire, sirs . . . hostile and friendly. Might've charged cross the muzzle of a swivel, just as it lit off, accidentally-like, 'bout the same time as some Frenchmen got a few shots off, too."

There, that'll explain it, Lewrie told himself, trying to think of what Clotworthy Chute had told him of how to spot a liar, or how to read a card player; what cutty-eyed expressions liars and the confident wore, and tried to plaster the exact opposite on his face. Blink too much, or was it no blinking at all; shrug too deep, eschew a sheepish smile, make firm eye contact, what *was* it?

Truth to tell, someone aboard *Erato,* maybe two or three someones, had fired their swivels about the same time, in the general direction of the village's buildings, but had "sorta–kind of" *missed,* and had blown the entire party off their feet, all the wounds from behind, and no one had cared much at all. Even Lt. Cottle could not say who had done it, and, from the cutty-eyed way *he'd* looked when Lewrie had put it to him, Cottle most-like hadn't made all that much of an effort to find out who did it, and probably would not, in future, either!

Now, the Eratos would shut their mouths as tight as oysters, and shrug their collective innocence. Oh, it was murder most foul, mutiny and a death-sentence for everyone involved, whether by omission or commission; the ones who did it, and the ones who didn't, but kept mum, and abetted the perpetrators; for those who refused, for whatever reason, to investigate, or those who did but wrote a lying report!

"Indeed," Commodore Ayscough sternly commented, looking leery of such an explanation, making Lewrie feel as if his eyes would begin to water, if he kept eye contact with him very much longer. "You find it a tad *suspicious,* do you, Lewrie?"

"Yes, and no, sir," Lewrie tried to weasel

out, wondering where inspiration was when you really needed it. Oh, yes! "One may think that *Erato's* crew, the bulk of 'em, *might* have felt shamed by Kenyon's doings, and his blatant favouritism, and . . . personal tastes. Yet, on the other hand, it could have been accidental. Or . . . premeditated."

Here we go, premeditated, aye! Lewrie felt like chortling right out loud as a thought came to him, as if whispered into his ear by some perverse wee, winged muse.

"By Kenyon himself, sir," Lewrie stated.

"What? Kenyon!" "Oh, rot!" "Murder, and dumb mutiny!"

"Feature this, sirs," Lewrie went on, both hands on the table, and slowly rolling his port glass between them. "Commander Kenyon was sick enough to *know* he was failing fast, that the Pox was eating him alive. Despite his best intentions he *knew* he had little command of his lusts, and just enough wit left to see the reactions of his crew.

"He was aging badly, his hair and formerly handsome features going, too, sirs," Lewrie improvised, "wasting away to a scare-crow, and . . . I had put him on warning that if he sauced me one more time, he'd be charged for it, and brought before a Court for insubordination, and there went his naval career, drab as it was. He wasn't *fetching* anymore, d'ye see, sirs?

"Ye mentioned his family, Captain

Cheatham," Lewrie continued. "Far as I know, he *had* none. Or, if he had, they'd slung him into the Navy as a lad, soon as he began t'act on his sinful predilictions, most-like, and wrote him off, so . . . the Navy, the officers of his past and present rank, *were* his family, and, could he no longer command himself, his buried secret would come out, and that'd be lost to him. Revealed as a sodomist, quietly cashiered without half-pay if not brought before a court-martial, either way, he'd end up 'beached' without ten pounds to his name, and he'd die a miserable, ravin' death in Bedlam, or some, place worse, 'thout a shred of dignity, or honour."

"Mean t'say, he *deliberately* was the first ashore, *willing* to be killed at the head of his men, 'stead of . . . ?" Capt. Charlton said, his head cocked over to one side as if he found it hard to swallow, . . . yet with a knowing glint to his eyes.

"Boresome as our blockade work had been 'til now, sirs," Lewrie said with a hapless shrug, "it might have been his last chance to fall a hero . . . to go out brave and glorious. While he still possessed a last few shreds of rationality. For his good *name,* sirs! Perhaps . . . perhaps for the good of the Service, as well," Lewrie suggested. "In the old days, were one not aware of his perversion, one'd think Kenyon a hellish-good seaman, a very competent officer, and a fellow dedicated to the Navy. I learned a lot from him, in truth."

"Good of the Service," Capt. Charlton said in the long silence as they mulled all that over.

"Ahem," Commodore Ayscough grumpily said over the creaking and groaning of *Chesterfield*'s working hull. "Yayss . . . I see. We will never know what was in his mind at the time, if indeed it was Kenyon's intention to end his life, or, whether it was an unfortunate mistake."

"Or, whether he and his 'pretty lads' were intentionally slaughtered," Capt. Cheatham growled, "and the guilty aboard *Erato* have got 'way with it . . . so far, sirs. As our Commodore related to me, our casualties were extremely light, given the audacity of our landings. Some few wounded aboard the cutters in taking the galley, hardly any aboard *Savage* or *Mischief,* and very few wounded aboard my ship, *Chesterfield, Lyme,* or the seventy-fours. Most of the 'Discharged, Dead' came among the landing-parties, ashore. Yet *Erato* lost eight killed, including a *cabin steward,* despite never taking any serious fire from the French."

"Indeed, sir, most casualties occurred among the landing-parties," Capt. Charlton countered quickly. "And, *Erato*'s losses were a *part* of the shore parties, . . . bravely standing into the harbour of Le Verdon and right alongside the piers against an entrenched company of French soldiers, who had to be rooted out with the bayonet and cannon fire."

"That is very true, Captain Charlton, aye," Ayscough mused with a spritely grin. " 'Twould be a damned shame, was our victory marred by such a scurrilous suspicion. As well planned as our adventure was, all thanks to Captain Lewrie, no one could possibly expect to succeed with none of our own blood shed. Do you agree, Captain Cheatham?"

"Well, now sir . . ." Cheatham huffed up, taut fingers curling on the stem of his glass. "Mean t'say . . . ! Should we not delve into the matter deeper, put the question to the *Erato*'s people . . . ?"

"Rear-Admiral Lord Boxham must be informed," Ayscough went on. "He may wish court-martials held, which would result in *Erato*'s crew being broken up among the rest of the ships of our squadron, once the guilty are sifted out, and a new crew and slate of officers appointed into her."

"*I'll* not have any of them!" Cheatham hotly exclaimed. "There's no telling *what* they might imagine they could get away with, next time! Nor would I wish my *worst* watch officer to go into her."

"Rear-Admiral Iredell indeed must be informed of the *possibility* that Kenyon and his . . . favourites fell accidentally, intentionally, or by a mutinous deed of the moment," Capt. Charlton suggested. "But, it is *his* decision as to what to do . . . or, whether it is his appreciation of the matter that a rough form of Justice was done, either way, and the rot aboard her had been . . . excised. You make a good point, Commodore," he said. "Why mar a rare, if minor, victory? For the good of the Service, it might be best did Lord Boxham put an officer of *his* choosing in command of *Erato,* put the crew on notice that they'd best be True Blue Hearts of Oak from now on, and, with the chiefest cause of their grievance gone, well . . ."

I can't believe this! Lewrie gawped to himself; *Ayscough, and Charlton, turnin' a blind eye t'what amounts t'murder an' mutiny? For that's pretty much what it was, wasn't it. Never thought I'd see* either *of 'em bend the rules* that *far!*

"Send her home," Lewrie said into the tenseness, the heat coming off Cheatham's glowers.

"What?" they all pretty much barked at the same time.

"*Erato* can't keep the sea more than four months without replenishment of stores, sirs," Lewrie said with a shrug. "She needs to be victualled. Let Lord Boxham place officers into her, men of his own selection. Whoever is her acting captain will surely be confirmed by Admiralty as a Commander, so

563

long as the war continues. Pluck Cottle, her First Officer, out, and place him aboard one of the seventy-fours, as replacement for the Lieutenant whom Lord Boxham names as the second-in-command. Thurston, too, in charge of her Marines, for there's no guilt attached to him, either . . . yet, and there's no reason he should suffer. Then, once in a home port, *Erato* can be given a refit, whether she's due or not, and, in the interim, the crew . . . guilty or innocent, or merely suspect . . . can be re-assigned to other ships in the Channel Fleet.

"Even if it was Kenyon's intention to die by the enemy's hands," he quickly added, "and *no one's* guilty, the scattering of her people'd draw no unwanted notice, sirs. Happens all the time."

Captain Cheatham of *Jersey* still looked sour, but he did nod his head in sullen agreement, while Ayscough and Charlton immediately looked relieved, taking Lewrie's scheme as a sensible suggestion.

"Well, we must leave the details of it to Lord Boxham . . . agreed, gentlemen?" Ayscough asked. "A toast, then. Fill your glasses. Damme, the port's almost gone, and we'll need another bottle soon. Here's to the memory of Commander James Kenyon . . . a fallen . . . hero."

"Rather sir, if I may?" Lewrie stuck in. "Perhaps the *memory* of Commander Kenyon might be, uhm . . . best soon forgotten.'"

"Oh, quite! Lord, yes," Commodore Ayscough said with a cynical laugh. "All topped up, gentlemen? Then here's to the late Commander Kenyon . . . and the '*Erato* Guns.' "

They all drank their glasses dry, reflective of a ritual empty of real sentiment, and an uneasy silence fell over the great-cabins.

"D'ye think Hogue will keep his prize, sir?" Lewrie dared ask. "Or, is she not 'Good Prize'?"

"*Marvellous* prize!" Ayscough bellowed gleefully. "By the time *Mischief* was alongside her, not a shot fired, mind . . . her master and crew had gone over the side and rowed for Talmont like the very Devil was at their heels. Only people left aboard were a half-drunk ship's boy and a one-legged cook, and both of 'em swearing they were Danish, but all they could speak was Dutch, ha ha! Her master left so quickly, he abandoned her *three* sets of papers, so he was surely up to something beyond smuggling wine and brandy to Rotterdam."

"Bung-full of Bordeaux, Lewrie," Capt. Charlton confided with joy. "Casks and kegs and crated bottles of it. She's bound for England, not Lisbon. Wine to Portgual? Like carrying coal to Newcastle!"

"Wouldn't fetch a shilling to the pound in Lisbon, but, landed in England, she's worth *thousands!*" Ayscough heartily agreed. "Lucky dog, Hogue, his fortune's made, and no master or ship owner to sue for her return. Abandoned . . . *salvaged,* must he claim so, ha ha, *and,* in the merchant service of the Batavian Republic, a French ally."

"Something to cheer, sir," Lewrie posed with a smile. "Punch, sir? For you make a fine'un."

Even if we'll all feel like the Wrath o' God in the mornin', he told himself, but . . . they needed some good cheer. They had a *victory* to celebrate!

"A punch, by God, yes!"

" 'Give *me* the punch-ladle, I'll *fath*-om *the* bowl!' " Lewrie sang right out, pounding his fists and swaying from side to side.

"Now from France, we get brandy, from
　　Jamaica good rum!
Sweet oranges and ap-ples, from Portugal
　　come!
Add the good old hard cider that England
　　con-trols . . .
Give me the punch-ladle, I'll fath-om the
　　bowl!"

Even Capt. Cheatham joined in the chorus, getting into the spirit of things, as their spirits and flavourings were being mixed and the hot water was fetched, and they all swayed as they loudly sang along.

"I'll fathom the bowl, I'll fathom the bowl . . . Give me the punch-ladle, I'll fath-om the bowl!"

■ ■ ■ ■

EPILOGUE

■ ■ ■ ■

On the most exalted throne in the world, nothing but our arse.
                    Michel de Montaigne (1533–1592)

CHAPTER
THIRTY-SIX

The early afternoon was overcast and cold, requiring Lewrie to button the lapels of his uniform coat doubled over to trap what little warmth he had, and huddle inside the folds of his voluminous and heavy boat cloak, with the collar turned up to the base of his cocked hat so the light, but cutting, wind along the Strand didn't freeze his ears off as he, along with his barrister Mr. Andrew MacDougall, his clerk Sadler, and his brother-in-law Burgess Chiswick, paused in their stroll from Whitefriars Street to a chop-house in Savoy Street, near the Thames.

Normally, the walk was not all that difficult, but for the fact that it was two days before Christmas, and the Strand, the finest shopping district in the civilised world, was infested with hordes of people out to obtain their turkey, their ham or goose, new suitings and gowns ordered weeks before in which to preen at routs, drums, balls, holiday "at-homes," and Divine Services. Children by the thousands, noses and gloved fingertips pressed to large bay windows of stores to drool over the toys displayed, were underfoot as thick as roaches round a butter-tub, hopping, skipping, shrieking, and tittering in boundless expectations, and, when their parents weren't looking, practicing ice-sliding on the sidewalks where old snow had melted, then frozen overnight to a delightful slickness. Some imps without parental supervision, the usual street urchins, also practiced their aim with snowballs at the odd passerby, and all their parties' coats bore white smudges from successful hits . . . though Lewrie, MacDougall, Burgess, and Sadler had given as well they got.

Rich, titled, working class, the working or idle poor, criminal and honest, all were out looking for presents, alighting from coaches, embarking into coaches, walking afoot as densely crowded as corn rows, and could not help but jostle each other, now and then . . . which was just topping-fine for the pickpockets and snatchers.

"Aha, there they are, sirs!" Sadler cried, clapping his mittened hands together as they paused before Somerset House, where crowds briefly gathered — children, mostly — to gawp at the "*Erato* Guns." Parents stood by impatiently, for the most part, allowing their offspring a *brief* "edifying and patriotic experience," before dragging them off so they could be about their errands and gift-buying. There was a temporary wooden plaque, a brace of soldiers to guard the cannon, but that didn't stop young lads from crawling all over them, so thoroughly that not a speck of new snow remained atop the barrels or truck-carriages, as they peeked down the un-tompioned muzzles, pretended that they were loading and firing them, and competing in which lad could go *Boom! Bang!* or *Pow!* the loudest, while impatient governesses or dads tapped their toes.

"Let us see them," Sadler pled his employer, dashing across the street to paw them over and marvel for a moment or two.

"Seen 'em," Lewrie laconically said.

"Seen odder in In'ja," Burgess said, chuckling.

"Just clapped-out old naval pieces, sure t'burst with a proper charge down the bores," Lewrie added, feeling hungry.

"An outstanding feat of arms, e'en so, Captain Lewrie, thanks to you," Mr. Mac-Dougall congratulated, his own eyes alight though he would not lower his dignity to go cross the street and gawk. "Though you do not receive your proper credit for their taking. Were I an officer in the Navy, I'd sue."

Commodore Ayscough had been right; their victory in the Gironde, minor though it was, had been blown all out of proportion in the papers. The *Marine Chronicle,* the *Times,* the

Gazette had printed the official report released by the Admiralty, writ large on their front pages, as if it was as grand a triumph as the Glorious First of June, the Battle of Cape St. Vincent, Camperdown, or the Nile. And, Ayscough's canny prediction of how such news could enthuse the populace had proven true, as well. After seven years of unending war, new and higher taxes on a whole host of new items, the scandal of paper *fiat* money, soaring costs for just about everything, a couple of lean crops, and a dearth of good news from overseas, Britain *needed* cheering news, and the bulk of them had pounced upon it as eagerly as they would their Christmas gifts.

Unfortunately for Lewrie, though, who needed a deed to bolster his own odour with potential jurors, the papers had taken Lord Boxham's account as the senior-most officer involved, and Lewrie's name was mentioned in that report just once, in connexion with delivering Marines and armed sailors from *Lord Boxham's* ships, under command of *his* officers, to take the battery, with the brief assistance of cannon fire: "HMS *Savage,* 36, Capt. A. Lewrie, provided brisk fire upon the battery until our parties were ashore and well engaged."

"A career ender, that, Mister MacDougall," Lewrie said with a wry laugh. "Doesn't matter, really. Other senior officers sent their reports to Admiralty, so *they* know who authored the plan. Besides, if such a suit were possible, I doubt I could afford it, and, do I call a titled Rear-Admiral a liar in public, it'd be more a cause to duel than go to court."

"I only hope that some artist paints them before they're taken from public view," Mr. Sadler bemoaned once he rejoined them, feeling very patriotic at the moment. "Even a coloured wood-cut print. Won't *that* anger Bonaparte over in Paris, does he see a copy, ha ha! English lads capering all over his precious artillery, huzzah!" Sadler exclaimed enthusiastically, peering at the captured pieces as if he wished to paint them forever in his mind.

"Thumb in his eye, Mister Sadler, thumb in his bloody eye," Mr. MacDougall cackled in like joy. "Well, shall we go on, sirs? I must own to feeling more than a tad peckish, and the chop-house awaits."

They continued their walk, reaching the crossing of Bow Street and onwards towards Cecil Street and Fountain Court, nearing Savoy Palace . . . but, even before reaching the chop-house, the aroma of food and cookfires wafted off the Thames, forcing Sadler and Lewrie to hasten their steps towards the river, the piers, and the landing stages.

"Frost Fair, sir!" Mr. Sadler gaily declared. "The ice is not so thick as I recall when I was a lad, but the Frost Fair will likely go on forever. Just like England, is it not, sirs? A delightful tradition of an *English* Christmas!"

There before them, below the edge of the empty quay, the Thames was frozen over from one bank to the other, thick enough for carriages and sleighs to cross it, avoiding the toll for London Bridge, ruining the Lord Mayor's Christmas. Pedestrians plodded carefully over thick ice, or practiced their ice-sliding games, too, adults as well as children. Along with the wonderful scents from the many cooking booths or gaily coloured pavilions, the light, cold breeze brought them sounds of music, of cranked hurdy-gurdies, brass bands, of shrieking children and the snorts of pit-ponies put to work as rides, the jingle-jangle of belled harnesses and reins from the one-horse sleighs, and a happy *humm-umm* from the thousands of shoppers and celebrants, the precarious dancers who dared some saw-dusted places; all celebrating a delightful London tradition, time out of mind.

"Which would you prefer, Mister Sadler?" Lewrie asked the weedy little scribbler, "a chop-house feast, or a stroll through the Frost Fair, perhaps a sleigh ride, and something meat-ish on a skewer, like as not burned to charcoal?"

"No thankee," Burgess demurred, laughing. "*Been* to In'ja, as I said, and eaten more than my share of dubious."

Frost Fair, spread out wide before his eyes,

was a carnival, a circus, a series of epic snowball fights and impromptu football matches, even one criquet game in which the players spent more time on the flat of their backs than upright, and the ball could skitter half a mile or more on a good pitch, and Lewrie's eyes lit up with youthful joy as he considered spending the rest of the day down there, for he'd had little reason for holiday cheer, so far.

His appearance before King's Bench was firmly set in the first week of Hilary Term, just after Epiphany Sunday, and, with the date at last known, Admiralty had decided that a well-found Fifth Rate frigate such as *Savage* could not sit idle in port awaiting his return to her, if things went his way, which Admiralty obviously doubted, so . . . they had sent orders down to Portsmouth that he was to be relieved of command, and another Post-Captain sent into her.

So Lewrie was, for the first time since 1793, "beached," and on half-pay, and odds were, even were he most honourably acquitted, there would most likely *not* be a welcome return to HMS *Savage* and the circle of officers, warrants, petty officers, and hands he'd come to know so well. His solid support was now trimmed to Aspinall, his cook and manservant, Cox'n Liam Desmond and his mate Patrick Furfy, and the cats.

Once "beached," Lewrie feared there might

not ever be another sea-going command; it would be easy enough for Admiralty to look past him, let him slowly climb in seniority on the Post-Captains' List, pay him the portion of half-pay, and allow his "taint" slowly evaporate as a bad memory, like a fool or cripple who'd been "Yellow Squadroned."

Oh, when he'd delivered all his accounts to Admiralty, people there had been polite and civil, not even brusque with him at all . . . though there had been a few cooling their heels in the Waiting Room who had glared at him. Most officers and civil servants, once they'd either recognised him, or learned his name, had gone shy and cutty-eyed as if they really wished to cry "My God, you're *that'un!*" or turned so bland and distracted by other things that they might as well have given him the "cut direct." Some had seemed genuinely sympathetic, those who approved of his slave stealing, but some made cow-eyes to his face, and troweled it on much too thick, "pissing down his back" 'til out of his sight so they might snigger over his predicament, and Lewrie could not decide which half galled him the most.

He felt a raging *need* to hop down the nearest landing stairs and go do something innocent, silly, and mindless, go cut capers on the ice and plaster people with snowballs, chat up just anyone, even toothless harridans from Wapping or Billingsgate!

"Circus . . . cross the river, there," Burgess said at his elbow, in a soft voice. "Wigmore's Peripatetic Extravaganza. They've set up their winter quarters in Southwark, near Vauxhall Gardens."

"Peripatetic?" Lewrie scoffed. "He's found a dictionary. Was 'Travelling' no longer good enough?"

"Doing a grand business, I'm told," Burgess said, shrugging his shoulders; most-like to warm himself than anything else.

"Gentlemen, my feet are freezing," Mr. MacDougall griped, shivering, and punctuating his statement with an actual *Brrr.* "We need to thaw out in front of a roaring fireplace, at the chop-house."

"No chance we'll run into the Beaumans there, is there?" Lewrie asked as he reluctantly turned away from the river, after a final peek cross the Thames to see if he could espy anything exotic or circus-y. If he couldn't make a fool of himself at the Frost Fair, then dinner in a warm place would have to do, so long as the said warm place came with lashings of drink, and yes, at the moment, images of hot punch or mugs of mulled wine, laced with spices, and half-aboil from the insertion of a red-hot fire poker, would suit, as would hot chocolate heavily laden with sugar and rum.

"Lord no, Alan!" Burgess hooted as they resumed their brisk pace into Savoy Street.

"Your father, and Mister Twigg, have seen to that. The last I heard, the Beaumans had been hounded far out past Islington . . . ran out of London lodgings *months* ago."

"Lord, what have they done?" Lewrie wondered aloud.

"There are few hoteliers or lessors who want loud mobs in their streets, day and night. Rocks through the window glass, pamphlets put up 'gainst their doors, damning them as allies of slavers . . . heaps of horse dung piled on their stoops? People of the Quality barging in at all hours, denouncing them, and running off their other renters? Your father reckons that even the worst lodgings cost them four or five times the going rate, for the annoyance, and to cover damages."

"Their Black body-servants absconded," MacDougall added, cackling in glee. "Members of the Abolitionist Society made known to them that slavery doesn't exist in England, and that the Beaumans hadn't any claim over them. They took 'leg hail' just weeks after your appearance in court, and have found paying employment. Hugh Beauman and his regal young wife are now reduced to the very *dregs* of servants, who as soon as they're told how rich the Beaumans are, and how beastly, can demand *triple* wages!"

"And odd it is, Alan," Burgess gleefully told him as they neared the chop-house's doors,

580

"how so many of them who *will* take their wages and abide their brute ways, come from Mister Twigg's people. S'truth! There's more than bodyguards and bully-bucks in Twigg's employ. Servants hear and see *everything*, don't ye know. Hellish-good thing for the nation; to have ears and eyes working for foreigners who mean our country harm . . . or keeping an eye on devils in human guise."

"London became too hot for them," MacDougall said as he opened the heavy oak door, "even in *plain* clothing and disguises, every time they ventured out, here came a shower of shit and garbage. Think of it . . . no galleries, no shopping, no theatre! Drury Lane, the Haymarket, Covent Garden, a coffee-house, all denied them. I could almost pity them . . . almost, mind, that they could not obtain a decent meal. Such as we do now, ha ha! Good afternoon, Mister Sloane, a table by a fire!" he cried to the proprietor.

Just as Lewrie was about to enter, though, a snowball smashed into the back of his cocked hat, knocking it off his head, and he spun about, looking for the culprit, ready to scoop up a slushy handful and retaliate with a well-packed, icy "stinger" of his own.

"Damn my eyes, that's . . . !" he gawped. "No, couldn't be."

He got a glimpse of a young woman in a fur-trimmed green cloak, a hint of raven-coloured hair under the hood, before whoever it was disappeared round the corner of a building into the busy Strand. For just a fleeting second, he wondered if it had been Eudoxia Durschenko.

No, couldn't be her, he told himself as he entered the doors to hand over his hat, cloak, and sword belt to a servant. Though whoever had hit him had done it square, right in the centre of the up-turned back of his hat, and Eudoxia had been raised to be a crack shot with a firearm, or her recurved Asian bow. *Circus cross the Thames, we were talkin' of it, and* any *impish young miss with dark hair, I'd take for Eudoxia. Coincidence. Besides, hurt as she was in Cape Town when she found I was married, I'd more expect an arrow 'tween my shoulder blades!*

MacDougall was an enthusiastic regular once he had discovered a new place to dine, and evidently had given this new chop-house quite a lot of his custom, the last few months or so, and, in his line of work brought people he represented, as well, who most-like became regulars, too . . . assuming they hadn't been hung or imprisoned. That explained the grand table they were given, right by one of the fireplaces that was stoked and drawing so well that waves of heat could be seen coming from it in airy ripples, and air could be heard whooshing in the flue; it was almost medieval with all the brass and dark, polished oak walls, the overhead beams and stout tables and chairs.

Lewrie unbuttoned his coat lapels before sitting down, away from the waves of heat; some things could be over-done, and he didn't wish to be one of them by the time they had fed.

"Hot drinks all round?" MacDougall heartily suggested. "Mulled wine or hot cider? Punch, or candled brandy?"

"Mulled wine for me," Lewrie declared, as did Burgess. Sadler went for chocolate and brandy, obviously a man with a sweet tooth.

"Now, before we order, Captain Lewrie, I must tell you my good news," MacDougall said with a cherubic, impish smile worthy of a Puck, and rubbing his chilled hands together in joy. "We now possess all the affidavits and depositions necessary for your defence, sir, *including* a letter from your old friend, former Leftenant-Colonel Cashman, now of Wilmington . . . North or South Carolina, I can never keep which is which straight . . . stating that your Black volunteers intended to run away to sea as *true* volunteers, along with a dreadful account of how harsh were their lives had they not. Since he was a rueful slaveowner for a time himself, his account is most emotional, and compelling. I intend to have it read, just before putting your surviving Black sailors up to testify, so they may expand upon Cashman's . . ."

"Then you'd better grow wings, or learn

t'swim like a seal, if that's yer intent, Mister MacDougall," Lewrie all but yelped. "I'm no longer in command, and *Savage* has a new captain. For all I know, she may have already completed re-storing, and sailed for God knows where!"

"Hmm, that'll never do," MacDougall fussily prosed on, once he'd gotten his lower jaw back in place from a ghastly-looking gasp. "Good God above! Well, has she departed, we'll simply have to get her back, that's all there is to it. I'll have a word with Admiralty, get Twigg to toddle over there and use his influence. Failing that, the lack of live witnesses could be grounds for a continuance 'til their return."

"What?" Lewrie barked, astonished. "Mean t'say, I could wait months . . . 'til *next* Hilary Term t'get this settled? Is she ordered halfway round the world, it might be *years* 'fore she's back!"

You silly, bloody, civilian *sod!* Lewrie silently fumed; *I* knew *ye sounded too good t'be true, ye . . . Tom-Noddy! Just trot over and ask Admiralty t'whistle up a frigate? I'm good as hung . . . swingin' and danglin'! Don't ye know there's a* war *on, ye ignorant . . . Gawd!*

"Alan has allies in Commons, and Lords," Burgess said with a hopeful sound, somewhat akin to whistling past a graveyard to Lewrie's ears. "A bit of pressure from politicians might help."

"Exactly so, sir," MacDougall rejoined, sounding like a fellow clutching straws, too. "Wilberforce and his people, as well, who are in both Houses of Parliament, may employ *their* interest and patronage links with the Navy. They must be . . . oh, what is the military term for it, Mister Chiswick?"

"Mustered, sir?" Burgess eagerly supplied.

"Lashed aloft," Lewrie sourly muttered under his breath, after he had gotten his breath back.

"Mustered. Exactly," MacDougall perked up, as though this snag was but a minor quibble, soon to be amended. "Ah, our drinks are here! I dare say, though, that, foul as the weather has been, there is a good possibility that Captain Lewrie's ship . . . former ship, is still tied up in port."

Civilians! Lewrie fumed some more, aghast at the fellow's lack of knowledge; and wondering, did the Beaumans prevail, could he have a quiet minute alone with the man, so he could strangle him to death; *he must think we don't go t'sea in snowstorms, when it's too cold, or wet!*

"Even without Captain Lewrie's Black sailors, there are the former body-servants of the Beaumans," MacDougall blathered on after he had taken a sip or two of his hot, brandy-laced cider. "They can tell the court horrific tales of how badly they were treated.

Why, with any luck, they might have known some of the volunteers themselves, if they ever visited that particular Beauman plantation on Portland Bight, and may speak for them and their motives in 'stealing themselves' and seeking freedom in the Royal Navy."

"Uhm . . ." Now Burgess was doubtful, and was about to explain the vast gulf 'twixt house slaves and field slaves, and the prejudices the well-dressed, well-fed, and lightly worked house servants held about their darker, more helpless kind. Burgess matched eyes with Lewrie, a fellow who had also seen real slavery in action. The arrival of a man in a blue apron and the house's unofficial livery with the slate menu bearing chalked-in specials interrupted him.

"Oh, good!" MacDougall exclaimed chearly. "They have both the venison *and* the jugged hare today. Capital!"

Lewrie felt like lowering his head to the tabletop and banging away 'til he knocked himself temporarily senseless; that, or the urge to spend the rest of the day, and the evening, amassing a *ragingly* good drunk!

"Uhm, perhaps a dab of haste might be, ah . . . ? Lewrie hinted.

"Oh, right. Sorry, Mister Sadler, but I will make it up to you. Do return to the office and write out a special plea for those members of Captain Lewrie's crew to be kept handy for their appearance before the Lord Justice," MacDougall instructed, turning very business-like. "We have the names and ranks already, from the depositions and witness list. Copy to Admiralty, copy to Lord Justice Oglethorpe, and a copy to Mister Twigg. Fast horse to Portsmouth with the orders to stay in port as soon as you receive them, mind. Twigg will be grand help in that."

"Yes, sir," Mr. Sadler said with a resigned sigh, then finished his hot drink, wiped the cocoa froth from his upper lip, and arose to reclaim his hat and greatcoat and gloves.

"Even if she sails, 'twill be the fault of the Admiralty that I cannot present my complete defence," MacDougall gaily said, "and solid proof will be at hand that the Lord Justice issued an order for her to be held. A continuance will naturally be granted, instanter. Now . . . how does the turtle soup all round sound to you, sirs?"

" 'Scuse me, sir," another waiter intruded as the first began to scribble their desires. "You'd be bein' a Captain Lewrie, sir? Lady said t'give ye this, sir."

"A lady?" Lewrie found new cause to gawp aloud as he spun about on his chair and craned his neck to see who the lady in question was. All he could see in the chop-house's crowded tables, though, were men, and only the rare matron dining with her husband. He took the note and opened it, careful to act nonchalant; and not let either Burgess or his barrister get a peek at it over his shoulder.

The first couple of lines, though, were written in some incomprehensible script that put him in mind of his equally unfathomable lessons in Greek, long ago. For all he knew, it could be a bill from some foreigner's laundry service where'd he'd left a bundle years before and had never returned to reclaim, or pay for, yet . . .

Poor, darling man, I lern of trile to com, for taken Black felloes to mak them free, and am so angre they trect yoo so bad. Lern too yoo are alone now.

I forgive yoo for break my heart.

Holy shit! he thought, stunned; *it* was *Eudoxia who clobbered me!*

I think much of yoo all time since yoo sail away to fite French. I miss yoor company and never we go shooting or hav outside dinner, race horses lik we say we do sum day in Africa. Time I see yoo last I say *[something in Cyrillic]* in yoor leters is *paka snova* . . . meaning is see you latter in Rossiya. Circus is winter over river. If yoo com I wood desire see yoo. New dramas and commedys. I hav the truble write in English, but may be yoo teech me beter? I pray for yoo and be in cort is trile begin.

Eudoxia

"A lady, hey?" Burgess enquired, trying not to sound too eager to know who it was from; he'd been in the middle of the lather 'tween Lewrie and his sister Caroline since getting back from India, and any new dalliance would only make things worse. Not that things were anywhere *near* good, already.

"An admirer who wishes me well in court, Burgess," Lewrie lied, folding over the note again and slipping it into a coat pocket; not before the final line he'd first missed caught his eye.

I hit with snoball good, yes?

"And did the lady request a reply?" Lewrie asked the waiter who still hovered expectantly.

"Nossir," the man said. "Jus' popped in long 'nough t'point ye out and gimme th' note."

"Thankee for deliverin' it," Lewrie told him, digging into his breeches pocket for his coin purse, and giving the fellow a crown coin. He turned his full attention, pointedly so, to the other waiter who held the slate menu. "Roast venison and jugged hare, did ye say? That does sound toothsome. Turtle soup for me, as well, t'begin with. Seeing it is

589

Christmastime, I'd admire a bit of your goose with the raspberry jam sauce, somewhere along the way . . . a salad between, of course. Right?"

"Very good, sir."

"What?" Lewrie all but yelped once he looked up to his partners at the table, who were both eying him rather charily at that point. "A fellow can't have supporters, and admirers?"

"In your absence, Captain Lewrie," Mac-Dougall sternly said with several slow negative shakes of his head, "Mister Twigg, your father, Sir Hugo, and Major Chiswick here have adverted to me that your relations with your wife are . . . strained. And, they had confided to me the reasons *why,* d'ye see, sir. As your legal representative in a serious matter, it is my professional advice to you, Captain Lewrie, that such doings must be kept strictly in check, and the Reverend Wilberforce and other supporters of yours, who are so far true admirers of yours, must not hear of any *new* escapades, so long as your trial continues. Else, they will withdraw *all* support . . . publicity tracts, favourable letters to the papers, *and* monetary aid, placing the financial burden of your defence upon your own purse."

"Ye mean they haven't heard already?" Lewrie gawped, finding it hard to believe that his father's formerly bad repute would not be *enough* to put them right off, and "the acorn don't fall far from the oak" and all that nonsense. *Surely* Twigg must have filled them in, somewhere along the line, he could not help thinking!

"You are, sir, or so I have led them to believe with what little I have had to reveal," MacDougall most carefully said, "a victim of a jealous termagant."

"Oh, I say!" Burgess disputed, in defence of his sister.

"A Colonial Loyalist from the Carolinas," MacDougall prosed on, his voice low, and frowning heavily to show that it wasn't personal, as if he disagreed with a disagreeable charade. "Three children enough in her mind, and yet jealous in the extreme. And the long separation demanded by your service to King and Country hasn't helped her suspicions. Those anonymous letters, *complete* fabrications, have driven her to distraction, and you have been estranged from your wife almost since the war with France began. Primly moral the members of the Abolitionist Society, and the Clapham Sect, may be, but, they are also realists, at bottom, and know, as ministers of the Gospel surely must, the limits of a man's resistance to temptations of the flesh.

"They also know that such *temporary* dalliances, ones which don't result in rival affairs of the *heart,* and the rending of families, *are* sometimes unavoidable . . . as evinced by men of the upper class who take mistresses to spare their wives the perils of further childbirth. Deplorable, but sometimes necessary, d'ye see."

I can fuck, but I better not kiss on the way out the door? Lewrie thought in puzzlement; *the ministers tolerate prostitution? Mine arse on a band-box! Missed* that *wheedle in the Good Book!*

"I'm fine as a martyr to the cause of Abolition, ye mean, just shiny enough t'be their Paladin," Lewrie rephrased it most cynically. "So long as I don't blot my copy book before the trial."

"Uhm, that is pretty much it, sir," Mac-Dougall confessed. "So, it would redound to your vast discredit should you, ah . . . dally with anyone so long as your legal proceedings last."

"Else they throw me to the lions, wash their hands like Pontius Pilate?" Lewrie pressed. "Hustle me to the gallows, themselves?"

"Rapidly," MacDougall assured him with all gravity.

"I s'pose I can go out in publick, though, can I not? See some plays . . . dine?" Lewrie asked, trying to sound casual, and innocent as the driven snow outside . . . which, in point of fact, was turning into a grey slush from all the coal smoke and fly ash from the umpteen thousand chimneys in London. "Go see the circus, or . . . ?"

"Oh, a *very* bad idea, Alan!" Burgess quickly cautioned, wincing, for he knew exactly whom Lewrie might run into; he had met met the lovely, lithe Eudoxia in Cape Town. "Actresses and circus persons would be a *real* scandal! Better you take in the city's enter-tainments with Reverend *Wilberforce* . . . a pack of eunuchs."

"D'ye know where t'find some?" Lewrie quipped. "This side of the Ottoman Empire? Or a Venetian *castrati* choir?"

They peered at him like a brace of buz-zards, eyes flinty-hard.

"Well . . . you're right, both of you," Lewrie finally answered. "I see the risk, and I thank you for your sound advice."

Still, he thought, with mental fingers crossed; *they didn't ask me to swear an oath. My trial gets carried over . . . a continuance did MacDougall call it? . . . it'll be a long, bore-some winter, and a spring too. Me . . . ashore . . . where I always get in trouble. Idle hands the Devil's workshop, all that. No wife, no visits home. No seein' the children 'til they're back at their school. No home-made Christmas pudding! Would there be all that much harm if I saw the circus again, their new shows?*

He seriously considered that Eudoxia's father, Arslan Artimovich, still had his daggers and his spine-cracking whip, and his lion cubs might now have grown so large that they could be sicced on him to drag him down and *maul* him to death! Yet, she *did* need help with her spelling . . .

"I worry about you, Alan. I really do," Burgess told him.

"So do I, Burgess," Lewrie ruefully rejoined. "So do I."

AFTERWORD

The criminal justice system of Georgian England was much like a description of most people's lives in those times, or of a winter's day . . . nasty, brutish, and short. Lawyers could "double in brass," first for the defence, then for the prosecution at their next trial. Fears of the Star Chamber, procedures where people were accused but never met their accusers face-to-face, never were told the charges against them 'til they were dragged into that infamous courtroom, held *incommunicado* and tried in secret (no Sunshine Laws then) with no access to capable legal counsel, and executed the next day or so, kept England from developing a permanent, standing District Attorney system for quite a long time. Witnesses and accusers still could not be cross-examined at the time of Lewrie's proceedings, and the accused could not testify for himself, but merely beg for mercy if the verdict went against him.

So I'd like to thank John Kitch, attorney-at-law here in Nashville, for enlightening me on the deadly maze of justice as it was practiced in the late 1700s and early 1800s. Believe it or not, he did it for *free;* quite unlike some learned, and tenured, law professors at one of our prestigious universities which shall remain nameless (three syllables, rhymes with Wilt) who, I was cautioned, would charge for their information by the billable hour (fifteen minutes equals an hour!), like I had staggered into a house and killed all eleven people inside, just because they were home . . . or needed *another* divorce!

Reference books to order, and keep forever as is my wont, on how English Common Law was practiced in court in those days are "scarce as hen's teeth" as we say down here in the South, though *Albion's Fatal Tree* by Hay, Linebaugh, Rule, Thompson, and Winslow (Pantheon Books) was helpful, even if it dealt more with capital punishment than court procedures; as was a chapter in *What Jane Austen Ate and Charles Dickens Knew* by Daniel Pool (Simon & Schuster). Other than that, even the ever-helpful folks at Davis-Kidd Bookstores shrugged like Turkish rug merchants and went "Ah dunno" after doing Books in Print searches for me. If someone out there knows of a better source, get in touch with me, for I fear that Alan Lewrie's legal troubles are not yet over, and he might end up in one of those hundred-year cases in Chancery!

I bludgeoned my editor at Thomas Dunne Books, John Parsley, to include a map of the mouth of the Gironde, and the southwestern coast of France this time (more like begged and pleaded, really), so readers could flip to it and mutter every now and then when a place-name was mentioned. So far as I know, there were no forts or batteries erected at the narrows of the Gironde during the French Revolution or the Napoleonic Wars . . . though had *I* been Napoleon Bonaparte, I would have insisted upon them, fitted with bloody-great 42-pounders, to boot. Médoc, Saintonge, and Aquitaine *are* rather flat, much like the Carolinas' and Georgia's Low Country, as Lewrie pointed out, and it's a great pity no one every really *goes* there . . . not even the French. When it comes to vacation or holiday time, most Frenchmen and Frenchwomen head for the Mediterranean, to Provence, and the southeast coast, the Côte d'Azur from Toulon to Nice . . . even if the beaches are gritty and gravelly, the rentals and hotel rates are astronomical, and the sea is as oily as the Houston Ship Channel . . . perhaps light, sweet crude and diesel fuel saves on suntan lotion.

The whole stretch of coast from Rochefort to the Spanish border, where Lewrie blockaded, *could* be a European Myrtle Beach. Sadly, there is only one touristy development mentioned in my guide book, an ultramodern sort of low-rent Disneyland by the small town of La Palmyre. (It was mentioned in the novel, so flip back to the map at this point, find it and go "Huhh," and ain't this educational?) It's on the North bank above Royan (flip back to the map, again).

All in all, even the guide book doesn't call southwest France all *that* picturesque and "quaint," but then, neither are Beaufort, North Carolina, or the dunes at Hatteras, unless you delight in places like Ye Olde Shipwreck Tavern . . . Come on in, get Wrecked! . . . which I do, and have the tee-shirt to prove it. The châteaux of the region, though, *do* produce some of the finest wines in the world, and give testing tours like the Napa Valley, and, do you see a sign that reads *Dégustation,* it does *not* mean "throw up here," but means you can go into a local restaurant or tavern and sample local wines by the glass. Well, maybe it *does* mean "throw up here" if you stay long enough.

Commander James Kenyon and his secret life . . . well. Sir Winston Churchill once quipped that life in the Royal Navy was, in the bad old days, ". . . nothing but Rum, Sodomy, and the Lash." If you thought that gay men these days have it rough, most of them preferring to stay "in the closet" to avoid trouble, consider what it was like in 1800! Being found out, caught in the act, could result in being put in the stocks, outdoors in all weathers, subject to the abuse, rocks, rotten fruit and vegetables of passersby, and *could* result in death. Some could, after release from the stocks, be branded and marked forevermore, much like a thief, which resulted in a much *slower* death-sentence of shunning, unemployment, being hounded from one parish to the next, and ultimate starvation. In the Royal Navy, the punishment decreed in the Articles of War was indeed draconian; you're caught, you hang.

Oddly though, life in the Royal Navy for common seamen was like the aforementioned "winter's day" . . . nasty, brutish, and short, as well. Desertion rates were so high that sailors were not trusted off of their ships with shore liberty very often. Instead, after six months or so at sea, bumboatmen rowed out to ships Put Out of Discipline, fetching shoddy goods, smuggling rum and gin, and renting out whores for as long as a sailor could afford to keep her on his rations and rum issue, his "temporary" wife; hence, "a wife in every port," and the mess decks became the scene of drunken orgies, with coupling 'tween the gun-carriages with some blankets hung from the overhead for privacy. So, be careful when you call someone "a real son of a gun," for that's what the bastards resulting were called.

Obviously, keeping up to eight hundred men aboard a Third Rate ship of the line from a good drunk, a run ashore, a chance to "put the leg over" a girl in a real bed, not a hammock, in *privacy,* was un-natural, *causing* desperation and "it's just for now" Sodomy and Buggery; much like the temporary homo-sexuality found in prisons today. During World War II, many U.S. Navy ships in the Pacific, in constant active service of two or three years' duration with only quick port calls for fuel, ammo, victuals, and new mov-ies, perhaps an afternoon on an island beach with two beers and some ball equipment called "Liberty," were *rumoured* to have developed "Daisy Chains" belowdecks; much like prisons, indeed, and the old Navy term of "Pogey Bait" equalled the modern-day "Bunk Punk"; a young lad who must yield or get hurt *real* bad by older, harder men.

Equally obvious is the fact that only a *tiny minority* of sailors submitted, took part, or developed a taste for such doings, for most of them were "righteously" heterosexual, and had been raised in those more strictly reli-gious times to think it a mortal sin. Yet, there would always be some who, until they were "pressed" into the Navy, leaned that direc-tion, and found one or two fellows of their persuasion aboard any warship, no matter the dire punishment if discovered.

There is also something else working in such situations, as it does in prisons today; harsh conditions make harsh men of the survivors. Some might have developed a taste for the sense of power and control over the weak, meek, and obedient.

Whatever the reason, Sodomy in those days was always a worry for officers to stamp out; but, when it's one of the *officers* who is homosexual . . . ! As I write this in late October 2006, Masterpiece Theatre on PBS is running William Golding's *To the Ends of the Earth,* from his trilogy of the same name, and the very first episode deals with the death of a parson who might have been weak, certainly naïve, who dared go into the fo'c'sle to preach the Gospel, but ended up drunk and sodomised by some of the sailors, and one of the officers aboard was there to witness it, and possibly urged them on, resulting in his dying from the shame. Was he a *willing* participant, or not? Blame the victim as a "Secret Molly," he brought it on himself, and get out the brooms, to whisk it out of sight, and out of mind!

I've always felt a sympathy for James Kenyon, from the first two Lewrie novels in which he appeared; shoved off to sea by his family to "make a man of him," then dismissed from their cares; banking his life in a naval career at which he's rather good, yet . . . tiptoeing in dread of being found out, and having to play the hairy-chested, upright man, the bluff Jack Me-Hearty expected of a Sea Officer and "tarpaulin man."

Everyone in the eighteenth century was two-faced; one projected one's Publick Face, a carefully crafted creation that pleased Society, and a Private Face, when the shoes were kicked off, the neck-stock undone, and one could cuss, spit, and belch. There was an odd character named Col. Hanger, a British Army officer who sometimes wore his uniform, sometimes civilian suitings, and sometimes ladies' dresses and hats. Make fun of him, and he'd challenge you to a duel, and most-like slice you into ribbons! He, as a member of the Squirearchy, in an honourable profession, was merely thought "eccentric," and delving into his private doings was almost always fatal with that gingery, testy bastard.

In later Victorian times, eccentricity became a British staple; they may still be able to bottle and export it, even in our Politically Correct era. There were many respected men who were alluded to as "perennial bachelors." What'd *that* mean, huh? Something caught at Oxford?

Kenyon is more to be pitied than despised; throw in the power of command, and a long-ago acquired dose of the Clap, which was all but incurable in those days, and throw in it turning into Tertiary Syphilis so that the Publick Façade and the Private Face become confused, and he really had no choice but to hope to die in harness, before getting caught in the act, revealed as a sinful fraud, cashiered, and "branded" in Society. There still was such a thing as Shame in those days.

For those who *still* think me a bigot, let me advert to you what another of my tee-shirts says: "I'd Rather Be Historically Accurate Than Politically Correct." If one writes historical novels, one has to accept, not condemn, how people felt and thought in the chosen period, warts and all, their prejudices and detestations, with no sugar-coating or glossing over . . . no cop-outs such as Mel Gibson's *The Patriot,* where his Black farm workers, when taken away by the British, swear that they *aren't* slaves, they just *work* for him . . . uh-huh. Like *that* could happen in South Carolina in 1780! Other than that, I still think it was a helluva movie.

So, here we are, with Alan Lewrie removed from command of his frigate, twiddling his thumbs alone through the holidays, and sweating bullets in dread of what will happen to him in court. The Beaumans, distanced though they are out past Islington, are still capable of getting at him, hot as they are for his heart's blood. There's Caroline, now utterly estranged from him, despite their attempt at reconciliation. And, of course, there's Lewrie's penchant for getting into *some* sort of trouble when idled ashore, and his near-idiocy when it comes to women that he must squelch.

Will he follow good advice and keep his breeches buttons chastely done up? Or, will he trundle cross the Thames to Southwark to see the circus just once more, take in those new dramas and comedies that Eudoxia mentioned.

Might he, in a truly benevolent and avuncular spirit of charity, instruct the delectable and exotic Eudoxia Durschenko in proper English grammar, spelling, and syntax? Will he be found with his head missing in Vauxhall Gardens, reeking of lion piss?

What do *you* think? Right, so do I.

ABOUT THE AUTHOR

Dewey Lambdin is the author of thirteen previous Alan Lewrie novels and an omnibus volume, *For King and Country*. A member of the U.S. Naval Institute and a Friend of the National Maritime Museum in Greenwich, England, Lambdin has been sailor since 1976, and he spends his free time working and sailing. He makes his home in Nashville, Tennessee, but would much prefer Margaritaville or Murrell's Inlet.

The employees of Thorndike Press hope you have enjoyed this Large Print book. All our Thorndike and Wheeler Large Print titles are designed for easy reading, and all our books are made to last. Other Thorndike Press Large Print books are available at your library, through selected bookstores, or directly from us.

For information about titles, please call:

(800) 223-1244

or visit our Web site at:

http://gale.cengage.com/thorndike

To share your comments, please write:

Publisher
Thorndike Press
295 Kennedy Memorial Drive
Waterville, ME 04901